# let's get it on

welcome to leo's

sisterhood of shopaholics

rosie's cut and weave

della's house of style

island magic

Don't Miss These Fabulous Anthologies from St. Martin's Press

**welcome to leo's**

**sistahood of shopaholics**

**rosie's curl and weave**

**della's house of syle**

**island magic**

# let's get it on

## With Stories from

**Rochelle Alers** **Donna Hill** **Brenda Jackson** **Francis Ray**

ST. MARTIN'S GRIFFIN  NEW YORK

www.stmartins.com

Book design by Jonathan Bennett

Library of Congress Cataloging-in-Publication Data

Let's get it on/with stories from Rochelle Alers...[et al.].—1st ed.
    p. cm.
    Contents: Love lessons / Rochelle Alers—Lady in waiting / Donna Hill—
Irresistible attraction / Brenda Jackson—The blind date / Francis Ray.
    ISBN 0-312-32592-4
    EAN 978-0312-32592-3
        1. American fiction—African American authors. 2. African Americans—
Fiction. 3. Love stories, American. I. Alers, Rochelle.

PS647.A35L47 2004
813'.08508896073—dc22

                                                                    2004046804

D 15  14  13  12  11

# CONTENTS

# ACKNOWLEDGMENTS

Special thanks to Monique Patterson, editor extraordinaire, who believed in this project, and to the wonderful fans who warmly embraced *Welcome to Leo's* and wanted the Hardcastles to have their own story.

let's get it on

Rochelle Alers

love lessons

*We may make our plans, but God has the last word.*

—PROVERBS 16:1

# ONE

Viola Chapman opened the door to her duplex apartment, sighing in relief as the yawning space welcomed her home. She had waited patiently for nearly a year to move into the four-thousand-square-foot loft in an industrial-turn-residential Washington, D.C., neighborhood. Formerly a warehouse taking up an entire square block, the property was sold to a developer who had divided more than sixty thousand square feet of space into ten luxury apartments.

She had been one of the first to purchase a unit, and the last resident to move in. An architect's rendering had reconfigured open spaces and a towering ceiling into a designer's showcase with recessed lights, fireplaces, skylights, an open staircase leading to an upper level, and the careful positioning and detail of internal walls. The final result was that her home radiated a sense of space, light, and warmth.

Viola placed her oversize leather handbag on a straight-back chair next to a corner table in an expansive foyer as she slipped out of her shoes. Reaching into the bag, she retrieved a letter addressed to her at Carver High School. The embossed logo on the envelope indicated the letter had come from Leo's, a trendy supper club in the District of Columbia.

Leo's was one of twenty-two other business establishments in the D.C. area she had solicited for the high school's annual Career Cooperative. As the lead teacher for this year's career initiative, she had set up meetings with local business owners to garner their cooperation for internships for eligible students interested in a future as entrepreneurs.

She made her way in nylon-covered feet across the oak floor laid out in a herringbone design to an alcove. Sitting on a cushioned built-in widow seat, she opened the envelope and withdrew a single sheet of beige parchment.

Viola's gaze raced quickly over the type, lingering on the last paragraph: *I am curious about your school's cooperative proposal. Please contact me at the number on the letterhead, so we may discuss this further. Cordially, Tyrell Hardcastle.*

"Yes!" she whispered, a wide grin parting her lips. Picking up a telephone, Viola dialed the number. It was answered on the third ring.

"Good afternoon, Leo's." The male voice was deep and resonant. James-Earl-Jones deep.

"I'd like to speak to Tyrell Hardcastle."

"This is he."

She smiled. He had used the proper pronoun. She had taught English and literature for nineteen years, and factured verbs or pronouns made her shake her head in despair.

"Mr. Hardcastle, I'm Viola Chapman, a teacher from Carver High School. I just read your letter, and I'd like to set up an appointment with you to discuss our school's vocational Cooperative Initiative."

"I'm only free on Mondays, Ms. Chapman. Will that pose a problem for you?"

"Not at all." She quickly recalled her Monday schedule. Her last class ended at two-thirty.

"What time would you like to meet?"

"That depends on where we meet, Mr. Hardcastle."

"We can meet here at Leo's."

She estimated it would take her at least twenty minutes to drive from the school to the restaurant, barring no traffic delays. She opened her mouth to say three, but quickly changed her mind.

"Four."

"Then, four it is."

Even though the man on the other end of the line couldn't see her, Viola smiled. "Thank you, Mr. Hardcastle."

There was a pause before he said, "Don't thank me yet, Ms. Chapman. As I indicated in my letter, I'm merely curious."

"The word curious means a desire to learn."

"What are you implying, Ms. Chapman?"

She registered the censure in his tone. "Only that we're never too old to learn. I'll see you Monday at four." Depressing a button, she did not give him the opportunity to come back at her.

A shiver of annoyance snaked up her spine. Either Tyrell Hardcastle was interested or he wasn't. She did not have time to waste on someone who was merely "curious" about what had become a positive and successful component to Carver High's academic curriculum.

She moved off the window seat, mentally dismissing Tyrell Hardcastle. It was a Friday afternoon—the end of what had become a hectic week and the beginning of a weekend for which she had nothing planned except to relax. The most strenuous task she'd intended to undertake was a couple of loads of wash.

She had completed her lesson plans for the following week, visited the full-service salon where she'd had her hair trimmed and her weekly manicure and pedicure. She had even turned down an invitation to go to a concert with the school's football coach because she hadn't wanted to give him the impression that they were now a couple.

Evan Richards had asked her to attend a jazz concert with him last spring, and she had accepted. The one date led to several more over the summer months, and Viola suspected the handsome science teacher had come to like her more than she liked him. He'd hinted that he wanted to take their relationship to another level, and she knew that level was intimacy. What Evan failed to realize was that she wanted friendship, not intimacy—especially with someone with whom she worked.

She had learned this valuable lesson the hard way. Fifteen years before, at the age of twenty-five, she had met and fallen head over heels in love with a teacher at a high school in Richmond, Virginia. A whirlwind romance resulted in a quick engagement. However, her rosy world was shattered after she was left standing at the altar when her fiancé eloped with another teacher.

Viola Reba Chapman would celebrate her fortieth birthday within three months, and she had made it a practice to never make the same mistake twice.

The bell rang, and Tyrell Hardcastle glanced at the monitor of the closed-circuit television in the restaurant's office. His clear brown eyes widened appreciably at the face on the screen. A sandy-brown eyebrow lifted.

"Good," he murmured, smiling. "At least she's on time."

It was exactly four o'clock, and he knew the woman who had rung the bell was Viola Chapman. His smile vanished, replaced by a slight frown. He had been taken in by her beautifully modulated voice until her parting remark about his not being too old to learn. No only did she claim a quick tongue, but a sharp one, too.

Rising to his feet, he walked out of the office, making his way to the restaurant's entrance. He unlocked the door, coming face-to-face with Viola Chapman. Tyrell did not know what to expect, but the closed-circuit monitor had deceptively distorted the exquisite beauty of the woman standing in front of him.

She was tall, her heels adding several inches to her towering height. Her face was incredibly round, with a delicate chin he found enchanting. High cheekbones, a generous mouth, and large slanting dark eyes in a sable-brown face held his rapt attention. His gaze shifted upward to her short, naturally curly salt-and-pepper hair, then surveyed what lay below her long, graceful neck. A tailored burnt-orange gabardine suit with a slim skirt and hip-length jacket skimmed her curvy body. The hem of her skirt ended at her knees, permitting him an unfettered view of a pair of shapely legs.

A knowing smile tilted the corners of Tyrell's mouth upward. When he attended school *none* of his female teachers ever came close to Viola Chapman's startling beauty.

Unconsciously Viola's brow furrowed. The golden eyes appraising her reminded her of a predator contemplating its next meal. Tyrell Hardcastle's eyes were figuratively eating her up.

She lifted a delicate eyebrow. "Mr. Hardcastle?"

He nodded, opening the door wider. "Please come in, Miss Chapman. It is Miss Chapman?" he asked, glancing at her bare fingers.

"*Ms.* Chapman."

Nodding, Tyrell closed and locked the door. "Well, Ms. Chapman, if we're going do business together, I don't think we should stand on formality. I'd prefer you call me Tyrell."

Viola shifted, staring at the tall, slender man dressed entirely in black. The V-neck pullover and slacks were the perfect foil for his gold-brown skin, eyes, and close-cropped sandy hair. It was her turn to visually devour his lean face with its attractive mole on his left cheekbone and his hypnotic cleft chin.

"What happened to your curiosity?"

He smiled for the first time, displaying a mouth filled with large white, straight teeth. The gesture reminded her of the rising sun, an inviting expression she found infectious.

"Oh, I'm still curious, Ms. Chapman. It's going to be up to you to convince me to become a participant in Carver's Career Cooperative."

She wanted to tell the very smug Tyrell Hardcastle that she was an educator, not a saleswoman. Either a business owner accepted the concept or rejected it. And if she had not wanted to meet her projected goal of a minimum of ten businesses she would have turned and walked out of Leo's soon after she'd walked in.

Forcing a smile, she crooned softly, "Only time will tell how convincing I can be. Is that not right, Mr. Hardcastle?"

His smile vanished as quickly as it had come. The timbre of Viola's voice had dropped, the dulcet sound sweeping over him like a sudden blast of heat from a hot oven. He nodded numbly, his gaze fixed on the brown-tinged orange color on her full lips.

"I insist you call me Tyrell," he said, recovering his voice, "because there are several other Hardcastles involved in the day-to-day operation of Leo's."

Cupping her elbow, he led through the darkened waiting area into the restaurant's dining room. He pushed two buttons on a panel on a wall, and the space was flooded with soft golden recessed lights. A soft gasp escaped Viola. "It's beautiful."

Dropping his hand, Tyrell stared at her stunned expression. "You've never been to Leo's?"

"No," she said, shaking her head. "And it's not as if I haven't heard wonderful things about the food and music from friends and colleagues."

Tyrell lifted an eyebrow. "You're soliciting Leo's participation without knowing anything about my family's business?"

Viola registered his heavy sarcasm. "My decision to solicit Leo's is based upon its reputation. On occasion I do private tutoring. And as the coordinator of this school year's cooperative, I surveyed the parents of these students to determine which businesses I would solicit."

"Is the same core group used to determine which businesses become involved in the cooperative?"

"I wouldn't know that."

"Why not?"

"Because every year the teacher chosen to lead the cooperative uses his or her own method for solicitation. This is my first year, so I thought, who better than the parents of these students? They have the money and clout to avail themselves of the best of everything in the capitol district. It is not my intention to flatter you, Tyrell, but Leo's consistently ranked at the top of the dining establishments."

He inclined his head. "If that's the case, then I'm going to have to give you a very special welcome to Leo's."

She frowned. "How?"

He smiled again, and this time a flicker of apprehension swept through Viola. There was something about Tyrell that was very attractive, yet the man wearing the somber colors radiated an air of danger—a danger that assaulted all of her five senses.

She had forced herself not to react when he cupped her elbow, while the clean masculine scent of his aftershave cloaked her in a sensual cocoon from which she did not want to escape. His face was undeniably male and stunningly handsome, his voice triple-X-rated. All that remained was taste. Her gaze went to his mouth, and she wondered if he would taste as good as he looked.

Realization hit her like a dousing of ice-cold water. Why was she lusting after a man she'd just met? A stranger? She didn't even know if he was single, or married with children!

Angling his head, Tyrell regarded Viola closely. He had interacted with a lot of women—literally hundreds of them since he had become Leo's executive chef—but none had come close to the perfection of the woman standing less than three feet away. She projected an air of poise, confidence, and sophistication he'd found lacking in the others. It was as if she wore a banner across her chest that touted: *I am the one.*

He wondered if she was or could be the one—the one to calm his restless spirit; the one who would help him to manifest his dream to open a culinary school in Washington, D.C.

His hand went to the small of her back as he directed her around rosewood tables with seating from two to eight. Each table claimed small Tiffany-style lamps and curvy glass vessels filled with wicks floating in colored oil.

"I'm going to prepare dinner, while offering you a little background on Leo's." Viola stopped short, causing Tyrell to bump into her. His hands touched her waist, steadying her. "Is something wrong, Viola?"

Glancing over her shoulder, she met his questioning gaze. "I thought you were the owner, not the chef."

His lids came down slowly, shuttering his gold eyes. "Leo's has four equal partners. My older brother Noah is responsible for the overall operation of the restaurant, while my twin brother Tyrone can take credit for the music. Then there's our first cousin, Ayanna. She's the accountant, and I must admit a financial genius. From the first day Leo's opened for business we have never had a week when we didn't realize a profit."

Viola's mind was a gamut of confusion. "My plan is to place students at Leo's who are interested in restaurant management."

"When your letter arrived, Noah gave it to me. Right now his schedule will not permit him to mentor any students, because they would have to work late afternoons and evenings to experience the full effect of interacting with our patrons. The volume of people coming through our doors on any given evening is much too great to take the time to train a student. Perhaps if we decide to open another restaurant, then it would be feasible."

"What made you more amenable to the idea than Noah?"

Tyrell decided that if he and Viola were going to work together, then he would have to be honest with her. "I'm planning to open a culinary school—"

"Where?" she asked, interrupting him.

"Here in D.C. If I decide to accept your students, then it will give me the hands-on experience I'll need to work one-on-one with aspiring chefs."

Her eyebrows shot up. "You want to use *my* students as guinea pigs for your own project?"

Crossing his arms over a broad chest, Tyrell shook his head. "Don't tell me this is a case of the pot calling the kettle black? You've solicited Leo's participation for your Career Cooperative, and now you're acting put out because I want the same thing you do. What's it going to be, *Ms. Chapman?*"

Viola bit down on her lower lip to keep from uttering a few colorful and profound epithets for which she usually chided her students. But on the other hand, she had come to Leo's to present Carver's vocational initiative, and she wasn't going to let Tyrell's self-serving arrogance dissuade her. There had been times when she had been threatened by street thugs, and she hadn't backed down. And there was nothing about Tyrell Hardcastle that hinted of thug.

Glancing up through her lashes, she affected a sensual smile. "What's for dinner, Tyrell?"

He came closer without actually moving. "What would you like?"

"Anything."

"Anything covers a lot. Meat, fowl, fish?"

"I'll take the fish, but only if it's fresh."

His fingers closing protectively over hers, Tyrell directed Viola to a enormous kitchen at the rear of the restaurant. He led her to two large tanks. One was filled with lobsters in varying sizes, the other with catfish.

"Fresh enough?"

Pulling back her shoulders, she tilted her chin in a gesture he quickly interpreted as defiance. "Yes."

"Good." He released her hand, a smile of contentment softening his even features. "Why don't you tell me about your proposal while I prepare dinner?"

# TWO

Looping the strap of her shoulder bag over the back of a tall stool, Viola sat down, watching the measured actions of Tyrell as he washed his hands in a stainless-steel sink before drying them and looping a bibbed apron over his head.

Waiting until he tied the apron around his slim waist, she said, "This is the cooperative's third year. The mission is to link up students with business establishments in the D.C. area. After an orientation, they will work one day each week in lieu of attending classes."

Tyrell pulled on a pair of large black rubber gloves. "How do you determine which students are eligible?"

"A vocational survey is administered to all incoming freshmen, and based upon the results of a computer analysis, we can usually determine a student's career focus. We then extrapolate those with an interest in the business sector."

"Do all of the grades participate?"

Viola shook her head. "No. The initiative is geared mainly to seniors. There was an exception this year because the committee selected a junior." Viola wanted to tell Tyrell that this student had expressed an interest in restaurant management. "The participants are paid a stipend, usually above minimum wage."

Tyrell glanced at Viola, admiring the long leg she had looped over the opposite knee. How, he wondered, were high school boys able to concentrate on their studies when their teacher looked like a high-fashion model?

"Are they permitted to work beyond the one day per week?"

"Yes. But not more than twenty hours each week."

Reluctantly he pulled his gaze away, reached into the tank, and caught a large thrashing crustacean. He placed it on a scale, peering closely at the numbers before returning it to the tank. He selected another lobster and weighed it.

"How much does that monster weigh?" The lobster on the industrial-size scale was huge.

"Sh-hh," Tyrell whispered. "Don't let Brutus hear you." She laughed softly, unaware of how the low, subdued, and sensual sound affected him. "I've been saving him for a special occasion."

Viola lifted an eyebrow. "Is this a special occasion?"

"I'd like to think so, Viola." He gave her a long, penetrating stare. "You've come to Leo's because you want something, and I'm thinking of accepting your proposal because I, too, want something." He didn't say was that something was a desire to know more about Viola Chapman.

She felt her pulse quicken. She hadn't thought it would be that easy for Tyrell to accept the initiative. Leo's would be a perfect venue, except that she wanted to place students at the restaurant who were interested in management, not cooking.

"None of the students have expressed an interest in becoming chefs."

"Have you asked them?"

A wave of heat rushed to her face. "No."

"I suggest you do. Chefs have come a long way since Julia Child came into our homes on public television more than thirty years ago. We now have our own cable channel, the Food Network."

Viola nodded in agreement. Cooking segments and celebrity chefs had become a part of the American landscape. Most morning shows highlighted regional dishes and restaurants. Devoting an entire channel to cooking had verified the country's passionate obsession with food.

"Tyrell?"

He smiled at her. "Yes, Viola."

"I'd like to ask a favor of you."

"Ask."

"Please don't cook Brutus."

He stared at her for several seconds before throwing back his head, roaring with laughter. The rich sound came deep from within his chest. Viola sat up straighter, pretending indifference. She didn't know what was so funny. All she'd asked was that he not cook the lobster.

Tyrell picked up Brutus, smiling. "You've been spared, old man, because of a woman who's not only soft-hearted, but also quite beautiful." Taking several steps, he returned the spared lobster to the tank.

Sighing in relief, she smiled. "Can't you prepare something that you don't have to kill?"

"But you said you wanted fresh fish."

"I do."

"I have shrimp and catfish already cleaned and filleted."

"Okay." There was a tremor of relief in her voice.

Opening a walk-in refrigerator-freezer, Tyrell picked up two labeled plastic containers. Viola's not wanting him to kill the lobster revealed a lot about her. She was compassionate. He had dated some women who were so competitive and aggressive that it usually diminished their femininity. In their goal to make it or become the best, they'd forgotten they were women first.

It wasn't that he did not admire a woman who wanted a successful career, but not at the risk of forfeiting what made her female. Everything about Viola Chapman indicated success, down to her choice in attire and accessories, yet her success had not overshadowed that she was wholly *woman*.

He placed containers on a countertop. "Do you eat pork products, or are you allergic to peanuts?"

Uncrossing her legs, Viola slid off the stool and closed the distance between them. Three inches of heels put her at five-ten, yet he still eclipsed her height by another five or six inches.

"Yes and no." She moved closer. "What are you going to make?"

"Sesame-crusted catfish with a Geechee peanut sauce."

"My grandfather was a Geechee. I never understood half of what he said."

"Where was he from?" Tyrell asked.

"Edisto Island. He taught me a proverb that says: *'If oonuh ent kno weh oonuh dah gwine, oonuh should kno weh oonuh come f'um.'*"

"'If you don't know where you're going, you should know where you come from.'"

Her eyes glittered with excitement. "You understand the language."

"There happen to be a few Geechees in the Hardcastle family tree."

Tyrell admired her enchanting profile. Her gray-streaked black shiny hair was the perfect style for her face. His gaze lingered on the straighter strands lying in perfect precision on her long neck. He'd tried guessing her age and failed. Despite the salt-and-pepper hair, her face claimed no lines or wrinkles. He was thirty-three, and he estimated that if she was older than that, it could only be by a few years.

"Would you like some help?" she asked, her dark gaze meeting his golden one.

He drank in her stunning beauty. "Do you cook?"

"Not much."

"How much is not much?"

"I can broil a steak, bake potatoes, and boil rice in a bag."

"What about vegetables?"

"There's always bagged salad and frozen vegetables."

He stared, complete surprise on his face. "No wonder you're so skinny."

Her jaw dropped. "I'm not skinny."

"Thin, skinny. It's all the same," he countered, waving a hand.

Folding her hands on her slim hips, Viola thrust her face close to Tyrell's. "You're a fine one to talk."

He gave her a placating smile. "I'm willing to bet that I'm closer to one-ninety than you are to one-twenty."

Viola wanted to tell him she weighed one hundred twenty-five pounds. But her vital statistics were none of his business. She had come to Leo's to present Carver's career initiative, not argue about whether she was too thin for Tyrell Hardcastle's personal tastes.

"If I can't help, then maybe I can watch you and *learn* something," she retorted, all business again.

His eyes narrowed slightly. "You've got a sharp tongue, Viola."

"It comes with the profession, Tyrell. After all, I teach high school."

"What subject?"

"English."

He grimaced. "My worst subject."

"Did you excel in any?"

"In fact, I excelled in all of them except English. It was the only course where I couldn't pull an A."

"What did you get?"

He paused, and then said, "B."

"Touché," she whispered softly.

Nodding, Tyrell leaned down and kissed her cheek. The scent of her perfume lingered in his nostrils after he'd raised his head. Reaching for her hand, he held it gently within his warm grasp. "You can help me by setting one of the tables."

Viola set a table for two with china, silver, and crystal in a corner of the dining room near a wall of stained glass. The shifting late-afternoon autumn sun streaming through the glass sparkled like diamonds, emeralds, rubies, sapphires, and citrines.

Tyrell had turned on a sound system from which flowed the soft sounds of contemporary jazz. Within minutes all of the accolades she'd heard about Leo's were manifested. A massive rosewood bar with a gleaming brass railing reflected overhead recessed lights.

Her fingers traced the luxurious fabric on the backs of padded stools lining the bar. It was apparent the Hardcastles had spared no expense when it came to decorating their upscale supper club.

Tyrell walked into the dining room, smiling. An overhead light created a halo around his head and face, turning him into a statue of molten gold.

"What's your wine preference?"

"White."

He winked at Viola. "I'll be right back."

She watched Tyrell as he made his way to a door at the opposite end of the dining room, admiring his loose-limbed walk. Five minutes later he reappeared, cradling a bottle of wine in the crook of one arm.

"Like Brutus, I've been waiting a long time to open this."

"What year is the vintage?"

"1974."

She lifted her eyebrows. "That's thirty years old."

He stared at the label. "But it's not really old. There are people who have private collections that are more than sixty years old. I read about someone in Europe who bought a 1938 Lafite Mouton Rothschild at auction for an astronomical price."

Viola smiled. "My mother was born in 1938."

Picking up a corkscrew, Tyrell opened the bottle, permitting the wine to breathe. He poured a small amount into a glass, handing it to Viola before he repeated the action for himself. Touching glasses, they sampled the vintage wine.

Nodding and smiling, she said, "It's wonderful."

"You get what you pay for," Tyrell confirmed.

"What did you pay for this bottle?"

He winked at her. "I'm not telling. I found it at a vineyard in the Loire Valley several years ago."

Resting her elbows on the bar's gleaming surface, Viola stared directly at the man who had more than aroused her curiosity. He was much more complex than she'd originally thought.

"Do you speak French?"

"French, a little German, Spanish, and Italian. My brothers and I were army brats. By the time we were eighteen, we'd lived on army bases on three continents."

"How did your mother adjust to being a military wife?"

"She never bonded with the other officers' wives because she was a teacher."

"What did she teach?"

"High school math. Even after Leo retired and returned to the States, Mom continued to teach. She finally retired last year."

Viola raised her wineglass. "Here's to a noble and rewarding profession."

Tyrell leaned closer. "Has it been rewarding?"

"For me it has been."

"How long have you been a teacher?"

"Nineteen years."

Tyrell's Adam's apple moved up and down in his throat as he tried to form the words to speak. "How ... how long?"

"Nineteen years. I entered college at sixteen and graduated at twenty. I will celebrate my twentieth year next fall."

"You're forty?"

"Not until December twenty-third."

He whistled softly. "Damn," he said softly. "You don't look more than thirty-four, maybe five."

She silently accepted his compliment. "How old are you?"

"Thirty-three."

There was something about Tyrell that made him appear very worldly to Viola. He did not look old, yet his demeanor wasn't that of a man in his early thirties.

"Why did you decide to become a chef?"

Tyrell smiled at Viola. "I'll tell you over dinner."

Viola was totally charmed by her dining partner as they shared an appetizer of chilled shrimp with a fiery cocktail sauce, followed by sesame-crusted catfish with a peanut sauce, brown roux, and sautéed okra.

She listened intently as he told of his fascination with cooking and the ingredients that made up any dish. After graduating high school he'd entered the Culinary Institute of America. Years later he returned to France, enrolling in graduate courses at the La Varenne École de Cuisine.

"Every February I take a month off from Leo's and travel either overseas or to other states to study with chefs featuring regional cuisine."

Viola touched the corners of her mouth with a linen napkin. "You feel you're ready to open a cooking school?"

Tyrell stared at her over the rim of his glass of sparkling water. "More than ready."

"Do you have a site for your school?"

He nodded. "I closed on a building two months ago."

"Where?" When he told her Viola gasped. "That's two blocks from where I live."

A wide smile curved his strong mouth. "You live in that new development with the loft apartments?"

"Yes."

"Well hello, neighbor," he said softly.

Suddenly she felt the need to put some distance between her and Leo's executive chef. Glancing at her watch, she noted the time. It was six-twenty. She had just spent more than two hours with Tyrell Hardcastle.

Placing her napkin beside her plate, she attempted to stand, but Tyrell was beside her, pulling back the chair. "You're leaving?"

"I've taken up enough of your time."

He stared at her from under lowered lids. "Why don't you let me be the judge of that?"

Tyrell was standing so close Viola could feel the whisper of his breath in her ear. "I have to leave, Tyrell. My workday begins at seven-twenty."

He took a step backward. Her day began early, while his did not begin until late afternoon. There was so much he wanted to know about Viola, but hadn't asked her. He would find out what he needed to know about her using an unorthodox method. It wasn't on the up-and-up, yet it wasn't illegal.

She smiled. "I'll talk to the students about rethinking a career in culinary arts."

"I would appreciate that. I expect the school to begin operating next fall. The space has to be renovated and outfitted with all of the necessary equipment before I'm licensed by the Department of Education, and it has to pass inspection by the fire department."

Viola nodded. "Thank you for dinner. Your cooking is incredible."

Tyrell wanted to tell Viola *she* was incredible. He couldn't remember the last time he had felt so relaxed, at ease with a woman.

"Perhaps we can do it again, even if your students decide they don't want to be chefs."

"Of course. I'll be certain to add Leo's to my favorite restaurants."

Successfully masking his disappointment, Tyrell smiled at her. "I'll look forward to that." He didn't want her to become another face in the crowd at Leo's. "How about next Monday?"

Viola wanted to reject the offer outright, but something wouldn't let her. "I'll call and let you know."

He escorted her back to the kitchen to retrieve her handbag, then walked with her to the parking lot. There were only two vehicles in the lot—her Honda and a late-model Toyota SUV.

Waiting until she was seated behind the wheel, Tyrell winked at her. "Get home safe."

Smiling up into his sun-lit eyes, Viola flashed a sexy smile. "I will. And thank you for everything."

*No, Viola. Thank you.* He closed the door, stepped back, and watched as she drove away. He was still standing in the same spot long after her car turned the corner.

Slipping his hands into the pockets of his slacks, he angled his head. Viola Chapman had cracked the shell he had put up around him to shield his heart ever since the woman he thought he'd love to his last breath deceived him.

The fact that Viola was an older woman never entered Tyrell's mind until he lay in his king-size bed—alone—later that night. He smiled in the darkness, then turned over on his belly to ease the growing hardness between his thighs. Just thinking about Viola had sent his hormones into overdrive.

It wasn't that he was celibate, but whenever he took a woman to his bed it was not in passion as much as it was for a physical release. He had given one woman all of his love and his passion. He recalled the woman with a lying tongue, a woman who had promised to share her life with him, only to fulfill that promise with another man. That had been three years ago.

Viola stood in front of the full-length mirror on the bathroom door, surveying her nude body. *No wonder you're so skinny.* She wasn't as skinny as she was slender. Her hips were small, inherited from her paternal grandmother. However, her breasts and legs more than compensated. Her breasts weren't large, yet they appeared fuller because of her narrow rib cage.

"Forget you, Tyrell," she whispered to her image. No man had ever complained about her body before; besides, at nearly forty she knew she looked good.

Damn good.

Slipping a pale pink silk gown over her head, she readied herself for bed.

# THREE

Tyrell set the truck alarm with a remote device. Then, with a determined stride, he left the parking lot and walked to the entrance of Carver High School. His footfalls made swishing sounds over the highly polished vinyl floor as he walked into the general office.

A young, attractive woman with braided extensions smiled at his approach. "Good morning. May I help you?"

He returned her friendly smile. "I'd like to see Ms. Farmer."

The receptionist glanced down at the large appointment book spread out on her desk. "Do you have an appointment Mr.—"

"Tyrell Hardcastle," he said, supplying his name. "No, I don't."

"Are you the parent of a student?"

*Damn!* he thought, *Do I look that old?* As soon as the question entered his head, he dismissed it. He supposed he could be old enough to have a son or daughter in high school if he had fathered a child at seventeen. At that age he'd been more interested in playing basketball and securing a driver's license than having sex. His older brother had teased him, saying he was a late bloomer when it came to women.

"I'm a friend of Ms. Farmer."

"Your name again, sir?"

"Tyrell Hardcastle. Please inform Ms. Farmer that I won't take up too much of her time."

He waited, glancing at the various bulletin boards covered with information for the school's faculty and staff. Sixty seconds after the receptionist dialed her boss's extension, the door to the principal's office opened.

"Ty Hardcastle! What a pleasant surprise. Please come in."

He turned his two-hundred-watt smile on a tall, full-figured woman in a conservative navy-blue suit, and white silk blouse, a double strand of perfectly matched pearls falling over her ample bosom.

Waiting until he was closeted in the principal's office, he kissed her scented cheek. "It's good seeing you again, Miss Anna."

Anna Farmer's hazel eyes crinkled in a smile. "Please sit down." She retook her seat behind her desk, waiting until he was seated on a worn brown leather chair. "What do I owe the pleasure of your company at Carver High?"

Tyrell studied the woman who happened to be his mother's best friend. The two women had grown up together, dated the same boys, but lost touch once Rosalind married Leo Hardcastle and settled into the life of a military wife. They had reconnected after Leo retired and the elder Hardcastles returned to the D.C. area.

"I need some information on one of your teachers."

The principal lifted an eyebrow. At fifty-nine, never-married Anna had devoted her life to educating children. Her khaki-hued smooth skin and sparkling hazel eyes had caught many a man's eye, but Anna had successfully thwarted their attempts to change her marital status.

"Which one?"

"Viola Chapman."

Resting her arms on her desk, Anna laced her fingers together. "What is you what to know about Ms. Chapman?"

"She came to me about your school's vocational initiative."

"Is Leo's interested in participating?"

*"I am."* The two words were emphatic.

Anna gave her friend's son a long, penetrating look. "Is this about the career initiative or Ms. Chapman?"

Tyrell crossed his legs and folded his arms over his chest. "Ms. Chapman." If he had been bold enough to come to Viola's school to inquire about her, then he knew he had to be direct with her boss.

A knowing smile softened Anna's face. "You want to know if she's married?"

Tyrell nodded. "Married, engaged, dating…"

She forced herself not to react to the talented chef's query. The last time she and Rosalind had gotten together, Rosalind had lamented that she didn't think she would ever become a grandmother. It appeared as if not one of her three sons appeared remotely interested in marrying and settling down. Rosalind feared Leo's had become their wives, girlfriends, or lovers.

"Neither of the above. But, let me clarify something. There has been talk that she and our football coach have gone out a couple of times. But, I don't think it's anything too serious, because he's also dating another teacher."

An unconscious smile displayed Tyrell's perfect white teeth. "Thank you, Miss Anna."

"Would you like to see her?"

"Now?"

"Sure."

Tyrell's pulse quickened. "Are you certain it will be all right?"

"This is my school, and if I say it's all right, then it is all right."

"You've made your point, Miss Anna."

They rose in unison, sharing a smile. "Come with me." Anna told her private secretary that she was going to Ms. Chapman's class and would return shortly.

Tyrell felt a shiver of apprehension as he followed the principal. He had come to Carver High because he wanted personal information as to Viola's marital status, never suspecting he would reunite with her less than twenty-four hours after their initial meeting.

Viola walked into her classroom, closing the door behind her. Within seconds all conversations came to an abrupt halt. Twenty-six pairs of eyes in an equal number of youthful faces were fixed on the tall, slender woman who strode deliberately to the desk in front of the room.

Placing her handbag in a drawer, she rounded the desk. She leaned against it, crossing her legs at the ankles. A slight smile softened her mouth. "Good morning."

"Good morning," came a chorus of masculine and feminine voices.

Viola's gaze swept over her students. Most were seniors, and quite serious about graduating in the spring. "How many of you completed the reading assignment?" Most of the hands went up. She eyed a tall, lanky boy slouching on his chair in the back of the room. "Please sit up straight, Mr. Keyeson, then tell me why you didn't complete your assignment."

James Keyeson shifted just enough so that the backs of his knees touched his chair. He had had enough run-ins with Miss Chapman not to blatantly challenge her.

"I read it, but I couldn't understand anything that Shakespeare dude was saying."

"Word," mumbled several other students in agreement.

Viola smiled at the students' response. "Using a show of hands, how many understood *Romeo and Juliet?*"

One girl raised her hand amid groans from the others. Racine Howard claimed a 4.0 grade point average, and was rumored to become the upcoming valedictorian.

"She must have read the *Cliffs Notes*," someone called out.

Racine's dark eyes gave off angry sparks. "I did not!"

Viola held up her hands. "Enough!" There was complete silence. "Over the next two months we're going to study two plays of the Bard, as people fondly call William Shakespeare. Born in 1564 in a small provincial town of Stratford-on-Avon, England, he became a prolific playwright, penning forty plays and sonnets before he died at the age of fifty-two. Reading Shakespeare for the first time is difficult because it is written in Early Modern English."

"It's like reading the King James Version of the Bible."

"Kyle's right," Viola said. "Shakespeare's pronouns are slightly different from our own and can be confusing." Walking to the chalkboard, she picked up a piece of chalk, drawing two columns, illustrating the differences in modern pronouns and those of Shakespeare's time.

Turning, she faced her students. "I've chosen *Romeo and Juliet* because it's about a young man and woman who fall in love despite their feuding families. I've also selected *Othello* because the central character is a Moor, a black man from North Africa."

"Shakespeare wrote about the brothers?" came a question from the back of the room.

Viola nodded. "Outside of *Othello*, the only other black person, male or female, present in Shakespeare's body of work is Aaron the Moor from *Titus Andronicus*."

Racine raised her hand. "If Shakespeare wrote so many plays, why did he only write about two black characters?"

"Good question, Racine. Just before we get into *Othello*, I'll give you an overview of English history during the time Shakespeare wrote his plays. Some critics argue that because of cultural stigmas of his day, Shakespeare would never have intended for a black man to be the hero in any of his plays. I'll let all of you determine this after viewing the video with Laurence Fishburne."

"Yo, isn't he the brother who played Morpheus in *The Matrix*?" James asked.

"Get out!" another boy shouted. "He ain't played in no Shake-speare thee, thy, and thou."

"Yes, he did," Racine countered. "I saw it."

The boy ripped a sheet of paper from his notebook, rolled it into a ball, and threw it at her. "Shut up, Racey."

Viola glared him. "Flirt with Racine on your own time, Philip." Red-haired, light-skinned, freckled Philip Jones flushed a bright pink. Turning her attention to the sniggling students, she continued. "Shakespeare was born more than four hundred years ago, yet he wrote about the things we see and read about today: love, lust, jeal-ousy, deception, murder, and betrayal."

James raised his hand, garnering her attention. "Miss C, can we write our own play, using our language?"

"Give me an example."

"Juliet calls Romeo. And he says, 'My sweet?' Then she asks, 'At what o'clock-tomorrow shall I send to thee?' Then he says, 'By the hour of nine.' All of that could've been said like, 'Yo, Romey, what time do I git with you tomorrow?'" The entire classroom erupted in laughter.

Viola smiled. "Now, you see what I'm talking about. Today's ver-nacular would've sounded as strange to Shakespeare..." Her words died on her lips as the door opened. Tyrell and the principal stood in the doorway. Everyone in the classroom sobered quickly.

Anna nodded at Viola. "Mr. Hardcastle wanted to come by and ob-serve your class." As silently as she had come, Anna closed the door.

Viola stared at Tyrell, shock rendering her motionless and mute. She saw things about him she hadn't noticed before. Maybe it had been the subdued lighting in the dining room, or that she had been more interested in getting him to accept the school's initiative than the man himself.

His shoulders seemed broader then she'd remembered. A leather jacket in a soft shade of butterscotch gold offset a chocolate-brown turtleneck, matching wool crepe slacks, and loafers. Her gaze moved slowly over his face, lingering on his distinctive cleft chin.

"Please have a seat in the back of the room, Mr. Hardcastle."

Heads turned and eyes followed the tall man as he made his way to the rear of the classroom. He sat down in the last row. Then, as if on cue, the students turned and stared at their teacher.

Tyrell stared at Viola as she wrote on the board the words "Capulet," "Montague," and "Verona," knowing they were discussing the timeless story about a pair of star-crossed lovers.

Completely enthralled, he watched her every move. No motion was wasted as she engaged her students in a discussion of a writer's work that had always eluded him. Perhaps if Viola Chapman had been his English teacher he would have been a straight-A student.

He wanted to retract his statement that she was skinny. A twin sweater set in a soft pale peach shade and a slim black skirt were more than flattering to her slender body. Each time she inhaled and exhaled, he watched the gentle rise and fall of her full breasts.

The bell rang, signaling the end of classes, but Tyrell did not move as the classroom emptied. It was only when Viola made her way toward him that he rose to meet her.

"What are you doing here?" Her voice had come out in a breathless whisper.

"I came to see you?"

"What for?"

"I'm willing to become a participant in your Career Cooperative."

Her eyes widened. "But, I haven't talked the students about—"

"When do you intend to talk to them?" he asked, interrupting her.

"Today."

"Will you call me if any are receptive?"

"Yes."

He gave her a lingering look. "Thank you."

"You're welcome."

He still had not moved. "Viola?"

She did not know why, but she loved hearing him say her name. It came out sounding like the instrument for which she'd been named. "Yes, Tyrell?"

"You look very nice."

Heat suffused her face. "Thank you."

"I'll see you around."

The four words were pregnant with a confidence that lingered with Viola beyond the end of classes.

She returned home and found two messages on her answering machine. The first was from her mother, reminding her that she was sending her a ticket for a flight to the Caribbean for the Christmas recess. The second message was from her best friend, confirming their once-a-month Friday-night dinner meeting. She and Paulette hadn't decided on a restaurant where they would dine, but Viola would suggest Leo's.

Picking up Tyrell's letter, she dialed the number on the letterhead. Her call was answered on the second ring. "Good afternoon, Leo's. How may I direct your call?" Instead of Tyrell's baritone voice, this one was distinctly feminine.

"I'd like to make a reservation for two for Friday evening, and also leave a message for Tyrell Hardcastle."

"At what time would you like to dine, ma'am?"

"Seven-thirty."

"The name, please?"

"Chapman."

"That's two for Chapman, Friday at seven-thirty. What is the message you'd like me to give Ty Hardcastle?"

"Please inform Mr. Hardcastle that Ms. Chapman's students have accepted his proposal."

"If he has to get back to you, Ms. Chapman, does he have a number where he can reach you?"

Viola wanted to tell the woman that Tyrell knew not only the number but also the address to Carver High School. And because time was of the essence, she decided to leave her home number. The cooperative initiative was scheduled to begin within two weeks.

The woman repeated the number and said, "We look forward to serving you, and I'd like to thank you for choosing Leo's for dining pleasure."

Viola smiled. "Thank you."

Depressing the button, she called Paulette Warren, informing her of their reservation at Leo's.

"Fabulous choice, Vi. Leo's features live music on the weekend."

"You've been to Leo's?"

"Twice. The service is superb and the food fabulous. I'm sorry to cut you short, but I have a dental appointment in half an hour. I'll meet you at Leo's on Friday."

Viola hung up, a satisfied smile curving her lush mouth. Leo's: superb service, fabulous food, and a very sexy executive chef—a most winning combination.

# FOUR

As Viola prepared dinner for herself, she thought about what she'd told Tyrell about her culinary prowess. She was not as skilled as he, but that did not mean her simple meals weren't nourishing and palatable. Tonight's fare was garlic-and-tarragon-flavored broiled chicken breast, a baked potato, and steamed frozen spinach. After filling a glass with chilled white cranberry juice, she carried a rattan tray with her evening meal into a room that doubled as her studio/library.

This space was the most lived-in area in the loft. Built-in shelves were crowded with books, sleeves of magazines, CDs, videos, and DVDs. An entertainment corner held a television and a state-of-the-art sound system. Comfortable chairs, love seats, and floor pillows invited one to come in and stay awhile.

Placing her tray on a side table, Viola folded her lithe body onto a cushioned chair with a matching footstool. Picking up a remote device off the table, she turned on the television to view the evening news. She watched the footage of a horrendous vehicular accident on the Beltway filmed by a news helicopter crew, her mind drifting to the discussion she had had earlier that afternoon with the students who had expressed an interest in careers in restaurant management.

What had surprised her was that the four were amenable to considering a career in the culinary arts. And when the two female students had mentioned they occasionally watched the Food Network, Viola had breathed a sigh of relief.

The soft chiming of the telephone pulled her thoughts away from her students and her gaze from the television screen.

She picked up the receiver after the second ring. "Hello."

"Good evening, Viola."

Her pulse quickened when she recognized the deep, distinctive voice. "Good evening to you, too."

There was a slight pause before Tyrell's voice came through the earpiece again. "I got your message that your students are interested in becoming apprentices here at Leo's. Did it take much convincing?"

"Hardly any," she admitted, smiling.

A soft chuckle came through the wire. "Smart kids."

"I'll agree with you on that. What I'm going to need from you is a curriculum with a corresponding time line."

"When do you need it?"

"As soon as possible."

"Let me check my schedule." There was the distinctive sound of pages turning. "I probably can have it for you by Sunday."

"I'll come by and pick it up Monday after classes."

"That's going to be a problem, Viola."

"Why?"

"I'm not available this Monday."

Viola remembered Tyrell saying that he was only free on Mondays. "What time on Sunday?"

"Two."

She nodded, although he could not see her. "Two is fine."

"I'll come by, pick you up, and we'll cook together."

"I don't want to cook with you, Tyrell."

"Bye, Viola."

Viola held the receiver to her ear, listening to the drone of the dial tone. He had hung up on her!

Returning the phone to its cradle, she thought of the first time she'd spoken to Tyrell and had abruptly ended their call. "Now we're even," she whispered.

Viola arrived at Leo's before Paulette, and sat in the waiting area with several other couples. She stared at a tall, impeccably dressed man talking quietly to the maitre d'. His coloring was darker than Tyrell's, as were his eyes, but there was no doubt they were brothers. Both claimed high cheekbones and a distinctive cleft chin. He had to be Noah, because she knew Tyrell had an identical twin.

Several minutes before seven-thirty, Paulette arrived and within minutes she and her friend were shown to a table for two. They ordered glasses of a white Zinfandel from the sommelier as soft laughter, subdued lighting, the sounds of ice tinkling in glasses, a quintet playing jazz selections, and the tantalizing aromas of food wafting from dishes carried by silent, efficient waiters and waitresses created an atmosphere of dining elegance in the richly appointment D.C. jazz supper club.

Viola stared across the table at her best friend. She and Paulette had formed a bond from childhood. They had grown up in the same neighborhood, attending the same schools, and both had decided on teaching careers. Paulette, older than Viola by a year, was her physical opposite: petite, ecru-hued complexion, large doll-like hazel eyes, and auburn hair, the college history professor attracted men like moths to a flame. She had recently celebrated her eighteenth wedding anniversary to her pediatrician husband, and although they were unable to have children of their own, Paulette and Thomas Warren had remained passionately in love with each other.

A waitress wearing the standard restaurant uniform of a white blouse with a Mandarin collar paired with a black skirt, approached their table, a professional smile in place.

"Good evening, my name is Shirleen, and I'll be your server for your dining pleasure. I'd like to tell you about tonight's specials." Viola and Paulette listened intently as the waitress enumerated dishes not listed on the menu.

A slight frown furrowed Paulette's forehead. "What is *sole meunière?*"

"Lightly pan-fried sole covered with a lemon butter sauce garnished with fresh parsley."

Paulette's frown vanished quickly. "I'd take the sole with a baked potato and the steamed vegetable medley."

Viola continued to study the menu. "And I'll have the deviled *poussin* with rice pilaf and marinated vegetables."

Shirleen smiled. "I'll bring your salads."

Waiting until the waitress walked away, Paulette leaned over the table. "What's been happening with you and Evan?"

"Nothing."

Lifting an eyebrow, Paulette gave her childhood friend a long, penetrating stare. "Why are you pushing him away?"

Viola schooled her expression to conceal her increasing annoyance. "I'm not pushing him away because he was never *there.* And you of all people should know how I feel about becoming involved with a coworker." Paulette was to have been her maid of honor at a wedding that now seemed a lifetime ago.

"What about Gregory? He wasn't a coworker."

Shaking her head, Viola rolled her eyes. "Now, I know you didn't go there. The man has been married three times, and I have no intention of becoming wife number four, thank you."

"But, he's so nice."

"Nice and certifiably crazy, Paulette." Dr. Gregory McDaniel, chief of psychiatry at a D.C. municipal hospital was tall, dark, incredibly handsome, and eccentric. He put on an oversize bib when eating and continually flicked his tongue, reminding her of reptile.

"Are you at least looking for someone, Viola?"

"No."

"Why not?"

"Because I don't want someone, Paulette." And she didn't. It had taken a long time, but she was now at peace with herself and the direction of her life.

"You know, you're still not too old to make me godmother to your children."

A bemused smile crossed Viola's face. "What's the matter with you tonight, Paulette?" She leaned closer. "Give it a rest."

A slight frown furrowed Paulette's smooth forehead. "I can't, Viola. Last week I dreamt about fish. And you know what it means when you dream of fish."

Viola wagged her head. It was an old Southern superstition that if one dreamt of fish, they were certain to hear of a pregnancy.

"You'd better check out some of your female relatives and colleagues, because I have no intention of getting pregnant."

"If you met a man and fell madly in love with him, would you at least consider having a child?"

Viola shrugged a shoulder. "I would if I married him."

Paulette sucked her teeth, then took a sip of wine. "Right. And we both know you'll never get married."

She knew Paulette was right. She had never wanted to marry. There were times when she wondered how it would feel to come home and share a roof with a man, go to sleep and wake up beside him day after day, and watch her belly grow with his seed. But all of those thoughts and dreams had been dashed fifteen years ago. Not only had she been left standing at the altar, but her fiancé had also eloped with another woman who had been their colleague. What Viola hadn't known at the time was that Frank had been sleeping with the foreign-language teacher, and that the woman was three months pregnant with his child. His deceit had been compounded twofold.

Embarrassed yet grateful that the school year had ended, Viola had tendered her resignation, moved from Richmond to the capital district, and applied for a position at a D.C. high school. With time, the pain and bitterness eased, and distrust of all men had taken their place.

The waitress returned with their salads, and the topic of marriage and children came to an abrupt end. Viola and Paulette spent the next two hours sipping wine, eating their delicious entrées, and listening to the talented lead singer of the quintet sing a repertoire of songs ranging from Billie Holiday, Etta James, Natalie Cole, and Sade to Alicia Keyes.

The two friends said their good-byes in Leo's parking lot, promising to see each other again in another four weeks.

Viola returned home, washed her face, brushed her teeth, and showered before she crawled into bed—alone. A slight smile softened her mouth when she recalled Tyrell Hardcastle's hauntingly attractive face and his deep, resonant voice. She finally slept, albeit uneasily. She was plagued by an erotic dream—one in which she was locked in a passionate embrace with Tyrell. She woke up, breasts heaving, her breath coming in short pants, and her body throbbing with a desire she had not felt in years. It took more than an hour before she fell asleep again. When she awoke late Saturday morning, it wasn't to the peace that always greeted her but an uneasiness that made her question whether she should meet with him the next day.

Viola heard the chiming of the intercom echo through her apartment at two o'clock Sunday afternoon. Walking over to a panel near the door, she pressed a button and saw Tyrell's image on a small closed-circuit screen. Pressing another button, she disengaged the lock to the outer door. Then she waited for him to walk the short hallway leading to her front door.

Thirty seconds later, she met Tyrell's brilliant gold gaze. A swath of heat suffused her face the moment his smile deepened the attractive lines around his eyes. Was she imagining an intriguing invitation in his eyes?

"Good afternoon," she said, opening the door wider. "Please come in." He was more casually dressed than on the other two occasions she had seen him. Like herself, he wore a pair of jeans that had seen so many washings they looked more gray than blue. He had paired his jeans with a gray golf shirt with a navy-blue collar and piping around the sleeves. It was the first time she had seen his arms, and she silently admired the corded muscles rippling under his deeply tanned, golden-brown skin. He looked nothing like the chefs on television, who looked as if they'd sampled their dishes more than necessary. Tyrell had the trim, hard physique of an athlete.

Tyrell's smile widened. "Good afternoon to you, too." Inclining his head, he pressed a soft kiss on her scented cheek.

In that instant, everything that was Viola Chapman became a part of who he was. Something intangible, mysterious, communicated to him that she was Adam's Eve, Romeo's Juliet, Napoleon's Josephine, Othello's Desdemona—women whose beauty and strength had totally bewitched their men.

And there was something about Viola that he found enchanting. He wasn't certain whether he liked her better in her business attire or in a long-sleeved, navy-blue polo, body-hugging jeans, and a pair low-heeled leather boots. Her casual look made her appear more relaxed, more approachable. The soft, clean scent of her perfume lingered in his sensitive nostrils. A knowing smile softened his mouth as he stared at her bare face. Her dewy skin was flawless, radiant.

He moved past Viola as she closed the door, his gaze sweeping the spacious entryway. He walked into a living-dining area. Free-standing curved walls and gleaming wood floors provided the perfect backdrop for eclectic furnishings ranging from a Louis XVI–style settee in the entryway to a contemporary table and chairs made of glass and steel tubing.

Light poured in through wide windows along exposed brick walls as well as through overhead skylights. A curving wrought-iron stair-case led to a second-story catwalk. It was apparent that Viola had taken meticulous care in renovating the loft from its former indus-trial setting to a residence for personal living.

Tyrell stared at Viola. "How many rooms do you have on the sec-ond story?"

A knowing smile parted her lips. Most people who visited her loft for the first time were intrigued by its layout. "Four. Would you like to see them?"

He returned her smile. "Yes, please."

The rubber soles on his running shoes made soft swishing sounds on the highly polished wood floor as he followed Viola across the length of the first level and up the curving staircase. His gaze was fixed on the outline of her slim hips inside her jeans and the narrow-ness of a waist he knew he could span with both hands. Viola may have been approaching forty, but she had the body of a woman half her age.

Viola slowed her pace when she reached the top of the staircase and turned to Tyrell.

"This is my bedroom."

A single glance at the room told Tyrell everything he needed to know about Viola: she was hopeless romantic. The all-white room evoked a sense of calm and innocence. A mahogany four-poster bed was draped in creamy sheer netting, and the ruching on a graceful love seat and wing chair complemented an off-white rug in a dramatically textured petit-point-and-honeycomb pattern in the adjoining sitting room. A vase of newly opening white roses in a milk-glass vase added to the absence of color that blended with textures and shapes.

"Perfect," he whispered in awe. He could not pull his gaze away from the pillows on the chairs in the sitting area, inviting him to come and stay while, and wondered, if he did get to know Viola well, whether she would ever invite him to spend the night.

"The next two rooms are my guest bedrooms. Unlike my bedroom that has an adjoining full bath, these have half-baths."

Her drawling, dulcet voice pulled Tyrell from his reverie. Like himself, it left no doubt that Viola was a native Virginian. "I thought you said you had four bedrooms."

Threading her fingers through his, she pulled him along the length of the catwalk. "This is what I call my aromatherapy room. I spend time here whenever I'm stressed out."

He did not know what to expect, but it wasn't a solarium. Glass walls and skylights let in the outdoors, and sunlight shimmered off the splashes of color against a white backdrop. Lush green flowering plants, baskets filled with magazines, coffee-table books, and candles, and white wicker furniture covered with floral-print cushions and pillows in sunny yellow and vibrant greens were conducive to total relaxation.

Squeezing the delicate fingers cradled in his large hand, Tyrell said, "It's incredible." What he wanted to tell Viola that *she* was incredible—perfect, with beauty, brains, style, and an innate, elegant sophistication that most women spent most of their lives trying to acquire.

love lessons

Viola pulled her fingers from his loose grasp. "If you want, we can have afternoon tea, either here or downstairs, while we go over your curriculum."

Ribbons of brilliant sunlight had turned Tyrell into a statue of molten gold. It reflected off the layers of gold in his skin, eyes, and hair. He lowered his gaze and a sweep of thick dark lashes resting on high cheekbones concealed the desire shimmering in those orbs.

"I didn't bring the curriculum."

Viola went completely still. He had promised to have the curriculum today. "You didn't do it?"

"I did it."

"Then, where is it?" Her voice had risen slightly.

Tyrell continued to stare down at her under hooded lids. "It's at my apartment."

Her eyes narrowed. "Your apartment?"

"Yes. Didn't I tell you that I would give you cooking lessons?"

"I don't need lessons, because I *can* cook," she retorted quickly. "And, instead of telling me what you want me to do, may I suggest asking."

"And because," he continued as if she hadn't spoken, "you eat rice you've boiled in plastic, bagged salad greens, and frozen vegetables, I decided we'll prepare a traditional Sunday dinner at my place. After dinner we can go over the curriculum together." He glanced at the watch strapped to his left wrist. "I suggest we leave now."

Turning on his heel, he walked out of the solarium and retraced his steps along the catwalk, leaving Viola to follow. Quickening her pace, she caught up with him as he descended the staircase.

"Tyrell." He stopped, but did not turn around. She stared at the breadth of his broad shoulders. "If we're going to work together over the next eight months, then I'm going to insist that you not make plans unless you consult with me first."

Rochelle Alers

"I remember distinctly telling you that I'd come here on Sunday at two to pick you up. It's after two, and I'm ready to eat."

Without saying another word, he walked down the curving staircase, leaving Viola to stare at his departing figure. Galvanized into motion, she followed him. She picked up her keys from a table in the entryway and grabbed her purse from a hook in a closet near the front door.

Tyrell stood at the door, waiting for her to open it. She squinted at him, successfully curbing her rising temper. "Let's get one thing straight before I walk through this door with you."

His stoic expression did not change. "What?"

"This is not a game or a competition. It's a cooperative. And that means we have to work together, not against each other."

He took a step, bringing them inches apart. "I suppose I'm going to need a little tutoring, because I'd always managed to get a 'needs improvement' in 'works and plays well with others.'"

The natural scent of Tyrell's body mingling with the clean, masculine fragrance of his aftershave and cologne brought a rush of heat to Viola's face. He was too close, potently masculine, and she knew if she did not put some distance between herself and the chef she would embarrass herself.

"You're too old for me to tutor," she hissed.

A smile crinkled his eyes. "Didn't you say I'm not too old to learn?"

That was true. She had told him that seconds before she'd hung up on him the first time they communicated. "Touché, Tyrell."

His smiled widened. "What's it going to be, Viola? Are you willing to give me lessons?"

"I'll have to think about it."

Lowering his head, he kissed her cheek again. "Don't take too long."

"Are you coming onto me, Tyrell?"

"Yes, ma'am," he murmured.

"But..." Her words trailed off.

"But what, Viola?"

"I'm too old for you."

Tyrell chuckled, a deep rumbling sound echoing in his throat and chest. "I wouldn't know anything about that because I can't count above thirty."

It was her turn to laugh. "I thought you were a straight-A student, with the exception of English."

Instead of replying, he winked at her. "Let's go, Viola. We'll discuss my grades and curriculum after we eat dinner."

Viola thought Tyrell was aggressive and arrogant, but decided to placate him this time because she needed Leo's for the Career Cooperative. She locked her door, and then, with Tyrell cradling her hand, they made their way out of the building to the visitor parking lot. Ten minutes later, after she had walked into Tyrell's Georgetown townhouse, she had forgotten all about being seven years older than Leo's executive chef.

# FIVE

Viola knew instinctively that Tyrell was a bachelor. Nothing in the living and dining rooms of his apartment hinted of a feminine touch. The raw qualities of natural fabrics in shades of brown and cream complemented the earthy tones of brick walls, a tan marble fireplace, and a leather seating arrangement. Photographs lined the fireplace mantel, and she recognized the somber image of the man who had greeted her and Paulette at Leo's on Friday night. He had to be Noah Hardcastle.

Tyrell watched Viola study his family's photographs, his gaze roaming leisurely over her slender body. Everything about her—from her professionally coiffed hair to her classic casual attire—screamed elegance. She was beautiful, exquisite, and he wondered why some man hadn't claimed her as his wife. Moreover, he wanted to know if she had ever been married.

"I met your brother the other night."

Tyrell went completely still. "Noah?"

"Yes."

"When did you meet him?"

Viola turned to face him. "Friday night at Leo's. I was there with a friend."

He opened his mouth to ask her if the friend was a man, but decided against it. He had no right to question Viola about whom she dated. "You should've let me know you were there. I would've prepared something off the menu for you."

"That wasn't necessary. I really enjoyed the deviled *poussin*."

His smile widened as he extended his right hand. "Are you ready to assist me in the kitchen? I'm going to show you exactly how I will interact with your students the first time I show them the inside of Leo's kitchen."

"Speaking of Leo's, don't you work on Sundays?"

"No. I'm off Sundays, and of course on Mondays and occasionally on Tuesdays, which is traditionally a restaurant's slow night. The assistant chefs are more than capable of running the kitchen when I'm not there."

Viola put her hand in Tyrell's as he led her out of the living room and into his kitchen. She had assumed that because he cooked at the restaurant he never would cook at home, but the number of pots, pans, and utensils hanging from overhead hooks said differently. Outfitted with the latest equipment and gadgets, the kitchen was the perfect setting for composing a gourmet masterpiece.

"I thought it would be nice if we dined on the patio." Releasing her hand, he pointed to a large room off the kitchen.

If Tyrell had been shocked by her solarium, his patio held her in awe. Floor-to-ceiling pocket windows provided the backdrop for an oasis. Towering potted cacti, ferns, palms, and bamboo, along with a corner waterfall, set the mood for total escape and relaxation.

Sparsely furnished in an Asian décor, the minimalist room was a delicate departure from the furnishings in the living and dining rooms. A white-textured rug covered the wood floor. The soft strains of classical music filled the air. A round glass table was set with polished glasses, gleaming silver, and votives in crystal holders. In the center was a rectangular glass vase overflowing with a profusion of white lilies.

"How beautiful." The words spilled from Viola's lips in a hoarse whisper.

Tyrell moved closer to her, inhaling the hauntingly sweet scent of lilies on her skin. He had purchased them earlier that morning because their fragrance reminded him of the woman who unknowingly had ensnared him in a web of desire.

He did not know why, but he had been driven to see her, hear her beautifully modulated voice, touch her silken flesh, and inhale the scent of the perfume that blended with her natural feminine bouquet. Everything about her assailed all of his five senses, leaving him to drown in a maelstrom of longing that had kept him from a restful night's sleep.

His gaze was drawn to the nape of her long, slender neck. "What do you want to eat?"

Viola felt the whisper of Tyrell's moist breath and shivered noticeably. "What are my choices?"

"French, Italian, and Southern."

"Italian," she said without hesitating.

"How does roast pork loin with garlic and rosemary, zucchini sautéed in olive oil and chopped shallots, and carrot batons in a Madeira sauce appeal to you?"

Her smile was sensuous. "It sounds delicious."

Tyrell leaned closer. "Will you assist me, Viola?"

She closed her eyes, taking deep breaths, hoping the rapid pounding of her heart would slow down enough for her to maintain control. She didn't want to embarrass herself.

"Are you going to grade me?"

"Not this time. I'll get an apron for you, then we'll begin."

---

Viola spent the next ninety minutes watching and listening to Tyrell as he gave her an overview of the utensils and appliances. She sat on a tall stool at the cooking island stripping rosemary leaves from their stems, adding them to the garlic, peppercorns, and salt in a food processor, while Tyrell trimmed the excess fat and sinew from a pork loin. It took him less than a quarter of an hour to prepare the loin and stuff the pulverized garlic, rosemary, peppercorn, and salt into the natural flap of the meat. Using separate pieces of string, he tied the string at one-inch intervals to hold the pork together during cooking.

It took her longer than Tyrell would've taken to complete it, but she managed to slice the zucchini at the perfect angle while he cut up the carrots. He was quick with his praise and gentle in admonishing her when she failed to follow his instructions. Whether he was aware of it or not, Viola knew he had the potential of becoming an excellent instructor. They moved easily around the kitchen, each engrossed in their own tasks as if they had worked together for weeks instead of an hour.

Tyrell washed the bowl of the food processor at one of the two sinks on the cooking island. "Would you like dessert?"

Viola smiled at him across the expanse of granite countertop. "Yes. What are we having?"

"*Crostata di fragole e lamponi.*"

She lifted a delicate eyebrow. "And that is?"

"A strawberry-and-raspberry hazelnut tart."

She cooed softly, shaking her head. "Now you're really talking to me. I have a serious weakness for berries and nuts."

Drying his hands on a towel, Tyrell rounded the counter and took the knife from her. "You're going to make the tart by yourself."

"No, I'm not!"

"Yes, you are, Viola. It's easy. I'll tell you exactly what to do. Traditionally, Italian fruit tarts are simple—often nothing more than fresh fruit on a pastry crust. We'll use red berries on top of a hazelnut pastry, then we'll decorate it with Marsala-flavored whipped cream."

Her apprehension eased as she followed Tyrell's instructions to the letter. By the time the pastry had baked to a golden brown and she had transferred it to a serving plate to cool, the full flavor of the roasting pork blended with the intensified nutty smell of the hazelnuts.

She pointed at the pastry bag on the countertop. "I'm not dealing with that."

Tyrell's light brown eyes twinkled. "Come on, Viola. You've done the hard part making the pastry dough."

Crossing her arms under her breasts, she shook her head. "No."

Moving over to her, he curved his arms around her body, pulling her to his chest. Her arms fell to her sides. "Don't tell me you're going to wimp out on me now."

Tilting her head, she stared up into the golden orbs. Her gaze caressed the sharp angle of his cheekbones, the minute mole high on his left cheek, and his chin.

"Calling me names won't get me to change my mind, Tyrell."

"Are you always so stubborn?"

A slight smile played at the corners of her mouth. "Only when I have to be."

Tyrell studied her face, feature by feature, committing each one to memory. His expression changed, suddenly becoming serious. "You're incredible."

A frown furrowed her smooth forehead. "What are you talking about?"

"I'm talking about you, Viola."

"What about me?"

"You're beautiful." There was so much awe in his compliment that she almost laughed aloud. "I'm certain men tell you that all the time," he continued softly.

Viola shook her head. "No."

"No, because you believe you're not, or is it no that they don't tell you?"

"Both."

"I can't believe not one man has said it to you."

She closed her eyes. "One did, but that was a long time ago."

Lowering his head, Tyrell pressed his mouth to her ear. "When?"

"Fifteen years ago."

"What happened?"

Viola had to ask herself whether she was ready to open up to Tyrell—a stranger she hadn't known two weeks. A man who would cease to become a stranger over the next eight months because of her school's Career Cooperative.

"He left me standing at the altar, because he was marrying another teacher who just happened to be pregnant with his child."

Tyrell tightened his grip on Viola's body, unaware that he was hurting her until she gasped aloud. He eased his hold as his lips feathered under her ear and along the column of her long neck.

"It's all right, baby," he whispered. "He didn't deserve you."

Closing her eyes, Viola shook her head. "That may be true, but it still hurts. I'll never forget the humiliation on my father's face, or the tears in my mother's eyes. Meanwhile, I'd been too numb to cry. I told my parents that we would hold the reception anyway, but they refused. Things got ugly when Daddy went after my father-in-law-to-be, screaming that his son was a sonofabitch. My maid of honor pulled me out of the church just as the police were arriving."

Tyrell turned Viola around to where he could see her face. "Did your father at least kick his butt?"

She managed a trembling smile. "He did get in a few licks before some of my male cousins broke it up."

"Good for him."

She gave him a measured stare. "Don't tell me you condone violence."

"Only when it's absolutely necessary. Whatever happened to the snake?"

Viola chuckled. It was the first time in fifteen years that she could actually laugh about the incident. "He slithered away."

"You never heard from him again?" She shook her head. "And you never married?" Again Viola shook her head. "Don't you *want* to get married? Have children?"

She knew it was too easy to get lost in Tyrell's look of desire and yearning, and it wasn't vanity that told her that he was interested in her because of her looks. He made that quite obvious.

"I don't give it much thought," she said primly.

"Is it because you don't want to, or because you haven't met the right man?"

"Both."

It was easier for Tyrell to accept her not having met the right man than her not wanting to marry at all. There had also been a time in his own life when he'd planned to marry and share the rest of his life with a woman, but, unlike Viola, his nuptials were thwarted before the church ceremony. Four months before he was to exchange vows with Rachel Harrison she'd returned his ring, tearfully claiming she wasn't ready for marriage. He had accepted her decision without question, but less than a month later she married a man who had been her high school sweetheart.

Rachel's deceit would have destroyed him emotionally, had it not been for his involvement with Leo's. He'd supervised the kitchen every day the restaurant was open for business, catering weddings and private parties, literally working around the clock. His workaholic tendencies disappeared once he came up the idea of establishing a culinary institute.

"Tyrell?"

Viola's voice broke into his reverie. "Yes?"

"That tart will never get done if you don't let me go."

His arms dropped. "I'll finish the tart, but the next time you're on your own."

She flashed a sassy smile, wrinkling her nose. "I didn't know I was going to be one of your students."

"Think of it as a reciprocal arrangement. You teach me how to work well with others, and I'll teach you how to cook."

Viola folded her hands on her hips. "I told you, I *know* how to cook."

"If that's the case, then I want you to cook for me." Her eyes widened at his challenge, and Tyrell decided to press his attack. "I want you to cook for me next Sunday. It can be here or at your place. If you want to cook here, then just let me know what you need and I'll have it on hand for you."

Viola knew she had walked into a trap of her own choosing, but decided to accept his challenge. "I'll cook, but nothing fancy."

"Fancy doesn't always mean palatable."

"Oh, will be palatable."

He smiled. "Your place or mine?"

"Mine."

"Good."

That was the last word they exchanged on the matter. As Viola watched, Tyrell sliced the large strawberries into quarters with a minimum of effort, poured heavy cream in a chilled bowl and blended it with a whisk until it formed soft peaks, then he added confectioners' sugar and Marsala wine, whisking the cream some more. Using a metal spatula, he spread two-thirds of the Marsala whipped cream evenly over the cooled hazelnut pastry, just to the edge, then filled a pastry bag with the remaining third.

His voice broke the silence. "Now pay close attention, Miss Chapman," he teased. "Starting with the outer edge and working inward, I'm arranging the strawberries in concentric circles over the cream. Once this is done, I'm going to arrange the raspberries in a pile in the center." Tyrell worked quickly as he lectured. "But," he emphasized, "I'm leaving a half-inch space between the strawberries and raspberries. This is essential because it's going to be filled in with a piping of cream rosettes."

He picked up a pastry bag fitted with a startipped tube. In less than sixty seconds he had decorated the tart with a ring of cream rosettes between the strawberries and raspberries, and made eight large rosettes around the outside edge on the strawberries. He finished the dessert masterpiece by garnishing each large rosette with a toasted hazelnut. Balancing the plate on his fingertips, he walked over to the stainless-steel refrigerator-freezer, opened the door, and placed it on a shelf to chill.

Using her fingers, Viola scraped the bowl and licked the cream as she had done as a child whenever her mother baked a cake.

Tyrell returned to the cooking island and smiled. "Good?"

"Uh-huh," she moaned, closing her eyes.

"Let me have a taste."

Without warning, he caught her hand and ran his tongue along the length of her fingers. Viola went completely still, but he continued his sensual assault on her hand as he flicked his tongue over her palm.

Then, without warning, he licked at the corner of her mouth. "Oh, yeah," he whispered. "It *is* good." His head came up and he met her startled gaze. "You had cream on your lips."

She nodded like a marionette being manipulated by a puppeteer. She hadn't wanted him to kiss her and remind her of what she had missed—what she was missing. His nearness made her senses spin, as if she had been caught in a vortex of longing that had no beginning or end.

"I think we should get back to the cooking lesson."

Tyrell blinked once. The spell was broken. He did not know why he had kissed Viola, other than he had wanted since first meeting her. There was something about the petulant curve of her lower lip that intrigued him. There was just enough of a pout to make her appear to be sulking.

He glanced at a clock over the oven. "I'll check the pork, then I'll show you how to sauté the squash and carrots."

Twenty minutes later Tyrell escorted Viola to the patio. Smiling, he took a step backward. "Come sit, and I'll serve you."

He pulled out a chair at a place setting and she sat down. Tilting her chin, she smiled. "Thank you."

Tyrell nodded, returning her smile. He picked up a lighter wand and lit the candles. She stared at his retreating back as he walked out of the patio to the kitchen.

Eyes closed and motionless, Viola listened to the haunting strains of a Mozart sonata played by a string quartet. Her eyes were still closed when Tyrell returned, pushing a serving cart. Within minutes he had set the table with salad plates of field greens tossed in a light oil-and-vinegar garlic dressing, a chilled bottle of rosé wine, and several serving dishes.

She opened her eyes, meeting his gaze as he stood opposite her. "Everything looks and smells wonderful."

Tyrell placed the pork on a cutting board, quickly and expertly slicing them into three eight-inch pieces. He spooned two tablespoons of Madeira sauce onto a plate, added slices of pork, zucchini, and carrots, then placed the plate in front of Viola.

"*Buon appetito!*"

Taking his seat, he filled a plate for himself.

Lowering her head, Viola said grace, then picked up her knife and fork. It had taken only a taste of the pork and vegetables to conclude that Tyrell Hardcastle was a gifted chef. He had to agree with her. The meal so far had met his high standard of excellence. The pork stuffed with garlic and rosemary was tender and aromatic, while the accompanying vegetables added color to the appetizing presentation.

She smiled at him across the table. "I'm thinking of hiring you to become my personal chef."

Tyrell lifted an eyebrow. "That can be arranged."

She met and held his gaze. "Are you serious?"

"Very serious. Aside from supervising Leo's kitchen, I cater private parties, luncheons, and weddings."

"When do you find the time?"

"I get up early and either cook here or at Leo's before the restaurant opens for business."

Viola took a sip of wine, staring at Tyrell over the rim of the glass. "How will setting up your own cooking school affect your position at Leo's?"

"I will continue as one-fourth owner, while the top two graduates of any class will be offered the opportunity to work at Leo's. I've reassured Noah that I will always be available for the restaurant's private parties."

"It sounds as if you have quite an undertaking ahead of you."

Tyrell smiled, his jeweled eyes shimmering like multifaceted citrines. "I'm looking forward to the challenge. How about you, Viola?" he asked, deftly shifting the focus away from himself.

"What about me?"

"How many more years do you plan to teach?"

"Next year will my last."

His jaw dropped. "You're retiring?"

She nodded, successfully concealing a smile when she noticed his shocked expression. "I plan to take a year off, then open a tutorial center with a friend."

"Where?"

"In D.C."

"Have you inquired about space?"

"Not yet."

"Do you plan to buy or rent?"

"It would depend."

"On what?" Tyrell asked.

"On the purchase price."

"If you're serious about buying, then let me know."

A slight frown formed between her eyes when Tyrell affected a mysterious smile. "What aren't you telling me?"

"The property where I'm setting up my school is owned by an uncle of mine. I'm certain I could talk him into offering you a good deal if you're interested."

"I am interested," she said quickly, thinking how she could walk to the center from her home. She had always conducted her private tutoring in a student's home.

"How much space do you think you'll need?"

"I'm not sure. Several classrooms and one or two private offices."

"How does six thousand square feet sound to you?"

"I'm certain that will be more than enough."

"I'll talk to my uncle, then I'll get back to you." Rising to his feet,

Tyrell pushed back his chair. "Please excuse me while I get my curriculum. Would you like coffee with dessert?"

"Please."

Two hours later, Viola stood in the entryway to her home, holding a colorful shopping bag filled with plastic containers of sliced pork, vegetables, and hazelnut tart. Tyrell had packed the containers, along with a copy of his curriculum in its own protective plastic envelope.

She returned his smile. "Thank you for everything."

"Are you still cooking next Sunday?"

"Of course."

"What time do you want me to come?"

"Three."

He smiled, moved closer, and brushed his mouth over hers. "Thank you again for your company."

Viola blinked once and he was there. She blinked again and he had opened the door and was gone. A sensual smile softened her mouth as she made her way to the kitchen to put away what would become dinner for the next several days.

She had to admit to herself that Tyrell was a bit brash and arrogant, but that did not stop her from liking him. What she did not want to do was like him too much. That could happen if she failed to keep their association on a business level.

"It's only business," she admonished herself. She repeated her warning several times until she had convinced herself that the last four hours she had spent with Tyrell was exactly that.

# SIX

Viola glanced at her watch, surveyed her dining room table, and found it perfect. She had set it with her best sterling and china, and the crystal stemware she had inherited from her maternal grandmother. The antique linen tablecloth and matching napkins were housewarming gifts from her mother after she had moved into the loft. A crystal vase cradled a dozen petite calla lilies and curly willow.

She had spent almost two hours in the cooking section of a bookstore Friday afternoon, trying to decide what she would prepare for her Sunday dinner with Tyrell. She was not a chef, but she could read. She believed that by following a recipe to the letter, there was no doubt that the dishes would turn out like the ones in the glossy photographs. Tyrell had prepared Italian cuisine for her, so she had decided to reciprocate with French.

It wasn't until she had placed her credit card on the counter after the salesclerk rung up her purchases that she realized she had spent nearly a hundred dollars on cookbooks. Fortified with her recipes, she had headed for Williams-Sonoma for utensils, measuring cups, spoons, pots, and pans, then returned home and pored over the books until she came up with a menu: roast chicken with an apricot-fig stuffing, asparagus with tarragon butter, and stuffed turnips. Her dessert selection was a crème caramel.

The doorbell rang exactly at three, and as she went to answer it, she reminded herself once again that the dinner was a business matter. Pressing a button, she saw Tyrell's image on the tiny screen. The sight of him caught her breath. She pushed the button to disengage the lock to the outer and opened her apartment door. There he was, smiling as he came closer, a large black shopping bag in his right hand.

His all-black attire of sharply creased slacks, a mock-turtleneck sweater, and a lightweight trench coat made him look taller, slimmer. She struggled with her excitement and hoped it didn't show. It had been a week—seven days—since she had seen Tyrell and she had spent the entire time waiting to see him again. During that week there *had* been nothing but business between them. She had the English Department secretary send him a letter approving his curriculum for the Cooperative. The letter listed the names of the students who were expected to arrive at Leo's Monday morning at nine. She also enclosed a memorandum of understanding for his signature, outlining his commitment and responsibilities as a Career Cooperative participant.

Tyrell's pulse accelerated as his gaze swept over Viola's lithe figure in a black wrap skirt that ended midcalf, a tailored white long-sleeved blouse with generous cuffs, and a pair of black leather high-heeled sling-backs. Her coiffed hair, her satiny face, and her body's sensual fragrance sent his hormones into overdrive. He could not understand why this woman had such an effect on him. He had dated at least half a dozen others since Rachel had walked out of life. His smile widened when she lifted her chin to give him a shy smile.

"Hello again, Viola."

"Hello." She opened the door wider. "Please come in."

He handed her the bag. "Here's a little something for your home."

Viola peered into the bag. Tyrell had given her a sago palm bonsai plant in a traditional Japanese ceramic bonsai pot. Her dark eyes were glittering with delight.

"It's exquisite, Tyrell. Thank you so much. But you didn't have to bring me anything." She set the bag on a side table.

His expression was impassive. "Yes, I did. I wanted to give you something for approving my curriculum."

"I approved it because it's exactly what I was looking for." She extended her free hand. "I'll take your coat." Droplets of rain clung to the silken garment.

He removed his coat but did not give it to her. Opening the hall closet, he hung it on a hook on the door. Raising his head, he sniffed the air. "Something smells quite good."

"Oh, that must be my boil-in-bag rice," Viola teased, deadpan. Tyrell stared at her, a stunned expression on his handsome face. She gave him a sweet smile. "It turned out very nice this time. Usually I don't boil it long enough and it ends up with the consistency of roasted nuts. But, then again, I once overcooked it and it stuck together like a glue ball."

"And—you ate it?"

"Of course," she said flippantly. "It's not too bad when you serve it with Spam."

He moaned under his breath but managed to keep a straight face. "You eat Spam?"

"At least three times a week." Viola reached for Tyrell's hand. "I hope you brought your appetite."

Tyrell followed Viola, praying silently he would be able eat what she had prepared without regurgitating. *Spam!* A slight shudder shook him.

His gaze widened in shock when he saw the dining room table.

Moving closer, he stared at the delicate cameolike figures from classical mythology on the distinctive Wedgwood-blue china pieces. The multifaceted lead-crystal glasses and goblets matched the vase holding the calla lilies.

A slow smile deepened the lines around his eyes. "Exquisite."

Viola clasped her hands together. "Thank you. I hope you're going to enjoy what I've prepared."

Tyrell forced a smile he definitely did not feel. "Do you need help with anything?"

"Yes, thank you."

He followed Viola into the kitchen. On a sideboard she had assembled, hot from the oven, a platter with two golden brown, stuffed chickens, a clay dish of stuffed turnips, and another of white asparagus with tarragon butter.

She handed him the platter. "I'll bring the vegetables."

Tyrell glared at Viola under lowered lids. "You know I'm going to pay you back for playing with my head."

Moving closer, she kissed his cheek. "What's the matter, Ty? Can't you take a joke?"

"*Spam*, Viola? Mystery meat?"

She winked at him. "Don't knock it. In certain parts of the country it would win out over filet mignon by ten to one."

A hint of a smile curved his sensual mouth. "I still owe you one."

Picking up the clay dishes, she shook her head. "I can't believe you would hold a grudge because I teased you."

"Didn't I tell you that I need improvement in learning to work well with others?"

"After dinner, we'll work on it."

Dinner was accomplished with a minimum of conversation as Tyrell had two servings of the moist, succulent chicken stuffed with

love lessons

61

chopped dried figs, apricots, fresh rosemary, thyme, and topped with a glaze of apricot jam and balsamic vinegar. He also ate two turnips stuffed with pork sausage, chopped hazelnuts, dried currants, fresh sage, and at least half a dozen stalks of asparagus.

Viola was pleasantly surprised that everything tasted as good as it looked. There was no doubt Tyrell would give her a high grade for presentation. Instead of wine, she had squeezed lemons into a pitcher filled with strawberry syrup and sparkling water. The result was a tart yet sweet refreshing beverage.

Patting his flat belly, Tyrell touched his napkin to his mouth. "You get an A, Viola, for taste and presentation."

She blew out her breath. "Thank you. Just don't ask me to cook for you again."

He lifted an eyebrow. "Why?"

"I spent two hours shopping for the ingredients and another chopping herbs. Then I got up early this morning to wash and stuff the chickens and turnips. It took two attempts for me to get the dessert right." She affected a sexy moue. "And I don't care what you say. There's nothing wrong with eating rice or salad from plastic bags."

Pushing back his chair, Tyrell rounded the table and eased Viola to her feet. He cradled her chin in his hand, his light-brown eyes moving slowly over her delicate features.

"You don't have to cook for me if you don't want to. I'd be honored to cook for you—every day—that is, if you want me to."

Her eyelids fluttered. "I'm not saying I didn't enjoy preparing dinner once I saw the results, but it was just that it took me a long time to chop up the herbs and spices. Then I had to make certain I did not put the sage in the butter for the asparagus instead of the tarragon."

"Shh," he whispered against her lips. "You will never have to cook for me again," Tyrell repeated, then pressed his mouth to her parted lips.

Viola leaned into the kiss, and her curiosity as to how he tasted was finally assuaged—delicious! His mouth was firm and soft, demanding, masculine, and addictive. She had been kissed before, but not like this. He was placing soft, nibbling kisses at the corners of her mouth that sent shivers of desire racing up and down her body. Heat, hotter than the one that came from her oven, settled between her legs. She moaned softly as a tremor inside her heated thighs grew stronger until it throbbed with a long-forgotten desire.

Tyrell inhaled the mingled fragrances of Viola's hair and skin. He wanted her! He had wanted her the instant she had walked into Leo's. Even when he hadn't known whether she was married or engaged he had wanted her, so much that he had boldly gone to her school to seek her out, just to see her again.

He had never chased a woman, but here he was, doing just that. Not only did he want Viola in his bed, he wanted her in his life. It had taken three long years of mourning for what had been and would never be again. Rachel was gone, and since meeting Viola he had come to face the reality that marriage to Rachel would have never lasted beyond the first year. He had been in serious denial thinking he could have made Rachel forget her first love.

But Viola was different. She had loved and lost, and for fifteen years she had kept men at a distance because she did not want to repeat the scenario. He had also loved and lost, but he knew instinctively that with Viola he could learn to trust and love again. She was secure as a woman and in her career. She had gone through highs and lows, and now it was time for her to soar.

He trailed his lips along the column of her long neck. "You smell so good," he crooned, breathing a kiss under her ear.

Viola's throbbing escalated until she wasn't certain whether her knees would support her. "No, Ty. Please."

His hand came down and he curved his arms around her waist,

bringing her flush against his belly. "No, what? You've been hurt and so have I. Meanwhile, you've had fifteen years to heal. I have not had the luxury of that much time. Three years ago I pledged my life and future to a woman who abruptly ended our engagement. What I didn't know was that she was in love with another man. The invitations were in the mail, the church had been notified, and the honeymoon was paid in full. In less than a minute she gave me back my ring and walked out of my life.

"Leo's became my wife, my lover, where I worked every day that the restaurant was open until there were times when I could hardly stand up straight. I catered weddings, private parties, bar mitzvahs, baby showers, and office and birthday parties. I wanted to die, but I was too much of a coward to kill myself, so I decided working myself to death was more heroic."

A frown appeared between Viola's dark, slanting eyes. "It could not have been that bad." Her voice was barely a whisper.

"It is when you love with all of your heart."

"Are you saying I didn't love Frank?"

He shook his head. "No, sweetheart. I'd never attempt to tell you how or what you felt. I'm merely saying that everyone reacts differently to pain."

Lowering her head, she rested her forehead on his solid shoulder. "You're right. I've had a long time to recover from the deception."

"Do you trust men?" Viola's head came up, and she gave Tyrell a long, penetrating look. "Do you?" he repeated.

She averted her gaze. "I don't know."

"Do you believe me when I say that I like you, Viola? Like you a lot." She nodded, and he smiled. "Like you enough to want to want to take you out." She nodded again. "Do you at least like me a little?"

It was her turn to smile. "Yes, Tyrell. I happen to like you a lot. If

I didn't, then I never would've gone through the machinations of cooking for you."

"You've never cooked for a man?"

"You're the first."

Seconds ticked by as he stared at her upturned face. "I'm honored."

Her arms curved under his shoulders and she rested her head on his chest like a trusting child. "You'd better remember this day for a long time, because I don't think it will come again anytime soon."

Tyrell kissed her soft curls. "You don't have to worry about cooking. All I want is for you to give me love lessons."

Viola went completely still. "Love lessons?"

"Yes. Teach me to love again."

"But, how?"

"By being you."

"What is that supposed to mean?"

"Don't change into someone other than Viola Chapman."

She looked confused. "Viola is all I know how to be. But, what I don't—"

"Good," he said in a quiet voice, interrupting her.

The brilliance of his smile fired the gold in Tyrell's eyes as Viola's face clouded with uneasiness. "Am I to understand that you want me as your therapist to help you learn to trust a woman again?"

His smiled vanished quickly. "I can't believe you'd ask me that. Especially since you have a doctorate."

She went completely still. "Who told you I have a doctorate?"

"You did. The letter I got from you approving the curriculum was signed 'Viola R. Chapman, Ph.D.' "

Viola nodded. "The English Department's secretary signed my name."

"So, Dr. Chapman, are we going to become a couple?"

Her eyes widened. "You and me?" She liked Tyrell, but not enough to consider having a relationship with him.

"Yes. You and me."

"It's not going to work."

He lifted his eyebrows. "And why not? We're both single adults who have confessed liking each other. I'm disease free, and I've never been arrested. I have no children, so there won't be any baby-mama drama. I have a career *and* a job, so I'm not a deadbeat. I'm currently not involved with a woman, which also rules out girlfriend drama. I don't smoke, I drink occasionally, and I've never taken drugs. Is there anything else you'd like to know?"

"Yes, Tyrell, there is something else I *need* to know."

"What is that, Viola?"

"How do you expect this friendship, liaison, association, or relationship between us to culminate?"

"In happily-ever-after, of course."

Viola fought the dynamic masculinity Tyrell exuded. He was so sure of himself and his rightful place in what he had created as his world. She was also secure, but only in her profession. As much as she had tried to deny it, standing in a church waiting for a fiancé who would never show up because he had married another woman had left scars—deep and ugly—and, whenever she least expected it, her distrust of men would raise its frightful head to send her running in the opposite direction.

She had lost count of the number of men she had dated and then rejected after a second or third time. Those who got past three encounters did not know they were the lucky ones. It also had been a long time since she could recall sharing her bed with a man, and it wasn't until her erotic dream wherein she and Tyrell were locked in a passionate embrace that she realized how sexually bereft she had been.

Could she take a chance at a normal relationship with a man? Would Tyrell be able to fill the void left by Frank?

She gave him a direct look. "What if I decide to accept what you're offering, but can't promise you a happily-ever-after?"

"Then I'll take here and now."

A satisfied smile curved her mouth. "Then, Mr. Hardcastle, you have yourself a deal."

Lowering his head, Tyrell pulled Viola closer as his mouth covered hers, sealing their agreement. He wanted to tell her that she had negotiated a deal with the wrong Hardcastle. Of the four owners of Leo's, he was the most proud and he didn't like losing.

He moved his mouth over Viola's, savoring its softness as her lips parted, permitting access to the sweetest honey he'd ever tasted.

"I promise not to hurt you," he crooned as he pressed a kiss under her ear and another along the column of her scented neck.

Reaching up, Viola touched his mouth with her fingertips. "No promises, Tyrell."

"No promises," he repeated as he continued his sensual assault on her mouth. The two words echoed in his head until, gasping, her full breasts rising and falling heavily, Viola pulled away and buried her face in the crook of his shoulder.

"Do you want dessert now?"

Tyrell smiled, wanting to tell her that he had just sampled dessert and had found it spectacular. "Yes," he said instead.

# SEVEN

Tyrell watched two male and two female students deftly wield knives as they diced onions, peppers, and meats to top individual-size pizzas.

It was the third week of the Cooperative, and it was the third time all of them had shown up at Leo's before their nine o'clock starting time. He took this to mean they were responsible, mature, and serious culinary students.

Their first session had begun with a two-hour orientation when he answered their questions about the advantages of a career in the culinary arts. Most were interested in how much they would earn after they graduated. Once he quoted the salary range, all revealed a sudden interest in becoming a chef.

He demonstrated how the many utensils and gadgets are used in food preparation, advising them that restaurant recipes were written using measurements in ounces as well as the metric system.

Initially, the female students complained about ruining their hairdos when Tyrell insisted everyone wear hairnets, but after he related stories of restaurant patrons pulling strands of hair from their mouths, causing a disturbance, they relented. They also learned to wear disposable gloves when preparing cold foods.

Rochelle Alers

Earlier that morning, he had taken them on a field trip to a wholesale greengrocer where he identified fresh herbs, fruits, and vegetables, and showed them how to determine which were of the best quality. The students watched in fascination as he selected produce for Leo's varied menu. Future scheduled field trips were to include a fish market and meat plant.

Arms crossed over his chest, Tyrell watched the students closely as they prepped the ingredients. Of the four, he was most impressed with Derrick Brown. He only had to demonstrate a technique once, and Derrick duplicated it with little effort. What he hadn't told Viola or the students was that the most talented of the quartet would be offered a full scholarship once Tyrell opened his school.

Thinking of Viola elicited a smile. His relationship with her was calm and uncomplicated. They usually spent Sundays together at his place, where he cooked enough food for her to last a week. All she had to do was reheat the portions in a microwave. Despite his working nights at Leo's, he had rearranged his Friday-night shift in order to take her to a Baltimore comedy club. They had spent ninety minutes laughing, sometimes hysterically. Tyrell couldn't remember the last time he had had so much fun without censuring himself.

"I'm finished, Mr. Hardcastle."

Derrick's voice broke into his musings. Moving closer, he examined the student's six individual-size pizzas, each three inches in diameter, with a variety of toppings—cheese, bacon, minute meatballs, onion and pepper, sausage, and mushrooms.

"Excellent, Derrick. Your toppings are small and evenly diced, and the thin crust means the dough won't overwhelm the toppings."

Derrick flashed a wide grin. "Thank you."

Tyrell returned the grin. "No, Derrick. Thank you for making my job as an instructor an easy one."

At first he had been uncertain of his teaching technique. Whenever he supervised newly hired chefs at Leo's, he had found himself short on patience and stingy with compliments. He felt that as graduates they should be adept at coping with the sometimes frenetic pace and flaring tempers in a restaurant kitchen.

However, his approach with the four high school students was different—more nurturing than critical. And because they hadn't had any prior culinary experience, they came to him completely open and objective.

Tyrell examined each of the pizzas, measured them, and graded each student for preparation and presentation. He glanced at his watch. It was two-fifty, ten minutes before the arrival of the school bus.

"It's too late to cook and eat your samples, so pack them up and take them home. I'll see everyone in two weeks. Remember, next Monday is a holiday."

"What holiday?" Eddie Robinson asked as he stacked his pizzas in a round plastic container.

"Veterans Day," answered Makita. She was the one who had complained about wearing the hairnet.

"Even though we don't have school, can't we still come, Mr. Hardcastle?" Derrick asked.

Tyrell shook his head. "Sorry, Derrick, but even I need a day off. You'll still be paid for the day." This announcement elicited wide grins and high-fives. He had agreed to pay each of the students ten dollars an hour for their six-hour day. The money came from his share of Leo's weekly profits. Sixty dollars a week wasn't much money, but that, along with eating whatever they had prepared, had become an added benefit for the four adolescents.

The students packed away their food, notebooks, and printed materials in the manual Tyrell had put together for them. Derrick lagged behind the others as they went outside the restaurant to await the bus.

"Mr. Hardcastle, can I talk to you?"

"Sure, Derrick. What's up?"

He glanced at the floor, a slender, medium-brown-skinned young man who did not favor the fashion of his peers. His short-cropped hair and ultraconservative dress and glasses had earned him the sobriquet of the Professor.

"I'd like to work at Leo's after school."

Tyrell's impassive face did not reveal his relief that his prize pupil was the first to accept the Cooperative's work-study initiative.

"As soon as I get the approval from Ms. Chapman, I'll let you know when you can begin. But remember, if your grades slip because of your work-study involvement, then you're out of the Cooperative."

"I know that, sir. I'll make certain to keep my grades up. My last class ends at twelve-ten, which means I can get here at one. I can work from one to six Tuesdays through Fridays, which will add up to twenty hours. That leaves me plenty of time to do my homework, and I can always study on the weekends."

Tyrell nodded. "You'd better get out of here before the bus leaves without you." He watched Derrick race out of the kitchen to catch up with his peers, and then turned to survey the flour-strewn countertops. He usually had the students clean up after themselves, but they had run behind schedule today because of their trip to the greengrocer.

Turning to an industrial-size aluminum sink, he filled it with hot water, rinsing the bowls and utensils before stacking them in the dishwasher. It took him less than half an hour to clean up the kitchen and post the menu on a bulletin board for the week's specials. After setting the code for the security system, he locked up Leo's and headed for the parking lot. He whistled softly under his breath as he started up the truck, maneuvered out of the lot, and pulled out into early D.C. rush-hour traffic.

He had promised to meet Viola at four to give her the progress reports on his apprentices. They were terrific, his career goal was progressing well, and the woman he had come to look forward to seeing every day was perfection, so much so that he had fallen in love with her.

Viola opened the door for Tyrell, smiling. Removing a pair of glasses, she lifted her face as his lips slowly descended to meet hers. She had come to look for his kisses as much as she had come to anticipate their next encounter.

It had only taken a little more than a month, but she had found herself completely enthralled with Tyrell Hardcastle. Each meeting was more intense than the one before. There were times when she feared being too close to him, that he would become aware of how much she needed him—needed him because she was a mature woman who had denied her female nature for far too long.

Tyrell deepened the kiss, his tongue slipping between Viola's soft lips. Everything about her—the crush of her full breasts against his chest, the hauntingly sweet perfume clinging to her skin and hair—made him a prisoner of his own desire.

He realized he had lusted after her from the first time she had walked into Leo's, and it had angered him because he did not want a woman to have that kind of power over him. But Viola did have the power, even if she did not know it. She had softened his heart, and in doing so she had also taught him how to love again, a love that was different from the one he had shared with Rachel. It wasn't frantic or competitive, but gentle, comfortable, and yet exciting.

Easing back, he kissed the end of her nose, smiling, his gaze still fixed on her soft lips. Then he remembered they had business to take care of.

He then removed the envelope containing the progress reports from his jacket's breast pocket and handed it to her.

"Thanks," she said, taking the envelope.

Tyrell peered down at Viola under lowered lids. "What are you reading?"

"Comparative literature term papers."

"I didn't know you wore glasses. They really make you look like a schoolteacher."

Viola returned his smile. "I only wear them when I do a lot of reading."

He kissed the end of her nose again, peering closely at the puffiness under her eyes. She looked tired. "Who are your students comparing?"

"The works of Jane Austen and Mary Wollstonecraft Shelley to Willa Cather and Toni Morrison."

"Brilliant women writers."

"That they are. I'm sorry, but I'm forgetting my manners. Would you like something to eat or drink?"

"I'd like a cup of tea, thank you." Tyrell did not actually want anything to drink, but if it meant spending more than the few minutes needed to give her the progress reports, then he would take as much time as he could sipping the tea.

"Please wait in the library, and I'll bring it to you."

He watched the gentle sway of her slim hips in a pair of leggings as she made her way to the kitchen. As during his previous visits, Tyrell was awed by the design and furnishings in Viola's home. And it was a home, warm and welcoming.

He walked into Viola's library, noting the smoldering fire in the fireplace. The summer heat was gone, replaced by cooler-than-normal autumn temperatures. Moving over to the fireplace, he stared at the photographs on the mantel. There was one of a very young Viola with her parents. She had inherited her mother's feminine beauty and her father's hair. There was another family photo, this one with a young man in a military uniform who was the image of Viola's father. No doubt he was her brother. In that instant that Tyrell realized he knew very little about the private Viola Chapman. She knew more about his family than he did about hers.

"He was my brother."

Tyrell spun around. Viola had entered the library without making a sound in her sock-covered feet. "Was?"

She nodded. "He was killed during Desert Storm. His death nearly destroyed my parents. After burying Vincent, they retired and moved to Puerto Rico."

Tyrell closed his eyes, unable to imagine losing his brothers, especially his identical twin. He and Tyrone had grown up inseparable, doing every thing together. It was only when they decided on different career choices that they finally saw themselves as separate entities.

He opened his eyes, noting the pain in her own. "I'm so sorry, Viola."

She nodded. It had taken years, but she had finally recovered from losing her sibling. "The tea should be ready in a few minutes." Taking several steps, she closed the distance between them, her gaze fixed on the smoldering wood. "This is my favorite time of the year, because it's not cold enough for a lot of heat, yet just right for a fire."

Curving his arms around her shoulders, Tyrell pulled her to his chest. Without her shoes, the top of her head didn't reach his chin. "How would you like to spend the holiday weekend with me?"

She lifted her face. "Where?"

"I have a little place near Chester Gap that I go to whenever I feel the need for a change of scenery. We can go for walks in the woods, fish, cook over an open fire, and sit out at night and look at the stars."

"I'd love to take you up on your offer, but I have a lot of papers to grade."

"Bring them with you."

She lifted an eyebrow. "You're asking me to go away with you, and we may not be able to spend that much time together."

"It doesn't matter. I'll fish and cook while you grade Willie Shakespeare and the rest of the sister-girl wordsmiths."

Her smile crinkled the skin around her eyes. "You're no better than my students. They won't even give the Bard a chance."

"That's because the dude talked funny."

"He's not that difficult to understand."

Tyrell lifted his eyebrows. "Speak for yourself, beautiful."

Viola moved closer until she could feel the whisper of Tyrell's breath on her forehead. "You have to open your mind."

He tapped her forehead softly. "Open *your* mind, Viola, and come away with me."

The smoldering flame in Tyrell's golden eyes ignited a wave of heat in her face that traveled downward like a slow-moving river of hot lava. There was no doubt he wanted her—as much as she had come to want him.

"Okay," she whispered. "I'll go away with you."

Lowering his head, Tyrell tasted her mouth, tentatively at first, then he deepened the kiss until a rising passion left both of them breathing heavily.

Easing away from his lips, Viola held her gaze. "I'd better see to the tea."

Waiting until she left the library, Tyrell walked over to a chair and dropped heavily onto it. Now all he had to do was wait and count the days.

Four days.

And he prayed they would come and go quickly.

# EIGHT

Tyrell met with his chefs Friday morning, briefing them on the twenty-fifth wedding anniversary celebration that was to be held later that evening in the larger of the two private rooms at Leo's. The pastry chef had come in at dawn, baked an eight-tier lemon cheesecake, and decorated it with butter-cream icing and miniature edible yellow pansies.

The guest of honor was a former president, his first lady, and their closest friends. Although the president no longer lived in Washington, D.C., he had been a regular at the restaurant while occupying the Oval Office; the patrons at Leo's had become accustomed to the presence of Secret Service agents silently guarding the country's commander-in-chief.

Checking his watch, Tyrell wished his staff the best, then rushed out to the parking lot. He still had to shop for food provisions for the weekend. He had closed on a house near the Shenandoah National Park as a getaway retreat after Rachel informed him they would not marry. It had been vacant for more than a year until Tyrone used it one summer. This prompted him to purchase furniture for the three-bedroom, chalet-style structure. It was only after sleeping under the roof for the first time that he came to think of it as a refuge.

He parked his Toyota SUV near the capitol district, then dashed from one specialty shop to another until he had purchased everything on his list. It was already three by the time he maneuvered into a parking spot in front of Viola's building, and she was waiting for him.

He put the Toyota in "park" but did not turn off the ignition, pressed a lever to open the hatch, then got out and walked over to Viola. A flicker of excitement lit up her dark eyes. It was apparent she was as happy to see him, as he was to see her.

He kissed her cheek. "Hey."

She gave him a sensual smile. "Hey, yourself."

Tyrell took a large canvas bag from her loose grip, feasting his eyes on her. She wore a pair of brown corduroy slacks with leather hiking boots and a white turtleneck sweater under a hip-length fleece-lined corduroy jacket.

She smiled up at him. "Do I need to get my sleeping bag?"

He glared at her. "I do have beds."

Viola registered the plural. She didn't know if Tyrell had invited her to spend the weekend because he wanted to sleep with her, but she was more than prepared. She had stopped at drugstore and purchased an ample supply of condoms. What she hadn't known was the size, so in the end she had selected the extra-large, ribbed variety.

Her decision to buy the condoms was the result of Paulette's dream of fish. There was no way that at nearly forty years of age she was going to become an unwed mother. She had worked with teachers who, unmarried, had opted to raise a child without benefit of a spouse. Viola thought of herself as liberal, but not quite that liberal. She had grown up with a mother and a father, and she wanted no less for her child.

Tyrell assisted Viola as she stepped up into the SUV. Waiting until she was seated and belted in, he closed the door. Rounding the truck, he sat down behind the wheel and secured his own seat belt.

"How long will it take to get there?"

"If I take the back roads, we should make it in a little over an hour."

Viola pressed the back of her head against the headrest and closed her eyes. When she had agreed to spend the weekend with Tyrell, she hadn't known her week would be so hectic. She had had to fill in for the head of her department at a national conference for teachers of English and language arts. The three-day event was held in Baltimore, which meant she had to endure the heavy commuter traffic between the two cities. It was not for the first time she had appreciated Tyrell's prepared meals, because she had been too tired to do anything more than heat up the portions, eat, shower, and go directly to bed.

Tyrell took a quick glance at Viola, noticing the steady rising and falling of her chest. There were dark circles under her eyes, which hinted of exhaustion. He had called her one night when he had a break, and from the sound of her voice he knew she had been asleep. It had been eight-thirty, and she was in bed. One thing was certain, and that was she would rest this weekend.

Tyrell shook Viola gently. "We're here."

She came awake immediately, blinking and looking around her. There was still enough daylight to make out a chalet-style structure nestled in a copse of towering pine trees.

*So much for roughing it*, she thought.

"Nice." The single word spoke volumes.

Tyrell nodded. "Thank you. Wait, and I'll help you down." He got out and assisted her until her feet touched the pine needle–littered earth.

Viola slid her arms around Tyrell's waist, inhaling a lungful of clean mountain air. "It smells wonderful."

He pulled her closer, resting his chin on the top of her head. "You smell wonderful."

Tilting her chin, Viola tried making out his features in the waning afternoon light. The words she longed to say were poised on the tip of her tongue. She wanted to tell Tyrell that she had fallen in love him. She thought it ironic that he had asked her to help him learn to trust a woman again, while instead of the student falling for his teacher, she had fallen in love with him. It hadn't mattered that he was seven years younger than she was, or that she was rapidly approaching middle age. The only thing that mattered at present was that she wanted Tyrell—in her bed and in her life. She refused to think of marriage and children, because that was not an option.

Burying his face in her curly hair, Tyrell pressed a kiss to her scalp. "Are you ready to go in?"

"Yes."

Hand in hand, they walked up the path to the front door. Tyrell deactivated an alarm, unlocked the door, and then pushed it open. Flicking a switch on the wall near the door, the living, dining, and kitchen area was flooded with golden light.

The first thing Viola noticed was the smell of wood. The second was the windows. And the third was the cathedral ceiling. Nestled under it was a ladder leading to a loft. A brick fireplace took up half of one wall. It was the perfect place to sit and watch a sunrise or sunset.

The furnishings and colors were reminiscent of those in Tyrell's Georgetown apartment. The country retreat was the perfect place to relax and become reacquainted with the splendor of nature's beauty.

"It's so clean," Viola remarked.

Tyrell smiled. "I had someone dust and air it out, then turn on the heat yesterday. Why don't you take a tour while I bring everything in."

Viola slipped out of her jacket and took off her boots so that she wouldn't track dirt over the highly polished wood floor. She walked through the living and dining area to an alcove inside a doorway to the master suite and stared at a massive oak antique tansu chest built into the wall. The many drawers and compartments eliminated the need for a dresser or chest-of-drawers. A king-size platform bed was the room's focal point. If it hadn't been for the pale gray upholstered chair with a matching ottoman and a ceiling fan, the room would have been empty.

She peered into an adjoining bathroom. Decorated in a sand beige, the whirlpool tub and large clear-glass shower enclosure made the room look and feel larger than it actually was. There were two smaller bedrooms on the other side of the living room, both similarly furnished in an Asian décor.

Viola joined Tyrell in the kitchen as he emptied a large portable chest and put perishable foodstuffs into a side-by-side refrigerator-freezer. "Do you need help?"

Tyrell glanced at Viola over his shoulder. "No, thanks. I thought we agreed you would relax, not work."

She moved closer, resting her elbows on a countertop, and stared out the tall windows at the deck and backyard. "I can't sit around doing absolutely nothing."

Tyrell wanted to tell her that, yes, she could. All she had to do was be Viola and look beautiful. "Do you want to set the table while I get dinner together?" Opening an overhead cabinet, he pressed a button on a radio, and the soft sounds of jazz filled the space.

She washed her hands in a bathroom several feet from the kitchen, and after Tyrell showed her where the dinnerware was stored, she busied herself setting the table. She slid open the door leading to the backyard and picked a bouquet of late-blooming fall flowers. The setting sun left streaks of orange on a dark-blue canvas of encroaching nightfall.

By the time she had arranged the bouquet in a vase, the mouth-watering smell of broiling steak filled the house. Potatoes covered in foil were baking in the oven and a salad of torn lettuce leaves filled a clear bowl. It had taken her twenty minutes to wash and dry dishes and flatware, set them out on the table, and pick flowers. In the same time Tyrell had cooked an entire meal.

He shook a cruet filled with a robust salad dressing, removed a cork from a bottle of wine, then pulled out a chair at the table. "Dinner's ready." Winking, he lowered his head and dropped a kiss on the end of Viola's nose. "The flowers add a nice touch." She sat down, smiling at Tyrell over her shoulder as he placed a steak on her plate.

She cut a small piece of the grilled meat and bit into it. Although it was thoroughly cooked, it was still tender and moist. There was something to be said about having a professional chef as a boyfriend.

*Boyfriend!*

Viola went completely still, her fork poised in midair. Was Tyrell her boyfriend?

"What's the matter?"

She stared at him. "Are you my boyfriend, Tyrell?"

He put down his wineglass, a stunned expression on his face, angled his head, and stared back at her. "Why would you ask that?"

She shrugged a shoulder. "I don't know. The thought just hit me that you're my boyfriend."

"I don't want to be your boyfriend, Viola."

She blinked. "Why not?"

A mysterious smile curved his strong mouth as he lifted an eyebrow. "Because a boyfriend is temporary, and I want permanence."

There was a lump in her chest, and Viola found it difficult to draw a breath. "Permanence how?"

"Didn't I tell you I wanted happily-ever-after?"

The constriction in her chest made breathing difficult. "But that's forever."

He smiled. "That's what I'm talking about."

Her eyes widened. "You want marriage?"

*love lessons*

Picking up his glass, Tyrell took his time draining it. "Marriage, children, the house in the country."

"Do you realize how old I am?"

Resting his elbows on the table, he glared at her. "You're old enough to marry without having to get your parents' permission. And old enough to have baby without being labeled a teenage mother."

She threw her napkin on the table, her eyes brimming with sparks of anger. "You've got a smart-ass mouth, Tyrell Hardcastle."

"Wrong, Miss Chapman. You're the one with the tongue that can stand in for a cat-o'-nine-tails." Her jaw dropped, and within seconds he stood up and rounded the table. He pulled her gently to her feet and his mouth covered hers in a hungry kiss that sucked the oxygen from her lungs.

"I love you, Viola," he whispered against her parted lips. "And loving you has made me a little bit crazy, because I've never chased a woman before. And right now I'm tired of running." In between each word he left kisses on her forehead, eyebrows, eyelids, cheeks, and chin.

Closing her eyes, Viola reveled in the sensual attack on her mouth. She wanted to sleep with Tyrell, but the thought of marrying him frightened her. She felt her knees weaken as he pressed his assault on her turbulent emotions.

Anchoring the heel of her hand against his shoulder, she pushed against him. "Stop, please."

Cradling the back on her head in one hand, Tyrell trailed kisses along the column of her neck. "Stop what, Viola? Stop loving you? Sorry, baby, but I can't. I'm in too deep."

Eyes closed, head thrown back, she shuddered. "Let's take it slow."

He raised his head. "How slow?"

"No promises about a future together. Let's just enjoy what comes without the promises."

Somehow Viola knew she had gotten through to Tyrell, because he nodded, smiling. "Okay."

Releasing her, he sat down and refilled his wineglass. He was on his second glass before she finished her first. She sat at the table pretending interest in the food in front of her while Tyrell left the table to clean up the kitchen.

"Are you finished eating?"

Her head came up with the soft query. "Yes. It was delicious, as usual."

Tyrell gave her a lingering stare. "Thank you."

Pushing back her chair, she stood up and slid back the glass door leading to the deck at the back of the house. A sprinkling of stars littered the inky sky. The sounds of nocturnal wildlife and the smell of burning wood were subtle reminders that she had left the big city.

She detected his smell, warmth, and his hard body as Tyrell moved behind her. Closing her eyes, she rested her head on his shoulder.

"Come, darling, let's go to bed."

Turning in his embrace, Viola rested her cheek over his heart. The strong, steady pumping under her ear said it all—Tyrell was calm, in control, while hers fluttered like a frightened bird's. And what did she have to be frightened of—the man holding her to his heart? A man who wanted to commit to a happily-ever-after while most men were sprinting from commitment?

"Give me a few minutes to shower, then I'll join you." Rising on tiptoe, her lips brushed against his.

She was there, then she was gone, but her warmth and scent lingered with Tyrell until he retraced his steps and walked back into the house, locking the door behind him. He stood motionless staring up at the nighttime sky, twisted a wand and closed the panels of silk over the wall of glass.

# NINE

Viola removed a nightgown and grooming supplies from the canvas bag Tyrell had left near the door, then walked into the bathroom off the kitchen.

A sense of peace had penetrated her as she brushed her teeth before stepping into the shower stall. She knew going to bed with Tyrell would change her and her life forever. He had confessed to being in love with her, and while she loved him, too, she had yet to tell him what lay in her heart.

The delicate fragrance of lilies lingered in the air as she dried and moisturized her body with a scented lotion. She stared at her reflection while she brushed her short damp hair off her face and forehead. She smiled, her slanting eyes inching upward with the gesture.

*I'm ready.*

And she was ready—ready for Tyrell and what was to come.

Her bare feet were silent as she walked out of the bathroom, through the alcove and into the master bedroom suite. A dim ray from recessed ceiling lights illuminated the large bed. The silk gray-and-white patterned quilt was turned down, but the bed was empty.

The door to the adjoining bathroom stood open, and she heard

Tyrell singing loudly. Moving closer to the bathroom, she peered in. He was in the shower.

Retracing her steps, she got into the bed, pulled a sheet up over her body, and closed her eyes. Within minutes she was asleep.

Tyrell walked into the bedroom to find Viola in bed. A gentle smile softened his features as he stood over her. She lay on her back, and her slightly parted lips and the gentle rising and falling of her breasts verified that she had fallen asleep. His gaze was fused to the outline of her firm breasts under the lace bodice of a pale-gray silk gown, forcing him to retract his initial opinion of her body. She wasn't skinny but ardently female.

Pressing a button on the wall, he extinguished the lights, then got into the bed. Viola stirred briefly, but did not wake up. Sleep had claimed her, while it took a lot longer for Tyrell. Turning to his right, he pulled her against his middle, her buttocks pressed to his groin. He inhaled her essence, and after awhile he, too, joined her in sleep.

Slivers of light had crept under the hem of the drapes at the windows in the bedroom when Viola opened her eyes to find herself imprisoned by the arm resting over her waist. She froze. She hadn't remembered Tyrell getting into bed with her. She tried inching away from him, but his hold tightened.

"It's too early to get up," he said.

Viola shivered when his moist breath seared the back of her neck. "I *have* to get up." The weight on her body eased. "But I'll be back."

Tyrell pressed a kiss to the nape of her neck. "Don't take too long." She slipped out of the bed and made her way to the bathroom.

He was sitting up, his back braced against a mound of pillows, arms crossed over his bare chest, when she returned. Lowering his arms, he extended them, and she jumped into his embrace.

love lessons

Pressing her nose to his smooth chest, she inhaled the lingering smell of soap from his nighttime shower. "Good morning."

Tyrell cradled her face between his hands, trying to make out her features in the darkened space. "Good morning, my love."

Slowly, deliberately, he kissed her. He was not disappointed when she returned the kiss with a passion she had not demonstrated in all of their encounters.

Viola kissed Tyrell with a hunger that belied her outward calm. The heat radiating from his body coursed down the length of hers, as the flush of sexual desire rippled under her skin in a slow, simmering burn.

Angling his head, Tyrell placed kisses along the side of her neck, over her collarbone and velvety shoulder. She was sweet, as sweet as spun-sugar confectionary. His flesh hardened quickly. He wanted her! He wanted to be inside her! The moan of ecstasy that had slipped through her parted lips snapped his control. With a minimum of effort, she was on her back and he was straddling her.

Only the sound of their breathing punctuated the silence, and Viola was fully aware of the arousal throbbing against the thin layer of fabric covering her nakedness.

Supporting his weight on his elbows, Tyrell pressed his mouth to her ear. "May I make love to you, Viola?" She closed her eyes and nodded. "I have to hear you say it, darling."

"Yes, Tyrell," she whispered. "You may make love to me."

His right hand moved up her leg, gathering fabric in his journey to claim what lay between her thighs. She was shaking, but she could not control it.

"Are you afraid?"

"No."

Tyrell smiled in the darkness. "Good."

Viola felt desire inch its way through her body, her blood, until she wanted to scream at Tyrell to take her—to end the erotic torment threatening to tear her asunder. His hand touched her, and she couldn't stop the gasp of delight or the gush of moisture flowing unchecked.

He removed her nightgown, and seconds later he began a sensual assault, sending shockwaves that scorched the area between her legs. Tyrell kissed, teased, and nibbled her breasts until her nipples were hard as rock candy. He tasted and kissed places where she had never been kissed or tasted.

Chills made her quake before heat seared not only her flesh but also her very soul. He tormented her when he inserted a finger into the secret place she had only permitted access to a few men.

"No more, Tyrell. Please." The last word was a lingering keening that resonated in the space long after she'd clenched her teeth to keep from embarrassing herself.

He released her, slipped off the bed and went to a drawer in the tansu chest in the alcove, retrieving a condom. He had opened the packet and rolled the latex covering down over his rigid flesh when Viola met him.

"I have my own."

He smiled. "Unless you have something in color, I'm certain this one will suffice."

She shook her head. "I'd rather use my own."

Tyrell gritted his teeth, praying he wouldn't lose his erection because Viola wanted to debate whose condom to use. "Okay, but you have to put it on."

Viola took a deep breath, her breasts trembling above her narrow rib cage. "I don't know how to put them on."

"Then this one will do," Tyrell said as he scooped her up in his arms and carried her back to the bed. "The next time we'll use yours, and I'll show you how to put it on." He brushed his mouth over hers. "I love you, Viola, and I would never deliberately do anything to make you feel uncomfortable." Her reluctance to use his condom meant she hadn't fully trusted him to protect her from an unwanted pregnancy.

There was a pulse beat before she said, "I know that." Her voice was soft, almost breathless, as Tyrell eased his hardness into her celibate flesh. She welcomed him into her body, sighing as pleasure sung in her veins like the sweetest song.

She was drowning, then within seconds she was soaring higher than she had been before, experiencing the ultimate freefall when she climaxed once, twice, then lost count as the explosions seared her in a fire that left her shaking from its scorching aftermath.

Tyrell knew the instant he joined his body to Viola's that she had been created for him. He had found the woman who was the light to his dark, the yang to his yin. Her candid, unpretentious, and gentle nature had soothed his restlessness, and every time he looked at her he saw his unborn children in her eyes.

She had reminded him that she was almost forty, which made her high-risk for bearing children. But with modern medicine, women were giving birth to healthy babies in their late forties and early fifties.

He felt the contractions in her womb closing around his flesh and gritted his teeth to sustain the pleasure. His heart pounded in his chest like a runaway jackhammer. Tyrell wanted the pleasure to last, but it was not to be. Lowering his head between her neck and shoulder, he growled out his climax like a triumphant big cat on the African savanna.

He collapsed, struggling for breath as his heart pumped painfully in his constricted chest. Somehow he managed to roll off her slight body. He lay on his back, one arm thrown over his head, and waited for his respiration to return to a normal rate. It was the first time he had experienced what the French called *le petite mort*. He had died the little death, and in doing so he had touched a little piece of heaven.

He lowered his arm and turned to face Viola. There was now enough daylight coming through the lined silk drapes to see her face. And what he saw stunned him.

Viola's smile was dazzling. Snuggling closer to her lover, she kissed his shoulder, tasting salt. "I love you, Tyrell."

He gathered her closer. They lay together, and when they finally got up to complete their morning ablutions both had bared their souls to the other.

Viola claimed the loft as her favorite place in the house. Resting her back against a pile of pillows on a divan, she spent hours reading and correcting term papers. When they were done, all she had left to do was review the progress reports of the student participants in the Career Cooperative.

She heard Tyrell when he left the house and drove away, and when he returned several hours later. Moving off the divan, she leaned over the railing to find him at the sink on the cooking island. The overhead light glinted off the stark white T-shirt stretched over his broad shoulders.

"What's for dinner?" They had gotten up too late for breakfast, so Tyrell had prepared a sumptuous brunch that included mushroom omelets, miniature cranberry muffins, country sausage links, and sliced melon with strawberries.

His head came up, and even from the distance Viola could see desire shimmering in his golden gaze. "Grilled fish, corn on the cob, sweet peppers, and cornbread."

"Where did you get fresh corn this time of year?"

"There are few farm stands that are still open."

"Do you need an assistant?"

He smiled. "I'd love one."

Turning off a floor lamp, she slipped her feet into a pair of slippers and made her way down the ladder. Her gaze widened when she saw two thrashing lobsters in the stainless-steel sink.

"I've changed my mind."

Tyrell gave her a questioning look. "What's the matter?"

She winced. "The lobsters."

"What about them?"

"They're alive."

"Of course they're alive, Viola. I would never cook a dead lobster."

"You could've cooked them before I saw them."

Curving an arm around her waist, Tyrell pulled her to his side. "I'm not going to throw them away."

She pulled out his loose embrace. "I'm going for a walk. Maybe by the time I get back they'll be cooked."

Throwing back his head, Tyrell laughed at her agonized expression. The woman he had fallen in love with was an enigma. She thought nothing of lashing him with the whip she called a tongue, yet she turned into mush when he had to cook something live. He remembered her plea not to cook the gigantic lobster swimming around the tank in Leo's kitchen. What she hadn't known was that Brutus had finally met a noble end. His meat was used in a lobster salad for guests at the former president and first lady's twenty-fifth wedding anniversary.

"Don't go too far. We'll sit down to eat in about forty minutes."

She glanced at her watch, nodding. "I'll see you later."

Viola returned from her walk through the woods in time to set the table on the deck. Tyrell had decided to grill outdoors, and the tantalizing smells lingered in the air long after they had retreated indoors.

They lay on a rug, holding hands, staring at the flickering flames dancing behind a decorative fireplace screen. Viola told Tyrell of her childhood in Richmond and her brother who had gone to a seminary to help save souls, but lost his own life in the desert when he went to the Persian Gulf as an army chaplain. Her voice was a hushed whisper when she told him that her parents never recovered from losing their son. They'd left positions as college professors, sold their home, and moved permanently into a San Juan condominium they had purchased years before as a vacation retreat.

"How often do you see your parents?" Tyrell asked.

"I always spend Christmas and spring break with them. And I also try to fly down for several weeks during the summer."

"Are going down this Christmas?"

"Yes."

*Six weeks,* he mused. All he had was another six weeks with Viola. Then when she returned, they would only have four weeks before he left for France. Every February he left Leo's to study with other chefs from around the world. One year it was England, another Spain or Italy. This year it was France.

He had promised her that they would not talk about a future together. However, that was easier said than done. Now that he had sampled her passion, being away from her for a day was certain torture.

A shower of sparks along with the popping firewood disturbed the cloaking silence. The next sound was the dulcet tone of Viola's voice.

"Tyrell."

"Yes, my love?"

"I'd like to go to bed now."

He glanced up at the clock on the mantel. It wasn't seven. "But, it's early."

She gave him a long, penetrating look. "Is it too early to make love? After all, you promised to show me how to put on a condom, and I'm ready for my lesson."

Shaking his head, he stood up and gathered her off the rug. "What am I going to do with you, Viola?"

"Love me," she said, giggling like a child.

"This is the easiest assignment I've ever been given." And it was.

# TEN

Heads turned as men dining with their female companions surreptitiously eyed Viola as she was shown to a table where Paulette waited. A stiff wind had rearranged her short-coiffed hair as if she had run her fingers through it, tousling the curls. Paulette had selected The Palm for their monthly dinner meeting. High-powered lobbyists and sports figures were known to frequent The Palm with its clubhouse atmosphere and steak-and-potatoes fare.

Paulette's gaze swept over her best friend's curvy body in a black knit turtleneck sheath dress as Viola was seated. "I don't know what it is about you, but you're radiating sex," she whispered.

"Stop it," she hissed through clenched teeth.

"Well, it's true. Whatever your man is doing to you, I hope he never stops. You're glowing, and if I didn't know you better, I'd say you're in the family way."

Viola went completely still, staring at her best friend. There was no mistaking the incredulous look on her face. "I am *not* pregnant."

"But you are having sex."

Suddenly Viola regretted telling Paulette that she was sleeping with Tyrell. It was just like her friend to conjure up all types of scenarios about marriage and babies.

"We use protection."

"Which isn't always one hundred percent foolproof."

"Are you wishing that I get pregnant?"

Paulette sobered. "Yes, I am. That way, at least one of us could become a mother."

Realization hit her like the blow of a sledgehammer. It was the first time in the eighteen years of marriage that Paulette admitted *she* wasn't able to have a child. In the past she had always said "Warren and I can't have children."

Reaching across the table, Viola took Paulette's hand. "Oh, Paul, I'm sorry," she said, using her childhood nickname for her best friend.

Paulette forced a smile. "Please, Vi, don't make me cry. I'm a little too bright to go around with a red nose and puffy eyes."

Viola had to laugh. Paulette had taken a lot of teasing as a child because of her fair coloring. "Am I still invited for Thanksgiving with your family?" she asked, deftly changing the topic.

"Now, you know if you don't come Mama will have my head. And why don't you bring your boyfriend?"

"I can't."

"Why not?"

"Because he has his own family. Remember, I'm the one with the parents who don't live on the mainland."

Their conversation ended when a waiter came over to take their beverage order. Paulette did not bring up Tyrell again, and for that Viola was grateful. They talked over the plans they'd made for their future tutoring center. It would be another two years before it would cease to be an idea and become a reality.

Tyrell glanced up at the clock when Derrick Brown strolled into Leo's kitchen. He was late—again.

He had gotten approval from Viola to hire Derrick for a twenty-hour-per-week work-study, and this was the third time Derrick had come in late. The first two times his excuse was that he had to stay after classes and make up an exam. He realized Derrick's first obligation was to maintain a B average, but that did not preclude him from calling to say he would not be able to come in as scheduled.

He met Derrick as he headed for a back room where the restaurant personnel stored their personal belongings. "Come with me." His voice was low, and those who were familiar with Tyrell Hardcastle knew he was close to losing his temper. "What's your excuse this time, other than not calling to say you'd be late?"

Derrick stared up at the ceiling. "I don't have one."

Tyrell's golden eyes darkened until they resembled black coffee. "Wait here."

Turning on his heels he walked over to a locker. With a flip of his wrist he turned the combination on the lock and opened the metal door. He reached into the pocket of his slacks and removed a money clip. Counting out several large bills, he returned the money clip to the pocket. He retraced his steps, extending the money to Derrick, who stared at three one-hundred-dollar bills.

"Take it."

"Why, Mr. Hardcastle?"

"I'm letting you go."

"You're firing me?" Derrick asked, his expression mirroring disbelief.

Tyrell nodded and shoved the money into Derrick's jacket pocket. "It's more than what I owe you, but I'm giving you this because I don't want to see you around here again. What bothers me most is that you have *it*, Derrick. Of all of the students you have a natural talent for cooking, but if you want to throw it away, then I don't care. Now, get out of my sight." The command was filled with anguish and disappointment. Running a hand over his face, Tyrell returned to the kitchen.

Viola spied Tyrell's truck as he maneuvered along the curb in front of his townhouse. Exiting her car, she crossed the street and caught up with him as he unlocked the front door. His expression indicated he was surprised to see her.

"Darling. What are you doing here so late?"

It was close to midnight, but she did not care about propriety. She wanted—no she *needed* to talk to Tyrell. "I have to see you."

Putting an arm around her waist, he pulled her into the entryway. A wave of heat swept over her, reminding Viola of how long she had sat in her unheated car waiting for Tyrell to come home.

"Have you come to spend the night?" Tyrell reached to take Viola's coat, but she stepped back.

"No, Tyrell. I want to talk to you about Derrick Brown."

Walking into the living room, Tyrell threw his leather jacket on a chair. Pointing to a matching chair, he said, "Please, sit down."

Viola shook her head. "I'd rather stand, thank you, because what I have to say to you won't take that long."

His gaze narrowed. "What's going on, Viola?"

"Why did you dismiss Derrick without checking with me first?"

Tyrell pushed his hands into the pockets of his slacks. "You've got to be kidding."

"No, I am not!" she shot back. "You know you can't dismiss or expel a student without a formal hearing. What you can do is put them on probation until we decide a course of action. You should know this because you signed an agreement attesting to this clause."

Sudden anger ignited the fire in his eyes. "I acted according to the circumstances, Miss Chapman. I am running a business, not a day care center. And if your students are irresponsible, immature, and insolent, then I suggest you send them for counseling. Based on Derrick's recent performance, I had every right to let him go. If he had been a regular employee, he would've been given two, not three chances."

"I, I, I," she threw at him. "All I hear is 'I'!"

"Would you have preferred that I'd said 'Leo's'?"

"I can't believe I've been such a fool as to have taken up with you. You're nothing but a stubborn, inflexible, controlling bully." A cynical sneer curled her upper lip. "I must say you had me fooled, because I was seriously thinking of accepting your marriage proposal. Thank you, Tyrell, for the advance notice."

She swiveled quickly, turned her back, and walked out his apartment and his life.

Viola did not remember driving home, or parking her car in its assigned spot, or falling across the bed fully dressed until she woke up the next morning, her throat raw and her eyes puffy from weeping. She had loved and lost—again.

Sitting up, she stared at the white-on-white striped wallpaper. Better she discovered Tyrell's negative traits now than after they had exchanged vows. And she hadn't lied to Tyrell. What Paulette had said to her at The Palm had stayed with her: *at least one of us could become a mother.*

She and Paulette used to play house in their respective attics, pretending they were mothers who stayed home, cooked, and took care of their children while their husbands worked. As they neared adolescence, both decided they wanted to become teachers like their parents.

Paulette had realized two of her three wishes; she had become a teacher and a wife, while Viola had realized one. But after falling in love with Tyrell she realized she could have the other two. She had never been pregnant, so she did not know whether could bear children, unlike Paulette who had had medical proof of her sterility. Now she would never know.

Forcing herself to get up, she went into the bathroom to get a cold compress for her eyes. If the swelling did not subside, she would be forced to wear her glasses at school.

On Friday morning Viola found a small envelope in her faculty mailbox. Running her finger under the flap, she pulled out a note card: *Dear Ms. Chapman, I would like to invite you to my home Monday evening to discuss my son Derrick Junior's future educational prospects. I hope you will not be inconvenienced by my offer, but it is important that I meet with you. If you are not able to make it, then please call. If you are, then I look forward to meeting with you at 6:00. Sincerely, Mrs. Derrick Brown Sr.*

Viola lifted her eyebrows, wondering what was going in the Brown household that had prompted Derrick's mother to contact her. The only way to find out was to accept the invitation.

Falling sleet sparkled on lawns and roofs as Viola slowed her car, peering at the numbers on houses in a modest working-class neighborhood. She managed to find a parking space several houses away from the Brown's. Turning off the ignition, she reached for the decorative shopping bag on the passenger seat and exited the car.

Her booted feet made crunching sounds on the wet sidewalk. It was three days before Thanksgiving, and winter had made an appearance in the form of the frozen precipitation.

Light filtered through lace panels at the tall narrow windows of the Victorian-style house. She walked up the stairs to the porch and rang the doorbell. Soon the door opened, and Viola smiled at Derrick Brown.

"Good evening, Miss Chapman. Please come in. I'll take your coat."

She placed the shopping bag on a drop-leaf table. "Thank you, Derrick," she said as she wiped her feet on a thick straw mat at the same time she sniffed the air. "Something smells wonderful."

Derrick smiled. "My mom and I made a special dinner." He took her coat, draping it over his arm. "I want to thank you for coming, Miss Chapman."

Viola registered his sincerity. There was no doubt Mrs. Brown wanted to discuss her son's discharge from the Cooperative and work-study program.

"I'm glad I came."

Picking up the shopping bag, she followed Derrick past a staircase, down a long narrow hallway, and into a living room decorated with overstuffed furniture from a bygone era.

Her body stiffened in shock when the man seated on a maroon brocade settee rose slowly to his feet.

"Good evening, Miss Chapman."

Viola nodded. "Mr. Hardcastle."

They stared at each other until a tall, heavy-set woman walked into the living room. "Mr. Hardcastle, Miss Chapman, I'm certain you two are familiar with each other."

"Yes," Viola and Tyrell said in unison.

Agnes Brown offered Viola her hand. "Miss Chapman, I'm Agnes, Derrick's mother."

Viola shook her hand. "My pleasure. Please call me Viola." She gave her the shopping bag. "This for you."

Agnes peered into the bag and smiled. "It's beautiful. It appears as if you and Mr. Hardcastle are on the same wavelength. Thank you for the plant. We'll talk about Derrick over dinner. He has just put the finishing touches on what he says is a very important project. Come."

Tyrell walked over to Viola, offering his arm. "Miss Chapman."

She rolled her eyes at him, and because she did not want to cause a scene, she rested her hand on the sleeve of his jacket. "Thank you, Mr. Hardcastle."

Viola and Tyrell walked into a formal dining room lit with shimmering light from an old-fashioned chandelier and several other lamps on a mahogany sideboard. Its surface was filled with platters and serving dishes from which wafted the most tantalizing smells.

Agnes removed the plant from the bag and placed it on an ornately carved credenza. The delicate pink orchids were the perfect compliment to Tyrell's gift of a frangipani.

An older version of Derrick sat in a wheelchair at the head of the formally set table. He nodded to Viola as Tyrell seated her. "I'm Derrick Brown. I'm sorry I can't get up to greet you formally, because this is my first day home. I've been in a residential facility where I had to undergo rehab for a hip replacement. That said, I'd like to welcome you to my home, Miss Chapman."

Viola smiled at Derrick's father. "I'm honored to be here."

Agnes placed a hand on her husband's shoulder. "Let me see what's keeping Junior and Leslie."

Tyrell sat on Viola's left. It hadn't been a week since their volatile confrontation, yet he felt as if it had been a year. It wasn't until after she had walked out of his apartment and his life that he realized what she'd said was true. He hadn't handled the situation with Derrick correctly because he knew he should not have dismissed the student without the proper course of action. Viola also had called him inflexible, stubborn, and a controlling bully. Those words did not wound him as much as her revelation that she had considered marrying him.

Viola had come to love and trust him enough to share her life and future with him, and he had blown it—big time! But he knew everyone was entitled to a second chance, and he was willing to sacrifice everything—including his stiff pride—to regain her trust.

Derrick walked into the dining room carrying a platter displaying an enormous herb-encrusted leg of lamb. He smiled at Tyrell. "I hope you're not going to grade me tonight."

Tyrell's expression was impassive. "But of course I am, Derrick. Until you graduate from culinary school, I'll continue to grade you."

Viola sat up straighter. "You've decided to go to culinary school?"

Derrick placed the lamb on the table. "Yes. Mr. Hardcastle and I talked about it over the weekend. He told me that if I complete my apprenticeship in the Cooperative, he would offer me a full scholarship to his school when it opens next fall. Meanwhile I can continue to work at Leo's during the summer."

Before Viola could react to Tyrell's generous offer, a prepubescent girl entered the dining room, kissed her father's cheek, and sat down opposite Viola. She was a feminine version of her older brother.

"Hi." Her greeting and smile indicated shyness.

Viola returned her smile. "Hello. You must be Leslie."

Derrick sat next to his sister. "Miss Chapman is my English teacher. She's the one who makes studying Shakespeare fun."

A loud groan went up from the elder Browns and Tyrell. Viola covered her mouth with her hand and laughed until her eyes filled with tears. The laughter ended, and when Tyrell rested his right hand along the curve of her back, a spurt of desire burned her flesh through her wool jacket and cashmere sweater.

She went rigid. Despite his arrogance and controlling personality, she still wanted him. Not just to see him on the weekend or on his days off, but every day and every night.

He removed his hand, and she was able to breathe normally again. Agnes proudly announced that her son had prepared most of the meal. Derrick had stuffed a whole cabbage, roasted the leg of lamb, and made side dishes of oven-roasted, herbed potatoes and buttery cornbread. Tyrell only offered one or two suggestions.

"Junior showed me how to make the salad dressing that Mr. Hard-castle uses at Leo's," Leslie said proudly.

"It's Leo's house dressing," Derrick said, gently correcting her.

It was during the next two hours that Viola uncovered why Tyrell had dismissed Derrick. While his father was in the rehab center, Leslie had a confrontation with another girl in one of her classes, and the girl had begun harassing his sister. Each day the girl and some of her friends would follow Leslie home, taunting her.

Derrick had been leaving the high school when his classes ended and walking a mile to his sister's school to wait for her. He then safely escorted her home, staying with her until their mother, a nurse working the eight-to-three shift, arrived. Because Derrick hadn't felt comfortable enough with Tyrell to confide this information, he had preferred to keep it a private matter.

Agnes smiled at her son. "Miss Chapman, my husband and I have raised our children to be responsible and respectful, and I've spoken to Junior about how he should've told Mr. Hardcastle about his situation with Leslie. His attitude about not letting other people get into his personal business has to change, especially when your employer is depending on you to do a job."

"I believe Derrick and I understand each other now," Tyrell said, winking at his protégé. Don't we, Derrick?"

Derrick ducked his head. "Yes, sir."

Agnes pushed out her ample bosom. "I can't wait to see my boy dressed in white with a toque on his head and his name, 'Derrick Brown Jr., Executive Chef,' on his tunic."

Tyrell nodded, smiling. There was no doubt it would become a reality. He would make certain of that.

Viola passed on dessert, which happened to be a double-chocolate-devil's food cake. She avoided chocolate whenever she was ovulating because it sometimes triggered headaches. Thanking the Browns for their wonderful hospitality, she smiled at Tyrell, but did not say good-bye, then walked out of the warm house and into a steadily falling snow.

The drive to her loft on the other side of the city took longer because of the weather. She was as proud of Derrick as were his parents, but seeing Tyrell again made her heart ache. This pain surpassed the one she had felt standing in a church in her wedding finery, waiting for the man who had pledged to love her forever.

Frank had walked out on her, and she had done the same to Tyrell, done to him what Frank had done to her! And it was the second time he had lost a woman he loved enough to offer marriage.

Biting down on her lower lip, Viola maneuvered her car into her assigned parking space. Determination shimmered in her dark eyes as she walked the short distance to her apartment.

Falling in love with Tyrell had taught her a valuable lesson: she had to lay pride aside and follow her heart. If he did not come to her, then she would go to him.

Viola slipped her feet into a pair of high-heeled silk sling-backs and wiggled her nylon-covered toes. The lace-topped thigh-highs were so sheer that the vibrant red color on her toenails was visible. Moving off the padded stool, she walked over to the vanity and peered into the mirror.

She smiled. She had showered and washed her hair, then applied a light gel to the wet strands. She had brushed out most of the curls, and the subtle touch of eye makeup and lipstick enhanced what she thought were her best features.

She left the bathroom before she could change her mind, reaching for the black silk trench coat thrown over the back of a club chair. Dimming the light on a table lamp, she slipped into the coat, belting it tightly at the waist. Her heels were muffled in the softness of the carpeting lining the catwalk. She descended the staircase and crossed the living room, stopping to pick up her keys and a tiny purse containing her driver's license.

Viola stepped out into the night, shivering against the cold. She hadn't taken more than half a dozen steps when she saw him. Tyrell was heading toward her, hatless, the collar of his coat turned up around his neck, and his hands shoved into his pockets.

His head came up, and he stared at Viola. "Where are you going?"

Viola wanted to tell him that was none of his business, but remembered what he'd said about her tongue. She didn't want to whip him with it, but kiss him—long and deep.

"I was coming to see you."

"Why?"

She took a deep breath of frigid air. "I have to tell you something."

Tyrell took her arm. "Let's go inside and talk."

Everything that was Viola swept over Tyrell the instant he touched her. He loved her: her passion, poise, intelligence, and her beauty. He had almost forgotten the flawlessness of her dark skin that reminded him of the smoothness of a whipped chocolate mousse. The delicate bones that made up her face and the lushness of her mouth that was made to be caressed all day and every day. Her smell—it was her hypnotic sweet smell that lingered with him, even when they were apart.

He waited until she unlocked her door, then he stepped into the entryway. Viola started toward the living room, but he stopped her. "What do you want to tell me?"

She met his direct stare. "I love you."

His lids lowered. "And I love you, Viola."

She bit down on her lower lip. "I wanted to say I was sorry that I misjudged you."

"Apology accepted, even though your assessment of me wasn't that far off the mark. I'll admit to being stubborn, inflexible, and there are times when I am controlling. But what I'm not is a bully." He touched his thumb to her lower lip, tracing its shape. "Is there something else you want to say to me?"

"Yes."

Lowering his head, he whispered, "What is it?"

Viola felt faint. He was so close. The heat coming from his body was incredible. "I have rethought your offer about marriage."

He lifted an eyebrow. "What about it?"

She groaned inwardly. He wasn't going to make it easy for her. "I accept."

Tyrell's heart stopped for several seconds before it started up again. It was beating so fast he thought he was going to pass out. Cradling her face between his hands, he kissed her gently as if she were a fragile piece of crystal.

"Thank you, Viola. Thank you," he whispered over and over.

Curving her arms around his neck, she kissed him back, opening her mouth to absorb his passion. Her thumbs traced the outline of his ears, cheekbones, and down to the distinctive Hardcastle cleft chin.

Her hands were busy pushing his coat off his shoulders while he untied the belt to hers. He went completely still when the silken garment parted.

Tyrell felt the blood pool in his groin as he ogled Viola's breasts spilling over a black lace bra that barely covered her nipples. His stunned gaze moved down to her flat belly, and still lower to a black lace thong. He closed his eyes, but not before he saw her long shapely legs in the thigh-high stockings. Men fantasized about Victoria's Secret models, while he had the real thing.

He opened his eyes, trying not to laugh. "You were coming to my place to seduce me?"

A rush of heat suffused her face. "Yes."

Bending slightly, Tyrell swept Viola up in his arms. "I happen to like what you're wearing, but you don't need skimpy underwear to seduce me, darling. You did that the first time you walked into Leo's, and you were wearing a lot more clothes than you are now. I'm going to take you upstairs where I'm going to show you how much I love you, then maybe if we're not too exhausted we can talk about setting a wedding date."

"I want something small and very private."

"I'll agree to anything you want." And he meant it.

Tyrell crossed the living room, heading toward the staircase. Taking the stairs two at a time, he carried her into her bedroom and placed her on the bed.

Time stood still as the lovers undressed each other before coming together in an explosive passion wherein they surrendered to a deeper level of ecstasy that made them one.

Loathe to pull out of her moist heat, Tyrell pressed his mouth to Viola's ear. "I have a homework assignment for you."

Smiling, she whispered, "What is it?"

"We get married Wednesday, then fly down to Puerto Rico for a honeymoon. And if we manage to find the energy to get out of bed, we can see your parents."

His proposal stunned Viola. "What about your brothers? Your parents, and Leo's?"

He laughed softly. "They'll all be here when we get back. We can throw a big reception after the first of the year, or when we renew our vows on our first wedding anniversary."

"I think I like that assignment."

Tyrell smiled. "I thought you would."

Viola wound her arms around her fiancé's neck, smiling. Yes, she could think of him as that now. "I have another assignment to give you."

"What is that?"

"You're going to learn to read and understand the work of Willie Shakespeare before you become a father."

Tyrell's head jerked up. Eyes wide, he stared down at Viola. "Are you pregnant?"

She flashed a sensual smile. "If you study extra hard after classes this week, then you should get an A in fatherhood."

Lowering his head, he kissed her taut breasts. "I believe we're going to have a helluva honeymoon." Slowly his hands moved downward, his fingertips caressing the silken skin on her thighs.

The fire he stoked in Viola spread to him, and minutes later they communicated in the most intimate way possible the magnitude of a love that promised forever.

# EPILOGUE

*Two years later*

Viola stood up and applauded with the others assembled in the large meeting room as Derrick Brown Jr. came up to the stage to accept his Associate of Science degree in Le Cordon Bleu Culinary Arts.

She froze when she felt a flutter. The child in her womb had moved for the first time. It would be another four months before her now-sixteen-month-old son would share a sister with his mother, father, grandparents, aunts, uncles, and cousins.

Once her second pregnancy was confirmed, Viola had decided it would become her last. After all, she was lucky—no, she was blessed—to have fulfilled her childhood dreams. Three out of three was good—very, very good.

She had retired from teaching and now was waiting for Paulette to return from an extended vacation with her husband before they would begin interviewing teachers for their tutorial center.

Her gaze met and fused with her husband's before he turned and greeted the second-highest-scoring graduate. Tyrell and his students had prepared a gastronomical feast for all of the attendees, and everyone talked about sampling every dish.

She sat down, reaching for her son who squirmed on his grand-mother's lap. Viola smiled at her mother, then kissed her soft scented cheek. The two women shared a knowing smile.

"I want to eat, Mama," Vincent Leo Hardcastle announced in a high-pitched voice that carried easily.

Viola pulled her son's head to her breasts. He had been named for his deceased uncle and paternal grandfather because of his chin. She sang softly in his ear until he quieted. Staring at the little boy in her arms, she still marveled how much he looked like his father. The only exception was his eye color. He had inherited her dark eyes, but there was no mistake that he was a Hardcastle.

When she had walked into a restaurant what now seemed so long ago, she never would have imagined that she would find love at Leo's.

Donna Hill

*lady in waiting*

# ONE

Noah heard the water running in the shower. He turned onto his side and peeked at the bedside clock through heavily lidded eyes. Three A.M.

Under normal circumstances he would join Tara in the shower, lather her body with her favorite soap, and run his hands along her full, silky curves. But these weren't normal circumstances and they hadn't been in more than a month. Two to be exact.

He flipped onto his back, throwing his right arm across his eyes, and wondered when things had gone so wrong between them, when he began to doubt that forever might not mean him and Tara.

They had been together for nearly three years and engaged for two. In the beginning he couldn't have been happier. They'd met at Leo's when Tara brought her best friend Jae there for her birthday. Jae caught the eye and heart of Noah's entertainment manager Clyde Burrell and married him soon after and Noah and Tara became inseparable. But Tara had begun to get impatient with their lengthy engagement.

"Do you really want to marry me, Noah?" she'd asked one Saturday night while they were dining at Leo's.

"Sure. Why do you ask that?"

Tara put her fork down and looked him in the eye. "Because it seems that every time I mention making some concrete plans and setting a date you get weird on me."

"Weird?" He shifted in his seat, reached for his glass of wine, and took a sip. "What's that supposed to mean?"

"You put me off. Tell me we can talk about it later. That you're busy. What's the rush? Weird, like I said."

He reached for his glass again, but found it empty. "I have been busy," he offered, suddenly scrambling for a new excuse.

"You're not busy now. Let's set a date." She folded her hands on top of the linen-covered table.

Noah signaled the waiter to bring another bottle of wine. "I really don't see what the big rush is, Tara."

"Rush? Noah, it's been two years. Are we going to stay perpetually engaged?"

He chuckled nervously. "Of course not. But I have a business to think about. I know you're going to want a long honeymoon and I can't see how I can take that kind of time away from the business right now. With Ayanna gone I've had to take over the books on top of all my other responsibilities."

"Ayanna is only gone until after the wedding. She'll be back. Your having to do her job is not forever."

"Is that why you're itching to get married, because Ayanna is getting married?"

"And your brothers... and Clyde and Jae are all married. Yes, I want to settle down. I want us to be official. I want to start a family before it's too late."

The waiter returned with their wine and refilled both glasses before leaving, giving Noah a moment to get his thoughts together.

"It seems like you have plenty of reasons—everyone else's reasons."

"Now, what is that supposed to mean?"

"Exactly what I said. You have yet to tell me you want to marry me because you love me. The only criteria seems to be that everyone else is doing it and your clock is ticking."

The pained expression in her eyes and the wavering of her mouth nearly made him eat his words.

"Is that what you think—that I don't love you, Noah?"

"You tell me."

She looked at him for what seemed like forever. "Then you don't know me at all." She tossed her napkin on the table and stood. "You tend to your restaurant, Noah, I'm going home."

That had been two months ago, and things had been tense between them ever since. He'd tried to make amends by promising they'd sit down and make some plans. It seemed to appease her for a while, but last night was the final straw for her.

They'd had a great meal, went to a play, and returned to his apartment where they'd made the kind of love you only dream about. That hot, no-holds-barred, wet, slippery, knock-the-bottom-out kind of love. If he'd died at the very instant that he'd climaxed inside of her heat, he would have died a happy man. But the euphoria was short lived. No sooner had they caught their breaths than Tara asked the inevitable.

"Are you ready to have that talk now, baby?" she'd whispered, sprinkling his bare chest with tiny kisses.

His body reflexively stiffened, but not from arousal. Gently he eased away.

"We're back to that again? Can't we just enjoy this moment? It's been a long time since we've been this way with each other."

Tara rolled away from him and sat up, pulling the sheet to cover her naked body. She drew her knees to her chest and lowered her head.

"It's okay, Noah. I won't ask anymore. Believe me, I'm not so desperate that I want to make you marry me if you don't want to."

Slowly she removed her diamond-and-sapphire engagement ring and placed it on the nightstand. "I hope you find what you're looking for, Noah, because it's clear it's not me."

She got up from the bed without another word, grabbed her clothes from the heap on the floor, and went into the bathroom.

Noah reached for the ring and twirled it between his fingers, its brilliance catching the intermittent light from outside.

What was wrong with him? Why couldn't he totally commit himself to Tara? He knew he loved her. *You know why*, his conscience taunted.

The bathroom door opened and Tara stepped out, silhouetted by the light behind her. She barely looked at him, but he could see that she'd been crying. She looked so hurt and vulnerable. He wanted to take her in his arms and tell her all the things she wanted to hear, but he couldn't make himself move or say the words.

"If it's okay with you, I'll come by one evening during the week and pick up my things. It'll probably be best if you're not here. I'll leave my key when I'm done." She waited, hope hanging in her eyes. "Don't you have anything to say, Noah?"

"I'm sorry," he murmured.

She looked at him and shook her head. "Yeah, so am I." She took her jacket and purse from the side chair and walked out.

*Go after her, man*, his inner voice urged. *Tell her you love her, that you'll work it out.*

He heard the engine of her car turn over in the still of the night. He listened as she tore out of the driveway. He listened until the car and Tara disappeared into the darkness.

# TWO

"What do you mean, the engagement is off?" Clyde asked, totally stunned by Noah's revelation.

"It's over. Tara gave me the ring back last night."

"Just like that, no reason? That doesn't sound like Tara."

Noah moved aimlessly around the confines of his office. He and Clyde Burrell had been friends for years. Not only did he depend on him as his entertainment manager but as his confidant as well. Clyde generally had solid advice and a patient ear, but right now Noah didn't want to hear any advice. He simply wanted to break the news to his buddy before Clyde's wife, Jae, did.

"According to Tara, she has reasons," Noah offered.

Clyde leaned forward in his seat. "What's the real deal, man, the truth?"

Noah hesitated. "Tara wants to get married now . . . and I'm not ready."

"Sounds like a bad case of cold feet. Hey, man, making that move is just like swimming for the first time; you have to jump in the water and hope you don't drown."

"Thanks. I feel better all ready."

"I thought you were in love with Tara."

"I am."

"So what's the real reason? You sure ain't getting younger."

Noah took a breath and slowly shook his head. "I don't know, Clyde. There's a part of me that knows I want to be with Tara. But there's another part of me that..."

"That what?"

He waited a moment, debating whether he should confess his deepest torment. "I don't think I've really gotten over Rachel," he finally admitted. "There was no real closure between us. She decided she wanted her music career more than she wanted us."

"So what part of that don't you get, Noah? She left you. Went off to greener pastures. She's been gone five years. When's the last time you heard from her?"

He glanced briefly at his friend. "About two months ago. She called me here at the club, said she was coming home, and when she did she wanted to see me... to talk."

"Aw, man." He threw his hands up in the air. "You've got to be kidding me." His features drew into a frown.

"I wish I were." He took a seat on the edge of his desk. "Ever since that call I've been second-guessing everything, questioning my relationship with Tara. Wondering about Rachel, what she's like now. And to be honest, until I get that part of me resolved, that part of my life settled, I can't commit to Tara. I'd spend the rest of my life asking, 'what if.'"

"Does Tara know about you and Rachel?"

He shook his head. "I never talked to her about Rachel."

"Maybe you should."

Jae Burrell waddled into the diner on Pennsylvania Avenue. Well into her eighth month, she was the picture of pregnant health. Tara watched her friend's approach and wished she could have a child, but now that dream was over.

"Hey, girl," Tara greeted, getting up from her seat and helping Jae into hers. She kissed her on her cheek. "You look wonderful."

Jae blew out a breath. "I'm glad I look good, because I feel like I'm going to explode." She laughed and rubbed her belly. "You, on the other hand, look miserable." She adjusted herself in the chair.

"I am."

"So, are you going to tell me before we eat or after?"

"It's a long story. Let's order."

"Why didn't you tell me things weren't going well between you and Noah?" Jae asked, stabbing her Caesar salad with her fork.

"You have enough to contend with...the baby, your husband, your job at the university. I didn't want to burden you with my stuff."

"Since when is our friendship a burden? You should have come to me, Tara." She reached across the table and covered Tara's hand with her own. "I always have time for you."

Tears spilled from Tara's eyes. All the hurt, confusion, and disappointment slid down her cheeks.

"I...I'm sorry, Jae. I didn't mean to start bawling." She reached for her napkin and wiped her eyes. "Everything just fell apart, and I don't know why."

"Did you try to talk to him?"

"Sure. But what he's saying isn't making sense."

"Do you think it's...someone else?"

Tara frowned. "No. I don't think so. He's never given me any reason to think..." She paused and stared at Jae. "*Is* there someone else?" Did Clyde say something to you?"

"No. I swear. Besides, Clyde and Noah are closer than brothers.

If there was someone else, Clyde hasn't said anything to me, I'm sure, out of loyalty to Noah. But," she quickly qualified her reply when she saw the distressed look on Tara's face, "Noah isn't the kind of man who would cheat on you. I know he loves you."

"I know he does, too. That's why this is so crazy. Every time I try to talk to him about setting a date, he starts making excuses. I just couldn't take it anymore. I gave him his ring back."

Jae's brows rose. "And what did he do?"

"He didn't *do* anything. All he said was that he was sorry."

"Oh, Tara. I wish I knew exactly what to tell you. Maybe you just need to give him some time. Let him know you're serious. He'll come around."

"I don't want to twist his arm into marrying me. The last thing I want is a man who doesn't want me."

"Oh, he wants you, alright. He just has to get his heart and head in sync."

"How is that going to happen?"

Jae leaned closer and lowered her voice to a conspiratorial whisper. "What we need is a plan."

# THREE

Rachel Beaumont watched the city of D.C. zip by her as the limo weaved in and out of the midday traffic.

She reclined against the soft, black leather interior. Five years, she thought. Five years since she'd been back to this town. Five years since she'd seen Noah Hardcastle. She wondered if he thought of her as often as she did of him. How many nights, flying from one city to the next, checking into one hotel after the other, did she question her decision to leave him to pursue her dream?

Rachel Beaumont was a household name in Europe and in the States. She had three Grammys and more nominations than she could count, for both her solo performances as a jazz pianist and her vocal virtuosity as well as her incomparable compositions. She had money, fame, notoriety, three homes, and a business manager to handle all of her affairs. She'd come a long way from her impoverished beginnings in Louisiana. The only thing missing from her perfect world was Noah, and she was as determined to get him back as she had been in the pursuit of her dream. She'd prove to him that the life he truly needed was a life with her.

She tapped on the Plexiglas partition. "Make a right at the corner, driver."

It may have been five years, she mused, but in five minutes she'd find out if the fire was still there between them.

Leo's had been open for about a half hour for the lunch crowd, and the upscale restaurant was already packed. Since Noah started "Noontime Jazz" on Wednesdays, business had been booming. The lunch was buffet; with everything from their famous house salad and country-fried chicken to their charbroiled catfish.

Clyde did a phenomenal job of scheduling the acts, mostly new-comers, but totally talented.

Noah moved from table to table, greeting his customers and en-suring that they had everything they needed. He'd just left the table of one of his regulars when he saw her.

She was standing by the bar, cool, controlled, and achingly beau-tiful. Her once short cap of curls was now a halo of spirals that hung to her shoulders, framing her near-perfect Creole features. A light suede coat in a soft camel color hung dramatically from her slender five-foot-seven frame, outlining a pantsuit of the same shade.

Rachel turned in his direction as if sensing his stare, and their gazes connected. A slow smile spread across her copper-colored lips.

For a moment everything around him seemed to disappear, and all that remained in the room were him and Rachel. His mind and emotions twisted as he recalled their turbulent times together, both of them passion-filled and stubborn, unwilling to give an inch, steadfast in what they wanted from life and from each other. The intensity of their personalities and their drive ultimately led to the demise of their tempestuous relationship. And since the day she left, when he'd watched her step onto the plane, there had been a hole in his spirit that he believed he'd filled when he found Tara. But ever since Rachel's call, and now seeing her again, he was no longer sure...of anything.

"Hello, Rachel. You look well."

"So do you," she said in that husky voice with the subtle Creole lilt. The same voice that had cooed to him in the dark, the voice that sometimes haunted him in the light of day, the voice that accompanied her compositions and thrilled millions with its unique charm.

"Is that it?" she softly teased, looking up at him. "No kiss, no hug for old times' sake?"

He leaned down with the intention of kissing her cheek, but she turned her head and caught his mouth instead, quickly flicking her tongue along his lips before stepping back. Her whiskey-colored eyes darkened the way he remembered just before...

He cleared his throat. "Where are you staying?"

"At the infamous Watergate." She smiled and reached for his hand. "It's good to see you, Noah. It's been much too long."

"That was your decision, if I remember correctly."

She lowered her gaze, then looked up. "I made a mistake, and," she squeezed his hand tighter, "I want to rectify that mistake."

"Rachel—"

"I know it's been a long time, but we can make up for it. That's why I came back."

"It's not that simple, Rachel. You can't just turn back the clock and magically make everything okay."

"I know that."

"Do you? Do you have any idea what you did to us... to me when you left?"

"Yes, and if you give me half a chance, I'll show you that I can make this work."

He exhaled. "How long are you in town this time?"

"As long as it takes."

"Rachel."

They both turned to the sound of Clyde's voice.

"Clyde!" She let go of Noah's hand and her expression swiftly shifted from sultry to engaging. She stretched out her arms and embraced him. "Looking as sharp as ever, I see. How are you?"

Clyde stepped back and gave her the once-over. "Looking pretty good yourself. I see your CDs everywhere, so I know you're doing well. Did Noah tell you I'm a married man now, with a baby on the way?"

Rachel glanced at Noah, then back at Clyde. "No, he didn't. Congratulations on both counts. You'll have to introduce me to the lucky lady." She turned her attention to Noah. "What about you, Noah? Do you have a lady-in-waiting?"

Images of Tara flashed through his head, what they'd had and what he'd let go. "No. Not at the moment."

The corner of Rachel's mouth curved in satisfaction. "Maybe all that will change."

A moment of uncomfortable silence hung over the trio until Clyde broke the tension.

"Hey, man, I need you to go over a few things before this shift is over."

"Yeah, sure," he answered, thankful for the reprieve. "I'll be in the office in a minute."

"Good to see you, Rachel." Clyde kissed her cheek and walked away.

"I need to get back to work," Noah said.

"Of course. Not a problem. I need to check into my hotel and unwind anyway."

He nodded.

"Can I call you later? Maybe we could have a late dinner."

"I don't think that would be such a good idea."

"Think about it. No strings. I just want to talk, spend some time with you—in a public place, if it makes you more comfortable."

He hesitated. "Fine. Call about ten. We close tonight at eleven."

"Ten it is." She turned and walked out, leaving Noah with a storm of confusing emotions.

Donna Hill

# FOUR

Clyde came in from work just before midnight. The club had been jumping from the opening bell, and the new act that he'd booked rocked the house. It had been a great day, but he was beat. All he had on his mind was a hot shower and curling up next to his wife. But the instant he crossed the threshold he smelled trouble as sure as his great-grandma could "smell" a storm coming.

Generally, by this time of night, his wife Jae would be fast asleep. When he saw her propped up on the couch with a book perched atop her stomach and "the look" that meant "We need to talk" on her face, his right pinky began to twitch.

In the year and a half that they'd been husband and wife, he'd come to dread that look, because invariably it meant he was in the hot seat about something. He often wondered, as he took his tongue-lashings from his wife, whatever happened to the shy, unassuming, church-going girl he met at Leo's? She'd turned into an assertive, self-assured, sexy siren who would rock his natural world as soon as do her nails or sing in the choir. What a woman.

He took a breath, tucked away his smile, and prepared himself to be dressed down for some infraction or the other, of which he was certain he was innocent.

"Hey, baby!" he greeted, putting on his best smile and all of his nightclub-player charm.

Jae folded her arms on top of the book on top of her stomach and pursed her lips. If he wasn't mistaken, he could have sworn she rolled her eyes at him. If she started rolling her neck, then he knew it would be "on."

He glided across the room as smooth as Smokey Robinson, eased alongside her, and planted a kiss on her cheek. "How are my babies tonight?" he cooed in her ear, knowing it was one of her weak spots. "Want me to rub your feet?"

"Don't try to get on my good side. I think you have something to tell me." She began tapping her foot—another bad sign.

Clyde definitely did not like how this was shaping up. "Don't I even get a hello, sugah, how was your day?" He needed a minute to do a quick mental inventory of possible scenarios. And then it hit him right between the eyes: Tara!

"Are you going to tell me what's going on with Noah? I know he spoke to you."

"Spoke to me about what?"

Her neck snapped to the right. "Don't play games, Clyde. You know what I'm talking about. Noah and Tara. He sent her packing."

It was Clyde's turn to jerk back in surprise. "Noah! He didn't send her packing. Tara said she wanted out," he said in defense of his buddy.

Inside, Jae smiled triumphantly, knowing that she had him just where she wanted him. "That's not the way I heard it. Tara is devastated. She's sure Noah is seeing someone else," she added coyly, watching his expression for any hint of homeboy loyalty. If she knew one thing about her husband, he was a lousy liar.

"Another woman." He chuckled nervously. "Don't be ridiculous." He got up and twisted his tie like it was a noose, then took off his jacket.

Got him! Anytime Clyde started messing with his tie, he was either lying or dodging a question.

"Who is it, Clyde?"

"It's nobody. It was over a long time ago." He squeezed his eyes shut in agony the instant he realized his mistake.

"So it is somebody!" Jae managed to push herself up from the couch and ambled around her husband to face him. "Is he seeing her now?"

"No. It's not like that."

"Then, what is it like?" she planted her hands on her hips.

"Look," he lowered his voice to a caressing whisper and gently clasped her shoulders. "Noah just needs some time to get his head right, that's all. He wants to finally put the past in the past so that he can move on."

"And this mystery woman is part of that past?"

"Something like that."

Jae lowered her gaze and sighed heavily before looking at her husband. "Baby, I know Noah is your friend and Tara is mine. I don't want to see her hurt. If there's something she needs to know, tell me."

"It's not my place, Jae."

"We're husband and wife. We aren't supposed to keep secrets from each other," she said, switching ploys.

"Jae . . . come on. Don't go there."

"You aren't giving me any other choice. We promised we would always be honest with each other, no secrets."

His shoulders sank as he tried to find a way out of this latest dilemma without betraying his friendship, but more importantly, without pissing off his wife. "Okay, look, Noah was deeply involved with Rachel Beaumont—"

Her brows rose in alarm and awe. "*The* Rachel Beaumont?"

He nodded. "Anyway, when she left . . . things as far as Noah was

*lady in waiting*

concerned were not totally resolved. Well, to make a long story short, she's back in D.C. and wants to reconcile."

Jae covered her mouth and wished she was still sitting down. "Oh, no," she murmured.

An avid music buff and a singer in her own right, she'd followed Rachel Beaumont's rising star, applauded her successes, and marveled at her talent and business savvy as well as her beauty. She could easily see how Noah—or any man—would be attracted to Rachel.

"Does he still love her?" Jae asked, practically holding her breath.

"I think Noah is in love with the idea of Rachel; he always has been." He put his arm around her waist and led her toward the couch, then eased her down onto his lap and gently rubbed her stomach. "She hurt him hon, deeply. He worked real hard to put it behind him, but he didn't, at least not totally. There has always been the lingering question: what if?"

"Is he going to go back to her? What about Tara?" Her voice cracked with emotion.

"If there is one thing that both of us have discovered about love, it's that those who belong together will find their way to each other."

Jae rested her head on her husband's chest and thought about how she could make sure that those two people were Noah and Tara.

# FIVE

The club was finally empty. The last of the customers were gone, the staff departed.

Noah sat in the center of the club with the lights dimmed and the music playing softly in the background. This was the time he enjoyed most, when it was quiet and the adrenaline rush of the day was behind him, when he could reflect on his successes and failures and plan for tomorrow. But he couldn't concentrate today, tomorrow, or any day. His now, his future, was still trapped in his past. The only thing running through his head was, *I'll be there before midnight.*

He glanced at his watch: 11:45. He should go home. Waiting for Rachel to show up couldn't lead to anything but trouble. But he knew he needed to confront his demon, sooner rather than later. He got up, walked to the back room, locked the night's receipts in the safe, and shut off the lights.

When he returned to the center of the restaurant there was a light tap on the locked glass doors.

*Rachel.*

Noah drew in a breath, walked to the door, and let her in.

"Surprised I'm on time?" she asked.

"Nothing surprises me these days." He held the door and

*lady in waiting*

stepped aside, catching a subtle whiff of her scent as she brushed by him.

"I see we have the place all to ourselves," she said, turning toward him as he approached.

"It seems appropriate that we'd pick up where we left off," he replied. "Our last conversation was here, the one where you told me you wanted more, more than this town or I could give you. Remember?"

"That was five years ago, Noah. People change. I've changed."

He reached for a switch on the side wall and raised the level of light. "The better to see your claws."

"Aw," she pouted, "I liked the dimly lit feel. More intimate, don't you think?"

He ignored her question and crossed the room to the bar. "Can I fix you a drink?"

"Sure. I'll have my usual." She walked over and slid onto the bar stool.

Noah looked at Rachel for a long moment, and suddenly she wasn't dressed in a form-fitting gray knit jersey dress, and her hair and makeup weren't done to camera-ready perfection. Instead, he saw her naked body covered with a thin sheen of sweat, her hair in damp ringlets pinned to her scalp, her mouth swollen from his kisses as she writhed and bucked beneath him, telling him how much she loved and needed him, that she'd never leave him.

"Yeah, I remember," he said finally. "Apple martini."

She smiled. "So…tell me how you've been, Noah," she said, taking the glass from his hand.

"I've managed to keep myself busy with the club."

"There has to be more to your life than this club. Everyone else seems to have gotten married in my absence. What about you? I know you haven't been alone all this time."

"I don't see what that has to do with anything."

She put down her glass. "Noah," she said quietly, "I know I messed up. I thought what I wanted I could find out there." She waved her right arm expansively. "But I didn't. There wasn't a day that went by that I didn't think of you."

"Then whey didn't you come back, Rachel?"

She glanced away. "I needed to see if I could make it. I had to try."

"What do you really want?"

She looked deep into his eyes. "I want you, Noah. I want us."

"And what's going to happen to us when you decide to take off again?"

"I won't."

He turned away. "I don't trust you, Rachel. It's as simple as that."

She got up and came behind the bar where he was. She placed her hand on his shoulder. "Look at me."

Slowly he turned around.

"Give me a chance. That's all I ask. I'll make you love me again." She cupped his face. "I swear I will." She reached up and brushed his lips with hers.

For an instant he was transported back to happier times when the only woman in the world for him was Rachel—the touch and feel of her, the sound of her voice, her scent, the way she made love to him. Then an image of Tara took her place—the look in her eyes the morning she gave him the ring back.

He eased away.

"Don't you want me anymore?" she asked in a voice thick with emotion. "It can be good between us again."

"I can't go back, Rachel. I won't. What we had...was five years ago. It's like you said, people change. Well I've changed too," he insisted, as much to convince her as himself.

*lady in waiting*

"We don't have to go back. We don't have to start over. We can begin today. Fresh." She paused. "Look, nothing will get settled in one conversation. I'm not asking you to make a decision right now. I know my turning up is not what you expected. Just think about it. That's all I ask. I'm willing to do whatever it takes to win your heart, if you'll give me a chance." She crossed the room and picked up her purse from the table, then headed for the door. "I'm a patient woman, Noah. And I'm willing to wait as long as necessary for you to see that we belong together."

She opened the door, then stepped out into the night and the waiting limo.

# SIX

Tara spent most of the night tossing and turning, reliving the moment when she walked out of Noah's apartment. In some versions he came after her, telling her how much he loved her. In others he laughed as she wept uncontrollably. And then there was the one where he simply said, "I'm sorry," before vanishing in front of her eyes. When she awoke she was achy, as if she'd been in a fight, and her eyes felt like they had tiny grains of sand in them.

As she drove the twenty minutes to her office in the center of trendy Georgetown, she sensed that it was not going to be a good day. She had a lunchtime meeting with a new client and felt totally unprepared. For the most part, she enjoyed her job as an international jewelry buyer. It afforded her the opportunity to travel around the world and meet some interesting clients. Somehow, she would have to dig deep inside herself to get through her day. She just hoped that the meeting went quickly and without too much effort on her part.

She eased her car into her reserved parking space, grabbed her purse and portfolio, set the car alarm, and headed inside.

" 'Morning, Tara," Becky the receptionist greeted.

"Is it still morning?" Tara answered in a monotone, removing her dark shades.

"Are you okay?" Becky asked. "You don't look like you're feeling very well."

"Rough night," she murmured. "Any messages?"

"Only one."

Her heart skipped a beat, hoping it was a message from Noah. She took the blue slip of paper and quickly glanced at the information. She handed the note back to Becky.

"Thanks. Give Mrs. Gibbs a call and let her know that I expect her shipment at the end of the week."

"Sure. Oh, and by the way, your one-o'clock is here."

"What?" She glanced at her watch. "It's only twelve-fifteen."

"I know. He said his meeting wrapped up early, so he came straight here. He's in your office."

Tara expelled a sigh through her teeth. She'd hoped to have a few minutes to get her act together before her meeting, but that notion just went out the window.

"Thanks." Reluctantly she headed down the carpeted corridor toward her office. With much effort she put on her best face and opened her office door.

"Mr. Miller," she said as she stepped inside.

Calvin Miller turned from the wall-to-wall window to face her, and Tara's stomach did a complete somersault.

Calvin Miller, upon first glance, was the man whose last name you wanted to add to yours.

He smiled and moved toward her with his hand extended.

"Ms. Mitchell. Sorry to barge in and camp out in your office, but my meeting concluded earlier than I expected. I hope you don't mind."

Somehow she found herself shaking his hand and muttering something inane about it not being a problem.

"Please... have a seat," she said, recovering.

Donna Hill

He opted for the couch, which forced her to take a seat there as well, unless she intended to conduct her meeting from across the room at her small conference table.

She opened her portfolio and extracted his file.

"I've gone over your requests," she began, trying to focus on her notes and not the manly scent of him. "And I was able to pull together a few samples of what I think would suit your needs." She fished in her portfolio and pulled out a dozen full-color photos of diamond and emerald stones, set in earrings, linked on chains, bracelets, and rings, and spread them on the table.

"These are——"

"You don't remember me, do you?"

Tara looked up and into his eyes, studying his face, and recognition slowly dawned on her.

"Calvin?" She squinted as if to get him in focus.

He nodded and smiled, and the room seemed to light up.

"I've changed just a little," he laughed.

Tara shook her head in disbelief. Calvin Miller was a scrawny, snot-nosed, knotty-headed little boy who lived down the street from her. The boys in the neighborhood took great pleasure in teasing him and chasing him home from school. She always felt sorry for him and would say hello if she passed him in the halls at school, or saw him sitting alone in the cafeteria. But the Calvin Miller she remembered was certainly not the handsome, self-assured man who sat next to her now.

"I can't believe it." She leaned over and hugged him. "Little Calvin."

He tossed his head back and chuckled. "Life has been good to me."

"So I see. Where are you living now?"

"Right here in D.C."

"Married? Kids?"

"No to both. I suppose I haven't found the right woman. What about you?"

Images of her almost-life with Noah Hardcastle flashed through her head. Absently she rubbed her hand that was now devoid of her ring.

She pulled in a breath. "No. Not at the moment."

"Maybe... we can get together for dinner or something. I'd love to catch up."

She thought about it for a moment. "Sure, why not? I think I'd really like that," she finally said. After all, what could be the harm in having a bite with an old school friend?

# SEVEN

"So what happened?" Clyde asked the instant he set foot in Noah's office and shut the door.

Noah barely glanced up from the stack of vendor bills on his desk.

"Good afternoon to you, too," he said and returned to punching numbers into the calculator. "I'll be glad when Ayanna gets back. This is not my thing," he grumbled, tore the tape from the machine, and hurled into the wastebasket.

"Don't avoid the question, Noah. What happened? I know Rachel came back last night. It's in her genes."

"Very funny." He tugged in a breath and pushed back from the desk, then glanced up and at Clyde before looking away. "Yeah, she came back, after closing."

"And?"

"We talked—sort of."

"Did you tell her about Tara?"

Noah's gaze snapped in Clyde's direction. "No, Tara's name didn't come up."

"So what exactly did come up—beside your libido?"

"I'll just ignore that last comment." He stood and crossed the room. "We talked about the past, what it was and what it wasn't. Bottom line is, she wants us back together and she sounded determined to make it happen."

Clyde made a disgusted noise in his throat. "And what did you say?"

"Not much."

"So essentially you left the door wide open for her to walk back in."

"Look, I know this may not make sense to you, and maybe you think I'm being a fool—"

"Think!"

"Are you gonna let me finish?"

"Go 'head."

"It's like I told you, things were never truly settled between me and Rachel. And it won't be fair to Tara for me to plow into a marriage with unresolved issues hanging over both of us."

"Do you love Tara?"

"Yes."

"Do you still love Rachel?"

There was a long pause before he replied. "That's just it, man, I don't know."

Rachel sat on the side of her bed in the penthouse suite of the Watergate Hotel. She'd barely been back in D.C. for twenty-four hours and already her room was filled with roses from studio heads, business acquaintances, and admirers. Her assistant, Carol London, was inundated with fielding phone calls from television and radio stations, not to mention the newspaper and magazine people who all wanted an interview, "just five minutes." Everyone wanted something, everyone wanted a piece of Rachel Beaumont.

Years earlier, when she'd set out on her rise to the top, she would have given anything for the admiration, notoriety, and accolades that had become hers for the taking. But she wasn't the same woman she was five years ago. She'd seen the inside of more recording studios, and slept in more strange beds to last her a lifetime. What she wanted now was a regular life, to have one place to call home, and Noah to share it with.

"This phone won't stop ringing," Carol said, strutting into the room as if it were a runway, her ever ready, leather-bound date book in her hand. "I'm still trying to figure out who spilled the beans and told everyone in the universe that you were in Washington." She flopped down on the chaise lounge and stretched out her long legs. "Whew. I'm really beat and it's barely lunchtime." She turned a bright smile on Rachel that quickly faded. "You look positively miserable. Are you feeling okay? Sleep well? Can I get you something?"

Rachel held up her hand to halt the barrage of questions. "I'm fine. Just trying to work some things out in my head."

"Can I help?"

Rachel was thoughtful for a moment. There were few secrets between her and Carol. They shared practically everything, at least that's what Carol believed. The truth was, Rachel had never fully shared the depths of her feelings for Noah, how terribly torn she was when she moved away to pursue her career, and how lonely she'd been without him. Maybe now was the time.

"Carol, we need to talk." She flashed a sheepish smile. "I need to talk. There are some things I want to tell you ... about me and Noah Hardcastle."

More than an hour later, Rachel was in Carol's arms, shedding the last of her story and her tears.

"Why didn't you ever tell me, Rach? I mean I kind of knew you liked the guy, but ... you always acted as if love and marriage were

*lady in waiting*

the last things on your mind. And I believed you. Maybe you should have gone into acting," she added with a wry chuckle.

Rachel laughed and sniffed back her tears. "I figured if I didn't talk about him, tried not to think about him and just focus on my career, I could put that part of my life behind me. But I was wrong. You're right. Maybe I should have been an actress instead of a musician. This has been a five-year performance."

"I should have known. Anyone who can write and play your kind of passion-filled ballads had to have experienced the real thing. I guess I simply refused to address it. I figured you were over him, so I just left well enough alone."

They were both silent for a few moments.

"So, what are you going to do?" Carol asked, brushing Rachel's hair away from her face.

A slow smile crept across Rachel's full mouth as she looked up at her friend. "Well...I've already made my intentions known. I stopped by the restaurant last night."

Carol giggled. "I bet you did."

"But five years stand between us. A lot happens in five years."

Carol watched the play of emotions across Rachel's face, how her mouth went from pouty and gentle to firm and resolute. Gone was the glow of the soft, love-struck woman of moments ago. In her place was the woman that Carol had come to know—a woman who got what she wanted.

Rachel eyes sparked with intensity. "I need to know about every minute of it."

# EIGHT

Jae sat behind her office desk with her swollen feet propped up on a little step stool she'd managed to get from one of the maintenance staff. She leaned back and sighed, rubbing her belly. The baby was restless today, and so was she. She needed to be doing something. She'd worked long and hard to become head of the English Department and she enjoyed the privileges and the esteem that came with the title and the paycheck. But there were days like today that she wished she were still doing the day-to-day stuff, mixing it up in the classroom, seeing the lights go on in student's eyes when they finally "got it."

She glanced around the office at the walls adorned with her degrees and certifications. She was going to miss the place, miss the daily challenges she faced. Although her job was exceedingly important and came with its share of responsibility, to be truthful, she was a bit more afraid of her new role as mother.

The baby gave her a swift kick in her right side, making her jump about an inch out of the chair. She gently rubbed the spot where she could actually see a little foot or a fist poking out. "Take it easy," she murmured and wished Clyde were around to see the little imprint.

At least she had Clyde, she thought, knowing he'd make an excellent father. She'd been so sure that Tara and Noah would soon follow in their footsteps, that she'd stand as Tara's matron of honor on her wedding day and Clyde would be best man. She couldn't believe that Noah would just let Tara go without a fight. She'd seen the two of them together, and no one could convince her that Noah didn't absolutely adore the ground that Tara walked on. The looks that he gave Tara when he thought she wasn't paying attention were the same looks that Clyde gave her—filled with love and longing. You can't fake those.

Jae couldn't imagine her life without Clyde and knew that Tara felt the same way about Noah. Her heart had almost broken when she listened to Tara tell her what happened between her and Noah. She knew how much her girl loved that man, and it was killing her to see her friend so unhappy. When she'd vowed the other day that they needed a plan—it was true. The sad part was, it was more bravado on her part than a concrete idea. She really wasn't sure what to do, other than snatching Noah by the collar and shaking some sense into him.

What haunted her more than anything were her husband's revelations about Rachel Beaumont. She thought she was going to have the baby right on the couch when he told her the news. "Of all the people in the world," she muttered. If what Clyde said about Rachel was true, then she and Tara had their hands full.

She glanced up at the clock on the wall, then checked her appointment book. She had one more meeting—but it could wait. She pressed the button on the phone for her assistant.

"Yes, Dr. Burrell?"

"Karen, I'm going to leave early. Would you please call Professor Driggs and tell her I deeply apologize, but if she's free, could we arrange to meet tomorrow at the same time?"

"Sure, Dr. Burrell. Are you feeling okay?"

"Yes, I'm fine. Something came up that I need to take care of."

"Okay, if you're sure."

Jae chuckled. "Yes, Karen, I'm sure."

"I'll call Professor Driggs now."

"Thanks."

Jae returned the phone to the base, collected her purse and her jacket, and slowly pulled herself up from her seat.

"Whew!" Gingerly she stood and slipped her feet back into her shoes, happy that her feet hadn't swelled. She smiled, thinking of the nightly foot massage that Clyde was sure to give her, and the way he would run his hands up and down her legs and across her belly and...well, there was no point in getting all worked up now. She switched off the lights and headed out. If people thought that pregnancy cut down on lovemaking, they were sorely mistaken. Tonight couldn't arrive soon enough.

"So how about dinner tonight?" Calvin said, picking up his briefcase. "I mean, if you're not busy." His dark eyes ran over her and sparkled when the light hit them.

"Umm. Tonight?" She hadn't expected him to make an offer so soon. Through force of habit she stroked her hand where her engagement ring once rested, then looked up at Calvin. "Tonight sounds fine."

Calvin's smile was slow and seductive. "Great. Where should I pick you up?"

"I finish around six."

"I'll be here." He headed for the door. At the threshold he stopped. "I'm really looking forward to dinner, Tara. Catch up."

"Yes, so am I."

He nodded and walked out.

Slowly Tara closed her office door behind him. She hadn't been out

*lady in waiting*

with another man since she'd started dating Noah. The emotional part of her felt as if she were betraying Noah somehow. But the rational part reasoned that, although she was the one who officially broke it off, Noah pushed her out the door.

It had been painfully clear for months that Noah was having second thoughts about marrying her. Going out with Calvin would be the perfect balm to soothe her wounded spirit and take her mind off what could have been.

She started to put away her portfolio when her intercom buzzed.

"Yes, Becky?"

"Jae Crawford is here to see you."

Tara's face brightened in surprise. "Send her right in." She stood just as the door opened. "Jae, what a—"

"Girl, we need to talk." She blew out a breath and headed for a chair.

Tara shook her head. "Can I just stick a pin in you and be done with it?"

"Not funny. Come on, sit down and close the door. This is important."

"Alright, alright. Are you and the baby okay?" She sat down next to Jae on the sofa.

"Yes, we're fine. Getting a little tired of each other, but we're doing okay," she said as the baby gave her another nudge in the ribs.

"So what's up?"

Jae turned her body to face her friend and looked her right in the eye. "Have you ever heard of Rachel Beaumont, the jazz pianist?"

"Of course, who hasn't? Why, you got tickets?" She giggled.

"You may not want tickets after you hear what I have to say."

"Well, get to it."

"Before you met Noah, he had a thing with Rachel Beaumont."

Tara had to take a couple of breaths and wait for the room to settle before she dared to speak. Her heart was racing as if she'd just run a mile. Noah and Rachel, one of the most famous, most beautiful black women in the industry? She swallowed hard and forced a smile.

"A thing." She shrugged. "So ... they dated a few times. Big deal."

Jae reached for Tara's hand, knowing that her friend was slipping into the denial mode. "Tara, it was a *serious* thing. Very serious."

Tara pulled back and glanced away. Suddenly she stood, folded her arms beneath her breasts, and paced the floor. "Everyone has had a serious relationship at some point," she said, mostly to fill the air as she tried to discern the full meaning of what Jae was telling her. Finally she stopped pacing and turned to Jae. "You must be telling me all this for a reason."

"Sit down, sweetie."

Tara's chest heaved in and out. "She's the reason why ... isn't she?"

Slowly Jae nodded her head.

Tara tugged on her bottom lip with her teeth. "And? I'm sure there's more."

"She's back in town."

Tara crossed the room and took a seat behind her desk. "I guess that would explain everything. He must have known all along that she was coming back." Her eyes began to fill. "Has he been seeing her? How long? Tell me!" He palm slapped down on the table.

"Relax. As far as I know, he hasn't seen her since she left town five years ago. She just got back."

"I'm sure they've been keeping in touch."

"You don't know that, Tara. Look, the reason I told you is I wanted you to have the right ammunition to fight with."

"Right ammunition!" She spat out a derisive laugh. "Have you seen her? I don't have the ammunition to fight against that."

"Love isn't about looks, Tara."

"Don't be naïve, Jae." She cut her eyes in Jae's direction, then looked away.

"Since when did you become such a pessimist? So what if she's famous and beautiful? You're cute and well known in small circles."

They both looked at each other and laughed, easing the tension in the room that had built to a boiling point.

Slowly Tara returned to the couch and plopped down. Her expression was a sketch of sadness. "What am I going to do?"

"The first thing you need to do is get your head right. As long as you think that she has something you don't, then you've already lost."

"Yeah, I guess," she murmured, not sounding too convincing.

"What we need to do is make Noah realize that the grass ain't greener on the other side."

"How are we supposed to do that?"

Jae frowned. "Hmmm. Good question." Suddenly her eyes widened and a slow smiled crept across her face. "We need to make him jealous."

"Jealous? Are you kidding?"

"Why should I be kidding? Jealousy works every time. Once Mr. Man realizes that you're moving on, he'll get on his game."

"You really think so?"

"I know so."

"But what if it all backfires, Jae? What if Noah finds out or sees me with someone and thinks the way is really clear for him and . . . and . . . what'shername?" She sucked her teeth in disgust.

"Then we need to give *him* somebody to worry about. He has to be good looking, polished, dress well, speak well, and hold up under pressure."

Donna Hill

"Well I don't—"

"What?"

"Life is funny." She looked her friend in the eyes. "Just today, Calvin Miller came into my office."

"Who is Calvin Miller?"

A smile stretched across her mouth. "He's fine, dresses well, he's polished, and can stand up under pressure."

"I think we have our plan, sister friend!"

# NINE

Carol sat with the phone in her hand, barking orders and taking notes. In a little more than two hours she'd gotten more information on Noah Hardcastle than the IRS could get on him. But more importantly, she'd found out about Tara. She printed out the e-mails from the computer and gathered up the faxes, then spread the material in front of her on the desk. Tara Mitchell by all accounts was a successful, well-respected businesswoman and Noah's fiancée.

Carol slipped off her glasses and put them on the desk next to the pile of papers. So Noah was engaged. How would Rachel handle the news? After talking with her, she saw Rachel in a completely different light. When she talked about Noah she became soft and giggly like a teenager, starry-eyed. She was no longer the diva who commanded the attention of millions, who had men dying to be with her and woman wanting to be her.

She tugged in a deep breath and stacked the papers into a neat pile before running them through the shredder, then tossed them into the trash.

Rachel needed to know, there was no question about that. She had to understand what she was dealing with and then decide if she wanted to. The catch was, if Noah wanted to marry this Tara person, then he must love her.

Carol turned in her swivel chair and began a Web search for Tara Mitchell. Within moments a list of Tara Mitchells popped up on the screen. By the process of elimination she soon hit pay dirt: not only a complete dossier but a full-color head shot as well.

"Hmm. So you're Tara Mitchell," she murmured as she studied the near-perfect face. She scrolled through the information and jotted down all the relevant details: business address and phone number.

"Who's that?"

Carol jumped and turned in her chair. "Uh, you scared me." She forced a smile.

Rachel stepped closer just as Carol minimized the screen.

"Another fan? Are they sending pictures now?" Rachel chuckled, took a seat, and sighed deeply. She looked at Carol for confirmation.

Her assistant glanced away.

"What is it, Carol? Something is obviously going on. Your face is as red as a tomato."

Carol stood and tugged on the hem of her jacket.

"It must be bad news. You only start tugging and pulling when something is really wrong. Now, tell me. What is it?"

"All right, all right." She took a breath. "I did some digging."

Rachel frowned. "And . . ."

"About Noah," she hedged.

"Okay." She unconsciously gripped the arms of the chair. "And?"

"Well, it appears that Noah is engaged."

Rachel's expression remained unreadable, but the light dimmed in her eyes. "I see." She swallowed over the sudden dryness in her throat. "Who is she?"

Carol swung in her seat back to the computer and restored the screen.

"Tara Mitchell," Rachel mouthed as she looked into the smiling face of the woman who'd captured Noah's heart. Her voice took on the commanding edge that Carol had come to know so well. "I want to meet her. Arrange it."

"So you're planning on going out with him?" Jae asked.

Tara slowly stood and crossed the room. "Yes. It's clearer now more than ever that Noah's heart is elsewhere."

Jae shook her head in denial. "I don't think so, Sis. I think Noah has a case of cold feet and some unresolved issues." She looked Tara in the eye. "That doesn't mean he doesn't love you."

"No, it doesn't. What it means is that he doesn't love me enough."

"I don't believe that, either. But I do believe that Mr. Man needs a wake-up call. And Calvin Miller is just the ticket."

"What do you mean?"

"A few well-placed comments in the right ears, and Noah will start seeing the light."

"What are you planning, Jae Crawford? I don't want to play games with Noah and I certainly won't use Calvin to get him."

"You won't be doing either. Trust me." Jae slowly pulled herself up from her seat. "I've never let you down and I don't plan to now. You and Noah belong together. It's as simple as that." She headed for the door. "And I intend to see it happen."

# TEN

Noah left his office to check out the after-work crowd. Clyde hired a new jazz band that featured an incredible singer, reminiscent of an early Billie Holiday. The band was in full swing and the songstress was belting out her rendition of "God Bless the Child."

The crowd seemed to enjoy the show, and the hostesses and bartenders were busy seating the stream of newcomers and keeping up with drink orders.

Noah stood along the side, secretly hoping to see Tara come through the door. This was usually the time she'd stroll in, flash that smile of hers, and make his day. But it didn't appear as if today was going to be one of those.

Since the night Tara walked out of his apartment door, he'd been tormented by what had happened. The questions ran after each other in his head: why didn't he stop her; why did he feel this overwhelming sense of doubt and confusion?

At night he lay awake for hours recalling their times together, her laughter, the soft and totally feminine way she looked after they'd made love. And then Rachel's face would appear. He'd hear her smoky voice, remember her touch and the way they once were with

*lady in waiting*

each other. It was maddening, and the ache he felt without Tara in his life only made it worse.

"Mr. Hardcastle, there's someone here to see you."

Noah turned toward Celeste, his senior hostess. "Who is it?"

"She said her name was Carol, a friend of Rachel Beaumont."

His eyes darted around the restaurant before focusing back on Celeste. "Where is she?"

"I had her sit at the bar. She's the one with the cream-colored suit."

Noah nodded as he spotted Carol with her back toward him. "Thanks."

"Mr. H, is she a friend of *the* Rachel Beaumont?" Her eyes widened with anticipation.

"I believe so."

"Oh, Mr. H, do you think you could get her to visit Leo's? I'd love to meet her."

Noah started to walk toward the bar. "I'm sure Ms. Beaumont is very busy," he said over his shoulder. He continued across the room until he stood behind Carol.

"My hostess said you wanted to see me."

Carol turned around on the bar stool and immediately understood why Rachel melted like butter when she spoke of Noah Hardcastle.

"Hello." She extended her hand, which Noah shook. "I'm Carol London, Rachel's assistant."

"What can I do for you, Ms. London?"

"Do you have a few minutes to talk?"

"A few." He took a seat next to her.

"I'll get straight to the point. I've worked with Rachel for the past five years. We've grown very close, and we're more than just business associates—we're friends."

"That's really nice, but what does it have to do with me?"

She expelled a long breath and gathered her thoughts. "Rachel has always been extremely focused, single-minded when it comes to her career. That's all she ever wanted."

Noah briefly glanced away. "I know that—all too well." He looked at her. "And I still don't see what it has to do with me."

"Rachel is ready to give it all up for you."

"Excuse me?"

"Everything she's worked for, dreamed about, she'd throw it all out the window for you."

"That's all very flattering, Ms. London, but I would never ask Rachel to do something like that."

"You wouldn't have to. But you see, as I said, I know Rachel and I believe that ultimately she'd be miserable and wind up blaming you. But at the same time she'd never be totally happy without you in her life. I want Rachel to be happy, Mr. Hardcastle."

"That's very commendable, but what do you want me to do about it? Rachel is a grown woman and quite capable of making her own decisions."

"You're engaged, aren't you?"

A jolt shot through his middle. "I don't see how that is any of your business."

"I didn't come here to fight with you. I simply wanted to lay the cards on the table. Stay out of Rachel's life. What she needs is her career. She just signed a new multimillion-dollar recording contract and she's scheduled to go back in the studio in the next few weeks. I won't sit by and watch her throw it all away."

Noah looked down into Carol's upturned face. "Thanks for stopping by. I'm sure you can find your way out."

Noah crossed the room, barely able to contain his anger. There was no way he was going to have a scene in his place of business.

If he didn't know better, he'd have sworn she threatened him. It was subtle but clear.

He strode into his office and slammed the door behind him. Pacing the floor, he replayed the conversation. Was Rachel willing to give up her career if it meant their being together? Her career, her blind ambition, was the wedge that drove them apart. She wanted fame and fortune more than she wanted a life with him. But now . . .

A short knock on the door jarred him out of his dark thoughts.

"Come in," he barked.

Clyde stuck his head in, then came inside. "What's up with you, man? I saw you tearing across the room. Everything cool?"

Noah grumbled something under his breath, then ran his hand across his close-cropped head. "I just had a visitor."

"Who . . . bill collector?" He laughed at his own joke.

Noah cut him a nasty look. "I wish. I got a visit from Rachel's assistant."

Clyde knew this was sit-down time and took a seat. Noah recounted his conversation with Carol.

"Whoa. That's pretty heavy, man. What are you going to do?"

"I think I need to pay Rachel a visit."

Clyde quietly shut his apartment door behind him and squinted through the semi-darkness into the living room. There was a sliver of light coming from beneath his bedroom door. He smiled. Jae was still up. Maybe if he rubbed her feet just the right way he could get some loving tonight.

He took off his shoes, tiptoed down the hallway, and eased open the door. A slight breeze could have knocked him over. Propped up on pillows, with candle lights shimmering from the mantle tossing an angelic glow on her face, was Jae. A slow, seductive smile spread across her mouth as she let the pearl-gray sheet accidentally slip down the rounded mounds and valleys of her ripe body.

"Hi," she whispered. "I've been waiting for you." She reached over to the night-stand and handed him a glass of his favorite white wine. "Thought you might be thirsty."

Clyde felt as if he'd been sucked into a real-life fantasy, the woman of his dreams within inches of his grasp. He crossed the room, tossing his jacket to the floor and loosening his tie. He took the wineglass from her fingers and set it back on the nightstand.

"I'd rather taste you." He lowered his head and let his tongue tease her parted lips until he knew she was eager for the completeness of his kiss.

She wrapped her arms around his neck and gently pulled him down on the bed next to her. "You have on much too much clothing for this time of the night," she cooed, kissing his eyelids, the tip of his nose, and his lips while simultaneously unbuttoning his shirt.

"And you are pretty agile for a... woman in your condition," he teased, running his hands along her enlarged breasts and swollen belly.

Her nipples hardened at his touch and she moaned as waves of pleasure coursed through her veins, exploding in her head. After her first trimester, when her body and mind had adjusted to impending motherhood, it seemed as though her libido kicked into overdrive. She was more hungry for her husband than she had ever been, close to insatiable. The passion, the urgency, and the heat that he'd ignited in her before her pregnancy had been magnified a hundred times. It made her almost dizzy with longing. If she didn't think she would hurt him, herself, and their child, she'd just toss him on the floor and have her way with him.

"Hmm, let's see what little mama has under this pretty pink, frilly thing," Clyde murmured, easing her short gown up over her hips.

*lady in waiting*

His eyes sparkled in the candlelight and a mischievous grin lifted his lips. "Nothing. Just what daddy ordered."

Jae giggled and adjusted her body on the bed.

"And I'm still so very … very thirsty." He planted tiny kisses along the length of her warm brown flesh, caressing her curves until she shivered with desire, mumbling his name as if possessed. Gently he parted her thighs, kissing the insides of them, nibbling tenderly, and when he was certain that she couldn't take any more he flicked his tongue along the hardened seed of her sex. Reflexively she arched her hips and Clyde held her there against his mouth, taking all that she had to give to him.

She tried to contain her cries of ecstasy by biting her lips, sticking her fist in her mouth, covering her face with a pillow, but she couldn't keep from screaming. Her husband was driving her up the wall of desire and into the valley of unspeakable release. Her entire body felt as if it were on fire, wired with electrical charges, as wave after wave of incredible sensation ripped through her and white lights danced behind her closed eyes. And just when she knew she couldn't take anymore and was ready to explode, he took her to another level.

"Clyde!"

He held her in the palms of his hands, drinking in every drop, until her tremors subsided and she lay weak and spent. Then he smiled. A long hard day at the office certainly had its payoffs.

"Hmmm, you are so good to me," Jae whispered in her husband's ear as she lay nestled in his arms.

"You deserve it, baby. I love you." He kissed the top of her head.

"We're so lucky to have found each other."

"Hmmm." Clyde felt the fingertips of sleep reaching out to claim him. His eyes drifted close as he cuddled against the warmth of Jae's body.

"Yeah...too bad about Noah and Tara. I was so sure they were heading for the altar. But now that Tara may have someone new in her life...well...you never know."

Clyde's eyes flew open and his antennae shot straight up. He tried to sound unconcerned. "Really, someone new, huh?" He yawned for effect. "You, uh, meet him?"

"No. But Tara said he's an old friend from school, a really nice guy who does very well for himself, from what she was telling me." She ran her fingers across his chest. "They were supposed to go to dinner tonight to catch up on old times. I'll definitely have to call over the weekend and see how it went."

Clyde grumbled something under his breath. Jae smiled and closed her eyes.

# ELEVEN

Noah drove around the Watergate Hotel for at least an hour, debating whether he should confront Rachel once and for all or simply go home. But the reality was that avoiding issues had gotten him into this position. He wouldn't walk away again and simply hope that things would work themselves out.

He pulled up in front of the hotel. Within seconds a valet was whisking his car away and the doorman was whisking him inside.

The female front desk clerk smiled brightly upon his approach and leaned forward. "Welcome to the Watergate, sir. How may I help you?"

By her body language, Noah could tell, she was giving off more than her trained hotel greeting. He cleared his throat. "I'm here to see Rachel Beaumont."

A look of disappointment bent the upward curve of her full red-tinted mouth until her smile disappeared all together. She pressed her lips together, then turned her attention to the computer screen. "Beaumont?"

"Yes."

She pressed some numbers. "Your name, sir?"

"Noah Hardcastle."

"You're one of the owners of Leo's, aren't you?" she asked, tilting her head to the side, her customer service skills switching back into gear.

"Yes, I am. Have you been there?"

"No, I haven't. But I've heard great things about it. I have some friends who go every now and then." She smiled shyly.

Noah dug into his inside jacket pocket and pulled out a business card, scribbled something on the back, and handed it to her. "Dinner on me for you and a guest. Just show this card to any of the hostesses."

She glanced at the card, then at him. Her eyes widened with excitement. "Thank you so much. This is so…people just don't do things like this."

"Not a problem." He looked at her name tag pinned to the lapel of her uniform jacket. "Come by one evening and enjoy yourself… Stephanie."

Her light-mocha complexion heated, turning her skin an almost honey brown. "Thank you. I will." She stared at him for a long moment before pulling herself together. Blinking rapidly, she then cleared her throat and reached for the phone. "I-I'm ringing her room now, sir. You can pick up the red phone on the table over there." She pointed to an ornate round table flanked by two overstuffed chairs.

"Thank you." Noah walked over to the phone and picked it up.

"How can I help you?"

Noah recognized the voice as Carol's. "Hello, Ms. London, this is Noah Hardcastle. I'd like to speak with Rachel."

"She's resting."

"I see. Well I'd really appreciate it if you'd wake her and ask her to come to the phone."

"I'm sorry, Mr. Hardcastle, but Rachel was extremely tired. I *won't*

*lady in waiting*

disturb her. But I'd be happy to give her a message…in the morning when she gets up."

"Don't trouble yourself. I'll be sure she gets my message. Have a nice evening." He hung up the phone, stood there for a few moments, then returned to the front desk. He drummed his fingernails on the countertop to keep from exploding while he waited for Stephanie to finish with another customer.

"Everything all right, Mr. Hardcastle?" she asked.

Noah snapped his head in her direction and an idea began to take shape. He leaned down and lowered his voice. "I know this may not be policy, but I need a favor."

She looked around for any signs of administration. "Sure…what can I do for you?"

Tara and Calvin stood outside her office building.

"It's really crazy for us to have two cars all night," Calvin said.

"Hmm. That's true."

"If it will make you more comfortable, I can leave mine here and we can use your car. I can always take a cab here and pick it up when the evening is over."

"I can bring you back. That's not a problem. Unless of course you do something really crass and I have to use my ejector button."

He tossed back his head and laughed. "Oh yeah, I hate when that happens. Sure, sounds fine."

Tara nodded in agreement. "Ready when you are." She walked toward her car and disengaged the alarm.

"So tell me, how did you get into the jewelry business?" Calvin asked as they weaved in and out of after-work traffic.

She smiled, remembering, and briefly glanced at him from the corner of her eye. "Let's be truthful, back in high school, I thought I was Ms. It." They both laughed, knowing it was true. "For as long as

I can remember I was always collecting beads, bracelets, chokers, earrings. I had tons of them, mostly fake but tons nonetheless. When I started working those after-school jobs, for some reason it was always in the jewelry section of the department stores. When I started college I was pretty clueless as to what I wanted to do, but somehow I drifted into a jewelry-design class, then I took marketing and found that I loved buying. Did some internships while I was in school and when I graduated I was hired as a buyer's assistant. And I've been clawing my way up the ladder to success ever since." She laughed.

"I'd say you've definitely made it, Tara. You should be proud of your accomplishments. How many people, especially African American men or women, can say that they've built a solid business and a stand-up reputation in that field from virtually nothing but an idea? I can probably count on one hand the number of African Americans who are running international businesses dealing with jewelry."

She tugged in a breath. "Yeah, I do have a lot to be proud of. I suppose I don't really think of it much, to be truthful. I stay so busy trying to remain on top of things. One of the perks is that I do get to travel a great deal."

"Yes, so do I. It can be rough, though, the traveling. Makes it very hard to form any real roots or maintain a relationship."

A nerve jumped under her left eye. Was that part of what went wrong between her and Noah, that she was on the road every few weeks? But he said he understood that and was proud of her. Was it all a lie?

"Something wrong? Your whole vibe suddenly changed."

Tara briskly shook her head to scatter the disparaging thoughts. "No. Sorry." She forced a smile. "My mind just drifted for a moment."

"Was it something I said?"

"Sort of."

"Oh...do you want to talk about it?"

She sighed. "No." She turned and looked at him, and saw the sincerity in his dark brown eyes. "Tonight is my night and I intend to enjoy it."

"You've got a deal, lady." His gaze held hers for a moment, the connection only broken from the blare of the car horn behind them. "That's what every man looks for," he said, "a woman who can stop traffic."

Tara pressed on the gas and darted through the intersection, laughing all the way. It was the first time in days that she'd felt remotely human. Maybe tonight was a good idea after all.

# TWELVE

Rachel turned off the water, stepped out of the shower, and reached for the towel hanging from behind the bathroom door, then wrapped it around her damp body.

All day, visions of Tara Mitchell's face had taunted her, she thought as she rubbed the towel over her skin. There was no doubt that Tara was an attractive woman. She could understand Noah's interest in her. How did they compare in other ways? she wondered. Did Tara kiss Noah the way she kissed him? Did Noah ever have visions of her when he made love to Tara? Could Tara make him call her name as she had done on so many occasions? She ran her hands across her warm body and faced the full-length mirror.

At thirty-eight she still had the body of a twenty-year-old. Her sugar-free diet, constant travel, and regular exercise kept her in shape. Of course there was always the ongoing battle with gravity, but so far she was holding her own.

Rachel sat down on the round paisley-covered settee, applying a thin layer of Honey and Black Seed lotion to her feet, legs, and thighs, and imagined that it was Noah's hands stroking her body. She loved how the lotion made her skin feel and the gentle scent was heavenly. It had been Noah's favorite.

She slid her feet into her slippers and put on a raw-silk robe in a fire-engine red. It had been a gift to herself on her last trip to Japan. Putting it on always made her feel daring and utterly sensual. If she had one wish, it would be to walk into her bedroom, tonight, and find Noah beneath the sheets, waiting for her.

She took one last look in the mirror, knowing that for now her prayer would not be answered. But it would be in time, of that she was certain.

When she stepped out of the steamy bathroom into the coolness of her bedroom, a slight chill ran along her spine, prickling her skin and hardening her nipples. She tugged the robe a bit tighter and was about to stretch out on the bed and read a book when she heard voices coming from the front of the suite.

"...I'm pretty sure I made myself clear earlier. Rachel is tired..."

"Carol...who is it?" Rachel stepped out into the living space.

Carol turned toward Rachel. "I...told him you were resting. I really don't know how he got up here in the first place. I'm going to report this to management—"

"Noah?" Rachel pulled her robe a bit tighter and came closer. "Is everything okay?" She glanced from Noah to Carol, who stood like a sentinel at the door.

"Rachel, you really need your rest," Carol insisted, then threw a daggerlike look in Noah's direction.

Rachel patted Carol's arm. "It's okay, Carol. I can take it from here."

"But—"

"I said it was all right." She spoke clearly and with deliberation.

Carol stiffened, but she held her tongue. "Fine."

"Thank you." She looked down at the floor, then slowly up at Noah. "Sorry about that. Carol can be...overly protective sometimes. Please come in."

Noah stepped across the threshold and Rachel closed the door behind him.

"We can talk in here," Rachel said, pointing to an intimate sitting room that faced the terrace.

"I can't stay long," he said.

"Preparing your escape already?" She laughed lightly. "I tried to tell you that I'm really quite harmless."

For an instant his eyes rolled over her from head to toe. "Rachel, you don't have a harmless bone in your body or thought in your head."

Amused, she slightly shrugged her shoulders. "Have a seat. Can I fix you a drink?"

"No, thanks. I'm fine."

That you are, she thought, taking out a bottle of rum. She quickly mixed it with Coke over ice and returned to where Noah sat, took a seat opposite him, and crossed her legs. Her robe fell open, revealing a long line of freshly scrubbed cinnamon-brown thigh. She took a sip from her drink.

"This little visit must be pretty important to pull you away from Leo's before midnight." She angled her head to the side and absently stroked her knee.

Noah trained his sights above her waist, but each time she took a breath, the swell of her breasts would crest the dip in her robe. Keeping his eyes above neck level didn't help, either. Her eyes seemed to hold all the memories of the times they'd shared. He blinked to clear his head.

"Your assistant paid me a visit today," he said.

She set down her glass on the black marble coffee table.

Rachel frowned. "What? She didn't say—"

"I'm sure she didn't say anything. But she seems to be very concerned about your well-being and for some reason believes that it's all linked to me."

Her voice took on a defensive edge. "I don't know what you're talking about." She set the glass down a bit too hard, spilling some of its contents on the black marble coffee table, which she ignored. "I certainly hope you don't think I *sent* her to you."

Noah replayed his conversation with Carol.

"You've got to believe that I didn't send or instruct or intimate that she should say anything to you. I wouldn't do that."

"It doesn't matter who sent her or if she got it in her head to do it on her own. Is there any truth to what she said? That's the only question I want answered."

Deliberately Rachel stood, folded her arms beneath her breasts, and crossed the room. "I'm going to put on some clothes and then we can finish this. I'll be right back."

Noah looked around while Rachel was out of the room. Every square inch screamed opulence, from the magnificent penthouse balcony view that only the rich and famous could afford, to the exquisite layout of the suite. This was the life Rachel dreamed of and had grown accustomed to, a life that he could never provide for her and in his heart believed that she would sorely miss if she gave it up.

He sighed heavily. There was a time in his life when he thought they were genuinely happy, irrevocably in love, ready to take on the world together. But he'd been slapped in the face with the icy hand of reality. Rachel Beaumont had risen above his means, and he knew he couldn't compete with what she'd attained. She'd done it without him as she said she would. But now she was back singing a different tune. He strolled over to the mantel and stared at the black-and-white photos of Rachel at awards ceremonies. Gently he fingered the glass.

"Sorry. I didn't mean to take so long."

Noah turned toward the sound of her voice. When he saw her, his pulse rate rose several notches.

The flowing accordion pants and halter top in a soft peach did wonderful things to her honey-toned skin that seemed to sparkle like diamonds. She'd pulled her hair up in a practiced, carefree style, allowing her natural curls to have their way and frame her face.

For a moment, as he looked at her soft smile, the light dancing in her eyes, the totally intoxicating scent that gently wafted around her, all the pain she'd caused him vanished. She was just Rachel again. Not the famous star, just Rachel.

Noah cleared his throat and stepped away from the mantel. "Not a problem." He shrugged. "It didn't seem that long."

She smiled, and her eyes picked up the light from the chandelier. "There was a time that you would be checking your watch and telling me that you could never understand what took women so long to get dressed."

The memory evoked a light laugh. "Hmm, but things have changed."

She pressed her lips together, taking his barb in stride. "Have you eaten?" She crossed the room and walked toward him.

"No."

"We can order something from room service while we talk, or we can go to the restaurant in the hotel. The food is fabulous."

"Where's Carol? Will she be joining us?"

"She went out. She took the service elevator. I suppose she thought we needed our privacy."

The last thing he wanted or needed was to be totally alone with Rachel in her hotel room. That was trouble waiting to happen.

"The restaurant sounds fine. My treat."

She arched a brow. "Whatever you say." She walked toward the private elevator and picked up her purse from the corner table, then pressed the button.

The doors slid open and they stepped into the narrow box. Noah looked down at the riot of curls on top of her head, then his glance slid down the silk of her bare back. He raised his chin and focused on the ceiling instead, thinking this had the potential of being a very long evening.

# THIRTEEN

Calvin raised his glass in a toast. "To rekindling friendships."

Tara tapped her wineglass against his. "I like the sound of that."
She took a sip of her wine then set the glass down on the polished
maple table. "I've never been here before," she said, taking a good
look around at the rich brown and burnt-orange décor. "This is really nice, and I've heard wonderful things about the menu."

Calvin pointed out several paintings that lined the wall. "Those
are all originals," he said. "Catlett, Bearden, Fielding. When the
owner purchased the property, he wanted it to be a combination of
new and old in terms of art and the layout. There's one wall on the
level above us that boasts slave etchings, and another with work from
the New Deal era under Roosevelt."

"It's all fabulous," Tara murmured. "I love what he's done with the
space. It's all so intimate with only two or three tables on graduated
levels. That is a unique idea."

"Yes, and you don't get the feeling that you're crowded."

Calvin went on to describe the history of the restaurant as the
waitress placed their grilled salmon appetizer on the table. He sprin-
kled some fresh parsley and several drops of lemon juice on his fish
as he spoke.

Tara gave him a sidelong glance before piercing her salmon with her fork. "Just how do you know all these things?"

Calvin looked up from his plate and gave her a wink. "The owner is one of my clients."

Tara lifted a piece of salmon to her mouth and shook her head, a soft smile spreading across her mouth. She looked him square in the eye. "Exactly what is it that you do, Calvin?"

He took a swallow of his wine. "I guess you could say I created a profession for myself. I was always interested in real estate, but I firmly believe that selling someone a piece of property should go a step further. So I began looking at the variety of options available to commercial real estate buyers and the kinds of businesses they purchased property for."

He went on to explain how he created the added services of interior development, as he called it, designing rooms with themes, making purchases that suited the mood and the pocketbook of his clients, connecting them with vendors, and marketing their business to the public.

"Wow," Tara said, duly impressed. "How many clients do you have?"

"At the moment, about forty in different parts of the country."

"How do you manage that?"

"I have a pretty solid staff. They're skilled in different areas and have no problem jumping on a plane at a moment's notice to soothe a client. Although I do try to keep my hand in it."

"And I thought my life was hectic."

They both laughed.

"Seems we have a lot in common," Calvin said, looking Tara in the eye.

Tara lowered her gaze to her plate and shifted in her seat. "Seems that way." She concentrated on her plate.

"Did I say something to make you uncomfortable?"

She glanced up, then looked away. Taking a breath, she put her fork down. "I really need to be honest with you, Calvin. This is the first time I've been out with a man in more than three years. I mean…not *out* with a man but out with someone other than one man in particular."

"I see." He leaned back in his chair. "How long ago was the break-up?"

She swallowed hard. "Three weeks."

"That's tough. I'm sorry. Do you want to talk about it?"

"No, not really. I only wanted you to understand if I act a bit off center it's not because of something that you've said or done."

"He must be one helluva fool to let you go," he said gently.

She pressed her lips together, too afraid to speak as a lump suddenly throbbed in her throat. "I'm sure he doesn't think so," she finally managed.

"Well, maybe just for tonight, we can think about the future. About being friends and all the things we have in common." He smiled as he reached across the table and patted her hand. "No strings, no expectations."

Tara swallowed hard. "That sounds fair."

Calvin raised his glass again. "Let's eat."

Tara smiled, feeling safe and comfortable in Calvin's company. She made a silent pledge to herself to put thoughts of Noah out of her mind and enjoy her evening.

"You were right about the hotel restaurant," Noah said, taking a forkful of saffron rice. "Great seating, too," he added referring to their window seat with its unobstructed view of the capital city.

"Glad you like it." Rachel hesitated a moment. "I want to be honest with you, Noah. I made a mistake five years ago. I put fame and wealth and my own needs above everything—including you. I be-

*lady in waiting*

lieved that was what it would take to make me happy." She looked into his dark, questioning eyes. "I'm not happy, Noah. I haven't been for a very long time."

Noah put down his fork and wiped the corners of his mouth with a white linen napkin. "It was a choice you made, a choice that I have come to live with." He inhaled deeply and placed the napkin on the table. "When I found out you were coming back, I didn't know what to think or how to feel. I began questioning things."

"Things? What things? Us, the possibility of us again?" she asked, hope lifting the pitch of her sultry voice. She reached across the table and took his hand. "It can work if we try. I know it can. I know what I've done wrong. I can fix it."

"It's not that simple. I made a life without you."

She pulled back. "Tara," she stated in a monotone.

Noah frowned. "How do you know about Tara?"

"I made it my business to know." She glanced down at her plate before looking across at him. "Do you love her?"

"Yes."

She lifted her chin a notch. "I see." Her jaw flexed. "Then why are you here with me?"

He was silent for a moment, caught off guard by her bluntness. But he shouldn't have been; it was the Rachel he'd always known.

"When I walked in here with you, I wondered the same thing. I asked myself the very same question the moment you stepped into Leo's: why are you bothering? The answer is simple. We have unresolved issues, you and me. And until I get them fully settled inside myself, I won't be good for anyone, including you."

"Do you still have feelings for me, Noah?" She leaned forward, waiting for his answer.

"I do, but I'm not sure what they are. If it's all Memorex or something real."

Donna Hill

She lowered her head and smiled. "I guess that's better than nothing."

"I'm not making promises, Rachel. I'm not offering anything."

She gazed into his eyes. "All I want is the chance to prove to you that this can work."

He lifted his glass and brought it to his lips. "We'll see." He finished off his drink. "I need to be getting back."

Rachel stood. "I'll walk you out."

"Thanks for dinner," Tara said as she and Calvin walked out of the restaurant. "I needed to get out more than I thought."

"It was my pleasure. Hopefully you'll let me take you out again."

"So, what else do you do in your spare time besides create fabulous spaces?" she asked, changing the direction of the conversation.

"Hmm, I love old movies. I'm a collector of sorts. Basketball is my next love. I usually play every other weekend with some of the guys from college."

"But can you really play?" she teased.

"I may not be a Michael Jordan, but I can hold my own." He did a mock dribble-and-shoot move.

"I'm mildly convinced."

"You wound me. You'll have to come out and see me play one afternoon. It's really a lot of fun."

She flashed a crooked smile. "Maybe I will. When are you playing again?"

"Sunday. We get the gym over at George Washington University from one to four."

"Maybe I'll drop by."

"Great." He placed his hand at the small of her back as they walked toward his car.

As Noah and Rachel strolled down the street, a couple passing on the opposite side caught Noah's attention. His stomach knotted as he watched Tara toss her head back in laughter and turn to the man next to her as if he were the most important thing in her life.

# FOURTEEN

Clyde sat in a chair in Noah's office and stretched out his long legs. He folded his arms and listened to Noah's rendition of the night before.

"Did you say anything to her?" Clyde asked.

"No. Of course not."

"How can you even be sure it was her? I mean..."

"I know Tara when I see her. Okay?" he ground out as he proceeded to wear out a path on the wood floor.

"Hey, look, can you blame her? You were the one who let her go, remember? And you were out with Rachel," he added with disdain.

Noah cut his eyes in Clyde's direction. "Whose side are you on, anyway?"

Clyde stood and slid his hands into his pants pockets. "This isn't about sides, man. This is about choices. You made yours and apparently Tara made hers."

Noah made a noise in the back of his throat. "Thanks. I feel so much better having spoken to you."

"Hey, don't shoot the messenger. If you want Tara, then you need to tell her. If it's really about Rachel, then you need to deal. The bottom line is, the ball in is your court. And you can't play for both sides and think you're going to win."

"It didn't take her long," Noah grumbled.

"Did you think she was supposed to wait around knitting while you made up your mind about what you wanted to do?" A guilty conscience made him shift in his seat. He didn't want to tell Noah that he knew about this guy from Jae. Noah would really flip.

"I didn't expect her to take up with the first guy that came her way," he tossed back.

"Look, why don't you just talk to Tara, really *talk* to her? Tell her how you feel. She's an intelligent, understanding woman. Maybe if she knew what she was dealing with..."

Noah shook his head. "I'm not going to her with hat in hand. If she's happy with this guy, then so be it."

"Just like that? Are you really willing to give up what the two of you had for what you know you had with Rachel—which was questionable at best? He could just be an old friend, for all you know."

"All I wanted was some time. I wanted to be sure that whatever residual feelings I had for Rachel were gone. I didn't want to go into a marriage with any questions or doubts. It wouldn't be fair to Tara or me."

Clyde sighed heavily. "You need to sit down and talk with her. That's the only advice I can offer you."

Noah sat down behind his desk. "Yeah. Thanks." He looked up at Clyde. "What if she won't talk to me?"

"You'll never know unless you give it a shot."

Rachel stepped out of the chauffeured car and looked at the office building. She checked the address against the information that Carol had given her. "I should be back in a few minutes," she said to the driver. "You can wait here." She walked through the front door to the reception desk.

"May I help you?" the receptionist asked, and then recognition set in. "Oh, my goodness," she squealed. "You're Rachel Beaumont! I listen to you all the time." She pressed her hand to her chest.

"Thank you. I'm here to see Tara Mitchell. Is she in?"

"I'll buzz her right away," she said, so flustered it took her several tries before she could get Tara's extension right. "Ms. Mitchell, you'll never guess who's here to see you. Rachel Beaumont! Yes, I'll show her in." She looked up at Rachel. "I'll take you to Ms. Mitchell's office. It's right down the hall," she rambled. "Oh, Ms. Beaumont, I would be so honored if you signed an autograph for me."

"Sure."

She grabbed her notepad and a pen and shoved it at Rachel.

Rachel quickly scribbled her name and "best wishes" and handed it back.

"Thank you so much. My friends will never believe I actually met you right here in the office!"

Rachel forced a smile. "I'm really pressed for time."

"Oh, oh, I'm sorry. Right this way." She led Rachel down the hall and knocked on Tara's closed door.

Tara brushed down her jacket and ran her fingers through her hair. "Come in." She straightened her shoulders as if preparing for battle.

The door opened and Rachel stepped in. Tara wasn't sure what she expected. She'd seen pictures of Rachel and watched her perform on television, but seeing her in person was a totally different experience. Rachel had a commanding presence, one that demanded attention. She had megastar written all over her, from the top of her perfectly coiffed head to the bottom of her designer-clad feet. So

*lady in waiting*

this was the woman that Noah loved before her and probably still did.

Rachel took a brief moment to assess her rival. She was certainly attractive but not in an overstated way, she observed. She was taller than she imagined, well-groomed, but wearing nothing that Rachel would ever consider. She could understand Noah's attraction to this woman, but she certainly couldn't see him spending the rest of his life with her. She was...ordinary.

Rachel stepped fully into the room. She extended her hand and put on the smile that had graced many magazine covers.

"Rachel Beaumont. I'm sorry to just barge in on you like this, but I thought we should talk."

Tara flicked her right brow. This hussy didn't waste any time, she thought. "Why don't you sit down?"

"I don't plan to stay." She strolled around the office, looking at the awards on the wall and the simple but tasteful furnishings. She noticed the photograph of Noah on the shelf behind Tara's desk. "We seem to have someone in common," she began.

Tara folded her arms. "I'm listening."

"I don't know how much Noah has told you about me...about us." She looked Tara square in the eye.

"Nothing," she said, and relished in seeing Rachel flinch.

Rachel set her purse down on Tara's desk. "Noah and I were planning to get married. I chose my career over a future with him. I made a mistake. And I'm back to rectify it."

"That's all very interesting, but what does that have to do with me?"

"I want us to be very clear, Ms. Mitchell. I intend to get Noah back at any cost. So if you have any...unresolved issues with him, I suggest you settle them so that he and I can get on with our lives."

"You have it all wrong, Ms. Beaumont," she said, spitting out her name. "It's over between Noah and me. So you're not only wasting my time, you're wasting yours as well by being here, and I'm quite sure that both of us have more important things to do. Now, if you'll excuse me, I'm expecting a client shortly." She walked to the door and opened it. "Thank you for dropping by and bringing me up to date. I wish you and Noah all the best."

Rachel was livid. No one spoke to her that way. She snatched up her purse from the desk and sauntered to the door, then stopped and glanced into Tara's eyes, her hands clenched into fists to keep from slapping the smug look off her face. "I can see why he left you." With that, she turned and walked out.

It took all of Tara's willpower not to slam the door behind her. She was so angry she was shaking all over. The nerve of that...Her breath rushed in and out in choppy waves. She felt her eyes burn, but she would not cry. If she was what Noah wanted, then so be it. Any iota of hope that she had of his coming back or taking him back was over. She was done.

Then why in the hell did she feel so utterly horrible? She sat down at her desk, lowered her head onto her arms, and let the tears flow.

# FIFTEEN

"What's wrong, girl? I can't understand a word you're saying," Jae said into the phone, trying to make sense of Tara's high-pitched tirade. "Take a breath."

Tara paced back and forth in her office with one arm across her waist and the phone tucked between her chin and shoulder while she held onto the receiver with a death grip.

"How dare she! Who in the hell does she think she is anyway... walking in here like she owns the place and telling *me* what *I* can do with my feelings for Noah. I could tell *her* what to do, alright." She huffed and paced.

"Tara, you need to relax. Don't make me have this baby early just so we can go over there and beat her down."

Tara stopped her pacing and broke out laughing. She couldn't begin to imagine church-going, most-of-the-time sanctified Jae beating anyone down. She would pay money to see that.

"Jae, don't make me laugh, girl. I'm supposed to be pissed off."

Jae giggled. "I *know* you are. But for what—over some woman who wouldn't put you out if you were on fire? Chile, please. She's just trying to throw her celebrity around like you're supposed to be intimidated by all that. If Noah wanted her so bad, she wouldn't have to be up in your face to tell you about it."

"It's all just as well," Tara said, finally sitting down. She spun the chair toward the window. "The last thing I want to do is to be getting into it with another woman over some man."

"Can I ask you something?"

"Sure."

"Did you and Noah ever really talk about marriage? I mean really talk… about what you wanted, your expectations, your pasts?"

"Sure… well…" She was thoughtful for a moment. "To be honest with you, we really didn't. It just seemed like the only thing that was important was us."

"Hon, you can't build a future together if you don't understand each other's past. Sure, you found each other, probably have a ball in bed, you look great together, you are both ambitious, intelligent, but did you really know each other—the things that scare you, the things that have hurt you? Those are the things that make a difference. And it's apparent that it's the conversation the two of you needed to have. There's a reason why Noah could only go so far with the relationship, and why it was so easy for you to say the heck with it and walk away."

Jae's logic was coming fast and furious, and Tara sucked in every word. "Since when did you get so wise and all-knowing?"

"When you have a football player roaming around in your belly all night and you can't sleep, you have plenty of time to think about other people's business."

They laughed.

"So now what, oh wise one?" Tara asked.

"That's up to you. Pray on it, girl. Open your heart. If it's really over for you, then so be it. But let it be over because you want it and mean it, not because some stuck-up so-and-so is making a move. You're a better woman than that. And I believe in my heart that Noah loves you deeply, but he's scared, too, and holding onto the past is easier than stepping into an unknown future."

Tara nodded her head. "You're right. Maybe I should go see him."

"Maybe you should..."

Rachel sat across the table from the reporter from *The Washington Post*. She'd been at the interview for more than an hour, and her patience was wearing thin. How many times would she have to answer the same inane questions? Couldn't reporters come up with anything original to ask?

"Ms. Beaumont, you've been all over the world, appeared in some of the most elegant venues, what brings you back to Washington? Someone special?" the young woman hedged.

Now, this was the kind of question she wanted to answer. Rachel smiled. "Actually...yes. I came back to rekindle an old love affair."

The woman's brows rose with interest. She checked her tape recorder to make sure there was enough tape and pushed it closer to Rachel, not wanting to miss a word. "Do you care to share who the special man is?"

"I don't mind at all. His name is Noah Hardcastle, co-owner of Leo's."

"Has the relationship been...rekindled?"

Rachel thought about Noah's reaction if he read the article. He'd be furious, but then, he'd know how serious she was to finally admit to the world how she felt.

"Absolutely."

"Can I get the correct spelling of his name?" She jotted down the name then looked across at Rachel. "Any wedding plans in the air?"

"We've been talking about it," Rachel smoothly lied.

"Really? How exciting." She jotted down some more notes. "How will marriage affect your career?"

Rachel leaned forward and lowered her voice. "This is off the record," she whispered, knowing that it wouldn't be. "I've been considering settling down for good and just being a wife... and mother." She smiled in triumph when she imagined the look on Tara Mitchell's face when she read the paper.

# SIXTEEN

Clyde leaned back in the kitchen chair and took a sip of coffee from his favorite NBA mug. He snapped open the newspaper and began flipping through it while listening to Jae's melodic voice in the background as she practiced for Sunday service. His eyes danced over the pages until they landed square on the smiling face of Rachel Beaumont. His stomach flipped and his hand began to shake as he read the article.

"Oh, damn," he hissed. He threw down the paper and darted over to the phone that hung on the lemon-yellow wall and dialed Noah. The phone rang and rang until his machine picked up. Clyde left an urgent message to call him immediately. He tried his cell phone and left a message there as well. He wracked his brain, trying to figure out where Noah could be. Leo's was closed until four and it was barely eight o'clock in the morning. His mind wandered in a direction he didn't want to go in, and he silently prayed that Noah wasn't with Rachel.

Carol, Rachel's assistant, opened the door to the suite and picked up the newspapers that were routinely delivered every morning. Rachel had a real penchant for reading the paper with breakfast. She wanted to be in the know about politics, religion, the budget, entertainment, and gossip. "You never know who you may run into," Rachel always said, "and sometimes you can get tired of talking about yourself all the time."

She tucked the papers under her arm and walked into the sitting room where Rachel was sipping tea and going over a song she was in the midst of composing. She looked up when Carol entered.

"I brought you the papers. Do you need anything else before I leave? I have some errands to run."

Rachel's eyes lit up. "Oh, no. You go ahead." She stretched out her hand for the papers. Her heart pounded in anticipation as she quickly leafed through the *Washington Post*, hoping that her interview was there. Right on the front page of the entertainment section was her picture and a full-page spread.

"Anything interesting?"

"Oh, just a little article with the interview I did yesterday," she said nonchalantly.

"It's out already." Carol stepped closer. "They don't waste any time. I hope they didn't misquote you like they usually do."

Rachel's eyes flew over the text until she found what she wanted. She smiled and handed the paper to Carol.

Carol went over the article and stopped cold when she saw the portion that talked about Rachel and Noah Hardcastle.

"Rachel, you actually said this?"

She nodded her head in satisfaction. "Maybe now Noah will take me seriously."

"But did you mean what you said about giving up your career?" She'd never believed Rachel was serious.

"If that's what it's going to take to get Noah back, then yes, I meant every word. Besides, celebrities make comebacks every day."

Slowly Carol sat down and read the article, word for word, then put the paper on the coffee table. "I hope you know what you're do-ing. What is Noah going to say when he reads this?"

"I can handle Noah. It will be fine. And now that his ex-fiancée is permanently out of the way..."

"What do you mean, permanently out of the way?"

Rachel told Carol about her encounter with Tara the day before.

"You're really serious about this, aren't you?"

"I've never been more serious about anything before in my life. I came back with the express purpose of winning Noah back. And I intend to get him."

Tara sat at the kitchen table. The food on her plate was uneaten, her coffee had grown cold. She re-read the article for the second time, making sure that she'd gotten it right. Everything that Rachel had told her the day before was true. Whatever naïve hope she'd held out for a reconciliation with Noah was gone.

How could he have done this to her? Did she mean nothing to him? Did what they'd shared together mean nothing to him? She jumped up from the chair and stormed into her bedroom. She pulled open the closet and riffled through the clothes, tossing anything that was Noah's onto the floor. From there she went to the dresser, and then the bathroom, doing the same thing. She felt like pulling an An-gela Bassett and setting the crap on fire.

Instead, she piled up everything and dumped it in a large black plastic garbage bag and dragged it to the door, just as the bell rang. Without thinking, she pulled the door open.

"Calvin! What are you doing here?"

"I know I should have called first." He glanced at the bag in her hand. "Do you need some help?"

"No. This is not a good time, Calvin." She tossed him a glare that he didn't deserve.

"Look, I'm sorry." He hesitated. "Are you okay?"

Her eyes filled and her throat grew so tight she could barely breathe.

"Tara, what is it?"

She blinked hard and fast to fight back the tears. "Nothing. I'm fine. I don't mean to be rude, but...I really need to be alone."

He took a breath. "You don't look or sound as if you want to be alone, but if it's what you want...call me if you want to talk."

She tugged on her bottom lip with her teeth and nodded, not trusting her voice.

"Take care." He gave her one last look before turning and walking down the hallway to the front door. "Excuse me," he said to the man coming in and stepped around him.

Noah stopped, turned, and watched the man walk to his car parked in front of Tara's building. Recognition hit him as Calvin got behind the wheel and pulled off. He'd seen Tara with him the other night. It was barely nine in the morning, which could only mean one thing—he'd spent the night.

He didn't know if what he was feeling was shock, anger, jealously, or all three. How could she have slept with someone else? Then Clyde's words of the previous day floated into his head... *did you expect her to sit around knitting?*

For several moments he stood in the entryway, uncertain about what to do. He looked down the hallway to Tara's apartment, then he walked to her door and knocked.

# SEVENTEEN

Tara stormed to her door, ready to give Calvin a piece of her mind. The last person she expected to see was Noah. She was so angry she couldn't speak.

"I ran into your overnight guest on my way out," he said, then wished he hadn't the moment the words were out of his mouth.

"What! You have some helluva nerve accusing me of anything." She spun around, grabbed her crumpled copy of the newspaper from the table, and threw it in his face. "I hope the two of you have a happy life together. Now get out and don't you dare come back!" She pushed the door shut and locked it before he had a chance to react.

Noah shook his head to clear it. What was going on? He leaned down and picked up the newspaper from the floor. The picture of Rachel stared back at him. He quickly read the article and began to feel ill. What had Rachel done?

He was going to deal with this once and for all. He banged on Tara's door. "Tara! Open the door. I want to talk to you."

"Go away! I don't want to talk to you."

"This is all a lie, Tara."

"Go away, Noah, before I call the police."

"Then call them, because I'm not leaving. There's nothing going on between me and Rachel."

"That's not what it says in print."

"It's a lie. She made all this up."

Tara walked closer to the door. "You must have given her reason to think that she could."

"Maybe I did," he admitted, "but I was wrong, dead wrong. Tara, please, open the door."

Silence.

"Tara . . . I . . ."

The door slowly opened. She jutted her chin upward and blocked the door with her body. "Talk."

"Out in the hallway?"

"It's either there or nowhere. Your choice."

He clenched his jaw. If there was one thing he knew about Tara, it was that she could be as stubborn as a mule once she'd wrapped her mind around something.

"I should have told you about Rachel a long time ago."

"Yeah, you should have." She rolled her eyes.

"I've been a real fool these past months. And none of it had anything to do with you. I guess I was . . . scared."

"Of what, Noah? Me?"

He tugged in a breath and released it slowly. "Of being truly in love again and getting hurt. Rachel became my excuse. I convinced myself that I wasn't over her, that I needed to find out how I truly felt."

"And?"

He swallowed and looked directly into her eyes. "I love you, Tara. I always have. What I feel for Rachel is gone. It's an attraction that is more illusion than reality. I know I could never have a life with her, not like the kind of life you and I can have together."

She hesitated, knowing that if she took this next step she would open her heart to him again. "I was fixing some tea," she said softly. "Would you like some?"

"Yeah, I would."

She stepped aside and let him in.

"Why aren't you dressed for church?" Jae asked when she walked into the kitchen and saw her husband sitting in the chair like a lump on a log.

He glanced up at her and tossed his head toward the paper. "I think you need to sit down and read that."

"Oh my goodness," Jae moaned as she read the article. She glared at her husband as if he were the culprit. "Do you know anything about this?"

He held up his hands. "No, babe, I swear. I'm just as surprised as you are."

"What if Tara sees this? She'll be devastated. Did you know that Rachel went to see her yesterday?"

"She did what?"

"You heard me. She went up to Tara's office and basically told Tara to get lost."

Clyde shook his head. "This is really getting ugly."

"You need to get your boy on the phone and find out what's going on."

"I tried that already. He's not answering."

Jae hoisted herself up from the chair. "Well, I'm calling Tara to make sure she's alright." She went to the phone and dialed her number. It rang three times before Tara picked up.

"Girl, are you sitting down? Have you seen today's paper?"

"Yes, I saw it, Jae. I'm fine."

"Fine? I don't believe it. And don't you believe it, either. Noah—"

"Noah is right here," Tara said.

Jae's brows rose. "He is? Is he still alive?"

Tara bit back a laugh. "For the moment. We're talking. I'll call you later. Okay?"

"Do you need me to come over? 'Cause I will, you know. The Lord will understand me missing church."

"You don't need to come over. I'm fine. Go on. We'll talk later."

"All right now. If you're sure."

"I'm sure."

Jae huffed. "Okay. But I don't want to see you on the eleven o'clock news with a raincoat over your face."

"Girl, you are too crazy. Good-bye."

"Bye." Jae hung up. "Guess who's sitting up in Tara's house? Noah," she said, answering her own question.

"Get out. Well it's about time. Maybe now they'll have that talk they should have had a long time ago."

"I hope you're right. Well, come on. Don't think you're going to get out of going to church. You have ten minutes to get ready." She marched off to the bedroom and Clyde groaned.

"I heard that!"

Tara sat down opposite Noah at the kitchen table. "I'm listening," she said.

Noah lowered his head a moment then looked across the table at her. "About eight years ago, I met Rachel when she came into the club..."

They talked for hours, really talked. Noah told Tara all about his doubts, how he'd become jaded after his relationship with Rachel ended, and how he had no intention of getting involved again until he met her. He told her about the letter he'd received from Rachel, and how all the unresolved issues rose to the surface as a result.

"It wasn't that I didn't love you, Tara. It was that I wanted to be sure that things were over between me and Rachel once and for all. I wanted to be fair to you and to me. She's shown me without a doubt that nothing about her has changed. She's still the same self-centered woman. That's not the kind of woman I want for my wife."

"Are you sure, I mean really sure? What if she comes back five years from now?"

"If she came back every day of my life for the rest of my life it wouldn't matter. I'm not in love with her. I'm in love with you." He reached into his pocket and pulled out the ring. He took her hand. "I love you and I want you to be my wife, Tara. Say yes."

Tara looked at the ring and then at Noah. She examined what was in her heart and balanced it against their reality. She knew that the pain she'd felt these past weeks and the promises she'd made to cancel Noah out of her life didn't matter anymore. All she wanted was him, to build a life with him, a family with him.

"Yes," she said softly.

Noah slipped the ring onto her finger. He got up and knelt down at her side, still holding her hand. "I promise to spend the rest of my life making you happy." He caressed her cheek. "To keep that beautiful smile on your face."

"Then I guess I can unpack those garbage bags filled with your stuff," she said, her voice light and her heart singing.

"You were really going to throw my stuff out into the street?" he asked, mildly appalled.

"You're damned right!"

He stood and pulled her to her feet, holding her close. "This is going to be an interesting life we're going to have."

"I'm looking forward to it."

"So am I," he whispered before lowering his head to seal their promise with a long-overdue kiss.

# EPILOGUE

*Six months later*

The small chapel of Ebenezer Baptist Church was filled with family, friends, and a profusion of flowers.

Noah and Tara stood before the pastor and, before God and man, pledged their love and fidelity for all time.

In the background baby Jada was squalling out her agreement of their union while her grandparents tried to keep her quiet.

Tara was regal in her floor-length fitted gown of champagne satin and lace, and Noah was certain he'd never seen her look more beautiful and radiant.

"If there is anyone present who believes this man and this woman should not be bound in matrimony, speak now or forever hold your peace," the pastor intoned, looking over the crowd. Finding no dissent, he proceeded.

"Do you, Noah Hardcastle, take Tara Mitchell for your lawfully wedded wife..."

"I do."

"And do you, Tara Mitchell, take Noah Hardcastle for your lawfully wedded husband..."

"I do."

"What God has joined together let no man…or woman put asunder. You may exchange rings and repeat after me…"

"By the power vested in me, I now pronounce you husband and wife. Turn and face your family and friends. Ladies and gentleman, may I introduce Mr. and Mrs. Noah Hardcastle."

The chapel attendees broke out in applause as the organ played the recessional march.

Outside, the newly married couple was showered with rice while cameras snapped and flashbulbs popped.

As they darted down the church steps to the waiting limo, they ran into Rachel, who was standing on the sidewalk.

She looked from one to the other. "I'm sorry for everything I did. I was wrong." She turned to the groom. "I want you to be happy, Noah, no matter what you may think. You made the right decision. I don't think I could ever really be happy if I wasn't traveling the world and performing in front of thousands of people. I know that now." Then she turned to Tara. "He truly loves you. You're a very lucky woman. I only hope that one day I can be as lucky. Have a wonderful life, both of you."

"Thank you," the couple said in unison.

Rachel got into a waiting car and pulled off.

Noah helped Tara into the white stretch limo and got in behind her. "She's right, you know," he said, settling in next to his wife.

Tara twisted her polished lips. "Right about what?"

"You are a very lucky woman," he said, laughing.

She gently elbowed him in the ribs. "Oh really? Well, let's see how lucky you can get when we arrive in Hawaii. I have a few tricks I want to try out on you."

He nuzzled her neck. "I can't wait."

Brenda Jackson

*irresistible attraction*

*So teach us to number our days, that we may apply our hearts unto wisdom.*

—PSALM 90:12

*To my husband, Gerald Jackson Sr.*
*and*
*A special young lady, Sydney Rashan Snow*

# PROLOGUE

Sydney Corbain smiled as she watched her brother Linc steal a kiss from Raven, his bride, as they waltzed around the room, their first dance together as husband and wife. Tears of happiness shone in her eyes and she took a deep breath, then exhaled. This was how it was supposed to be for two people who loved each other.

Her smile widened as she acknowledged there were actually six people dancing around the room who loved each other, happy and eager to start their new lives together. This was the first triple wedding she had ever attended, and she had to admit it was one of the most beautiful. It was evident that Leigh Walcott Alexander, the professional event planner, along with the owners of Leo's Supper Club, the Hardcastles, had worked hard to make the wedding and the reception special for the three couples.

She didn't think she had seen such beautiful brides as Raven and her two sisters, Robin and Falcon. They were simply glowing for their husbands and there was no doubt in Sydney's mind they were women well loved.

She glanced around the room and her gaze met that of Tyrone Hardcastle, one of the owners of Leo's. This wasn't the first time tonight that their gazes had met . . . and held. She could feel something

irresistible attraction

between them—interest, curiosity, awareness—as well as something else.

An irresistible attraction.

She sighed deeply, frozen in place, as they continued to look at each other. His gaze began moving slowly over her face, studying her feature by feature. She wanted to look away but could not. Her senses were on high alert and she actually liked the excitement. At twenty-six, a sexual attraction she could handle. An emotional connection she could not.

The two of them had been introduced last year when she'd come from Memphis to D.C. to see her brother Linc, and within seconds she had felt an aura of acute sexual awareness that radiated between them. It was there in the intensity of his gaze whenever he looked at her, making a shiver of heated desire course through her body. Even now she could feel her reactions being triggered. She knew from the psychology classes she'd taken in college that sexual attraction was normal and a part of every human's makeup.

Sydney sighed again. There was nothing normal about the desire she was feeling for Tyrone Hardcastle. She was an attorney, for heaven's sake, programmed to deal with facts—specifics and details. But at that very moment, Tyrone was making her too confused to play the role. The strange thing about it was that she had never felt these strong vibes from his identical twin brother, Tyrell. Her reaction to Tyrone was one sure way to tell them apart, as well as the difference in hairstyle. She hadn't spent enough time with either to know their temperament. Last October, exactly six months ago, she had learned the painful lesson that a person could be one way on the outside and totally different on the inside. Rafe Sutherlin had been the one to educate her. She was glad she had found out what type of inconsiderate person he was before she agreed to marry him.

So here she was, fighting off vibes she had never felt for Rafe or any man for that matter. Everyone who knew her was aware that she was levelheaded in some things and impulsive in others.

Like now.

She and Tyrone were flirting with each other without saying a single word, yet flirting just the same. But so what? It was fun, spicy, and harmless. Each time they saw each other their attraction became more tempting and enticing, and she felt that Tyrone Hardcastle was worth every minute she was putting into it. Juilliard educated with a doctorate degree, he was responsible for the music and entertainment at Leo's. She had to give him credit for how his skillful selection of music, every noteworthy tune, had enhanced the event. Those in attendance would remember the varied sounds and resonance of the reception as much as they did the wedding itself. Both had been crafted together in a way that made it one unforgettable event.

She could also give him credit for how he looked tonight. He was not dressed like a behind-the-scene worker, detached from the activities. Like the rest of the Hardcastles who felt a definite closeness to the three brides, he was dressed in formal attire like everyone else.

No man, she thought, should look that good in a tux and have such a striking profile. He wore his sandy brown hair in twists that fell to his shoulders. His skin was a golden brown and his eyes, still trained directly on her, were large, slanted, and clear brown. Like his twin, there was a distinctive mole on his left cheekbone and a strong cleft chin.

From what her sister-in-law Raven had told her, Tyrone was very much single, preferred to be called Roni by family and friends, and placed everything... including women... second to his music.

She shrugged. She didn't have a problem with that since she'd also been accused of placing everything second to her career. At least that's what Rafe had claimed. As she took a sip of her punch, thinking that even the fruity drink was first class, she decided to stop this game she was playing with Tyrone Hardcastle for now, since nothing could ever come of it.

But then, maybe, one day...

# ONE

*Nine months later*

Tyrone Hardcastle clasped his hands around a mug of hot chocolate while sitting in a café in New York City in the middle of January, with the temperature less than fifteen degrees outside. He almost envied the two brothers and cousin he'd left behind in D.C. to run things at Leo's.

*Almost but not quite.*

Even with the cold weather, nothing was better than being in New York in the wintertime. He had grown accustomed to New York winters while a student at Juilliard. In spite of the ice, snow, and cold, there was something invigorating about being back in the Big Apple, even for just a short while, especially since he was here to do something he got a lot of pleasure from—sharing his musical talent with others.

He thoroughly enjoyed his job as entertainment director at Leo's Supper Club, a restaurant he owned along with his oldest brother Noah, his twin brother Tyrell, and his cousin Ayanna. During the year he occasionally traveled to a number of places to keep his finger on the pulse of the music industry, which was the reason he was in New York. He had returned to work as a visiting music professor at Columbia University for six weeks.

Tyrone glanced up, looked out the window and studied the feminine figure moving across the street, then drew in a deep breath as a sudden feeling of heat slithered through his body. This was the second time he had seen her this week, and both times he had gotten this sudden feeling of acute desire. He wondered if she were someone he knew, but both times he'd only managed to catch a glimpse of her from the back. As she was also wearing a huge overcoat and a knitted cap, he hadn't been too sure. Still, a part of him wondered, what was the possibility of two women having that same sensuous walk? As far as he was concerned, Sydney Corbain definitely had a patent on it. She also had a patent on the sudden rush of passion he was feeling. In all his thirty-three years, she was the only woman who could make him feel such an irresistible attraction.

*Sydney Corbain.*

Thinking of Sydney, he recalled the last time they had seen each other at her brother's wedding nearly nine months ago. He would never forget that day. They had not exchanged a single word yet somehow managed to take the art of flirtation to a whole new level. They had been rather creative, and she had definitely gotten a rise out of him...literally.

She'd had all the qualities needed to attract a man's attention that day, and had definitely attracted his. From the moment she walked down the aisle as a bridesmaid his libido had gone into overdrive. Instead of the long gowns that most attendants wore, the three brides had decided to go with short bridesmaids' dresses. There was nothing like seeing a great pair of legs to turbocharge a man's mating instincts, and his had nearly overloaded. He couldn't forget the perfume he'd gotten a whiff of when she passed him on her way to the altar. It had been soft, sultry, and sexy as hell.

At the reception things had gotten even more interesting. After posing for enough pictures to last the brides and grooms until their silver anniversaries, Sydney had changed into an outfit that showed not only a lot of leg but also a nice amount of cleavage. He hadn't been the only man watching her, but he'd been the only man whose interest she had reciprocated.

Since he'd been technically working that day to make sure the music at the reception was everything the brides had wanted, he did not get a chance to speak to Sydney, but he had definitely enjoyed their flirting game. He had asked her brother Linc about her a few months ago when the newlyweds had patronized Leo's one Sunday morning for brunch. According to Linc, she was doing fine and was busy back in Memphis working on an important court case.

Tyrone sighed deeply and made a quick decision to solve the mystery of the woman across the street and why she had made him think of Sydney. When he saw her enter a neighboring shop, he stood, threw more than enough money on the table for his bill, placed the straps to his saxophone case on his shoulder, left the café, and quickly crossed the street.

The evening was still early, and for once he didn't have anything else to do.

Sydney smiled the moment she stepped across the threshold of Victoria's Secret. Closing her eyes, she inhaled the subtle scent of everything feminine, a trademark of every Victoria's Secret store she patronized. She liked feeling sexy as well as looking the part.

Opening her eyes, she walked into the store and immediately went over to a table where panties were on display. She was beginning to develop a fetish for sexy underwear, and before her were some of the sexiest. She picked up a pair of cotton low-rise V-string panties and definitely liked the feel of the material. She had begun wearing the scanty undies, liking the way they fit, the freedom of movement they provided, and the naughtiness of wearing almost nothing.

irresistible attraction

Her smile widened as she glanced at the tag. They were on sale! Deciding that a dozen or so were definitely a must-buy, she concentrated on selecting the size and the colors she wanted, then quickly decided that, while she was at it, she might as well buy the colorful sexy-looking bras to match.

"Can I help you, Miss Corbain?"

Sydney inhaled sharply, startled at the deep, masculine voice behind her, very close to her ear. Her heart started pumping enough blood to bring a dead man back to life, and a sizzle of awareness coursed rapidly through her body. She blinked to bring herself out of her sexy haze. Only one man had the power to make her feel overloaded from so much sensuous heat. However, *that* man was supposed to be in Washington, D.C.

Her arms filled with at least fifteen pairs of panties, she slowly turned around, tilting her head back to take a good look. Her eyes grew wide in surprise, and for a brief moment her words stuck in her throat as she tried to speak. Finally, after swallowing deeply, she found her voice.

"Tyrone Hardcastle! What are you doing in New York?" She allowed her gaze to soak up just how good he looked in his black leather overcoat, a sax case over his shoulder. And as always, his features were calm, composed, and utterly handsome.

Tyrone smiled and crossed his arms over his chest. "I should be asking you that same question, although I think it's obvious," he said, indicating the bundle of brightly colored panties she cradled tightly in her arms.

Sydney shook her head. There was no point in getting embarrassed, although it wasn't every day a man was present when she purchased her underwear. Even Rafe would not have dared.

She continued to hold Tyrone's gaze, transfixed. His smile was a complete turn-on, vibrantly alive, sensuous, and blatantly male. She had always appreciated his smile, but found that she appreciated it even more today. The weather was rather cold outside, but he was definitely thawing her out. "Well, these purchases are only part of the reason. They're an added perk, I guess you can say," she finally answered. "There's nothing like a Victoria's Secret sale."

Tyrone glanced around at all the scantily clad mannequins, then tilted his head at her. "You like shopping at this place, do you?" In his mind he was imagining her wearing some of the items he saw on display.

"Yes." She decided to quickly change the subject. "You never told me what you're doing in New York." She wondered what he would think if he knew that since her brother's wedding, he had been the object of her fantasies and a participant in many of her heated dreams.

"I'm in town for six weeks as a visiting music professor at Columbia University. And you?"

She smiled. "I'm getting much-needed rest. For the past four months I've been involved in a very taxing litigation case. I'm proud to say that I won, but it took a lot out of me. When a friend who's a television news correspondent asked me to come here and stay in her apartment and watch her dog for three weeks while she did an assignment in Barcelona, I jumped at the chance."

She glanced at the snowflakes falling lightly outside the store's display window and added, "Although I wish it could have been summer instead of winter."

Tyrone shook his head and laughed. "Sweetheart, winter is the best time to be in New York."

*Sweetheart.* Although she knew he hadn't meant anything by the use of the endearment, it sent shivers up her body just the same. And then it started happening—The attraction she'd come to expect intensified. She knew the exact moment that he picked up on it as well.

*irresistible attraction*

Her long sigh echoed simultaneously with his, and his eyes darkened as her gaze was drawn to his lips. He had such a pretty mouth for a man, one that was meant to kiss and be kissed. Then there was everything else about him: tall, muscular build, very nice features, and sandy brown hair. A woman couldn't do much better, unless she happened to meet his identical twin.

Sydney blinked upon realizing he had said something. "I'm sorry, could you repeat that?" she asked, embarrassed he had caught her staring.

A grin tilted both corners of his mouth. "I asked what were your plans for later. Would you like to go out to dinner with me?"

His grin did things to her insides. "Dinner?"

"Yes, dinner. And since I know that you like French food, an evening at Au Petit Beurre would be nice."

She raised a brow. "And how do you know I like French food?" she asked, although she already knew the answer.

He laughed then said, "A little birdie told me."

She couldn't help but laugh along with him. Since one of the grooms at the wedding, Franco Renoir, was part French and part African American, a number of tasty French dishes had been prepared, compliments of Tyrone's twin Tyrell, who was Leo's master chef. Sydney had spent a lot of time at the buffet table and, as Tyrone had watched her closely that night, he would have definitely noticed all her activities.

But then, she had watched him that night as much as he had watched her.

"So, what about dinner, Sydney?" More than anything he wanted to take her out. The attraction that had been there between them from the first still burned, and there was no way he could walk away from it this time.

She sighed deeply, knowing there was no way she could turn him down. "What time do you have in mind? I'd like to finish my shopping first, then go home and change."

He nodded. "All right. I need to go back to the hotel and change as well. And I want to call my parents. Today is their fortieth wedding anniversary."

Sydney smiled. "Oh, that's wonderful." And she really meant it. She was proud of the number of years her own parents had been happily married. They would be celebrating their thirty-fifth anniversary later that year, and she and her three brothers knew their parents were still very much in love. She always planned to have that sort of happy ending for herself. It had been her goal after finishing law school to meet the perfect mate, get married, and have his children. She had thought she'd found him in Rafe and discovered that was not the case. But she refused to give up. She truly believed there was a man out there somewhere who believed in love and marriage as much as she did.

"Thanks. I think it's wonderful how long they've been married, too," Tyrone said, although he'd never really given the longevity of his parents' marriage much thought. However, her words made him stop and appreciate what they had together.

He checked his watch and asked, "Would seven o'clock be okay?"

She smiled. "Yes, seven will be fine."

He nodded. "Give me your address."

She rattled it off to him and he wrote it down on a piece of paper. "Strivers Row? That's a real nice part of Harlem," he commented.

"Yes, it is. My friend is doing quite well for herself."

Tyrone shifted his sax strap to the other shoulder. "Well then, I'll see you at seven. He started to walk off, then turned around, smiled, and added, "You may as well get a purple pair, too. I think that color would look good on you."

She couldn't help but laugh again. "I'll think about it, Mr. Hardcastle." She watched as he left the store, keeping her eyes glued to him until he was no longer in sight. His nearness had really scrambled her brain. Before walking off to where the bras were located, she snatched an additional pair of panties off the table—purple—thinking it was too bad that he would never see her in them.

# TWO

Sydney checked her appearance once again in the mirror. She had no qualms about going out with Tyrone, in fact she was rather excited. Chalk it up to her still being on a high after winning that court case, as well as the fact that she was away from Memphis, where her behavior would not be scrutinized and used as a possible weapon against her father's reelection bid.

She smiled and for a brief moment thought how in New York she could do just about anything she wanted. Being the only daughter of Judge Warren Cobain was pretty difficult at times, especially when wanna-be politicians didn't play fair, ran dirty campaigns, and thought nothing of smearing someone's reputation. Such was the case in the last election, when her father's opponent had spread vicious rumors about her parents' marriage. Sydney had found out the hard way that no one was spared when someone was obsessed with winning.

She also had to confess there was another reason that she looked forward to her date with Tyrone, one she had only owned up to while getting dressed. She liked challenges, and Tyrone Hardcastle was definitely a challenge.

Raven had been full of information about him since her sister

*irresistible attraction*

Robin had dated Tyrone's twin brother Tyrell a few years back. Tyrone was known to date a lot of women but would not hesitate to put the brakes on any involvement that started taking precedence over his music. He was a born musician, a gifted artist, whose first love was his music.

Sydney tossed her hair back to apply her lipstick. Music or no music, the bottom line was that the two of them were deeply attracted to each other. He knew it and she knew it, and in that way the two of them had forged some sort of intimate bond. Whenever he looked at her she felt passionate, wild, filled with the most wanton kind of lust.

In a way, his attraction to her was comforting, especially after Rafe made it seem like she'd been lacking in the bedroom. He thought she had been criticizing him one night when she'd tried suggesting ways to boost their sexual pleasure—specifically hers. She'd read an article in a women's magazine about how a woman should be able to openly communicate with her mate and tell him what she wanted in the bedroom, especially if the pleasure was becoming one-sided. She had noticed that their lovemaking had started getting rushed and was usually over before she'd even reached sexual fulfillment. He would roll away, satisfied, and she'd be left wanting.

After reading the article, she decided to broach the subject with Rafe, and all she'd ended up doing was crushing his male ego. He'd said that if she wasn't getting anything out of their sex life, it meant she wasn't putting enough into it, which was her fault and not his. He further declared after a somewhat heated and downright nasty exchange, that he had no intentions of altering his style of doing things. As far as he was concerned, there was nothing wrong with his technique. He had left angry and had not called her for four days. That night had shown her he really didn't care about her feelings. The world revolved around Rafe and his wants. It had also shown her it was time to wise up and do something about her situation. Life was too short to have to put up with unnecessary foolishness.

The next time he'd shown up at her place, she had asked for her key and told him to get the hell out of her life. That had been over a year ago. In the beginning, he had called constantly and sent her flowers numerous times as an apology, but she hadn't felt inclined to forgive him for being selfish and inconsiderate. He had learned a hard lesson—that he had his ego, but she also had her pride.

Rafe had been the first guy she'd slept with. At the time, she thought they had a promising future together, not knowing then that he was the type of man stamped "Fragile, handle with care, and proceed with caution." She was grateful that she had too much confidence in herself to believe what Rafe had said about her being totally lacking. She may not have been a pro in the bedroom, but she hadn't been a complete failure, either. She believed there was a man out there whose buttons she could push and who could definitely push hers, and she needed to do some button-pushing, fast. Ever since her breakup with Rafe she had poured all her time and energy into her work. Now it was time to try and relax, loosen up, live a little, and have fun.

Her thoughts immediately went to Tyrone Hardcastle and the attraction they felt whenever they saw each other. He could make her toes curl and her breathing unsteady just by looking at her. No matter how tired she was at night, as soon as her head hit the pillow she had fantasies about him. It had been that way since their encounter at her brother's wedding last April. She didn't want to think of how her bedroom experience with him would be, if the real thing came even close to her fantasies.

She would give just about anything to find out.

Swallowing hard, she wondered if she had totally lost her mind.

irresistible attraction

She'd never been one to engage in casual sex. She knew a lot of her friends were into it, but for her, sleeping with a man meant love and a deep commitment, not to mention marriage and family.

A frown drew her brows together. After a year of avoiding any involvement with the opposite sex, the woman in her needed assurance that she was still desired and had what it took not only to capture a man's interest but to hold it as well. And for that reason alone, Tyrone Hardcastle—the man and his music—would be her biggest test since music and not any sort of relationship with a woman was his focus. She needed to know just where she would rank next to a saxophone. The big question of the hour was, did she have the guts to find out?

Tyrone leaned against a white column on the porch after walking up the steps and ringing the doorbell. Seeing Sydney earlier definitely had him looking forward to tonight.

Since arriving in New York a few weeks ago, he had spent the first couple of days with a few friends from college, but after that he had pretty much kept to himself. Unlike the other visiting professors he'd met, who usually went out on the town most evenings, he'd been satisfied just to go back to the hotel where he was staying in Manhattan and chill.

While waiting for Sydney to answer the door, he considered what he knew about her; information he'd been able to obtain over a period of time from Linc. She was twenty-six years old, a graduate of Spellman as well as the University of Tennessee law school. She came from a family of attorneys. Her mother, her two older brothers, Adam and Linc, and her younger brother Grant were all practicing attorneys. A couple of years ago, her father had stopped practicing law to enter the political arena.

Although Tyrone had never spent any time alone with Sydney,

she came across as someone who appreciated having a good time, and since Linc was someone whom he considered a friend, he knew he had to watch his step. Besides, an involvement with any woman was the last thing on his mind. He went to great pains to keep his relationships commitment-free. The last woman he'd been with had proven to be rather clingy and had questioned his comings and goings too often to suit him.

But he couldn't discount the attraction that he and Sydney shared. It was there when he saw her and at times when she wasn't there—like in his dreams. He had to admit, something had happened between them at her brother's wedding that had shaken him to the core. Never before had he felt such an intense need and desire for a woman. He grew warm just thinking about what had happened between them—from a distance and without any words being exchanged. For a man who prided himself on being relaxed, he'd been anything but relaxed that day. He had been gripped in a kind of tension that made his body tight, heavy, and hard.

When Sydney opened the door he drank in her scent, part store-bought fragrance and part natural. Together they formed a luscious aroma that was most definitely female. He held her gaze for a moment without saying anything. The only thought that came to his mind was that she was simply beautiful.

Gone was the knitted cap from earlier that day. Now her dark brown, shoulder-length hair was parted in the middle and shimmered with reddish streaks of highlight that enhanced her cocoa-colored complexion as well as the vibrancy of her dark brown eyes. Her brows were perfectly arched, and her lips were covered in a delectable shade of strawberry that made him want to lean down and taste the fruit right from her mouth. A black wool pantsuit clung to her shapely curves.

His gaze shifted back to her mouth when she moistened her lips with her tongue. At that moment, a vision of kissing that mouth entered his mind in the most provocative way. He was tempted to kiss her right then and there, but he held himself back, somehow found his voice, and said, "Your hair. I like what you've done to it."

She smiled at his compliment, pleased that he liked the highlights she'd let her beautician talk her into since the wedding. "Thanks."

She took a step back. "Would you like to come in and meet Denzel?"

He blinked and forced his gaze from her hair to her eyes, then raised a dark brow. "Denzel?"

Her smile widened. "Yes, the dog I'm watching for the next three weeks."

Tyrone shook his head, grinning. "Your friend named her dog Denzel?"

Sydney returned his grin. "Yes."

"Why?"

Her lips flashed him a playful smile. "Because she knew that he was the only Denzel she'd get in her bedroom," she replied, grinning. "And," Sydney couldn't help but add, "he's the only Denzel she'll have at her beck and call."

Tyrone chuckled. "Sure, I'd like to meet him."

He had taken one step over the threshold when a little black terrier appeared out of another room. He immediately came over and began sniffing at his shoes and circling his legs a few times. Having a love for dogs, Tyrone bent down, picked up the little terrier and held him in his arms. "Hey, little guy, how's it going?" he asked, giving him a playful scratch behind the ear. In response, the dog barked and began wagging his tail.

"I'll be ready to go as soon as I grab my coat."

Tyrone watched Sydney as she left the room, admiring the way she looked and feeling again the fierce tug of awareness that always consumed him whenever the two of them were anywhere near each other.

Putting the dog down, he decided to check out the framed pictures on the walls. He recognized the woman in the photograph immediately as Donna Burbank, someone he'd seen reporting the national news a number of times. The different photos showed her with well-known people. There were two of her with presidents, both present and past, one with Colin Powell, another with Samuel L. Jackson on one side of her and Will Smith on the other, and one with news reporter Ed Bradley. Then there was a photograph of a much younger Donna and Sydney together, dressed in caps and gowns in what appeared to be a high school graduation photo.

"So, you and Donna Burbank went to high school together?" he asked when he heard Sydney reenter the room.

"Yes, even further back than that. We've been friends since we were babies. Our parents went to law school together, and I've always considered her mom and dad as my second set of parents while growing up. At least I did until they got divorced."

Tyrone turned around. "And how long ago was that?"

"When Donna and I turned twelve. Her mother caught her father in an affair, but they got back together. Then less than a year later her father caught her mother in one. Her father moved to Atlanta and married the woman he'd been having the affair with and her mother remained in Memphis. Donna was close to her parents, and more than once she was caught in the middle when they played her against each other."

Tyrone shook his head. He'd had a friend who had gone through a similar situation with his parents while growing up. "That was unfair to her."

"Yes, it was. Since then, both her parents have had numerous marriages. They're both on their third."

*irresistible attraction*

For the second time that day, Tyrone thought about his own parents' marriage. His father, Leo Hardcastle, would not hesitate to let everyone know that his wife meant everything to him. Not too many women, Leo would say, would have willingly traveled around the world for over twenty years with her military husband and not complain about it. "Just like you said earlier today, Sydney, it's wonderful that our parents have stayed together for so long," he said in a tone filled with solemn conviction.

She nodded in agreement as she gazed up at him. His twisted hair style looked good on him, but then, everything did. He also had long eyelashes, the kind most women would kill for.

Sydney swallowed hard and her heart nearly missed a beat when he met her gaze with his own. In that short time, desire shimmered through her, and she had a feeling it shimmered through him as well.

She cleared her throat and clasped her coat in front of her to still a trembling that came over her, suddenly feeling unsure of herself where he was concerned. "Are you ready to leave?"

He smiled. "Yes."

Tyrone took her coat out of her hands and helped her put it on. Her skin suddenly felt hot with his nearness, and when he smoothed and straightened the coat on her shoulders, she shivered at his touch. Her breathing was becoming difficult and her breasts ached.

"Think we can handle things tonight, Sydney?"

Sydney quickly met his gaze. She knew what he was asking and why. He was being up-front and honest with her, and with each other, by acknowledging the strong attraction between them. The question of the hour was whether or not they would let it get the best of them.

This preoccupation was new, and troubling. After her first time making love with Rafe, she had thought that sex had been all right, but definitely not worthy of the hoopla she'd heard in college. She had a deep feeling that with Tyrone, things would be different. For some reason, she believed that he would not be a conceited and selfish lover, that with him she would experience the type of passion she'd only read about in those women's magazines.

She tightened her coat belt around her waist, tilted her head, and looked up at him. "Yes, I think we can handle things between us tonight, Tyrone. We have no other choice."

He met her gaze and the glint in his eyes, as well as the expression he wore, told her that he wasn't as confident about that as she was.

# THREE

The restaurant was quiet, quaint, and upscale, and the aroma of French food reached Sydney as soon as they entered. She felt the heat of Tyrone's hand in the center of her back when he touched her as they followed the waiter to their table. Just being with him made her appreciate being a woman.

"Would you like some wine?" Tyrone asked when they had been seated.

She wanted to tell him that she thought she needed something a bit stronger than wine, but refrained from doing so. "Yes, please."

Tyrone gave the waiter their drink request. After the waiter returned with their drinks and they gave him their meal selections, Sydney eased back in her chair and relaxed somewhat. She noted Tyrone did the same.

"So, what else have you been doing since the weddings, other than winning court cases?" Although he'd asked her a rather simple question, the heat in his eyes almost unnerved her. She cleared her throat and took a sip of her wine, hoping the liquid would somehow calm her nerves and cool her insides. "That particular court case took up the majority of my time," she finally found her voice to say. "It was a long, bitter battle and I'm glad we won."

He nodded. "What type of case was it?" he asked with genuine interest.

Sydney appreciated his response. She really liked her job, and with everyone in her family being attorneys, it was hard for anyone to want to talk shop at the end of the day. Even Rafe, who was also an attorney, used to get annoyed with her when she'd tell him how her day went or attempt to discuss some of her court cases, just to get another opinion.

"It was a David-versus-Goliath case, a little woman going after a major corporation that dropped the ball and didn't want to admit it. My client is a working mother of two girls, and for years she'd been tucking away money into one of these educational plans that guaranteed the money would be there when she needed it to fund her daughters' college expenses. Well, when her daughter turned eighteen and applied to colleges, evidently some of the rules for dispersement had changed without my client being notified, which included the fact that now only certain colleges and universities fell under their umbrella. As far as I was concerned, it was an outright case of a conflict of interest, since the majority of those schools somehow benefited from the company in the long run, as well as the fact that none of the schools on that list were ones my client's daughter wanted to attend. They made it seemed like she didn't have a choice. As her attorney, I had to send a message out there that she did have a choice. If she had one when she took out the plan then she had one at the end, especially if their change of policy wasn't dictated to her."

Tyrone nodded. While she'd been talking, he'd kept his gaze glued to her mouth. He liked the firm fullness of her lips and turned on by the color of her lipstick. He'd never been so attracted to a woman's mouth before. And when she stopped talking and nervously licked her lips before taking another sip of her wine, he knew that if he ever got a chance, he planned to feast on that mouth until he got his fill, then wondered if such a thing were possible. He had a feeling that across from him sat a hot-blooded woman, filled with passion of the highest degree.

He could feel it. And he wanted it.

Tyrone blinked when he realized that Sydney had asked him a question.

"I'm sorry, could you repeat that?" he asked.

She smiled, and the way that smile touched her lips made heat settle in the pit of his stomach. "I asked what you've been doing since the weddings."

*Nothing much, other than fantasizing about you,* he wanted to say. Dreams of making love to her had been the norm for months following the wedding. He would wake up at night in a cold sweat with visions of her naked, silky flesh entwining his. He could even hear her tiny cries of pleasure when they both came. He didn't think he would ever forget his vision of her moving beneath his thrusting body. On some nights, the only thing he could do to calm himself was to get out of bed and belt out a few, slow melodic tunes on his sax, or play a soothing number or two on his piano. One night things had gotten so heated he felt the need to beat out his frustrations on his drums, but in consideration of his neighbors hadn't done so.

Tyrone shifted in his seat and decided to give her what he considered a watered-down version of what he'd been doing since they'd last seen each other. "Most of my time has been spent booking entertainment for Leo's for the rest of the year. Wednesday nights will continue to be Amateur/Open-Mike Night, when we showcase new and upcoming talent, but we'll like to continue to bring class acts on Fridays and Saturdays, when we do live entertainment."

Sydney nodded. One weekend before Linc's marriage, the two of them had had dinner at Leo's, and Smokey Robinson had made a rare appearance. It had been a wonderful show. "Sounds like you've been busy," she said smiling. "Who's running things while you're away?"

"Clyde Burrell. He's the entertainment manager for the club. Normally when I'm in town we work together, and when I'm away I leave things in his capable hands."

"Do you get away a lot?"

"I take extended trips at least two to three times a year. Any dedicated musician needs to keep his fingers on the pulse of the music industry."

Sydney tugged on her bottom lip with her teeth as she listened. She could imagine those same fingers keeping a pulse on something else, too. She'd studied his hands earlier while he'd been taking a sip of his wine. They were firm hands, strong and beautiful, and she believed they were capable of giving a woman all kinds of pleasure. Her heart began beating relentlessly at the thought when suddenly she was reminded of the last time she'd had pleasure. It had been the kind she had with Rafe Sutherlin, the kind that had left her still wanting.

Suddenly she wanted to make love to Tyrone. She craved it with a desire so deep it almost took her breath away, and the way he was looking at her didn't help matters. She opened her mouth to say something, then closed it when the waiter appeared with their food.

She sighed, thankful for the timely interruption, since she'd been tempted to act more brazen than she'd ever been with a man by asking Tyrone to make love to her tonight.

"It was lovely evening, Tyrone, thanks for taking me to dinner." They stood in front of her door and she tried not to stare at him too much and too long. But when he nodded and let his gaze drift to her mouth, she knew he wanted to kiss her, that he would kiss her, and the kind of kiss he would give her needed to be done inside.

*irresistible attraction*

"Would you like to come in for a while?" She didn't include the phrase "for a drink" because she knew he would be coming in for something other than that. There was no use pretending otherwise. Curiosity between them had reached its peak, and they needed to sample this unusual, mind-blowing attraction before it got the best of them.

"Yes, I'd like to come in for a while," he responded in a voice that sent sensuous chills down her spine.

Sydney knew that if she'd had the presence of mind, she would have told him goodnight after thanking him for dinner. But she didn't have the presence of mind. The only thing on her mind was finding out if he tasted as good as he looked.

She slowly unlocked the door and opened it, all the while feeling the heat of his body standing close to her. Her breathing was irregular and her breasts ached. She didn't need anyone to tell her she was turned on to the third degree and had been all evening.

She heard him close the door behind her and turned around expectantly. Tyrone was glancing around the room.

"Where's Denzel?" he asked.

She lifted a brow. Her thoughts were focused on kissing him and his were on a dog? He evidently understood what she was thinking. "I don't want any interruptions, Sydney."

Her skin suddenly felt hot when she realized what he was saying. She swallowed deeply and then answered, "It's late. Denzel has probably turned in for the night. Not too much will wake him after that." She couldn't help but smile when she added, "He's not a very good watch dog."

Tyrone chuckled lightly. "Maybe that's a good thing, because I'm not sure I'd want him to watch this," he said, reaching out, taking her hand, and pulling her toward him. He gently eased the coat off her shoulders, then did the same for his, tossing both garments across a nearby chair.

When he met her gaze again, she felt her pulse increase its racing. As if he knew, he slid his hand up her wrist and touched the area that was beating out of control. While she watched him, he slowly lifted it to his lips and placed a kissed there.

It took everything Sydney possessed not to swoon. The touch of his lips to her wrist was hot.

"Do you remember that first time we met, Sydney?" he asked huskily.

She didn't have to rack her brain to remember that day. She and Rafe had broken up and, needing to lick her wounds, she'd shown up unexpectedly one weekend in D.C. At first it hadn't seemed like good timing on her part since Linc had had an argument with Raven. When Raven had shown up at Linc's apartment to make up and had seen her standing in the living room with nothing on but her slip and bra, she'd gotten the wrong idea. Needless to say, things had gotten straightened out and the three of them, along with Raven's two sisters and the men they loved, had met the next day at Leo's for brunch. That Sunday she'd been introduced to Tyrone.

"Yes, Tyrone, I remember when we first met."

He smiled. "And do you know the first thing that went through my mind when I saw you?"

She shook her head. "No."

He took a step closer; so close she could feel the firm peaks of her breasts touching his shirt.

"I had two thoughts. My first thought was that you had to be the most beautiful woman I'd ever seen. And I mean that sincerely, Sydney. It's not just another line a man would say to a woman."

He then placed his hands at her waist. "My second thought was that one day I wanted to taste you in every way."

The fire that had been smouldering in Sydney's veins all evening suddenly escalated into a blaze. Maybe it was the fact that that same thought had gone through her mind when she'd first seen him, too. Whatever the reason, they were in a position, a very good position, to find out.

Boldly she reached out and placed her arms around his neck. "Now you have your chance, Tyrone Hardcastle, and I have mine, since I had the same thought," she said honestly, too far gone to play games with him.

Sydney wasn't all that clear as to what happened next. All she knew was that Tyrone's mouth was slanted on hers, kissing her in a way she had never been kissed before, not even during the year she had dated Rafe. With the tip of his tongue Tyrone traced every part of the insides of her mouth before capturing her tongue with his own, mating with it and driving her wild.

His hand shifted from her waist to her hips. Holding her body against his, she felt his erection against her middle, leaving little doubt in her mind of how much he wanted her. By the same token, she could feel the heat between her legs intensify and the firmness of the tips of her breasts against him. He was rock-solid against her, and she imagined that hardness inside of her in a way she had only dreamed about for months.

She felt an immediate sense of loss the moment he ended the kiss, but not for long. After a deep breath of air, he was back at her mouth, kissing her relentlessly. In spite of the heat, she was shivering in his arms. Grasping his shoulders for support, she met the gentle rotation of his hips against hers, grind for grind. The musician in him had created a tempo, and the woman in her was stroking the tune he was playing.

Brenda Jackson

Tyrone was determined to give in to the desire that had been driving him mad since first meeting Sydney. Her body's response to him was making him that much hotter. She was pure temptation, and he wanted nothing better than to take her to the nearest bedroom and get inside of her. No woman had ever made him this out of control, and he had to slow down. He forced himself to think about her brother. Their relationship dictated that he not take advantage of her. Then he thought about Ayanna. He didn't have a sister, but he thought the world of his cousin. He would be mad as hell if any man wanted to use Ayanna's body just to satisfy an urge. He was determined to show Sydney the same courtesy and respect, even if it killed him...and walking away tonight, turning down what she was so blatantly offering, just might.

He reluctantly pulled his mouth away, but not before his tongue traced the wetness it had generated from around her lips. When she stretched her neck and groaned, he couldn't resist brushing his lips against her neck, tasting her there.

"I'd better go before we do something we'll both regret later, Sydney," he whispered hoarsely against her ear.

Sydney nodded, knowing what he said was true. She appreciated and admired his willpower, because at that moment she didn't have any. She'd never felt so out of control in her life. Never had kissing a man made her feel this way. If he'd had the mind to pick her up and take her to the nearest bedroom, she was so far gone in desire that she would have gladly participated in anything he had planned.

"I usually don't get this carried away," she murmered. She didn't want him to think of her as a loose woman, although at present she was not at all together.

"I know. I think the two of us bring out a certain degree of lust in each other," he said smoothly, still kissing her softly around her eyes and cheeks.

"Why do you think we do?" she asked curiously, since he seemed to understand more of what was happening between them than she did.

"We're deeply attracted to each other."

She chuckled good-naturedly. "Tell me something I don't know, Tyrone."

He grinned. "All right, when was the last time you slept with a man?"

She lifted a brow but answered anyway. "About fifteen months ago." Wondering where his line of questioning was going, she asked, "And when was the last time you slept with a woman?"

He frowned as he thought about her question. When it dawned on him that he also hadn't been with anyone since then, almost fifteen months, he decided to be as honest with her as she'd been with him. "I haven't slept with anyone since I first met you, Sydney."

Sydney's eyes widened. "Why?" she asked on a breathless sigh.

Again he decided to tell her the truth. "Because I'd made up in my mind that you were the woman I wanted."

Sydney shook her head. "If it's true that there was more than the obvious attraction between us, why didn't you say anything to let me know you were interested?"

He met her gaze. "Because I'd overheard Linc mention to Ayanna that the reason you showed up in D.C. unexpectedly that weekend was because of an argument you'd had with your boyfriend. For all I knew, once you returned to Memphis, the two of you worked things out and got back together."

"We didn't," she said quickly.

He continued holding her gaze. "Yes, I know. I asked Linc about you a few months later, and although I tried asking in the way of small talk, I think he picked up on the fact that I may have been interested in you." He smiled wryly. "So, I believe out of pity, every time he'd come into Leo's he would tell me some tidbit or two about you and how you were doing."

Sydney nodded, meeting his warm gaze. "Why didn't you make an attempt to talk to me six months later at the rehearsal dinner?"

"Because I still wasn't sure if you and that guy would get back together," he said quietly. "According to Linc, the two of you had dated for over a year, and that's a lot of history."

And a lot of selfishness on Rafe's part, she thought. She had finally seen just how inconsiderate he'd been to her. "There's no way Rafe and I can get back together," she said firmly.

Tyrone's deep voice filled her senses. "Although I pity the guy, I'm glad he's out of the picture."

Sydney was stunned by the seriousness in his voice and marveled at the thought that he felt that way. But a part of her needed to know the reason. Her throat tightened with emotion when she asked, "Why?"

He took her hand and folded it gently into his. "Because nothing has changed. I still want you."

"Oh." She was speechless. She and Tyrone barely knew each other and they definitely weren't in love. Yet, from the first, something monumental and totally unexpected had taken place between them. Seemingly they had been drawn together by something irresistible that went beyond common sense... at least her own.

"I really don't know what to say, Tyrone," she said softly. Even now she couldn't take her eyes away from his.

He reached up and skimmed his thumb against the softness of her cheek. "You don't have to say anything. Just consider it a 'tell me where you're coming from' night. And because I want you as much as I do, I won't take advantage of the situation. We've waited over a year to finally put these desires out there on the table, and I think that we'd be doing each other a disservice if we rushed into anything because of overloaded hormones."

irresistible attraction

He smiled warmly. "You never seemed to be the kind of woman who did anything without first thinking it through."

Sydney nodded. Her family had often accused her of analyzing things to death. Yet when it came to Tyrone Hardcastle, she felt wildly impulsive.

"If we ever decide to take things further, I want to know without any doubt that you understand what the relationship will be and also what it won't be."

She raised a confused brow. "Which is?"

His hold on her hand tightened. "What it will be is sharing mind-less passion by two people who are irresistibly attracted to one another. And what it won't be is a prelude to love or to a commitment. I'm not interested in either."

Sydney understood what he was saying. She couldn't remember how many men she had walked away from who'd offered her the same thing. It wasn't in her makeup to accept so little out of a relationship, but Tyrone was making her rethink that position. Even now, she felt her resistance to his offer melt away.

She was too confused to give him an answer about anything tonight. "You're right. I need time to think about all of this, Tyrone."

He smiled into her eyes. "Take all the time you need, and if you feel you can't handle the type of relationship I'm offering, then I understand."

She nodded. His tone was sincere, and she knew he meant what he said. Whatever they shared would be physical and not emotional. The big question of the hour was whether she could handle that sort of relationship with him. It seemed so detached. But then, she'd been in what she'd considered an *attached* relationship with Rafe, and look where it had gotten her.

"Can I leave you with something else to think about, Sydney?"

Tyrone's deep, sexy voice pulled her back in and she gazed into his eyes. Her heart began pounding furiously when she saw the deep desire in his gaze. "Yes," she said softly, and wondered why in heaven's name she was playing with fire.

He smiled and leaned down closer to her, and her mind suddenly cleared of everything except him. She opened her mouth under his, and again he took the time to kiss her. The intensity of his desire for her was still evident in the way he was kissing her, and she couldn't do anything but return the passion that seemed to be uniquely his.

Moments later, he slowly lifted his head to end their kiss and stared down at her. A frown knotted his forehead, and for a minute she wondered if he were as confused about what was taking place between them as she was.

He took a step back and got his coat off the chair that he'd thrown it across earlier. "What are you doing tomorrow?" he asked, in deep thought about something.

She shrugged, trying to regain the senses that his kiss had knocked right out of her. "I hadn't planned on doing anything special. Why?"

"Tomorrow is one of my free days, and I thought the two of us could spend some time together, starting with lunch. And if you're free tomorrow night, we could go to dinner, then attend a play afterwards."

She didn't say anything for a while. It had been a long time since she'd allowed a man to monopolize her time. She also made a quick decision about lunch and dinner. "And I'd enjoy spending time with you tomorrow."

He smiled. "Good. I'll be by to pick you up at noon."

She nodded. "All right."

He then took a step toward her, leaned down, and placed another kiss on her lips, taking his tongue and tracing the sweet seam of her mouth, reveling in her taste as if he needed the memory until he saw her again. "I'd better go while I still have the good mind to do so," he said huskily, finally pulling away.

He turned to leave. Before reaching the door, he turned around again, and after taking a long, hard look at her, he opened it and walked out.

# FOUR

"The food here is wonderful, Tyrone. Thanks for bringing me," Sydney said after taking the last sip of her iced tea. He had picked her up exactly at noon and had taken her to a restaurant near Times Square. She couldn't help but admire how he had braved the New York traffic to reach their destination.

"I'm glad you liked it. The Monetts have owned this restaurant for years. This place was a favorite of mine when I was a student at Juilliard."

Sydney nodded. Over lunch he told her about the years he had lived in New York while attending college, and the many friends he'd made. He also told her about his older brother Noah, his twin Tyrell, and his female cousin Ayanna. He described enthusiastically their decision a few years back to open a supper club in D.C. and name it after his father Leo, a man the four of them admired and deeply respected, who had encouraged them to fulfill their dreams from the time they were still in diapers.

Tyrone checked his watch and said, "Do you need to return to your place and check on Denzel?"

Sydney smiled and shook her head. "No, he'll be fine until we go back and change for dinner." At first she'd been surprised when

Tyrone had arrived with a garment bag, then realized it made perfect sense for him to use one of Donna's guest bedrooms to change for dinner instead of driving all the way back to his hotel.

"Do you want to walk off lunch?"

Tyrone's question interrupted her thoughts. "Sure, why not?"

Upon leaving the restaurant, he took her hand and desire flooded her insides. She was completely astonished that she could feel the heat of him through the leather gloves she wore, and from the way he was looking at her, she knew he was astonished, too. Instead of releasing her hand, he tightened his hold.

Then he smiled down at her and that gesture sent even more heat shooting through her body. Together they started walking, quickly merging with the pedestrian traffic at a pace a lot more hurried than their own.

The first place they decided to go was to Macy's, where Tyrone wanted to purchase another dress shirt. She sat on a sofa in a men's designer clothes department and watched the salesman help Tyrone with his selection, thinking of how easily she got aroused just from looking at him.

She let out a frustrating sigh. This arousal thing was completely new to her. Rafe could turn her on, true enough, but only when that was his intent. With Tyrone, he was able to get her hot and bothered without even trying.

Sydney sucked in a quick breath as she watched Tyrone remove his pullover sweater so the salesman could take measurements of his chest. Her hands suddenly began itching. She wanted to walk over to him, touch his muscular shoulders, and bury her face in his chest to inhale his scent.

He pulled his sweater back over his head and then, as if sensing her gaze on him, he glanced over in her direction, then stopped what he was doing. Evidently he read something in her eyes, because he stood there staring at her as if glued to the spot.

Sydney's heart began racing. Tyrone was the only man who'd ever looked at her like she was something he just had to have. That thought was so delicious, she felt her erect nipples straining against her blouse. The tips were so sensitive it was as if she wasn't even wearing a bra. And then there was the monumental heat settling between her legs.

She took a deep breath and continued to hold his gaze as the vibration of heated desire flowed across the room and enveloped them. Only when the salesman reclaimed his attention did Tyrone break the connection. Sydney took another deep breath, trying to regain control.

Moments later Tyrone appeared before her with a Macy's bag in his hand. They stood, not saying anything, since there was really nothing to be said, as they waited for an elevator. The doors opened and they stepped inside. They were alone. The moment the door closed, without wasting any time, Tyrone reached out for her. She went willingly into his arms, needing the feel and the taste of him.

His mouth met hers, mating his tongue with her own, feeding her desire, then reached beneath her coat and touched her backside, pulling her closer to him.

They were interrupted by an electronic peep, reminding them to press a button for their floor, which they ignored. "I couldn't wait," he whispered against her lips.

"And I didn't want you to wait," she responded honestly. She dropped her head to his chest to inhale his scent.

When the elevator began descending, she lifted her head and met his gaze, a question in her eyes she couldn't bring herself to ask. From the way he was looking at her, she could tell he knew what that question was.

He tightened his hold around her waist and they stepped back when the elevator stopped to let others on. As soon as they reached

*irresistible attraction*

the main floor and stepped out of the car he pulled her close to him. Her mouth went suddenly dry scorched by the look in his eyes. He reached out and touched her cheek, caressing it lightly, and chills of pleasure coursed throughout her body.

"The answer is yes, and if you want what I believe you're asking for, then come with me, Sydney," he said in the sexiest voice she'd ever heard. "Come with me to my hotel room."

Tyrone pulled his card key from his coat pocket as they entered the lobby of the Hyatt Regency Hotel, knowing that once he stepped inside his room with Sydney, things for him wouldn't be the same. He had a strong feeling that she was the type of woman who would leave a mark on him, and that was dangerous. No woman had ever branded him, but he knew without a doubt that Sydney would. Even knowing that, he still he wanted to make love to her so much it was almost painful. He glanced down at her, wondering if they were still of the same mind. She hadn't said much after they'd left Macy's, or while they had walked holding hands to his car.

She hadn't said anything on the drive over, either. Neither of them had. He'd been too afraid that if he had spoken, whatever spell they were caught up in would shatter and she would change her mind. He didn't know how he could handle it if she did. But still, he wanted to be fair to her. Only last night he'd told her he was willing to take things slow, that he didn't want her to feel rushed. When they reached the elevator to his room, he stopped and turned to her.

"Are you sure about this, Sydney?" he asked softly. "If you prefer, we can go someplace else, take in a movie or something."

She met his gaze, squelching the urge to tell him that the only thing she wanted to take in was him, that she had a passionate need to feel him inside of her, that she wanted to reach the highest peak of sexual fulfillment with him. While in New York she wanted to forget

Brenda Jackson

that she was the type of woman who needed love and commitment from a relationship. The only thing she wanted—what she felt she had to have—was to make love with Tyrone Hardcastle.

Deep down she wasn't surprised. The attraction between them had always been too potent for things to end otherwise. It would be their secret, and no matter what, she would always have her memories of the intimacy they would share.

"Yes, I'm sure," she finally answered.

He nodded with relief upon hearing her response and punched the elevator button. This time they were not alone, and in a way they were glad. The need to keep their hands off each other only added to their excitement.

When the elevator came to a stop on the twelfth floor, he again held her eyes to make sure she hadn't changed her mind. To show him that she hadn't, she quickly stepped out of the elevator. They walked in silence, holding hands, down the carpeted hall toward his room. Words weren't needed. They both knew what they wanted and what they intended to get there.

When they reached his room at the very end of the hall, he leaned his shoulder against the door and took in all of her. Before him stood the most beautiful woman he had ever seen, clutching his Macy's bag in front of her like it was the only defense she had against this irresistible attraction they had for each other.

He cleared his throat and asked gently. "Are you okay?"

She quickly nodded. "Yes, but I think I'll be a lot better once I'm with you inside in this room."

She watched him take a deep breath as his eyes darkened. Without hesitating any longer, he inserted the card key into its slot, turned the knob, and opened the door, then stepped aside for her to enter. She did so, knowing from this moment on her life was about to take a definite change.

*irresistible attraction*

235

The first thing Sydney noticed was that Tyrone's hotel suite had a separate spacious sitting area, a bedroom, and another room with a computer that he could use for an office. There was also a nice eat-in kitchen area with a bar.

The second thing she noticed was that he was leaning against the closed door, looking at her like she was something delicious to eat.

"Nice place," she said when it became apparent he preferred looking at her to talking. She removed her coat and placed it over a chair. "No wonder this room is at the end of the hall. I didn't know this hotel had rooms so large."

He nodded but didn't say anything.

"I guess, since you'll be here six weeks, you need all this space."

Again he nodded but still didn't say anything. He just continued looking at her.

He evidently liked what she had on—a short, purple wool dress with flesh-tone pantyhose and a pair of short black leather boots. His expression when he had first seen her that day had indicated as much. The dress clung to her curves like a second skin.

It was then that she noted how short her outfit was and how much thigh was showing. Pretending to smooth out the winkles in the dress, she tried to pull it down to cover more of her, she glanced up as Tyrone moved away from the door. His gaze was intense, deeply penetrating, profoundly predatory, and definitely hungry. And it was communicating a message to her that sent sensual chills all through her body.

He came within three feet of her, then stopped. "I consider your brother a friend," he said huskily.

She lifted a brow. "And?"

He frowned and gazed at her several long seconds before he finally responded. "And I'm not sure he would appreciate knowing what I intend to do to you."

She shrugged. "Do you plan to tell him?"

"No."

"Well then, why worry about it? Besides, if you haven't noticed, Tyrone, I'm a grown woman and old enough to make my own decisions about what I want."

He crossed his arms over his chest. "I got the impression that he liked your ex-boyfriend and was hoping the two of you would work things out."

Sydney shrugged. She knew her family liked Rafe and was clinging to that hope. "And I believe I told you that won't happen."

She decided to be completely honest with him so he would know why she was so certain of that. "Rafe wasn't satisfying me in bed like I figured he should be, and I thought we had the kind of relationship where we could talk about it, and be open to trying new and different things. So I suggested a few."

Tyrone nodded. "And I gather that he didn't go along with your suggestions?"

"No. In fact, he got upset over my having the gall to think that anything in our sex life needed improving. He had no complaints, so he felt if there was a problem, it had to be mine."

Tyrone shook his head, not believing that any man would be that inconsiderate to his woman. "What a selfish bas—"

"My sentiments exactly. I ended our relationship after that. He said a lot of things to me that were unforgivable. And when he showed up again at my place again like everything was peachy-keen between us, I was ready to tell him just where he could go."

Tyrone grinned. "Good for you."

She chuckled. "Yeah, I think so."

He took the remaining steps to stand directly in front of her. "And it's good for me, too, since I consider myself a very generous man. If I feel good, then I can guarantee that you'll feel even better," he said huskily, placing his arms around her waist and bringing her against his already hard body.

"Then I hope, Mr. Hardcastle, that you feel good," she said with labored breathing.

"I have no doubt that I will."

He lowered his mouth to hers, and Sydney immediately forgot Rafe's selfishness and everything else except Tyrone. All her mind could concentrate on was how good he tasted and how wonderful it felt being in his arms and being kissed by him. He might be a master artist with his musical skills, but that mastery also extended to his tongue and how well he used it.

He was stroking, teasing, and tasting her to oblivion, and she was driven by her desire to give him anything he wanted. From the way he was kissing her, he wanted a whole lot. He deepened the kiss to show her how much. His mouth tasted like the strawberry daiquiri he had at lunch, a sweet, fruity flavor that was making heat coil deep within her lower belly; where she could feel his hard and solid erection pressing against her. He pulled her closer to his strong, muscular body.

When he finally released her mouth, she grasped the lapels of his leather coat to keep from sinking to her knees, she felt that weak. Moments later, he removed his coat and tossed it on the chair with hers, then pulled her back into his arms.

Once again he succeeded in sweeping her away in mindless passion. He lifted up her dress to caress her backside, then he broke the kiss, lifted her into his arms, and set her down on the bar's countertop.

He leaned down and removed her boots, then straightened his tall frame to look at her. "Lift up so I can take off those pantyhose," he whispered. Without thinking twice about it, she raised her bottom while he eased the silky hose down her legs, caressing and massaging them as he went, then dropped the pantyhose on the floor.

"You have beautiful legs, Sydney," he said, lifting her right leg and letting it come to rest in his midsection, propped up on his hardness.

She swallowed. "Thanks. I think you have beautiful legs, too."

He lifted a curious brow and smiled. "And when did you see my legs?"

"That Sunday we met. You rode your bike to Leo's."

He nodded. "I like staying in good shape."

"As a woman I can appreciate that."

His smile widened as he placed her back on her feet. "Now for your dress," he said as he reached behind her for the zipper. He found it without any trouble and began easing it down. When he slowly removed the dress from her body, he exposed a purple bra and a matching pair of purple V-string panties.

He caught his breath as he stared at her, seeing all the purple with the purple dress in a heap at her feet and the purple underwear she was wearing. "Did you know that purple is my favorite color?"

She grinned. "Yes, I figured as much, especially after what you suggested that day in Victoria's Secret. And to think when I bought this set I thought it was a pity that you would never see me in them." She chuckled. "Boy, was I wrong."

Tyrone nodded, thinking she didn't know how wrong she was. A part of him had known he would see her this way, eventually.

"Now it's my turn," she said. She tugged his shirt out of his jeans and rubbed her hand over his bare stomach. The crisp hair there sent a thrumming sensation throughout her body.

She captured his gaze when she began removing his belt. "I've never undressed a man before," she said, thinking how most of the time Rafe was naked in bed, waiting for her, before she could bat an eye. "I think I like doing this," she added, tossing his belt aside.

"I happen to think you're pretty good at it," Tyrone managed to say when she went to the snap of his jeans and began easing his zipper down, grateful that she was taking her time. The bulge of his erection was so large, he didn't want her to cause him any permanent damage.

"You're amazing," she said in astonishment when he stepped out of his jeans and kicked them aside. He was now down to his shirt and briefs.

"Now it's my turn again," he said, pulling her into his arms, and liking the feel of having her there. He reached behind her and unhooked her bra, took the time to toss it with the rest of their discarded things, then fastened his gaze on her. Seeing her naked chest was nearly too much for him. Her breasts were perfect, and he couldn't help but reach out and cup them. He liked the way her breasts felt in his hand and the way the nipples hardened against his caressing fingers. Soon he felt an urge to taste her and he leaned down to capture a budding tip in his mouth.

With the feel of Tyrone's mouth on her breasts, Sydney became so aroused she begged him to stop, then begged him for more. His tongue was driving her insane with pleasure. Lifting her by the waist, he set her back on the bar, then began removing his shirt.

A lump formed in Sydney's throat. She'd never participated in

Brenda Jackson

240

this part of lovemaking with Rafe, and found that simply watching Tyrone undress was so arousing it only added to her sweet torture. He was in perfect condition, with a well-muscled chest, and she was tempted to rub her bare breasts against it.

She watched as he finally rid himself of his last piece of garment and let out a deep admiring sigh. The man was so beautifully made in every way it overwhelmed her senses.

"Now, take off your panties," he said heatedly. "I want to know all your hidden feminine secrets and I want to see them as well."

He lifted her off the bar, stood her on her feet, and slowly began tracing the outline of her panties with his fingertips. The sensuous caress made her moan with desire.

"These are so skimpy, it's like you aren't wearing anything," he whispered near her ear, his breath ragged. "This barely covers you."

Sydney shuddered from his touch. Her senses were approaching overload, and she didn't think she could handle too much more of his mind-blowing stimulation. "Tyrone, I—"

His finger slipped past the edge of her panties to find just what she wanted. Instinctively she widened her legs for him. Her smoldering groan was all the invitation he needed to slip his finger into the dewy essence of her heat and stroke her even hotter.

When she swooned, Tyrone picked her up in his arms and carried her to the bedroom. No sooner had he placed her on the bed than he joined her and removed the last barrier that shielded her body from him. Before she could react, his mouth replaced where his finger had been earlier and she all but screamed as he worshipped her body in a way no man had ever done before. His mouth knew the exact spot to increase the sensuous torture she was going through, and she couldn't do anything but enjoy the sensations.

When she thought there was no way she could possibly take any-more, he reached into the nightstand drawer and pull out a condom

*irresistible attraction*

packet. With one hand still covering the heat of her mound, he used his mouth to rip open the packet.

"Let me," she found herself saying, then wondered how it was done. She'd never put a condom on a man before. Rafe always went into the bathroom to put his on, saying it was something a man did in private. Evidently Tyrone didn't believe in that theory.

After he nodded his consent, she took the packet from his mouth. Easing herself up in the bed, her gaze went to his erection. She sucked in a sharp breath, wondering how she was going to get something that big into a condom that looked so small.

"I'll instruct you," Tyrone said huskily.

She glanced up at him. Evidently he sensed her distress over not knowing what to do. She breathed in deeply. His masculine scent was overpowering and was driving her out of her mind. She reached out and splayed her fingers on his stomach before moving lower and capturing him in her hand.

Following his instructions, she slowly sheathed him, liking the way the solid hardness of him felt in her hand. And for some reason she wasn't embarrassed by what she was doing. Tyrone had a way of making her feel that anything they did in the bedroom together was all right, and she appreciated his letting her share in such an intimate part of their lovemaking.

When she finished she eased back down on the bed and he positioned himself above her, his legs on either side of her waist and his hard erection directly over her feminine mound.

He held her gaze for a long moment. "I want you more than I've ever wanted any woman, Sydney," he said huskily, easing his body down on top of hers just a little. "From the moment I saw you I knew I wanted you," he said as he placed his hands under her hips and lifted her while he continued to gaze deep into her eyes.

She held his gaze and watched his eyes grow darker and darker and she released a trembling sigh. She had to admit that although she hadn't wanted to think about him that way, she had dreamed of them making love since she first met him. Something about the way he had looked at her that day had made her wonder about all the possibilities.

She sucked in a deep breath the moment she felt the tip of his erection, hard and hot, press against the very essence of her womanhood. She spread her legs as he eased down and then inch by inch, began filling her body and becoming a part of her. He went deeper and deeper until it seemed there was no place left for him to go. He was inside of her, snug, tight, and her body began clenching him, sending waves of pleasure escalating through her.

"Tyrone!"

As soon as his name left her lips, he began moving, slowly at first to let her acquaint her body with his, to let her savor the feel of him inside of her. Then he began pumping hard and steady, making her body rock with his, sharing the rhythm he was creating for them. Each thrust he made into her took her closer and closer to something she had never experienced before, at least not in the magnitude that she knew awaited her.

She sucked in a deep breath and held it when he increased the tempo. She knew he was playing her as expertly and skillfully as he would a musical instrument, and whatever tune he was playing for them was rocking and rolling her world. In the back of her mind, she could hear cymbals clashing, a drum beating, and a horn blasting, all at once. And she knew that only someone like Tyrone could let her experience such a thing. He made love the same way he made his music—all knowing, all caring, and all gifted. It was hard for her to believe that two people who supposedly didn't love each other could share something this beautiful, this special and profound.

She didn't have time to dwell on that thought when she felt

Tyrone's hand lift her hips even higher to him and locked down on her in a circular motion that became more erotic than anything she'd ever experienced. He touched areas inside of her that had never been touched before.

Her pulse pounded and her body suddenly exploded so hard and deep, she screamed. Tyrone's answering deep, guttural groan made her realize that he was experiencing the same intense pleasure as she when he sank deeper and deeper inside of her.

Another groan rumbled deep within his chest as he clutched her body tighter into the fit of his and shuddered from the force of his own climax. Instinctively she wrapped her legs tighter around him as he continued to thrust into her, causing her body to be swept up in an earth-shattering release for a second time. And she knew as the waves came crashing down on her yet again, that she wasn't alone. The man who'd been an active participant in her dreams for over a year was there with her, once again tumbling through the boundaries of total fulfillment.

# SIX

Tyrone stared up at the ceiling, physically sated and mentally drained. Sydney slept peacefully beside him with one of her legs thrown over his. He had watched her face during her first orgasm, and the expression there had been so utterly and incredibly beautiful, he had wondered how any man could deny her such a rapturous moment. He had been overwhelmed by the depth of her pleasure. Clearly her needs had not been met for far too long. Even now he was tempted to wake her up and make love to her again but decided she needed her rest.

And he needed to think.

He would never admit it but making love with Sydney had scared the daylights out of him. He didn't think he had ever felt that way with another woman. He'd been so caught up in the scent and feel of her that he'd almost forgotten to use a second condom. If she hadn't mentioned it, he would have engaged in unprotected lovemaking, something he had never done with any woman.

And he had never allowed a woman to put a condom on him before. He preferred doing something that important himself just in case his partner didn't do it right. He didn't believe in careless accidents and the last thing he wanted was to father a child, at least not at this stage in his life. But for once in his life the desire to have a woman

*irresistible attraction*

245

was overriding his common sense, and all he could think about was making love to Sydney, over and over again. As a matter of fact, he was just waiting for her to wake up so he could get back inside of her.

He scrubbed a hand across his face. The last thing he needed was to complicate his life by becoming attached to any woman. Having Sydney in his dreams was one thing, but dallying with the real Mc-Coy was another. He had to make sure he got things back in perspective and didn't let his emotions get wrapped up in what was nothing more than great sex.

He closed his eyes and wondered what had pushed him over the edge. God knows his body had suddenly seemed to become addicted to her. It was as if being inside of her with her body clenching him was the way things should be. After making love to her, the thought of making love to another woman was sacraligious. He wanted Sydney and no other woman would do.

He released a deep sigh, knowing he needed time alone to think. Easing her leg off his, he slipped out of bed, left the room, closing the door behind him, and went into the sitting room. Picking up his jeans off the floor, he put them on, went into the office, and closed the door. He picked up his sax, needing to hear the sound of it. Sitting in a chair, he began playing a soft tune, one he had composed over a year ago. He closed his eyes thinking, this is what he needed to clear his mind. His music always had a way of soothing him, of helping put things in perspective.

He couldn't recall just how long he'd been playing when suddenly, Sydney's scent wrapped itself around him. He opened his eyes and saw her standing naked in the doorway. He wondered how long she'd been there, watching him and listening to him play. He ended the tune, placed the sax on the desk and watched her watching him. His gaze swept her from head to toe. She was a beautiful woman and he appreciated the fact that she didn't have any hang-ups about being nude in front of him. He liked a woman who wasn't ashamed of her body, who wasn't embarrassed for her man to see her in all her natural glory.

*Her man.*

He shook his head. He was getting way ahead of himself.

"That was a beautiful piece, Tyrone," she said softly, breaking the silence that had engulfed them. "I don't think I've ever heard it before."

He smiled. "And you wouldn't have," he answered. "It's a number I composed over a year ago."

She nodded, her gaze lighted up in admiration for his skill as a musician. "What's it called?"

Tyrone's gaze left hers and went to the sax on his desk. It was one of his prized possessions, a gift on his eighteenth birthday from his parents. It was on that sax, the very night of the day they'd met, that he had sat in his darkened bedroom, closed his eyes, and composed the piece that he had simply titled "Sydney."

When he met Sydney's gaze again, he didn't want to think about the significance of what he'd done that night and he didn't want to give her false ideas by sharing it with her. "The name of it isn't important. I'm just glad you liked it."

She nodded. "I do. It has such a soothing and romantic melody. While listening to it I could imagine being swept away in peaceful surrender," she said breathlessly.

"In peaceful surrender?" A heady rush of need flooded him as his gaze moved over her nude body.

"Yes, it has that sort of an effect on me. It reminds me of some sort of love ballad. I can imagine a man playing that tune to the woman he loves, telling her with music just how much she means to him and just how much he wants her in his life."

Tyrone nodded and then, unable to help himself, he crossed the room to her, pulled her into his arms, held her close. Her naked body

*irresistible attraction*

felt warm and soft against his, and he wondered what would become of him when their time in New York ended and they went their separate ways.

Not wanting to dwell on that, he stepped back, unsnapped his jeans, pushed them down his legs, and stepped out of them. He reached out for her and pulled her back into his arms. He kissed her as if he were a starving man and her mouth was the only food he'd had in months.

Moments later he pulled back, needing to be joined with her in another way. He reached out to gather her into his arms and she quickly placed a condom packet into his hand.

"You almost forgot again," she said smiling sensuously at him. "It's a good thing I brought one out of the bedroom."

Tyrone could only nod and then took the time to do what was needed to protect her, again thinking how little control he had around her. He would hate for her to think that he wasn't a responsible person, because he was.

Picking her up in his arms, he carried her to the bar stool and placed her on it, widening her legs as he did so. As soon as her bottom touched the seat he was there between her legs, seeking entry inside her. He clenched his jaw as he slid inside her, leaning her back in his arms so he could go deeper, wanting to feel his body flush with hers.

She wrapped her legs around him, locking him in place when he began moving. "Sydney," he said her name as he pushed hard and began thrusting deep inside of her.

When he felt her body milking him the only thing he could do was press forward and let her take whatever she wanted from him.

He tried holding back, not ready for it to end, but she was clenching him too tight, her body's demand was too forceful. Then in a deep, shuddering release, he gave her just what she wanted, what he wanted. And when he felt her come apart in his arms, he pulled her closer to him and his mouth devoured hers as sensation after sensation washed over him.

A soft whine and an insistent scratching outside her bedroom door woke Sydney. She blinked, then realized that she was in her own bed and Denzel was on the other side of the door, letting her know that he needed to go out. She blinked again. It was barely morning, and Tyrone was sound asleep next to her.

After making love again at his hotel, they had dressed and come home to take care of Denzel's needs. Then they had changed for dinner and later that night to a play. Afterwards, they had stopped by his hotel only long enough for him to throw a few things into an overnight bag.

As she slipped out of bed, everything they had done yesterday and last night came back to her in full force. She inhaled deeply as she put on her robe, thinking that if she never made love again to a man, Tyrone had definitely given her enough to last her a lifetime. Last night she had slept soundly—relaxed, sated, and peaceful.

Now she realized with full clarity, just what she had been missing during the year she had spent with Rafe. Even in the beginning, when their relationship was new and passionate, she had never felt the way Tyrone had made her feel yesterday and last night. Tyrone had shown her what a monumental mistake she'd made by letting Rafe control things in the bedroom. That was not how lovemaking worked. A woman was supposed to reap just as many benefits out of it as a man.

Each time she had been with Tyrone, he had gone out of his way to make sure that she was right there, sharing in the pleasure with him.

When she reached the dresser, she glanced at herself in the mirror. Her hair was tumbled in disarray around her shoulders, her cheeks were flushed, and her mouth looked as if it had been thoroughly kissed. She looked just like the woman she was, a woman who'd been made love to practically all night by the man she loved.

Sydney whirled away from the mirror, her heart pounding. Love? There was no way she could use that word to describe what she felt for Tyrone. They had only spent two days together, so there was no way she could love him. Hadn't she decided after Rafe that she would not fall in love again, at least not for a long time? What she was sharing with Tyrone was just a fling, nothing more. Now was not the time to get lust confused with love.

Yet, as she slipped out of the bedroom and reached down to pick up Denzel, she knew she was only fooling herself if she denied her true feelings. She did love him, she had fallen in love with him the day they had first met. In a burst of clarity she knew that she had fought having any feelings for him because of Rafe and how he had disappointed her. She also didn't want to admit how quickly she had fallen in love with Tyrone. Truthfully, she had stopped loving Rafe months before she'd given him the boot. His overinflated ego had begun playing on her nerves and she had begun losing whatever feelings she thought she'd had for him.

Sydney glanced at the clock on the dresser. She needed time away from Tyrone to think, and walking Denzel was just what the doctor ordered. Tyrone had told her last night that he had a class at ten this morning. She decided to prepare breakfast for him so that he wouldn't have to worry about making a stop along the way. That was the least she could do for him.

And there was no way she would let him know how she felt about him. He had told her up front that what they shared was not a prelude to love or to a commitment since he wasn't interested in either. No matter how she felt, she had to respect his wishes and his feelings.

# SEVEN

Tyrone leaned in the kitchen doorway and watched Sydney as she stood at the stove doing something that looked very much like cooking pancakes. He smiled, liking what he saw of her from behind. Need was like a living, breathing thing inside of him as his gaze centered on the curvaceous body beneath her short silk robe.

He decided he could stand here and watch her like this all day. However, Denzel let out a rambunctious bark and raced over to him and Sydney quickly turned around and smiled.

"Good morning."

He returned her smile and crossed the floor to her. "Good morning."

She automatically tilted up her face and he leaned down and kissed her. He had intended to just brush his lips across hers, but the moment she opened her mouth beneath his, the kiss turned heated as he savored her taste while running his hand down the smooth valley of her spine, pressing her closer to him.

He released her when Denzel barked again. "What's his problem?" he asked, nibbling at the corners of her mouth. "Hasn't he been fed yet?"

Sydney chuckled against his moist lips. "Yes. I guess he's jealous."

*irresistible attraction*

Tyrone smiled. "Then I guess he'd better find himself a female of his own. Do you know if there's any available ones in this neighborhood?"

Sydney shook her head. "No, and besides I think he's been fixed."

"Ouch!"

Sydney burst out laughing. "Yes, a typical man would say that." She then returned to the stove. "I hope you like pancakes."

He cradled her from behind, enclosing her gently in his arms. "I do. I also like making love to you."

She turned around to him. "And I like making love to you, too. Thank you."

He raised a dark brow. "For what?"

"For making it special and for proving that all men aren't inconsiderate like Rafe."

Tyrone's gaze hardened at the mention of her ex-boyfriend. "Most of us aren't. You just picked a bad apple with that guy."

"Yes, I see that now."

His expression softened and he stroked her cheek tenderly. "Good, and let's not talk about him anymore. All right?"

"All right. If you'll have a seat I'll serve you."

He shook his head. "No, let's serve each other. Tell me what I can do to help."

She smiled. "Okay, since you're so eager to help, you can take down the glasses and pour the orange juice."

She drew in a shaky breath when he left her to walk over to the cabinets. She wondered how in the world she was going to handle downplaying the feelings she had for him for the next two weeks before going back to Memphis. A heavy feeling settled in her stomach.

"Sydney?"

She glanced over at him. Their gazes met. "Yes?"

"Thank *you* for yesterday and last night."

Brenda Jackson

She chuckled. "And just what did I do?"

He leaned against the counter. "After a solid fifteen months of celibacy, I got just what I needed and from the person I wanted it from. You're some kind of a lady."

She remembered all they had done and laughed. "A lady?"

His smiled widened as those same memories flickered through his mind. "Yes, a lady. A very sensuous lady."

Sydney's heart leapt at Tyrone's words. Rafe had never complimented her in bed although she'd known she'd pleased him. Words were important and evidently Tyrone knew that. "Thank you."

"You're welcome."

Sydney discovered that even after their day and night of wild abandon, there was no awkwardness between them. Together they set up breakfast, then sat down to eat, chatting amiably about Linc and Raven's plans to leave D.C. so Linc could return to Memphis and pursue a political career.

"My family is excited that he's returning home," Sydney said. "Everyone in the family works in our law firm, and when he left there was a huge void."

After breakfast Tyrone helped clean up the kitchen. Somehow, something as simple as sharing breakfast had been a complete turn-on. Sitting across the table from her and knowing she had nothing on underneath her robe had almost driven him out of his mind.

When he watched her reach up and place the last dish back in the cabinet, he pulled her into his arms, wanting her again. Their mouths met, the kiss was hot and explosive, carnal. Picking her up into his arms, he carried her to the bedroom and placed her down on the unmade bed. Immediately his hand began fumbling with the opening of her robe, and when he opened it and saw her naked body, his mind and his senses suddenly went over the edge.

He wanted to touch her everywhere and he did, making her moan

*irresistible attraction*

with pleasure. His hands explored her, stroking her to a fever pitch. Then he leaned down and kissed her again. She returned his kiss hungrily, greedily, which made him that much hotter for her.

"Sydney." He breathed her name and forced himself to pull back, remove his jeans, and prepare himself for her when he felt his sanity and control begin to slip again.

He quickly returned to her and gathered her into his arms, placing her beneath his throbbing body. He almost went weak in the knees when she grabbed hold of his erection and led him to her warm, moist center.

When she raised her hips to him, he flexed his body to go deeper into hers, wanting all of her, needing to claim every part of her as his. He reached out and caught her face in his hands and forced her to look at him, to marvel at what they were sharing.

"Look at me, Sydney," he whispered huskily, needing to see her reaction each time he thrust inside of her, wanting to see her features contort with a passion he knew no other man had given her, and wanting to know from the look in her eyes that she enjoyed his being inside of her as much as he did.

When she tightened her feminine muscles around him, clenching him with all her might, he growled in pleasure.

"You like this, don't you?" he asked as he slowly moved his body inside of her, setting a rhythm dictated by a particular tune that played inside of his head.

She sucked in her breath as he went still deeper. "Yes," she said breathlessly, straining to hold herself back as Tyrone's body leisurely pumped into hers, almost driving her crazy.

"Good, because I like this, too."

He thrust into her deeper, relentlessly, almost taking her over the brink, then slowed the pace again to prolong their pleasure. When it became so overpowering that her eyes fluttered and closed with desire, he urged her again to look at him so he could know just how his lovemaking was making her feel.

When they couldn't handle the exquisite sensations anymore, he sped up the rhythm, thrusting with a manic urgency. She cried out his name. Her face lit up with a climax so intense, the spasms that racked her body also racked his, pulling everything out of him and giving her more of himself than he'd ever given a woman. He screamed her name over and over, and when he thrust into her one last time, determined to go deeper than before, his world exploded and he knew that he could never get enough of Sydney, even if they were to make love every day for the rest of their lives.

A thought came to his mind as his body succumbed to the delight of her: how on earth was he ever going to walk away?

A while later, when he could find the strength to move, Tyrone eased onto his elbows and looked down at Sydney. She was looking at him with glazed eyes, flushed features, and a smile tilting her lips. "You are something else," she managed to say in a breathless sigh.

He leaned down and kissed her lips. "No, *you're* something else. I could make love to you all day and all night."

The smile on her lips widened. "I'm up for it if you are."

He chuckled. "Don't tempt me." He glanced over at the clock on the nightstand. "Besides, I need to get out of here if I'm going to make it to class on time. I don't want my students to think I've gone soft."

Sydney grinned when she felt his erection, hard as ever, pressing against her thigh. "Soft? I don't think you know the meaning of the word."

He laughed. "It's all your fault. I'm going to have to shower again before I leave, or I'll have the scent of you clinging to me all day and I'll never get any work done."

Moments later when he came out of the now steamy bathroom, Sydney was just where he'd left her, naked in bed. Her eyes were closed and he figured she had fallen asleep. He leaned against the dresser and stared at her, thinking once again that she was the most beautiful, senuous woman he had ever seen.

He knelt beside the bed and kissed her lips. Her eyes slowly opened. "You're leaving now?"

He smiled down at her, liking the way her features still reflected the pleasures he'd shared with her earlier. "Yes. What are your plans for today?"

She smiled. "I'd thought about catching the subway downtown to do some shopping. But I don't think I have the strength to move."

He leaned down and placed another kiss on her lips. "Well, when you get your strength back, how about dropping by the Cotton Club later? A group of friends from Juilliard who live here in New York and I will be this evening's entertainment. We're trying to raise money for the Harlem Music Festival."

She nodded. "What time?"

"Around five."

She smiled. "I'll be there."

"Good," he said, liking her quick response and he knew she would be on his mind until he saw her again. He also knew that getting all wrapped up in Sydney was not the smartest thing to do, but for now he couldn't help it. The woman had totally bewitched him.

He stood, knowing that if he didn't leave now, he would climb back in that bed with her and make love to her all over again. "I'll see you later."

As he forced himself to leave her, he realized it was the hardest thing he'd had to do in a long time.

# EIGHT

Sydney tapped lightly upon the glossy surface of her table at the
Cotton Club. Several groups had performed, but the one Tyrone was
a part of had yet to come on stage.

She glanced at her watch. She'd been here an hour already but
couldn't complain, as she was enjoying herself. She had felt joyful all
day. After Tyrone had left that morning she had gone back to sleep.
When she woke up she felt rejuvenated and energized. A day and
night spent making love with Tyrone had certainly been the thing
she needed.

The lights in the club dimmed, signaling that the matinee was
over and the next show was about to begin. She took a sip of her
drink, leaned back in her chair, and waited. Her heart raced when
four men and a woman appeared on stage. Everyone gave them a big
applause, and moments later the emcee introduced them.

"Most of you will remember this group of dedicated musicians,"
he said. "Years ago, while students at Juilliard, they used to come
play for free each week to benefit the Harlem Youth Choir and other
charitable events. Tonight they have returned in behalf of the
Harlem Music Festival that will be held this summer. Let's give them
another round of applause."

_irresistible attraction_

And the audience did just that. Sydney joined them, proud of the dedication of Tyrone and his friends on behalf of the Harlem community.

The lone female in the group went to the drums. Sydney lifted a brow when Tyrone went to the piano instead of the saxophone. Their first number was "A Fifth of Beethoven," Walter Murphy's upbeat jazzy style.

She tried ignoring a group of women sitting at the table behind her who were whispering loudly about Tyrone. They all agreed that he was the best-looking man on stage. "Look at that great body." One of the women crooned. "I bet he knows just how to use it in bed."

Sydney tried to force the woman's words from her mind but couldn't, especially since she knew firsthand how Tyrone could use his body to pleasure a woman. Just thinking about what they had shared yesterday and this morning sent sharp sexual awareness through her.

Then the music took over and she joined the audience that was rocking to the beat. She caught Tyrone's eye and her heart fluttered when he smiled at her. The women behind her squealed, thinking his sensual look had been directed at them. Sydney smiled back at him, enjoying the moment, confidant that she had been the recipient of that smile. After a few other numbers, most of them soft jazz, they turned the heat up again with a fast-paced number.

The emcee called for a break and the group left the stage to prepare for their final two numbers. Sydney raised her hand to get a waiter's attention for another drink, and he had just left her table when she heard the women burst into excited chatter behind her. Tyrone was heading in their direction. She couldn't help but admire his looks as she watched him walk towards her. Her smile widened when she heard the women's disappointed sighs when he stopped at her table. She could just imagine the envious looks they were probably giving her.

"Hi. Enjoying yourself?" he asked, snagging the empty chair at her table.

"Yes," she said, beaming, the luckiest woman in the place. "I'm impressed. Just how many instruments do you know how to play?" she asked. You played just about every one on stage. I've heard you play the sax, but it's incredible how you handle the piano *and* the guitar. You're really gifted, Tyrone."

He grinned. "I can play just about any instrument that's put in front of me. I love music."

Sydney nodded, believing him. She could tell from the expression on his face while performing.

"Are you hungry?" he asked her. "If you are, we can grab something when we leave here."

"I ate before I came but if you're hungry we can certainly go somewhere later."

"I'd like that. There's an all-night restaurant in my hotel." He lowered his voice and leaned over and whispered seductively, "And if you stay with me tonight, I promise to have you back in the morning to take care of Denzel's needs."

She agreed quickly since there was no way she could resist his invitation.

He leaned across the table and kissed the tip of her nose, then leaned in closer to kiss her lips as the women behind her sighed in unison. "I have to get back."

She watched him walk away, astonished once again at how anytime he came within two feet of her, her body came alive with wanting. She took a deep breath, knowing she was in trouble by letting

*irresistible attraction*

herself be drawn to a man who had made it clear from the beginning that he couldn't commit to any woman. But, for her, what had started, as merely a short fling was no longer casual in her mind, which proved that she was a woman who could only sleep with a man if her heart was in it. And her heart was in this so deep that it was beginning to get downright scary.

After leaving the club they had stopped at the restaurant in his hotel. She drank coffee while he ate a hearty meal of steak and potatoes. Then, barely keeping their hands off each other, they rode up in the elevator to his hotel room.

Once inside his suite, he had begun taking her clothes off. Then, not bothering to take off his own, he had picked her up in his arms and carried her into the bedroom, kissing her with a passion that had taken her breath away and had sent sensation after sensation rippling through her. After placing her on the bed, he removed his clothes.

She would never forget the look in his eyes just moments before he had entered her. For long moments they remained perfectly still, caressing each other with their eyes. Then he had slowly pressed himself inside of her, joining their bodies.

A look of satisfaction had spread across his face as he entered her to the hilt, and then the action began. He had literally rocked her world—her body, the bed, her mind—as he established a rhythm that was destined to drive them both to the edge. However, before the inevitable free-fall, he would slow down to extend the agony.

She begged him to give her what she craved, but he kept prolonging the moment until his control broke and he growled her name through clenched teeth, taking one final, hard and deep thrust inside of her, letting them explode in mutual ecstasy as they toppled over the edge together, yet another heightened pleasure she experienced for the first time with Tyrone.

Brenda Jackson

"Tyrone!"

His name came out as a whispered gasp on Sydney's lips as he pushed deeper inside of her. She felt as if she were on fire.

They had fallen asleep in each other's arms. The next morning, she opened her eyes to the sight of his sleeping features. She drew in a deep breath, not regretting what they had shared the last two days.

He opened his eyes, as if he could read her mind, and pulled her closer into his arms. Leaning over, he kissed her lips. "You're something else, Sydney."

She shook her head. "No, Tyrone, you're the one who's something else. I'm just glad we're both here. In this place and at this time."

He gently pushed a strand of hair away from her face. "No regrets?"

She shook her head. "No regrets."

Sydney knew that chances were that when she left New York she wouldn't be seeing him again, as Linc and Raven were moving to Memphis. That meant she would have no reason to go visit the nation's capital. It also meant that this New York trip was the only time the two of them would share such intimacies like this.

When she felt Tyrone shift in bed, she noted that all signs of sleep had suddenly disappeared from his face. Instinctively she went into his arms when he reached for her. As his mouth covered hers she knew she had meant just what she'd said. For her there would not be any regrets.

# NINE

Over the next two weeks Tyrone and Sydney settled into a satisfying and pleasurable routine. On the days that he taught classes, Sydney kept busy touring Harlem or catching the subway into Queens, Brooklyn, and the Bronx. There was so much to see and do. She shopped at some of her favorite stores and went to museums. On the days Tyrone didn't have a class he would join her. As he had lived in New York, he became her personal tour guide.

In the afternoon they would attend a play, go to some hot entertainment spot, or just enjoy a nice cozy dinner at a restaurant. Better yet were those evenings when they didn't make any plans but stayed in at his place or hers and talked. Then at night, they enjoyed each other. They had taken their intimacy to a new level, and it became the norm for them to wake up every morning, cuddled in each other's arms. Neither discussed what would happen when the fling was over since it was understood that in the end, she would go her way and he would go his. But Tyrone knew that the degree of intimacy they shared would stay with him forever. A culmination of three weeks of mindless, earth-shattering pleasure guaranteed that.

Tyrone heard Denzel scratching against the door. Deciding that Sydney needed her rest, he silently closed the door behind him as memories of the intensity of their lovemaking the night before flooded his mind. After making unforgettable love, they hadn't had energy to do more than fall asleep in each other's arms.

As he slipped into the clothes he had hastily tossed on the sofa the night before, he tried not to think about how he and Sydney had only two more days together. Her friend Donna was due back tomorrow and Sydney would be leaving for Memphis the following day. He had planned something special for her final night in New York, but now as he thought about it, he decided it would not be enough.

What could you do for a woman who in three weeks had shown you a side of passion you'd never seen before? What did you give a woman who made you appreciate the fact that you were born a man? A woman who made multiple orgasms appear like a common achievement?

Tyrone sighed deeply, not believing that he was that much into a woman. Since he had discovered there was a difference between the sexes, he had taken pleasure in dodging every beautiful woman who'd been intent on finding some definite place in his life. He always figured it must have been a "twin thing" because Tyrell was of the same mind, dodging them right along with him. Both saw a serious commitment as something to avoid. And he couldn't leave out his older brother Noah, who had been such a good role model for him and Tyrell. For years they'd watched Noah enjoy his life as a bachelor, much to the chagrin of their mother. She complained that it seemed her three sons would never settle down with wives, which was robbing her of grandchildren. Her complaints had fallen on deaf ears since none of them were serious enough about a woman to contemplate marriage.

His mother's obsession with grandchildren suddenly made him think of the two times he'd almost slipped in the protection department with Sydney on the first night they'd made love. Somehow the magnitude of what they'd shared hit him on an emotional level.

Tyrone shook his head. This can't be happening, he told himself.

*irresistible attraction*

The two of them were having a fling, nothing more. He'd had flings with women before, although he'd be the first to admit this one with Sydney was different. However, he couldn't lose sight of what was between them, which was nothing more than satisfying overactive hormones and an attraction that was more irresistible than any he'd ever known.

But even with all the intensity they shared, he was convinced that he was getting her out of his system, and confident that all the time they had spent together would do the trick. When she left for Memphis, he would remain in New York an additional week before heading back to D.C. to resume his daily routine. Their time together here would soon be fond memories.

He rubbed his hand across his face. Then why in the hell was he feeling so damn bad at the thought that in two days she would be leaving? Why did the possibility of not seeing her again once Linc and Raven moved to Memphis bother him?

He frowned, refusing to get emotional again. That wasn't his way. He buttoned up his coat while Denzel danced impatiently around his feet, reassured himself that he would make their last night together special, and when he watched her board that plane to go back to Tennessee, he would be okay with it. There was no reason for him not to be.

"Well, what do you think?"

Tyrone's slow, hot gaze traveled down the length of Sydney's body, as he gave her his hand to assist her out of the car. He took in the way the short, clingy dress hugged every curve on her body and how well it showed off her gorgeous legs. "I think you're tantalizing, Miss Corbain."

Sydney chuckled. "Thanks, but that's not what I was asking you. I meant what you thought of Donna."

"Oh." He shrugged. "She's nice, but then I figured she would be since she's such a good friend of yours."

Tyrone had met Donna when he picked her up at five o'clock.

She had raised a curious brow when Sydney announced that she would not be returning that night and would see her tomorrow. Donna knew better than anyone that a casual relationship with a man was not the norm for her.

The plans were that Tyrone would return her to Donna's place to pack in the morning and around noontime, when his class was over, he would take her to the airport. From the look on Donna's face Sydney knew that she and her best friend had a lot to talk about tomorrow while she packed.

After sitting and chatting with Donna for more than an hour, they had left for dinner.

Sydney smiled, thinking of their time together. For some reason she was glad Tyrone liked her friend. "So, are you going to tell me where we're going tonight?"

"No, I thought I'd let it be a surprise." Since his hotel was located in the heart of Manhattan, he left the car in the parking garage so they could walk the few blocks to their destination. He had made special plans for them to dine at one of the most elegant restaurants in the city, located on the sixty-fifth floor of Rockefeller Center, the Rainbow Room.

They entered the beautiful lobby of Rockefeller Center and caught an elevator to the sixty-fifth floor. She leaned back against a paneled wall on the long ride up and considered everything she now knew about Tyrone Hardcastle. Over the past three weeks they had made love plenty of times, but he had also shared a side of him that she had appreciated getting to know. The term "the man and his music" suited him. She had also discovered that he was warm and caring person who took up time offering free music lessons to underprivileged kids at a couple of the youth centers in the D.C. and Maryland areas. She also found out that he had played at the White House when President and Mrs. Clinton had been in residence, and he had been part of a group that had performed for President Bush's inauguration. What she had discovered most of all was just how giving he was. No matter how many times they had made love, and no matter how fierce a sexual hunger had raged within him, he had withheld his pleasure until he was sure she had gotten hers.

"Here we are."

Tyrone's words broke into Sydney's thoughts and she noted they were at the entrance of a very elegant restaurant. They stepped out of the elevator and her breath caught in her throat, in awe over how posh the place was. The walls were made of glass.

"Oh, Tyrone, this place is simply beautiful and the view of New York City at night from up here is incredible."

He smiled warmly, taking her hand in his. "I wanted to make our last night together special," he said, pleased with the unabashed look of happiness on her face.

"And you have." For Sydney, not only tonight, but the past three weeks she had spent with Tyrone were already special, a time she would not forget.

Dining with him at the Rainbow Room was nothing short of a dream. The food was excellent, the atmosphere elegant, but nothing could compare to the company she kept.

Tyrone was the most gracious of dinner companions. She sat across from him and marveled at just how sinfully, incredibly sexy he looked dressed in his dark suit.

A few hours later, Sydney sighed as she entered Tyrone's hotel room. When he closed the door behind them, he would be hers alone, their final night together. Since he had made dinner special for her, she wanted to make this part of their night special for him.

"I want to thank you again for tonight, Tyrone. Everything was wonderful."

"Like I said earlier, I wanted it to be special." His voice was deep and soft rumble of a sound that immediately made Sydney's entire body tingle from that irresistible attraction they had given into for three weeks, and in spite of the hunger they had constantly fed over those three weeks, it was now at its sharpest.

"If I live to be over a hundred years old, I'll never come to understand this sexual chemistry that exists between us, Sydney," he said, placing his hands at her waist. "I've never experienced anything like it in all my days."

She met his gaze while red-hot desire pooled in her body and knew that she would never love another man the way she loved him. It would be a love she would take to her grave.

She moistened her bottom lip with her tongue as she eased her short leather jacket off her shoulders, then slid the thin straps of the little slinky black dress she was wearing, and within seconds it had slithered down her body to join her leather jacket on the floor. She then stepped out of her high-heeled shoes and stood before him wearing nothing but a black lacy bra-and-panty set and silky black thigh-high stockings with a lacy top.

Tyrone's breath caught in his throat as he gazed at Sydney. During the past three weeks, he had come to expect that what she wore underneath her clothes was just as sexy as what she wore on the outside, which only made him anticipate what was to come. He had gotten more than a glimpse of her passion for sexy, skimpy, and revealing underthings, and her curvaceous body was made for them.

Like his body was made just for hers. She constantly made him remember what a hot-blooded male he was, a man who appreciated the sight of a gorgeous woman.

"Strip for me," he said silkily, hoping that she would. All the other times he had been the one to undress her, but now, tonight, he wanted to see her bare it all for him. Her breath rushed from her lungs and she flushed. Although over the past weeks the two of them had shared one wild sexual fling, in essence there was an innocence about Sydney that always touched him. He was well aware that having casual sex wasn't anything she normally did, and a part of him was grateful to be the man she felt comfortable enough with to have this one-time liaison. For some reason, the idea bothered him that she might one day decide to engage in this sort of activity with someone else. His heart thundered in his chest at the mere thought that some other man would one day share the same pleasures.

He pushed that idea to the back of his mind, and when Sydney began to slowly unfasten the front hook of her bra and her lush breasts spilled from their confinement, he became excited beyond reason. His tongue tingled in anticipation of devouring the generous swell of flesh exposed before him.

He tensed and his breathing became labored as he watched her hand move slowly down her belly toward the waistband of her panties. She was wearing a pair of the sexiest, most provocative pair he had ever seen on a woman, and the flimsy, itty-bitty garment was contoured just for her shape. It teased more than it covered.

His erection hardened at the thought of what was beneath that scrap of material and just how much he wanted it. He lifted his gaze to meet her eyes and without speaking a word, he told her blatantly what he wanted to do to her. He silently told her how he wanted to use his mouth on her, and how he wanted to get between those long, gorgeous legs of hers.

He saw her flush of excitement as she slowly began easing the panties over her hips and down her legs. He gritted his teeth at the sight of the bounty she was uncovering and his body ached to touch it, taste it, and get connected with it in the most primal way. When she had finally stepped out of her panties and kicked them aside, she stood before him completely nude and completely gorgeous.

A satisfied smile touched his lips and his nostrils flared at the womanly scent she emitted. His gaze dropped to that part of her and his vision caressed it as intimately as his tongue soon would.

He began removing his clothes, giving her the same strip show she had given him, although he took off his clothing a little more hurriedly.

He heard her huge sigh of anticipation when he began removing his briefs. Her reaction to seeing his erection was sensuous and he knew he wanted her with a passion that overrode any common sense he had left.

Tyrone felt a compelling need to take her now, to sink his body into hers, as a hunger more fierce than he'd ever experienced before tore through him.

His control snapped when a desperate need to brand her as his own filled his head. He lifted her into his arms, carried her into the bedroom, placed her in the middle of the bed, and immediately joined her there.

"I have to get inside of you," he groaned against her ear, too filled with emotions he had never felt before and too out of control to think straight. Hunger for her gripped him. Intense. Enthralling. Wild.

Automatically she spread her legs open for him and when she took her soft fingers and wrapped around his throbbing erection, his entire body shook. He knew if he waited even a second longer before possessing her, he would go mad.

As soon as the velvety tip of him touched her wet opening, he thrust deeply inside of her while her moans of pleasure filled his mind. Her inner muscles had him in a tight grip and she did some branding of her own when her fingertips raked his back, urging him to move.

*irresistible attraction*

And he did.

The thought that this would be the last time he experienced passion this rich, mind-boggling, and provocative made him move faster and thrust deeper. Never before had he been filled with such raw desire for a woman, and with a growl of need that rumbled through his clenched teeth, he relentlessly pumped his body into hers.

She clutched a fistful of his twisted hair and the pain was overshadowed by the intense spurts of pleasure that ripped through him each time her muscles tightened around him.

"Tyrone!"

Her scream of pleasure as she climaxed sent sensations tearing through his insides, and when she went for a second round he released another growl, this one of extreme satisfaction.

Lifting her hips, he gave one final, deep thrust into her, and with that powerful thrust he met her gaze. Over the past three weeks they had given into the irresistible attraction that had consumed them from the first, and now, with an unexpected surge of emotions that had consumed him from the moment she had dropped that final piece of clothing, he lowered his head and kissed her at the same moment that he exploded inside of her, sending his release deep within her womb.

His heart turned over in his chest upon realizing what he'd done, but there was nothing he could do to stop it. Then the thought that he was possibly giving her a part of him that he had never dared share with another woman sent a surge of unexpected tenderness through him. And for a moment, the idea that she could get pregnant filled him in a way he didn't think he could ever be filled.

And when another orgasm approached its crest, he clenched the muscles of his buttocks, wanting his release to go into the deepest part of her, as yet another wave of pleasure consumed them both.

Brenda Jackson

# TEN

Sydney glanced down at her watch. "I have another hour before my plane leaves. You don't have to wait with me if you have something else to do."

Tyrone tipped his head back as he studied her. Even now, that all-too-familiar irresistibility flared between them. Last night had done nothing to tame it. Not that they had tried taming it. They had ridden its crest to get their fill of each other, only to discover their hunger was never ending.

He let out a deep sigh. "We need to talk, Sydney," he said huskily.

Sydney lowered her gaze, knowing what he wanted to say. They had made love last night, numerous times, without protection. While one part of her wanted to assure him it was all right, that the chances were she hadn't gotten pregnant because the timing was wrong, another part wished she had. It was the part of her that loved him and had decided that if she couldn't have his heart, then his baby would do. The thought that she would have a part of the man she would forever love touched her deeply, although she knew the ramifications.

"About last night, Sydney," Tyrone began, breaking into her thoughts. "I owe you an apology for not acting responsibly, and I will—"

She suddenly reached up and placed a finger to his lips to stop any further words. "We promised, Tyrone, no regrets."

He met her gaze. "This isn't about regrets, Sydney. It's about being man enough to admit a mistake and taking a stand to do the right thing. I should have used protection, and if you're pregnant I want to know."

She saw deep concern in his eyes. "Tyrone, I don't—"

He cupped her shoulders. "No, Sydney. If you're pregnant it will be *my* baby. *Our* baby. And I will take full responsibility for our child and for you."

Sydney swallowed hard, fighting the tears that threatened to fall. Tyrone Hardcastle was such an honorable man in every sense of the word, which was why she had fallen so helplessly in love with him. And although he didn't love her, even now his actions proved that he did care.

"You will let me know one way or the other, won't you?"

He moved closer and tucked a stray strand of hair away from her face. The look of tenderness in his features caused her heart to ache. "I'm probably not pregnant. The timing isn't good," she said softly, trying to reassure him.

"But still, there's a possibility, and I want to know one way or the other." He pulled one of his business cards out of his wallet and flipped it over, then took a pen from the top pocket of his coat and wrote a phone number on the back.

"This is my home number. If you can't reach me there, I'll probably be at Leo's." He handed her the card and met her gaze intently. "Promise that you'll call me."

She took the card and slowly nodded. "I promise."

A smile tilted the corners of his lips and he gently pulled her into his arms and kissed her, deeply, hungrily, and she returned the kiss in equal measure.

Brenda Jackson

He released her but kept her close to him and whispered, "I will never forget these three weeks, Sydney."

She forced herself to smile at him. "And neither will I."

Then she caught his face between her palms and kissed him, a kiss she felt all the way to her heart. And for a moment, she wanted him to feel it too, and to know just how much he had come to mean to her.

And to know that, no matter what, she would never have any regrets.

Three weeks after her return to Memphis, Sydney placed a call to Tyrone to let him know she was not pregnant. She could not reach him at his home or at Leo's and called his home again and left a message on his answering machine, merely telling him, "I'm fine and everything worked out the way you wanted." She hadn't been able to say, "the way *we* wanted," because a part of her had held out until the last, hoping she was pregnant.

When a week passed and she didn't get a return phone call from him to acknowledge he had received her message, a part of her felt hurt at the thought that he could so easily toss aside what they had shared in New York. To rid herself of that pain, she became absorbed in her work and eagerly worked on a new case. Several times she had caught her parents looking at her with concern over what was causing her dismal mood, but it was something she could not talk about to them, although she had come close to confiding in Raven a few times when they talked on the phone.

Sydney, who'd never had a sister, had bonded with her sister-in-law, thanking God for not only giving her brother a wonderful wife but also for providing her with the sister friendship she needed. Although she and her mother shared a rather close relationship, telling one's mother about an intense three-week fling wasn't anything she felt comfortable doing.

Although she tried not to think about Tyrone, each day she missed him fiercely and when she went to bed at night she was reminded of all the things they had done together, not just sexual things but other things as well, such as the conversations they'd shared and the places they had visited. He was a talented musician and a very intelligent man. He knew a lot about law, and she had discovered that talking to him about some of the cases she'd handled had fascinated him.

She checked her watch. Her mother and brothers had left the office over an hour ago with instructions that she close up shop within fifteen minutes. She tossed aside the file she'd been reading as she thought about her plans for that night. It was Friday and although she had gotten a call from Rafe earlier, inviting her to dinner, she had turned him down flat, not wanting to see him again. After Tyrone, Rafe no longer had a place in her mind or her heart. Besides, Tyrone had shown her how a real man treated his lady in the bedroom.

She stood, stretched, and decided to stop by the bookstore on her way home and pick up Walter Moseley's latest novel. After preparing something quick for dinner, she would spend the rest of her evening in bed, reading.

Sydney turned another page. Already she was up to page one hundred. The story held her spellbound. She had come home and taken some left-over spaghetti out of the freezer, fixed a salad, and enjoyed a tasty dinner. Then she had taken a relaxing shower before slipping into her nightgown and getting settled for the night.

She had been curled up in bed with her book for a few hours when she heard her doorbell ring. At first she didn't want to answer it, thinking it was one of her brothers, then decided she was really in a bad way if she wanted to avoid them, whom she adored tremendously, although she didn't think she would be good company for anyone tonight.

Slipping out of bed, she put on a robe and made her way to the door, flicking on a light as she moved around the room. Taking precaution, she opened her peephole and when she looked through it, her heart stopped.

She held her hand to her heart and quickly opened the door, barely able to catch her breath. "Tyrone, what are you doing here," she asked breathlessly, not believing he was really there. Her throat felt tight and her eyes burned with tears that she refused to let fall.

He looked so good, so darn good. And seeing him standing there, under the soft lighting of her apartment doorway, she became even more aware of just how handsome he was. He was dressed casually in a pair of jeans and a pullover Washington Redskins sweater, and she thought that no man deserved to look that good.

"May I come in?"

She nodded and took a step back to let him enter. When she closed the door and turned to face him, her throat went dry at the way he was staring at her, and that all-too-familiar shiver of sexual arousal coursed through her once more. She took a deep breath and cleared her throat. "Didn't you get the message I left for you last week?"

He nodded slowly, not taking his eyes off her. "Yeah, I got it, but something you said bothered me."

Sydney looked confused, trying to remember just what she'd said that could have bothered him.

"I don't understand. What did I say?" she asked.

"You said that everything worked out the way I wanted."

She nodded. "Well, didn't it work out the way you wanted?"

"No."

His response threw her off balance. She brought her hand to her heart. "And why didn't it?" she asked softly.

For a long moment he didn't say anything. He just stood there and studied her as if he were trying to find the right words. Finally he spoke. "I lost my control that night and unintentionally placed you at risk of getting pregnant, Sydney. But once you left New York, I discovered that I lost something else that night as well."

Sydney's pulse began beating rapidly. "What?"

"My heart. And because I lost my heart to you, a part of me wanted you to be pregnant. It may have been wrong and unfair to you, but I wanted to get a phone call from you saying that you were carrying my baby inside of you."

Sydney leaned back against the door as her knees went to jelly. "What are you saying, Tyrone?"

He took a step toward her. "I'm saying that I love you more than I thought was possible for a man to love a woman. I'm saying that I wanted you to be pregnant with my child. And what I haven't said yet is that I don't want things to end between us."

Sydney nodded, still confused. "Are you saying that you want us to continue our fling?"

He shook his head. "No. I want it to become something else, like a very serious relationship that will eventually lead to us getting married." A gentle smile touched his lips. "Although it would suit me fine if we skip the serious-relationship part and move on to marriage."

He took another step toward her, until he was so close that her back was pressed against the door. "But you can only say yes if you love me as deeply as I love you. I may be wrong, but I think you do. I believe that only a woman who truly loves a man could give herself to him the way you gave yourself to me. And a part of me wants to believe... has to believe... that you love me. Do you, Sydney?"

Sydney couldn't hold back her tears any longer. The man she loved had just told her that he loved her and wanted her to have his baby.

"Sydney?" He tenderly lifted up her chin with his finger and met her wet gaze.

"Yes," she said softly. "I love you, but I didn't think I could tell you since we had agreed not to take things seriously. But I couldn't help loving you. I even admit that I fell in love with you that same day we met in Leo's."

Tyrone smiled. "It took me a bit longer to admit it, but I fell in love with you that day we met, too. I stayed up most of the night writing that piece of music you heard me play on my sax in my hotel room. I had composed that entire piece while thoughts of you filled my mind. Even when you asked me the name of it, I couldn't let myself tell you that I had named it 'Sydney,' after you."

A huge smiled spread across her face. "Oh, Tyrone, you did?"

"Yes. So you were right, it *was* a love ballad. Without realizing it, I was telling you with my music just how much you meant to me and how much I wanted you in my life."

His expression then grew serious. "After you left New York, I kept thinking about everything, all my feelings and emotions, and I was forced to put two and two together. Then I knew that I loved you and began missing you something fierce. Over the last three weeks I haven't been able to eat, sleep, or think straight."

She nodded. "I've been missing you something fierce, too."

His smile widened at her admission. "So what do you think we should do to get out of our misery?"

Instead of answering him, she rose on tiptoes and brought her mouth to his, slipping her tongue between his lips. His mouth opened wide over hers, taking everything she was offering.

Moments later he pulled back, breaking the kiss, reached into his pocket, and pulled out a small white jewelry box. "This is for you."

With shaking fingers she took the box from him and opened it, then let out a gasp of happiness when she saw the beautiful diamond

*irresistible attraction*

engagement ring. "Oh, Tyrone," she said as more tears filled her eyes.

"Will you marry me, Sydney, and be my best friend, lover, confidante, wife, and the mother of my babies?"

Sydney's heart soared with all the love and happiness she felt. "Yes!" she said through misty eyes as he placed the ring on her finger.

"And I don't want a long engagement," he said immediately.

"Neither do I," she agreed.

Smiling, he met her gaze. "Do you have any qualms about moving to D.C.?"

She shook her head happily. "No, none."

"Good." He took a step closer, bringing their bodies in contact, and she felt the largeness of his erection pressed against her. "Do you have any qualms about my carrying you into your bedroom and making hot passionate love to you?"

"No, none whatsoever," she said in a deep, sultry voice.

"All night?"

"Yes, all night," she said, wrapping her arms around his neck. "We have a lot of lost time to make up for."

"I agree." Tyrone picked her up in his arms, she pointed out the direction he needed to take, and he carried her into the bedroom, knowing that the irresistible attraction that had once consumed them had transformed into a love that would sustain them for the rest of their days.

He placed her on the bed, then joined her there. "Let me love you, Sydney," he pleaded in a deep, raspy voice that was filled with emotions, the same heartfelt emotions that were shining in his eyes.

And she did. She let him love her with all the love the two of them could generate as they sealed their future and reaffirmed their love in a very special way.

# EPILOGUE

*Six months later*

Flashbulbs went off as Tyrone and Sydney stepped out of the huge brick church where her parents had gotten married over thirty-five years ago.

Cheers went up from the multitude who had come to see the beautiful bride emerge on the arm of her handsome groom. Sydney glanced up at the man who was now her husband and didn't think she could ever feel as happy as she was this very moment.

The wedding had been beautiful, and no doubt the society column of tomorrow's paper would boast of the forty-piece orchestra, all friends of Tyrone, who had performed "Irresistible Attraction," a special musical piece that the groom had composed and dedicated to his wife.

Tyrone turned to Sydney. Although he hadn't liked the idea of waiting six months to get married, he had to admit that it had been well worth it. Rosalind Corbain, Sydney's mother, had gone all out to make their wedding day one with a perfect fairy-tale ending, including the horse-drawn carriage that awaited them in front of the church.

He leaned down and kissed her as more cheers went up from the crowd. He brushed his fingers against her cheek. "I love you, Mrs. Hardcastle."

Sydney's smile was radiant. "And I love you, Mr. Hardcastle."

His hand tightened on hers as he glanced at the crowd. It seemed the Corbain family was popular in Memphis, because a lot of people had come to see the judge's beautiful daughter get married. "Are you ready?" he asked her softly.

She nodded as she glanced around at all the crowd. "Yes, I'm as ready as I'll ever be."

Tyrone nodded. "All right then." He reached down and tightened his hand around hers. "Hold on tight. We're going to make a run for it." Tyrone and Sydney raced down the steps toward the waiting carriage as pelts of rice showered down on them.

Once inside the carriage, he pulled Sydney into his arms and kissed her, thanking God for bringing her into his life and for providing that irresistible attraction that had been the magnet that pulled them together—permanently.

When he slowly and reluctantly removed his mouth from hers, he met a gaze that was glazed with desire. They both knew they had a huge reception to endure before they could finally sneak off to start their honeymoon, a week in Hawaii, compliments of her parents, followed by another week in the Virgin Islands, compliments of his. It seemed that both sets of parents were eager for them to start making babies.

Not able to help himself, Tyrone's lips sought possession of her mouth once more, and when he heard the soft moan that rose within her throat he was tempted to strip her naked then and there.

Reluctantly he pulled away and blew out a frustrated breath. The wait was killing him.

Sydney's hand covered his, understanding how he felt. They had agreed to stop being intimate three months before the wedding to make their wedding night extra special. And now the two of them were burning up in anticipation. "Just think, sweetheart, two weeks all alone, together."

He smiled and looked at her lips with yearning. They were slightly swollen from the enthusiastic kiss he had given her when the minister had proclaimed them man and wife, as well all the kisses that had followed. He shifted his gaze away from her lips to look into her eyes. "No," he murmured softly. "We have the rest of our lives together."

Then he pulled her into his arms and kissed her yet again.

Francis Ray

# the blind date

# ONE

Tanner Rafferty, one of the most sought-after bachelors in Washington, D.C., had been stood up. In his thirty-six years he could count on one hand the number of times that had happened. However, if his sister Raine had been called out of town unexpectedly on business, at least she had ensured that he'd have a wonderful dinner at Leo's.

Tanner sat back as his waitress, dressed in a slim black skirt and white blouse, cleared the remnants of his rare prime rib, cooked to perfection, while another waitress brought the coffee he'd ordered to be served after his meal.

He nodded his thanks and picked up the fine china cup. In the two weeks he'd been in town he'd heard a great deal about the popular supper club. Everyone from politicians to college students flocked in droves to Leo's to dine, unwind, and lose themselves in the ambiance. Tonight, a Thursday, taped jazz flowed through the room like a haunting melody. It seemed the accolades he'd heard about the place weren't superfluous after all.

No wonder Raine had insisted they dine here when she dropped in from Charleston that morning for an unexpected visit. A smile tugged the corners of Tanner's sensual mouth. His baby sister was checking out the competition.

Raine was beautiful, intelligent, and as competitive as they came. It wasn't a coincidence that she had chosen to have dinner at Leo's, since she had recently added a supper club in Atlanta to her growing list of restaurants. In fact, the new supper club had been the reason for her quick departure. He didn't have a doubt that whatever the problem, Raine would solve it. She'd go over, around, or through you, as tenacious as her two older brothers and father when it came to getting what she wanted. None of them believed in settling for less than the best or having their clients settle, either.

Their father, Thomas Rafferty III, had taught them never to be satisfied with the status quo, and that service was always the bottom line. As the smiling waitress approached Tanner's table to refill his half-empty coffee cup, Tanner gave Leo's additional points for an attentive staff.

He glanced appreciatively around the crowded restaurant with its elegant yet comfortable décor of Tiffany lamps on rosewood tables covered with white linen, the stained-glass, floor-to-ceiling narrow windows behind him, and the intricately patterned parquet area for dancing. Leo's had style, something else he valued.

Tanner nodded to a U.S. senator from Texas and her escort who were leaving. The table was quickly cleaned and another couple seated. Knowing Raine would want a full report, he relaxed in his chair, sipping his coffee. It was a rare moment and he planned to take advantage of it. As a hotel developer and chief operating officer of ten Rafferty Hotels dotting the coast from Florida to D.C., he usually had nonstop twelve- to sixteen-hour days.

With the scheduled opening of his newest hotel, The Rafferty Grand, six weeks away, his life was about to become even more hectic. He didn't mind. He loved what he did. There was a huge amount of responsibility but also the freedom to travel, to move from one city to the other where something new and different always waited for him. He was easily bored. His mother had often lamented that it was the reason he never stayed with one woman longer than a few weeks. In the hotel business, boredom was impossible.

In the weeks he'd been in D.C. he'd been confronted with numerous problems, from pacifying the temperamental consulting concept chef over the design of his kitchen, to the delay of the custom-made crystal chandeliers for the ballrooms, to the imported marble for the bathrooms in the suites. He'd solved each problem to his satisfaction. The opening of The Rafferty Grand would be on schedule and would be as spectacular as he had envisioned. The guests would be pampered in luxury and treated with the kind of old-fashioned southern hospitality and graciousness that he'd grown up with in Charleston.

Like Raine and their brother Adrian, who ran the Rafferty Resorts in the Virgin Islands, Tanner prided himself on service and customer satisfaction. All of his hotels were four-star. His aim was for The Rafferty Grand to be five.

He was about to put down his coffee cup and signal for his check when he looked up and saw *her*. For a long moment he just stared. In his lifetime he'd seen many beautiful women, but never one who stopped him in his tracks the way she did. Wondering why he hadn't seen her sitting there before, he finally put down the cup as he realized the four men who had been sitting at the table in front of him had been obscuring his view of her.

The men's bawdy conversation had been of easy women and tough choices in life. Tanner had tuned them out. He had excellent hearing, much to the chagrin of many of his employees. They had learned over the years that whispering was useless when he was around. Now he had no intention of ignoring the conversation of the woman in red whose skin was the color of sun-warmed honey.

A broad-shouldered man in a black raw-silk sports jacket showed a young couple to the vacant table. Tanner's frown turned into a sigh

the blind date

of relief when they sat next to each other, leaving an unobstructed view of the woman. She was wearing a red sleeveless top with a high collar that framed her stunning face. Seated across from her was another young woman who waved her left hand expressively in the air as she talked. A diamond ring glinted on her third finger.

From the resigned expression on her face, the woman in red wasn't thrilled with what was being said. One small, fine-boned hand, unfortunately the right, rested on the table near a half-full glass of red wine, then shoved its way impatiently though lustrous, short black curls.

Tanner absently stroked his full beard, then leaned forward and placed his arm on the table as if he were continuing to relax. He smoothed out his features and prepared to eavesdrop. He didn't consider it rude, just necessary, if he were to find out more about the woman... like if was she already taken.

"Ayanna, George Collins is a fantastic catch," Sheri said, her voice excited and rushed. "He comes from a very wealthy and influential family in Rochester. He's been here about six months. He's one of the best tax attorneys in the country. You two would have lots in common since you're the accountant for Leo's. You just *have* to go out with him Saturday night."

Ayanna Hardcastle barely kept a grimace from her face as Sheri finally wound down and stared expectantly across the table at her. Sheri had been Ayanna's best friend since high school. She agreed to meet her for dinner because she genuinely liked and admired her... when she wasn't trying to fix her up. At least Sheri had waited until they'd finished dinner and Sarah, their waitress, wasn't likely to return as frequently and learn that her boss couldn't get a date on her own.

"Please, Ayanna," Sheri said into the lengthening silence. "I'm sure you'll like George much better than the others I set you up with."

Which wasn't saying much, since the last three in a four-week period had been self-centered and rude. Trying to keep a smile on her face, Ayanna said, "Sheri, summer is the restaurant's busiest season. I appreciate your effort, but I really have to say no this time."

"You can't," Sheri wailed, her expressive brown eyes staring at Ayanna in alarm. "He's too good to let get away. I met him a couple of months ago at a fund-raising dinner. He's a good conversationalist and a great dancer. You know you love to dance."

Ayanna resisted draining her glass of wine then asking Sarah to bring her a double gin and tonic. The only thing she'd accomplish would be a splitting headache in the morning, and if she drank that much Sheri would still be after her to date another total dud. "Sheri, just look around you. I have payroll, worker's comp claims, insurance, financial reports, and bills to pay. I don't have time for dating."

Sheri jerked straight in her chair, causing the multicolored scarf draped stylishly over one shoulder to slide off. "But you have to, Ayanna! How else are you going to find a man and get married? I can't imagine my life without Reginald. He's everything to me."

The double gin and tonic was looking better all the time. Sheri was a hopeless romantic, in love with Reginald since they were in the seventh grade. Four months ago, Ayanna had been Sheri's maid of honor when she'd married Reginald in a lavish garden wedding. Two hundred guests were in attendance. Sheri was happier these days than Ayanna had ever seen her and, unfortunately, even more determined that Ayanna experience the marital bliss she'd found... whether Ayanna wanted it or not.

"I'm happy for you and my cousins, too, but I simply don't have time for a relationship," Ayanna insisted. Now, more than ever, with her cousins and partners in Leo's taking on the added responsibility of wives, the business needed to maintain its profit margin. It didn't matter that the wives were financially solvent. Her cousins were surprisingly old-fashioned that way. Ayanna didn't plan on letting any of them down. She'd always be thankful to them for asking her to be a partner and for naming the restaurant after Leo Hardcastle.

Unfortunately Sheri's attack didn't seem to be abating anytime soon. "I love being married and I bet they do, too. Please, just one more blind date. You and George can double-date with Reginald and me to Judge Wyman's sixtieth birthday party. Like your father, George's father and the judge go way back."

The noose closed tighter around Ayanna's neck. Judge Wyman had been a friend of her father's since he'd been a cadet, fresh from the police academy, and the judge, right out of law school, had been a public defender. They'd fought bigotry and cussed meanness each day, just to do their jobs. The other police officers hadn't wanted to be a partner with her father; Wyman's clients wanted a white lawyer. Her father had gone on to become the chief of police in D.C. before he died from a stroke ten years ago. The judge sat on the U.S. Circuit Court of Appeals.

"Come on, Ayanna. You'll be there anyway," Sheri pointed out. "So will your mother."

Ayanna went into a full panic. Her mother was worse than Sheri when it came to trying to get her only child married. It was time for some straight talk. "Sheri, I couldn't love you more if you were a sister, and Reginald is a wonderful man, but you have a bit of difficulty picking out men for me." Ayanna refrained from pointing out it was probably because she hadn't dated any man except her husband.

"What do you mean?" A frown worked it way across Sheri's brow.

Ayanna raised her right hand and enumerated, one finger at a time. "Blind date number one thought he should get a discount on the meal because we had dinner here." Up went another finger.

"Number two wanted to know about my portfolio before we got to his car. Number three thought the evening should end in bed."

Shock broke out Sheri's face, then it quickly cleared. "You won't have to worry about any of that with George. He's wealthy, and since we're double-dating, the three of us can pick you up last and drop you off first. It will be perfect."

Ayanna refrained from beating her head against the table. Sheri worked in the Department of Education as a reading specialist. She had to deal with enough governmental red tape not to become discouraged when something hit a snag. She simply tackled it from a different direction. Ayanna would have to do the same.

"I already have a date for Saturday night," she lied.

Sheri had already lifted her hand to brush aside any excuse by Ayanna. Her mouth gapped instead. "What? Tell me you aren't kidding."

Ayanna felt a twinge of guilt when she saw the excitement on Sheri's pretty nut-brown face, then thought of her horrendous experiences with the last three blind dates. "I'm not kidding."

Sheri's squeal garnered only a few interested looks. Ayanna wasn't surprised.

Besides being well known for its fine food and atmosphere, Leo's also had a reputation for people finding love there. It happened so often that the restaurant kept a supply of champagne on hand for these occasions. Her friend's squeal was hardly cause for a celebration. She just hoped Sheri would believe the fib she'd just told.

"I'm so happy." Sheri leaned forward and propped both arms on the table. "Details. I want all the details of how this great event came about."

Ayanna floundered, then took a sip of wine to gather her thoughts, realizing why honesty was always the best policy. Sooner or later the lie came back to nip you on the backside. She was putting together the next one in her mind when a dark-eyed man sitting two tables over caught her attention.

Men had stared at her before, but she'd never felt the need to stare back, or the slight tingling sensation that was now racing over her. She had always been attracted to men with beards. His was midnight black and neatly trimmed, just like his hair. The beard lent a roguish quality to his handsome face. The civilized trappings of a tailored gray pin-stripe suit and crisp white shirt with a burgundy silk tie couldn't quite mask the untamed glint in his dark eyes. The erect set of his shoulders announced to the world that he was ready to take it on if necessary. He was a throwback, a renegade, a man who took what he wanted.

Ayanna shivered. She sensed that everything she'd read about Tanner Rafferty had been true. She'd never met him, but she recognized him from all the press he'd received since coming to D.C.

Tanner Rafferty, hotel developer, was the newest darling on the city's social scene. His family owned one of the largest conglomerates in the country. They had started out in manufacturing and then diversified. Tanner, his younger brother, and his sister Raine each headed their own successful division of the company. The well-heeled and well-connected had been doing back-flips in glee over him since his arrival. He was on everyone's "A" list, feared in the boardroom and coveted in the bedroom.

The women were welcomed to him, Ayanna thought. She'd loved her father and he had loved his family, but he had been passionate about his work. Ayanna and her mother had always known that his job came first.

From what she'd read about Tanner, he felt the same way about his hotels. One article had reported that The Rafferty Grand was almost booked to capacity for its first year. No one had to tell her that his time was seldom his own. If she ever decided to dip her toe in the shark-infested waters of a relationship, she'd come first or not at all.

"Ayanna?"

She started, then looked at the frown on Sheri's face and realized she must have been trying to get her attention for some time. "What? I'm sorry."

"What were you looking at?" Sheri asked. Glancing in the same direction of Ayanna's stare, she gasped. "My goodness! It's Tanner Rafferty. What an eyeful! He's even better looking in person. I wonder if the stories I've read about him are true. He's known as 'The Renegade' because he doesn't always stick to rules of business or society. He takes what he wants."

"I believe it," Ayanna answered, her gaze unerringly returning to Tanner, her voice husky.

Sheri's attention bounced from Ayanna to Tanner. "My goodness, he's looking at you! Like—" Sheri gasped again. "It's him, isn't it? your date. It has to be. You never pay attention to men and he's looking at you as if he wished we'd all disappear. This is absolutely fabulous!"

Ayanna attributed the sudden racing of her heart to relief that Sheri had inadvertently provided her with a way out, and not to the way she said Tanner was looking at her. Ayanna smiled knowingly and looked at her plate.

"Oh, girl, I should be upset with you for not telling me, but I'm just so happy for you!" Sheri twisted around, grinned at Tanner, then confronted Ayanna. "Introduce us."

"What?" Ayanna's head came up with a jerk. "I can't do that."

"Why?" Sheri asked, obviously perplexed.

Ayanna looked at Tanner and thought she saw an amused smile on his dark, handsome face. She twisted in her seat and took another sip of her drink. "We're keeping it a secret."

Sheri rolled her eyes. "This is D.C. Nothing stays a secret for long. Certainly not this. You're both too well known. Please," she cajoled. "I want to meet the man who's the talk of the town."

Ayanna faltered, promising herself that she'd never tell another lie if somehow she got out of this situation. Just then Tanner, lean and elegant, rose from his table. Relief swept over her. He was leaving. Everything was going to work out. She wouldn't have to admit she'd lied, or embarrass herself and upset Sheri.

"I bet he's coming over here," Sheri said in excitement, turning toward the approaching man.

Ayanna wasn't paying attention. Her mind was racing, trying to think of a way to explain why Tanner wasn't stopping without breaking the promise she had just made not to tell another lie if she got out of this mess.

"Good evening, gorgeous. I couldn't stay away a moment longer."

Ayanna went very still. Although she had never heard Tanner's voice, she instinctively knew it was him. The smooth baritone rumble made her skin prickle. She was instantly aware of the close proximity of his lean, powerfully built body, his hand that rested lightly on the back of her chair, the light pressure of his knuckles brushing against her silk dress. Heat and an unwanted something she didn't want to think about zipped though her.

She jerked her gaze up and stared straight into the deepest, most hypnotic black eyes she had ever seen. They promised to fulfill a thousand fantasies. No wonder women fought to be in his bed.

"It seems our secret is out, sweetheart, and I'm afraid I can't deny myself another second." A smile curving his sensual lips, his head descended toward her upturned face.

Instead of telling him no or, at the very least, placing a hand on his magnificant broad chest to stop him, Ayanna simply stared and waited for his kiss.

# TWO

Tanner watched her eyes widen. They were deep chocolate, beautiful, and alluring. If he'd seen fear in them, he would have stopped the slow descent of his head toward the flawless perfection of her honeyed-colored face. He was a man who seized opportunities where he found them, but never without warning.

He'd heard the women's entire conversation. His relief that she was unattached was short lived when he heard her say she had a date. He was stunned moments later to hear his own name.

Women had tried to trap him since he was old enough to shave. He might have thought she had similar thoughts if he hadn't seen the desperation in her face when she was trying to get out of the blind date, and then the shocked look on her face when her friend insisted on meeting him.

Now he watched her long, sooty lashes drift shut just before his lips brushed lightly against her cheek. A jolt of awareness shot though him. From the sudden intake of breath, she felt the same sensation.

His eyes narrowed. He hadn't expected that to happen and apparently neither had she. He enjoyed women, but it took more than a kiss to excite him. *Interesting.*

*the blind date*

"Ah, hmmm." Sheri cleared her throat and grinned as Ayanna avoided her eyes and Tanner straightened. "Mr. Rafferty, I'm Sheri Moore, Ayanna's best friend. At least, I thought I was until she kept you a secret."

Tanner straightened and flashed a smile that had been charming females since he had his first tooth. His hand remained on Ayanna's chair. He was a possessive man and made no bones about it. "Please, call me Tanner, and I hope you'll allow me to call you Sheri."

Her smiled widened in pleasure. "Please do."

Tanner glanced back at the silent Ayanna. He wanted to see her reaction when he said her name for the first time. "Forgive the secrecy. My fault entirely. It was my idea, not Ayanna's."

She swallowed and licked her lips. Pleased, he said to Sheri, "I hope you and Ayanna will join me at my table."

Sheri glanced at her watch, then shook her head with regret and stood. "My husband is out of town and he's going to call me in less than thirty minutes. If I'm not at home, he'll worry."

"I understand," Tanner said graciously, aware that Ayanna remained silent. "Perhaps another time."

"That would be nice. Good night, Tanner." Sheri looked at Ayanna. "I'm calling you first thing in the morning." With those words of warning she walked off.

Tanner took the seat next to Ayanna. "I seem to have forgotten where you live and where we were going. Perhaps you can help. I certainly wouldn't want to miss our first date."

Ayanna heard the unexpected teasing note in his deep voice, and shook herself to keep from being affected by it. It was easy to see how he had gained such a notorious reputation with women. However, she didn't plan to be next on his list. A momentary lapse in judgment was one thing; going headlong into certain heartache was another.

"Mr. Raf—"

"Tanner, please."

Ayanna moistened her lips, wishing he'd move back. His body wasn't crowding her, his overpowering presence was. "Please accept my deepest apologies for involving you. It wasn't intentional."

"I know. I heard you trying to get out of the blind date." His grin widened. "And I was your way out."

Ayanna finally stopped being embarrassed long enough to realize he must have been listening to their conversation. "You eavesdropped on a private conversation?"

"For which we both should be thankful," he said, not seemingly the least disturbed by her hard stare, "since we both get what we want."

She folded her arms over her chest. Another egotistical, rude man. "And what exactly is that?"

He leaned closer until she caught a whiff of his citrus-and-spice cologne and a scent that was elementally male and dangerous. "You get out of a blind date you were dreading, and I get an introduction to you that might lead to a date." He stuck out his wide-palmed hand. "Tanner Rafferty, and you are Ayanna..."

It was the smile in his eyes that had her unfolding her arms and extending her hand. She'd always liked men who didn't take themselves too seriously. "Hardcastle."

His hand closed gently but firmly over hers. "Where would you like to go Saturday night, Ayanna?"

She pulled her hand free and sat back, ignoring the tingling that started in her hand and radiated all over her body. "I'm busy—"

"Sheri will be unhappy to hear that."

Ayanna made a face. "She'll get over it."

"I won't," he said, his voice drifting over her like a caress.

Ayanna felt her body heat up. He should wear a sign that said "Lethal to Females," she thought, twisting in her seat. He moved closer.

the blind date

"You two at it again?" Sheri picked up her scarf from the floor. "I can never keep track of my scarves."

Ayanna tried not to look guilty. "At least you still have that one. You'd better hurry if you're going to be home for Reginald's call." Sheri lived twenty minutes away, near the marina.

Sheri turned to Rafferty. "Tanner, I hope you to see you Saturday night at Judge Wyman's party."

"I wouldn't miss it," he said easily.

"Good. I'll see you two tomorrow night." Looping the scarf around her neck, she turned and left again.

Ayanna waited until Sheri neared the mahogany front doors and the hostess opened it for her to exit. "Why did you do that?" she hissed. "I am not going anyplace with you."

This time Tanner was the one who folded his arms. "I have an invitation to the judge's party."

She might have known. Judge Wyman's wife, Edith, was a renowned hostess. The elite of D.C.'s society vied for an invitation from her. Sheri would want to know what happened if they weren't together.

"She'll probably introduce you to my replacement," Tanner commented lazily, as though he'd read her mind.

Pointing out that he didn't have a replacement since she wasn't going out with him didn't seem as important as trying to figure out how she was going to get out of the mess she had put herself in. As hard and as long as she thought, nothing came to mind that didn't require her admitting she lied, which, since Sheri had introduced herself to Tanner, would embarrass her best friend as well.

"My mother will be there," Ayanna mumbled, not sure if she wanted reassurance or to frighten Tanner off.

He gave her reassurance and a smile guaranteed to make a sane woman act irrationally. "Mothers like me."

Ayanna resisted, but it wasn't easy. What mother wouldn't want to see her daughter with him? He was handsome, successful, charming. She'd envision cuddling beautiful dark-haired grandchildren who looked like him.

Ayanna blinked, berating herself for that unwanted thought. Her body had picked a heck of a time to come out of sexual hibernation. And definitely with the wrong man. She *was* telling the truth when she told Sheri she was busy. She didn't help out in the restaurant at night unless they were busy, but she did catch up on paperwork at her home office.

"I could pick you up, we could wish the judge a happy birthday, and be on our way in thirty minutes," Tanner suggested persuasively. "Sheri would be happy, and I'd have the pleasure of taking you out. It's a win-win situation."

It sounded nice and simple, but simple wasn't a word she'd associate with a renegade like Tanner. "Are you really dateless on a Saturday night or is some woman going to want my scalp?"

"Your scalp is lovely right where it is," he said, lightly brushing his fingers through her short curly hair.

"You have a date and you're just going to dump her and take another woman?" Ayanna asked, her voice incensed.

Tanner studied the outrage on Ayanna's face on behalf of a woman she didn't know. Obviously she was someone with principle, another reason not to let her get away. "I don't have a date, but I'd very much like to take you."

Resistance melted like snowflakes on a hot stove. Ayanna chalked it up to the beard and the fact that it was the only way out of a difficult situation. "We're in and out?"

"In and out," he repeated, having the good sense and manners not to gloat. "Where and what time should I pick you up?"

Ayanna gave him the information and her phone number, just in case he had to cancel.

the blind date

"Not in this lifetime." He stood. "I better get back to my table and take care of the bill before my waitress thinks I'm trying to sneak off."

"Let me take care of it." Ayanna lifted her hand, then jerked as Tanner's large one closed around hers. She hoped he didn't feel her pulse skittering.

"There's no need for that," he said. "Until Saturday night." He kissed her palm.

Ayanna tried to calm herself as he paid his bill, then sent her a smile that upped the temperature in her body fifty degrees. When he left, she slumped back in her chair. What on earth had possessed her accept a date with a renegade like Tanner Rafferty?

The tingling in her body wasn't the answer she wanted.

The phone on Ayanna's nightstand rang seconds after the six-thirty alarm went off Friday morning. She didn't have to look at her caller ID to know it was Sheri making good on her threat. With a baleful look at the phone, Ayanna debated about whether or not she should let Sheri think she had already left for her morning jog. Deciding to do just that, she bounded out of bed, but couldn't quite make herself continue to the bathroom. Sheri was a good friend.

Plopping back on the side of the bed, she picked up the phone. "How's Reginald?"

"Fine. Details," Sheri said. "And don't leave out anything."

Ayanna refused to squirm, even if her conscience was beginning to beat up on her. Sheri had been trying to help. It wasn't her fault Ayanna didn't like hurting people's feelings. "There's nothing much to tell. It just sort of happened."

"Ayanna Hardcastle, I can't believe you're not giving me anything! My best friend is going out with the yummiest man in town and you act like it's no big deal."

"It isn't. Tomorrow night will be our first date," Ayanna said slowly, glad that much was true. "It might not lead anywhere."

"If the way you two were staring at each other is any indication, I have a good idea where it's going," Sheri said frankly.

Ayanna chose to ignore that remark. Sheri had never been shy about her sex life with Reginald. They might have recently married, but they had lived together, much to the chagrin of her parents, for the past three years. "Just promise me you won't try and fix me up with any more blind dates if it doesn't?"

"I won't have to because you're too smart to let a man like Tanner Rafferty get away," Sheri said with a smile. "George is a great guy, but not many men could measure up if they were put up against Tanner."

Ayanna didn't have to meet George to know Sheri spoke the truth. "I'd better get going or else I'm going to get caught in traffic."

"That's your own fault," her friend said unsympathetically. "With your income you could get a wonderful place here instead of fighting the crazy traffic from Baltimore twice a day."

Ayanna gave her friend her usual and truthful answer. "I love living in a house with a yard and a garden that I can afford. Now let me go. I'll see you tomorrow night."

"All right. Everyone will be trying to outdo each other, so wear something that will keep Tanner's eyes on you."

"Bye." Ayanna hung up the phone and headed for the bathroom. She had no intention of dressing to impress Tanner because one date was all they were ever going to have.

Ayanna arrived at Leo's at nine sharp. Parking her Lexus in her designated spot on the side of the supper club, she grabbed her attaché case and headed inside. Her cousins' three spots were empty. Since they kept the place going until closing, they didn't come in until

the blind date

around two in the afternoon. In the meantime, Ayanna had the restaurant to herself, except for the security guard and the maintenance crew. Waving to the cleaning crew, she went directly to her office in the back.

Cozy was the only way to describe the converted closet, but it was functional and chic. She stepped behind her mahogany desk with ball-and-claw feet and sat down with a sigh. Across the room were mahogany file cabinets and bookshelves. On the walls were paintings by her favorite artists to add color. A six-by-three-foot mirror in a heavy ornate frame on the opposite wall added depth. She and her mother had gone searching for the office furniture soon after she'd accepted her cousins' offer to be their partner/accountant for Leo's.

Thinking of her mother bought back the present problem. Ayanna loved her, but one look at Tanner and she was going to start thinking of him as a potential son-in-law. Patricia Hardcastle was a level-headed woman. She had to be since she was an elementary school principal to over twelve hundred lucky children, but practicality went out the window when it came to the possibility of her daughter's marriage.

Ayanna leaned back in her chair, forgetting about the invoices she had planned to pay that day. Her mother had married the day after receiving her master's in education from Howard. Two years later, when she was twenty-four, Ayanna had been born. To her mother's and Ayanna's family's way of thinking, at thirty-three, Ayanna was getting perniciously close to being at an unsafe age for childbearing—*if* she found a husband—which it didn't look as if she would.

Perhaps things would have been different if her father had lived. The shock of his sudden death had been hard on everyone. Ayanna hadn't been dating anyone at the time and it had taken a couple of years to get back into the social swing of things. When she had, she'd found it increasingly difficult to be the same carefree woman she had once been. She didn't believe in forever so trustingly anymore.

She'd spoken to her father the morning he died. He and her mother had planned on coming to her apartment for dinner, but he never made it. It was then she discovered that the next hour wasn't promised, let alone the next day. As a result she'd guarded her emotions, perhaps too well. She hadn't dated seriously since.

Occasionally she'd feel a twinge of remorse that she wasn't married, didn't have children, but not enough to worry about it. Despite what her family thought, she had time. Tanner certainly hadn't thought she was past her prime.

Ayanna dropped her forehead into the palms of her hands. Her mother wouldn't be the only one thinking about Tanner for Ayanna. Like the gooey candy her parents had forbidden her to eat as a child because it was bad for her teeth, but which she had craved and frequently eaten anyway, Tanner was just as tempting. But he could be a lot more hazardous to her well-being.

## THREE

It was nine AM Saturday morning and Tanner had already been up for three hours. After his routine morning workout and a two-mile swim, he'd gone to his hotel, an impressive twelve-story structure of rose marble. Many hotels were going modern with lots of black and chrome; he planned to stay with elegance and sophistication. Guests of The Rafferty Grand would be treated to the genteel refinement of the South in the most stylish setting imaginable.

Arms folded, Tanner stared across the street at his hotel. He noted the twenty-foot palms in rose-colored ceramic pots, the graceful curve of the decorative ironwork of each balcony. He could envision the uniformed doorman, the bellmen whisking luggage and harried travelers into the cool serenity of the atrium lobby.

Crystal bowls of miniature wrapped Belgian chocolate with The Rafferty Grand in gold letters would be at each check-in station. Once the guest had registered they'd receive a key to activate the oak-paneled elevator, which would take them swiftly to their floor. In their room they'd find complimentary chilled bottled water next to a mouth-watering picture of the cuisine they'd be tempted to order through room service or by dining downstairs.

Thoughts of dining brought Tanner's mind back to Ayanna. Twin lines radiated across his brow as he jaywalked across the busy street. He'd spent more time than he cared to admit thinking about her since Thursday night. Women usually didn't occupy so much of his attention.

Opening the heavy glass door, he was greeted by the sounds of workers and machinery and pushed Ayanna from his mind. After more than ten months, the outer structure was complete. Now they were putting the finishing touches on what would make The Rafferty Grand unique. He sidestepped two men rolling carpet, another three carrying one of the specially commissioned mirrors that would be hung off the main lobby, then stopped to check with the project manager before heading for the curving stairs and his office on the second floor.

On the landing he glanced back, satisfaction swelling within him. Everything was on schedule. The confirmed guest list was a who's who of the business, political, and entertainment world. He wanted their first impression to be of a well-run hotel committed to excellence. He planned to start by giving them an event to remember, *and* by opening on time.

As he opened the door to his outer office he caught a flash of red out of the corner of his eye. It took only a second for him to realize that the woman coming into the hotel was a worker in a red shirt and not Ayanna. He accepted his disappointment and the undeniable fact that she wasn't going to be as easily forgotten as other women in his past. Not sure how he felt about that, he entered the office and closed the door.

Right up until thirty minutes before Tanner was due to pick her up, Ayanna had told herself she wasn't going to dress to impress. She then looked at herself in the mauve floor-length gown that had been a great buy but did nothing for her and quickly whipped it off.

With almost desperate haste she hurried to her closet and began shoving aside the padded hangers until she found what she was looking for, then quickly took out a long-sleeved black dress of clinging jersey and laid it on the bed. She exchanged the flesh-toned hose she was wearing for sheer black, took off her bra, then slipped the ankle-length gown over her head. The fit was perfect and totally provocative—the neck high and innocent, the back completely bare, stopping a scant inch above her hips. She'd bought the dress on a whim when she and Sheri were shopping for her wedding gown and had never worn it.

Looking over her shoulder at the cheval mirror in the corner of her bedroom, she admitted she'd never had the nerve. So why was she wearing it now?

The ringing doorbell was her answer. No matter how much she'd tried to deny it, she'd enjoyed Tanner's attention, enjoyed the little zip his touch caused, enjoyed being with him. He had a keen wit and he made her smile. He wasn't looking for anything long term, so there was no need for her to guard her heart. Why not just enjoy herself for the evening? In the process she'd show her family that she still had what it took to attract one of the most sought-after bachelors in the country. And she'd show Sheri she didn't need any help getting a date. Afterwards she could go back into hibernation.

Picking up a large wicker gift basket wrapped in iridescent paper with one hand, she stuck her small black beaded clutch under her arm with the other, then went to the front door and opened it. Tanner stood bathed in the soft yellow glow from the wrought-iron lantern on the porch, smiling down at her. Ayanna couldn't prevent the leap of her heart. Tanner in a black tux, bib-front white shirt, and black bow tie was even more devastating than he had been in a business suit.

"Hello, Ayanna. You look beautiful."

"Hello, and thank you," she said, pleased that her voice sounded normal.

"Let me take that for you." He lifted the basket filled with chocolate goodies and a bottle of wine. "The judge is going to be a happy man."

"He loves chocolate-covered nuts and Sweet Temptation has the best in the city." Stepping over the threshold, she turned to pull the door closed.

"Ayanna!"

She froze. There was as much reverence as admiration in the way he uttered her name. Slowly she turned to face him.

"You're beautiful," he whispered.

"I think you already said that," she said, inordinately pleased.

"Certain things bear repeating." Taking her by the elbow, he led her to the black limousine waiting by the curb. "I hope there'll be dancing tonight."

She glanced up at him. "You like to dance?"

"Sometimes." He waved the driver away and opened the door. After helping her inside, he placed the basket on the seat across from them and slid in beside Ayanna. "Do you think we might get in a few turns around the floor before we leave? I have a feeling we'd both enjoy it immensely."

Ayanna moistened her lips as the driver pulled smoothly away from the curb. She didn't have a doubt that Tanner knew just how to hold a woman, stroke her, make her burn. "I don't think we'll have time."

"Pity," he said, watching her with hooded eyes.

Ayanna felt like a baby chick in the henhouse with a sharp-toothed fox. She had forgotten one important thing: Tanner was a renegade. He made his own rules. What he wanted took precedence over the desires or plans of others. And he wanted her, a thought that both chilled and excited her. She glanced out the tinted window

*the blind date*

as the car headed up the ramp to the freeway into D.C. and tried hard not to think about how much she wanted him.

"How have things been at work?" he asked, breaking the silence.

She glanced over at him. "Routine," she said, omitting to tell him that she hadn't been able to get him off her mind. "How are things going at The Rafferty Grand?"

"We're right on schedule," he said simply. "What made you want to be an accountant?"

No man had ever asked her that before. She got the distinct impression that Tanner wasn't just being nice or needing to fill the silence; he genuinely wanted to know. "One of my father's second jobs was doing income taxes. I used to help him and found I had a skill for mathematical computations."

"What did he do?"

"He was a policeman, a very good one," she said with pride in her voice. "He'd tried to get work as an off-duty policeman in security because it would have been steadier and paid more, but very few of those jobs were given to minority police officers. Eventually the system changed and he was able to get the recognition and respect he deserved. At the time of his death he was the chief of police."

Tanner's hand closed gently over hers. "Our forefathers went through a lot, but I think it made us stronger, more resilient. You might not have known where your talent lay if not for your father's other job. Because of what he went through, he certainly understood those coming after him."

"That's what he always said."

"Sounds as if he was a wonderful man."

"He was."

"From what I've seen so far, so is his daughter."

Warmth curled though Ayanna. She forgot caution and let Tanner continue to hold her hand. A moment or two longer wouldn't hurt.

Traffic was backed up two blocks away from the Hyatt. Cars, limos, and taxis jockeyed to get to the door and drop off passengers. Tanner had attended enough social events in D.C. to expect the snarled nightmare. "I see it's business as usual tonight. Parking will be at a premium."

Ayanna smiled at Tanner. "One of the reasons I live outside of the city. Even on the one-way street in front of Leo's accidents have occurred. They've tied up traffic for hours and drastically cut into business."

"One of the requirements for the location of The Rafferty Grand was easy accessibility," he said thoughtfully. "The owners of Leo's would do well to think about the traffic situation. You never want to be vulnerable."

"I agree," she said, crossing her long legs and drawing Tanner's attention. "The building behind Leo's is for sale, but it's overpriced, even in D.C.'s inflated market."

Tanner withdrew his gaze from her trim ankle. "The owner has a problem, then."

"Owners," she corrected casually, then added, "But not an insurmountable one for us."

His brows bunched in shock. "You own part of Leo's?"

Her smile made him want to kiss her breathless. "Full partner with my other three male cousins. Leo's is named after their father."

He laughed, shaking his head. "Why am I not surprised? You continue to amaze me, Ayanna. You have quite an establishment there, but I guess you already know that."

"Yes, but it's always nice to hear it, especially from a man of your reputation," Ayanna said.

"Don't believe everything you read about me," Tanner cautioned, his knuckles brushing across her cheek.

Her breath stalled and she eased back in the seat, glancing out the window, desperately trying to calm her racing heart. "The driver may run out of gas before we get to the hotel."

Tanner allowed her escape. For now. "Pete has been my driver for six years. He knows his business."

Ayanna glanced toward the front of the limo. "You have him full time?"

"He's not a frivolous luxury. I don't have time to waste waiting for taxis, locating an address, or returning rentals. Besides, while I'm in transit, I can return phone calls or work on the lap top."

"That makes sense," she said. "You're a busy man."

"I'm going to get a lot busier when The Rafferty Grand opens. I plan for it to have five stars by the end of the first year," he told her.

"You'll get it, too," she replied with complete confidence. Few things could probably withstand the force that was Tanner Rafferty. The thought caused her a moment of unease.

"We might as well get out here, if you don't mind," he said when the car idled through another green light. "Unless you want to wait until the driver can get closer."

"This is fine."

"Let us off here, Pete. Don't bother to get out," Tanner said to the driver. "I'll call you when we're ready to be picked up."

"Yes, Mr. Rafferty," the driver said as he eased to the curb.

As soon as the car stopped, Tanner retrieved the basket, helped Ayanna out, then did what he'd wanted to do ever since he saw the enticing bare curve of her slender back. He placed his hand on that smooth, bare skin.

She jumped and whirled around. Her eyes were huge, her chest heaving with fury.

Her skin had felt like warmed silk, but if he wanted to touch it again, he knew he had better back off. He took her arm and they walked down the street toward the hotel. "Temptation is a terrible thing," he said contritely. "I had a weak moment and I'm not sure I won't have another."

Ayanna glanced up at him, no longer upset. He'd done it again. Made light of what could have been an embarrassing moment for her and, at the same time, made her aware that he thought she was desirable. "You believe in speaking your mind," she said.

"Always." He opened one of the small glass side doors to the entrance of the hotel. "Tonight is for us to have a good time. I also plan to make it a memorable one."

Ayanna didn't doubt him for a second.

The Imperial Ballroom was a moving sea of people. The sparkle of the women's gowns and their jewelry rivaled that of the ten immense chandeliers in the vaulted ceiling. A five-piece band played Judge Wyman's favorite songs, made unforgettable by jazz legend Miles Davis. Food and drink were plentiful and people were taking full advantage of both.

Ayanna and Tanner hadn't gone five feet before the first of many guests came up to speak to him, welcome him to the city, or invite him to join a club or a business organization. Every few steps the process was repeated. With the ease of a man used to being fawned over, he thanked them and moved on without committing himself.

Ayanna would have to be blind to miss the speculative looks and outright stares she received, or the envy in many of the women's eyes. She tried to recall if Tanner's name had been linked to any woman since his arrival and drew a blank. She certainly didn't want to be the first. Having fun was one thing; being known as the first woman Tanner dumped in D.C. was quite another.

"What's the frown for?"

"Just considering how it's going to feel to be known as the first of many you dated while in D.C.," she said.

"I wouldn't worry about that if I were you," he said, handing the basket to an attendant at one of the three tables reserved for gifts. Two security guards stood nearby.

She was about to ask him why when she spotted Sheri dragging Reginald and another man toward them. Somehow she knew the slender man with the long, serious face in a tailor-made black tux was George.

"I think we're about to meet my would-be replacement." Tanner's hand moved from her arm and curved possessively around her waist. Ayanna looked up and saw the hard glint in his eyes. He was definitely staking a claim, and she wasn't quite sure how she felt about it.

Sheri, pretty in a pale blue gown, quickly made the introductions. Reginald had a wicked sense of humor and soon had all of them laughing... except George. He seemed more interested in letting them know of his family connections and how brilliant he was. Ayanna caught Sheri's pained looked and hoped fervently that she would now stop trying to fix her up. A few minutes later Reginald saw his parents and they went off to meet them.

"We'd better find my mother and Judge Wyman," Ayanna said, trying to peer through the growing crush of people.

"Do you bare a striking resemblance to your mother?"

"Yes. Why?" she asked.

"Because, if I'm not mistaken, they've found us."

Ayanna followed the direction of his gaze. He was right. Her mother and Judge Wyman, arms linked, were heading straight for them. And both were grinning as if they'd won the lottery.

# FOUR

Patricia Hardcastle, slim and lovely at fifty-six years old, had never met a stranger, Ayanna thought. Her father used to say she'd talk to a sign post. Two minutes after meeting Tanner, she was chatting with him as if they'd known each other for years. She even managed to get in a plug for her school. If Tanner ever considered being a sponsor, or if any of his staff wanted to mentor, her elementary school would be grateful.

"I'd be happy to discuss it with you when things settle down a bit," he said.

After he'd sidestepped so many requests and invitations that evening Ayanna couldn't hide her surprise. Only Tanner noticed. She had a feeling that very little got past him.

"Children need to know adults care. The earlier, the better," he said sincerely.

"Exactly," Patricia said, beaming. "Thank you, Mr. Rafferty. It would mean so much to my kids."

"Please call me Tanner," he said with urbane charm.

It would have taken a woman of stone not to melt when all that charm was directed at her. Her mother actually blushed.

Ayanna had been the recipient of that soulful voice and mesmerizing eyes, so she understood her mother's reaction. From the first she had labeled him as dangerous to the female population. Any woman who went out with him would either have to be very self-assured or so enamored of him that she didn't care that he attracted women like bees to a honey pot.

As if aware of her thoughts, Tanner smiled at her. Again heat shimmered through her. She was acutely aware of his hand on her bare skin. *Dangerous.* So what was she doing here with him, doing all this pretending, instead of being home with a good book?

"I see, as usual, you've managed to find the best," Judge Wyman said, his shrewd black eyes staring at Tanner. The judge was dressed in a black tux that fit his slender body perfectly.

"I try." Tanner smiled down at Ayanna.

She flushed and decided it was best to lighten the mood. "Judge Wyman, it's a wonderful party."

"Glad you could come." The judge looked her over and nodded his gray head approvingly. "Leo would be proud of you." He glanced at Tanner. "But he'd also be a bit concerned."

Ayanna sighed. Her ploy to keep things light hadn't worked. However, before Ayanna could speak, Tanner said, "He wouldn't have to be. I hope you and Mrs. Hardcastle won't be, either."

After a moment, the judge nodded. "You can be a ruthless SOB, Tanner but you're a fair one."

"I trust my daughter's judgment until you show me otherwise." Patricia's eyes, the exact color of Ayanna's, narrowed. "Mess up and you'll regret it."

Ayanna flushed in embarrassment. "It's just a date, Mother. We'll probably never see each other again."

"Not if I have anything to say about it," Tanner said firmly, taking her arm. "If you'll excuse us, I'd like to have at least one dance. I promised Ayanna not to keep her out too late."

"Why so early?" her mother asked with a frown.

Tanner looked at Ayanna and she forced herself not to squirm. "I have a lot of paperwork."

"You work too hard," her mother admonished with a frown. "For once, just enjoy yourself."

"Patricia is right," the judge said. "I'd like to know that people had a good time at my party."

Everyone knew the judge's wife threw the birthday party as a social event. "I suppose we could stay a little while longer."

"Then let's dance." Tanner didn't wait for an answer.

As soon as he put his arms around her, she knew she was in trouble. Nothing in her wildest dreams could have prepared her for the erotic sensation of the feel of his hard body against hers, the arousing touch of his hand on her skin.

Warning bells went off in her head, but overriding them was the seductive pull of his body against hers. Without thought, her body softened, fitting itself against his. When the music stopped and he looked down at her, she saw reflected in his eyes her own naked desire.

"I never knew need could be this intense," he said huskily.

"Neither did I," she said without thought and watched his eyes narrow, his nostrils flair. His head started to descend. "T-Tanner."

His hand clenched in hers. He seemed to shake himself. "Would you like something to drink or eat?"

She didn't, but it was safer than another dance. "Yes."

They walked from the dance floor, their bodies brushing against the other with each step. Neither thought of moving away.

the blind date

*This is it*, Ayanna thought as Tanner unlocked her front door. The big moment when you had to decide on the good-night kiss. With her recent dates, there hadn't been any question. She'd thanked them politely and then went inside... alone.

With Tanner her body had been in a humming state of arousal since they had left the party. They'd stayed about forty minutes longer, then bade everyone good night. As if both were aware their emotions were being held in check by a delicate thread, they had not returned to the dance floor, nor had Tanner touched her except on her arm.

Holding the front door open, Tanner stood aside for her to enter. The key was still in his hand. She could wait for him to give it to her, or go inside and get the kiss her body craved.

Silently she walked inside, heard the door close behind her, and turned around.

In the next second she was in his arms, his mouth devouring hers. She heard her purse land on the terrazzo floor. His hands on her burned with feverish delight. She couldn't seem to get enough of him.

He jerked his head up, his breathing harsh and deep. Ayanna's eyes flickered open and she stared into the glittering eyes of a man who ravaged and plundered to take whatever he wanted. She shivered.

He shut his eyes briefly, then drew her gently into his arms and held her. "I could kiss you forever and it still wouldn't be long enough."

Her breath shuddered over her lips. She knew exactly how he felt.

He stepped back and held her at arm's length. "I understand Leo's has brunch on Sunday. Care to join me if I can get reservations?"

Ayanna stared up at him. He hadn't phrased the invitation as a date but more as friends meeting. He also hadn't expected preferential treatment. "I'd like that."

"After I make the reservations, I'll call." He pulled her key from his pocket and handed it to her. "Good night."

"Good night." Her hand closed around the ring of keys and felt the lingering heat.

His lips brushed so softly against her cheek it could have been her imagination. Her eyes drifted shut again. When she opened them he was gone.

Sunday morning Tanner and Ayanna arrived at Leo's shortly before their 11:30 reservation. Her cousin Noah was in front helping with seating. His astute black eyes flickered from Ayanna to Tanner, then Noah smiled. Ayanna breathed a bit easier. When it came to men, all three of her cousins tended to act as if she were operating on less than half a brain cell. Apparently marriage had mellowed her older cousin Noah. The twins, Tyrell and Tyrone, were a bit more unpredictable.

"Hi, Ayanna. Glad to have you back, Mr. Rafferty," Noah said as he stuck two menus beneath his arm.

"Hi, Noah," Ayanna greeted. It didn't surprise her that Noah greeted Tanner by name. He prided himself on remembering Leo's patrons. "Tanner, this is my cousin and one of the other owners and the manager of Leo's, Noah Hardcastle."

The handshake was firm. "This way," Noah said, leading them through the already crowded restaurant to a quiet table in the corner of the room. "Is this all right?"

"Yes," Tanner said, seating Ayanna, then taking his own seat and accepting the menu.

"Can I get either of you something to drink, perhaps a mimosa?"

"Ayanna?" Tanner said, his menu still closed.

"Tomato juice."

"I'll have the same."

"Your waitress Sarah will be with you shortly."

Tanner opened his menu as Noah left. "What's good?"

"Everything," Ayanna answered. They smiled at each other across the table.

"I'll take your word for it," he said as their waitress came up to take their orders, then left. "Do the other cousins work here as well?"

"The answer to your question is coming this way." Tyrell and Tyrone were identical twins but opposites in the way they dressed, wore their hair, in temperament, and taste. Both had made artistic triumphs in their own right, Tyrell as a master chef and Tyrone as a musical genius.

They spoke to Ayanna, nodded at Tanner, put their drink order on the table, then flanked her, each twin placing a hand on the back of her chair, and stared at Tanner. Although they were a year younger than Ayanna they had grown up protective of her. Too much so, in her opinion.

"Be good," she admonished, then made introductions.

Tanner stood and extended his hand. "Glad to see you look after her. Not that she needs it," he added when Ayanna snorted.

"No, I don't," she agreed. "Tyrell, you're probably needed in the kitchen and, Tyrone, I believe we're supposed to have live music today and I want to hear my favorite."

Both men laughed and kissed her on the cheek. "She always was bossy," Tyrone told Tanner.

"I'd better get back to the kitchen if you want your orders on time. Bye."

Tanner chuckled. "That little episode reminded me of how my sister Raine reacts to me or Adrian stepping on her independence."

Ayanna smiled across the table at him. "The newspaper reported she was going to try and duplicate her brothers' successes by acquiring restaurants across the country."

Tanner frowned. "She hates it when anyone compares her to us. Some people act as if all she has to do is ask Dad for a check. She's worked hard, just like the rest of us did to get where we are. Nothing was handed to us. We were given two years to turn a profit or go back to basics and learn why. All of us got it right the first time out."

Tanner's defense of his sister endeared him to Ayanna a little more. She'd grown up with three surrogate brothers in her cousins. "Unfortunately, some people will never look at a woman's accomplishments, her hard work and intelligence, as being equal to a man's," she commented.

His dark head titled to one side. "I hear the voice of experience."

Sighing, she leaned back in her chair. "Although I was better qualified and had more seniority, I was passed over for promotion and then asked to train my male replacement, who didn't know a spread sheet from a debit sheet. It galled me, but I reasoned if I showed them I was a team player, the next time it would benefit me and I would get the promotion."

She made a face. "I was so naïve and so wrong. The second time I was passed over, I handed in my resignation."

"What happened then?"

"I moped, gained ten pounds eating junk food, thought of writing to the EEOC, and then Noah, Tyrone, and Tyrell came to visit one night and offered me a chance to be an integral part of their vision." She glanced around the restaurant that had become her salvation. "I'll always be thankful to them for having enough faith in me to bring me on as a full partner, for trusting me with their money, and especially for rescuing me from a downward spiral of self-pity."

His large hand covered hers. "Everyone needs someone sometimes. I'm just glad they were there."

She wanted to ask if he had ever needed someone, but Sarah arrived with their food and she pulled her hand free.

# FIVE

Ayanna grew increasingly quiet as their meal progressed. Tanner hadn't a clue as to what had caused the change in her, but he intended to find out once they were alone. He paid their bill, leaving a generous tip for their waitress, said good-bye to her cousins, then walked her to his rental. He planned to spend the day and possibly the night with her and, for reasons he hadn't yet figured out, he didn't want Pete to know.

He pulled out of the parking lot. He wasn't used to waiting for answers, but he didn't want her to be the object of the staff's gossip, or have her cousins interfering if the conversation went where he didn't want it going. There it was again, the protective instinct that kept popping up.

Stopping at a red light, his fingers tapping on the steering wheel, Tanner glanced at Ayanna. She quickly looked away. He sensed a vulnerability about her that pulled at him. Without thought, he brushed his knuckles against her cheek. Again he felt her shudder beneath his touch and he flexed his hand. The light turned green and he pulled off.

"Why so quiet?" he asked, unable to hold the questions back any longer.

"Just thinking."

Her answer told him nothing and left him with a vague sense of uneasiness that he was about to get the brush-off. That he wouldn't allow. "I've been to your place. How about coming by tomorrow to see mine?"

She was quiet for so long he guessed the answer. "That's very nice of you, but although the restaurant is closed on Mondays, I go in and work. I won't have time."

Tanner's hand gripped the steering wheel. People were practically lining up to be the first ones to see inside The Rafferty Grand. He had purposely kept the interior a secret to increase the buzz, but Ayanna had turned him down.

Shooting her a quick glance, he hit the freeway ramp with a burst of speed. Traffic into Maryland on I-95 was surprisingly heavy and he had to concentrate on driving. Finding out whatever was bothering her had to wait.

Thirty-five minutes later he pulled into her driveway. She lived in a quiet neighborhood of modest, one-story brick homes. The yards were well maintained. Scalloped tree rings filled with a profusion of flowers seemed a particular favorite of the homeowners.

He got out and went to open her door, but she got out by herself and started up the walkway. Tanner had little time to admire the graceful sway of her hips in a slim black dress that showed her long legs to perfection. He quickly caught up with her and took her arm. "Ayanna, what is it?"

"Nothing," she said, her key already out. "I had a wonderful time, Tanner."

"Do you really expect me to trot on back to the car and drive off?" he asked.

Ayanna had hoped . . . no, that was a lie, and she had lied to herself enough where Tanner was concerned. Tanner excited her as no man

the blind date

321

ever had. He stirred things in her that made her want to forget being safe, forget that caring for a man like Tanner could shatter her.

"A man like you could cause a woman a lot of trouble," she said at last.

He stepped closer. He was pure temptation dressed up in a suit.

"The same could be said of you," he said.

She tried one last time. "You have more experience at this than I do."

There was a subtle shift in his predatory posture. Something flickered in his dark eyes. "I told you not to believe everything you've read about me."

"If I hadn't read one word, I could tell." She shook her head, searching for the words. "It's in the self-assured way you carry yourself, your dogged determination to have your way in everything. Your refuse to listen to 'no' unless you're the one saying it."

His brow puckered. "You see that as bad?"

His genuine puzzlement made her want to throw up her hands. "Tanner, when has a woman ever been able to say no to you and keep saying no if you wanted a yes?"

"Do you really expect me to answer that?" he asked, his mouth tight.

She sighed. "No. Good-bye, Tanner."

"No," he said, then gritted his teeth as if remembering her comment about his refusing to listen to no unless he were saying it. "Could we please go inside and talk?"

Ayanna had lived in the quiet older neighborhood for five years and both she and her mother were acquainted with many of her neighbors. There would be enough questions from her mother as to why Tanner was no longer around without her hearing about their arguing on the front porch. Ayanna stepped aside. "I won't change my mind."

Tanner didn't say anything.

Closing the door, Ayanna waved him to a seat on the white sofa in the living room. She took a seat on the matching Queen Anne chair.

"The way I see it, my reputation has put me at an unfair disadvantage. The only way to change your mind and show you that I'm not ruthless or unconscionable is for you spend more time with me," he reasoned.

"That's not an option."

Tanner stared at her intently. "I want to see you. What would it take for that to happen?"

*Promise me you won't break my heart.* She folded her hands in her lap. Life had no guarantees. She already knew that.

Tanner leaned toward her and his hand closed over hers, drawing her gaze to his. He'd moved so fast she hadn't a chance to object or evade. It probably wouldn't have done her any good, anyway, as he was not a man who yielded or backed down. And honestly would she really want to date a man who wouldn't stand up and fight for what he believed in or wanted? She glanced down at their hands, felt the heat, and experienced the fear. "I need a few days to think about this."

His hand tightened on hers, then relaxed. "You'll call me by Wednesday?"

She almost smiled at his persistence. "Yes."

He turned her hand over and pressed his lips to the inside of her wrist. With a will of its own, her other hand cupped his cheek and felt the incredible softness of his beard. In the next instant his mouth, hot and avid, was on hers, and then they were somehow on the carpeted floor.

As she'd feared and known all along, resistance never entered her mind. When in Tanner's arms, his kisses heated her blood and made her burn. She heard him moan her name, and experienced a thrill of

the blind date

pleasure that she wasn't the only one caught up in the madness. Then she was tumbling headlong into passion, fierce and greedy.

She moaned. Tanner was right. The need was intense.

Tanner lifted his head and stared down into Ayanna's passion-flushed face beneath him. He wanted nothing more than to strip away their clothes—if he could wait that long—and sink into her softness. He knew she wouldn't stop him.

He pulled her to him and rolled over, bringing her with him until she was on top. He muttered when his knee bumped the coffee table.

"Tanner?"

"It's all right, baby. Just give me a minute," he said, stroking her back, making sure his hand went no further than her waist. "Nothing is going to happen."

Ayanna shifted, then stilled when she felt the rigid budge pressed against the notch of her thighs. "You positive?"

A ragged laugh tore from him. Uncertain if he heard regret or fear in her voice, he hugged her. "I control my body. When we make love we'll both be ready."

She buried her face between his neck and shoulder. He took what little comfort he could in the fact that she didn't deny his words.

"What time do you think I could come by tomorrow?"

Slowly, very slowly, he lifted her face with his thumb and finger. "You won't regret it."

"I already know that," she said, holding his gaze.

"Not that I'm not thankful, but what changed your mind?"

Her hand stroked his chest though his white shirt. "You did. You may be ruthless, but you didn't take unfair advantage of the situation."

"I wanted to. I still want to."

Ayanna scrambled off Tanner, inadvertently rubbing against the part of him that wanted to be buried deep in her satin heat. He groaned.

"Did I hurt you?" she asked, still on her knees beside him.

He gave her a look that made her blush.

Gracefully he came to his feet, bringing her with him. "If you can make it around noon, Stephen Pointe, the consulting concept chef, has promised to serve a sampling of the Mediterranean and Asian cuisine he plans to serve in The Jade Room, which will be the largest and most formal of the two restaurants in the hotel."

"I love Asian food. We don't serve it at Leo's and when I bring take-out, Tyrell has a fit," she said.

"Then I'll see you at noon." He kissed on her the cheek and left.

Ayanna watched him get in his car and drive off. She didn't know where tomorrow might lead, but she wasn't running from it any longer. The question was no longer if she'd go to bed with Tanner, it was how soon.

Tanner was whistling when he opened the door to his leased condo. He'd chosen the location for its proximity to the hotel, but also for its view of the Potomac River. Looking out on the river always soothed and calmed him. It wasn't a coincidence that all his hotels were located near the water. Adrian was the same way. They teased Raine about being a land lover. Only one of her three restaurants was near the water.

He was in his bedroom undressing when the phone rang. He hit the speaker button and jerked off his tie. "Tanner."

"About time you made it home. I called twice."

"Hi, Ra." Raine never wasted time with small talk when she had a point to make. "Guess I forgot to turn on the machine when I left this morning."

"Problems with the hotel?" she asked, concern in her soft voice.

He slipped off his Italian loafers; his socks followed. "Things couldn't be better. I was in a rush to pick up Ayanna Hardcastle."

*the blind date*

"Whoa, big brother. Ayanna Hardcastle? And since when have you been in a hurry to pick up any woman?"

Tanner paused in the process of zipping up a pair of jeans that seamlessly flowed over his long legs and hips. He frowned, then smiled, zipping and snapping. "I guess this is a first. How did things go in Atlanta?"

"That crooked manager I dismissed for skimming profits from the previous owner was trying to get the employees to walk out en masse." Her voice took on a hard edge. "Instead of being thankful that Holiday didn't file charges against him but let him get off with restitution, he tried to get back at me."

"Is he still in one piece?"

"Barely, but he won't pull that stunt again and neither will the staff, unless they want to find other jobs. I called a meeting, showed them a stack of applicants waiting to take their place, the same applicants who, if hired, would get a bonus proportionate to profits. They decided they didn't want to quit after all."

He chuckled. Raine was definitely a chip off the old block. Never hesitating to crush the opposition. "I'm glad you're on my team." Pulling a melon-colored polo shirt over his head, he picked up the cordless phone and walked into his home office. His long, narrow feet sank into the ecru carpet.

"That's the same thing Dad said this morning."

Their father was probably on the golf course bragging to his buddies about Raine's victory as they spoke. It was embarrassing at times, but their father always said telling the truth wasn't bragging. Tanner hit the speaker button on the office phone and deactivated the hand-held one.

"We'll celebrate when you come back. I already figured out why we had reservations at Leo's." He sat at the U-shaped workstation and booted up the computer.

"So give."

Tanner gave her a full report on Leo's in glowing terms. "It's a great supper club. Ayanna and her cousins have a right to be proud."

"Any vulnerabilities?"

Tanner scrolled though his e-mail for the weekly reports from each hotel. "Nothing that you have to contend with in Atlanta or any of your locations. Leo's is on a one-way street and a couple of times accidents have tied up traffic and cut down on business. But the restaurant has been packed each time I've been there."

"So Leo's *does* have a weak spot," she mused.

Tanner's attention wavered as he read the "Urgent" e-mail from Sidney Yates, his executive manager of The Rafferty House in Charleston. Tanner reached for the second phone on his desk and keyed in the number. "Have to run, Ra. I'll call you back."

"No need. You've given me the information I wanted. Thanks."

Thinking she meant a report on how to duplicate Leo's success, he gave his full attention to the problem in Charleston. "Yates," Tanner said when the executive manager answered her cell phone on the second ring. "Rafferty here. What is it, why couldn't you solve it, and why didn't you call?"

Yates didn't falter as she gave Tanner the details. A guest had slipped and fallen in the gift shop because of another guest's spilled drink on the floor. The incident raised suspicion in the executive manager's mind when the young woman, although claiming to be in a lot of pain and unable to stand on her own, refused to let the hotel doctor check her. She'd left with the assistance of the man she was with to seek private care.

"I want Slaughter to do a check on everyone involved," Tanner said, referring to the head of security for the Rafferty enterprise.

"He's already on it, and he's checking the computer for similar incidents."

the blind date

"Good. Now, why didn't you contact me sooner?" The episode happened when the shop opened at twelve. It was past three.

"I tried. You didn't answer at home and your cell was off."

Tanner muttered one succinct word. Not only had he forgotten to turn on his answering machine before leaving, he'd forgotten to turn his cell back on when he left Leo's. It had always aggravated him when people's cells went off in the theater or in restaurants. He'd been so concerned about Ayanna's sudden quietness, he hadn't thought about it. He had never overlooked something like that in the past.

"It won't happen again," was all he said. He didn't accept excuses or make them. "Keep me posted."

"Yes, sir."

"Yates?"

"Yes?"

"Good job."

"Thank you." There was relief in her voice.

Tanner hung up the phone, got up, and walked over to the window. Ayanna could cause him a lot of trouble and it seemed he was only beginning to realize how much.

# SIX

Ayanna spotted Tanner the moment she rounded the street corner that Monday afternoon. Hands stuffed into the uncuffed pants of his double-breasted olive suit, he was pacing the sidewalk in front of his hotel. She didn't have to check her watch again to know she was ten minutes late. Since she disliked waiting on people, she hurried over to him, words of apology already running through her mind.

When she was fifteen feet away, his dark head lifted abruptly and he stared directly at her, almost as if he had sensed her presence. The impact of all that intensity directed at her caused her steps to momentarily falter, her breath to quicken. What was it about this particular man that caused her body to react so strongly?

While she was contemplating the answer to that question, his hands came out of his pockets and he started toward her. All the people on the busy street seemed to disappear; the sounds of traffic faded away.

He was a couple of feet away when she blurted, "I had trouble finding a parking spot."

His expression didn't change as he took her arm and started back. "I should have sent the car for you."

"That's not necessary," she said, still unsure of his mood. She was used to seeing a glint of humor in his eyes. Today there was none.

the blind date

"The laundry truck came in early and I had to check the order before I left."

He pushed opened the glass door. "Welcome to The Rafferty Grand."

Ayanna's heart experienced a little pang. His words had all the warmth of an ice cube. "Tanner, if you're busy we can do this another time."

"I invited you," he said, continuing through the lobby.

Ayanna dug in her heels on the light blue Italian stone flooring in front of the receptionist desk. "Obviously you regret it."

Tanner looked at her, his mouth tight. "There was a problem at The Rafferty House in Charleston yesterday."

Instantly contrite, Ayanna placed her hand on his chest. "Was? Does that mean it's all right now?"

"Yes." His mouth was a narrow line.

"So why are you still upset about it?" Ayanna titled her head to one side.

He bought the full force of his gaze back to her. "Because it could have gone the other way if the executive manager hadn't been on her toes, and the head of security hadn't been able to find out the incident was a scam."

"I'm still trying to figure out why you're beating yourself over the head about it," she said. "You wouldn't have them working for you if they weren't competent enough to take care of problems."

"Because I was unreachable," he said, derision in his voice. "I have always prided myself on being available to the people who work for and with me."

Slowly Ayanna began to put everything together. "You weren't available because you were with me." It was a statement, not a question.

"I didn't turn on the answering machine when I left my place, and I failed to turn my cell back on after we left Leo's," he stated flatly.

"I can see how much that bothers you and I have the perfect solution. Good-bye, Tanner." She spun on her heels.

"No!" he said, grabbing her arm. The one word in the high-ceilinged space went through the room like a pistol shot, drawing the attention of the workers. "You can't do that."

"It was bound to end sooner than later."

"Says who?" he challenged, his eyes taking on a dangerous glint.

Ayanna was about to reply when she noticed that it had grown quiet. She glanced around and flushed at seeing they were the center of attention. Worse, a few feet behind Tanner and to the left stood a thin, middle-aged man with a neatly trimmed graying mustache wearing a chef's uniform. "I think your chef wants to speak to you."

"He can wait until we're finished." Tanner didn't even look away from her.

Ayanna's saw the chef's eyes flash. Temperamental, just like Tyrell. If Tanner wasn't careful he'd be minus a concept chef.

Sidestepping Tanner, she extended her hand to the glaring man. "Ayanna Hardcastle. Are you the wonderful concept chef Mr. Rafferty told me who is going to make my taste buds weep with joy?"

The man beamed and clasped her hand. "Stephen Pointe. Everything is ready." He looked at Tanner and his voice cooled. "If Mr. Rafferty is agreeable?"

"Of course he is," she answered for Tanner. "Why don't I walk with you and you can tell me about the delicacies you've prepared."

The chef smiled warmly at her, turning his back on Tanner. "Delighted. This way."

Ayanna walked beside the chef, a prickling sensation in her back. Tanner looked as if he could chew nails. She was trying to help, but she wouldn't put it past him to fire the chef and toss both them out of his hotel.

the blind date

331

Tanner wanted to toss the chef out the nearest window. Unfortunately, it was sealed shut. The scrawny man was fawning over Ayanna as he personally prepared her plate, all the time chatting with her as if they had known each other for years. The worse offense was when he took a seat at the table Tanner had ordered to be set with fresh cut flowers, linen, and sterling silver.

Tanner knew that his management staff was tiptoeing around him as if he were a ticking time bomb, but he couldn't seem to help it. He wasn't particularly surprised when, one by one, they quickly prepared their plates and left. If he hadn't already told them that he expected a report on the dishes served, he suspected the majority of them would have taken one look at him and left.

Ayanna certainly didn't appear concerned by the prospect of angering him, or of not seeing him again. She was sampling everything the chef put on her plate, then rhapsodizing over it as if she had never tasted anything so good. Tanner hadn't bothered to fix a plate. The one his executive secretary prepared for him sat untouched on a table several feet from Ayanna and Pointe. Tanner hadn't trusted himself to sit any closer.

"Not another bite, please." Ayanna placed her hand on her flat stomach and smiled at the chef. "You will have people begging to get a reservation. Your alliance with The Rafferty Grand will ensure that The Jade Room will create one of the most exciting dining experiences in the East." She tipped her head. "My compliments to you and Mr. Rafferty."

Pointe's thin nose tilted upward. He folded his arms. "I am in demand in my own right."

"Of course, but every star needs a stage, the right setting in which to create." She glanced around the high-ceilinged room with silk wall coverings and authentic art. "You have it here. A feast for the eyes is as important as a feast for the stomach. You and Mr. Rafferty have worked together to ensure both."

Slowly the chef's arms unfolded. "You are a wise woman." He leaned closer. "If you ever get tired of him, I'm available."

Ayanna blinked.

"That's enough," Tanner snapped, striding over to their table. "Ayanna, we need to talk."

The chef winked at Ayanna. Apparently he had wanted to get in one last jab at Tanner.

"Ayanna?" Tanner repeated, his hand on the back of her chair.

She extended her hand to the smug chef. She hoped he learned before it was too late that it wasn't wise to bait a tiger, especially when your hand was in its mouth. "Thank you again."

Pointe took her hand. "You have a standing invitation to The Jade Room. I hope to see you often." Inclining his head, he walked toward the back of the restaurant and disappeared through a swinging door.

Ayanna made herself look Tanner in the eye and prayed her voice didn't crack. "Tanner, I don't think there's anything to talk about and I need to get back to work."

His black eyes narrowed, then he turned and walked toward the open door. Ayanna bit her lip to keep from calling him back, thinking it was for the best. But instead of leaving, he closed both massive ten-foot double doors. She heard the distinct click of a lock.

"You're not leaving until we settle the issue. You're not walking out on me," he told her. He started toward her, a predator stalking its pray, a renegade who followed no rules but his own. It took all of her courage not to back up. He kept coming until he was so close she could see her reflection in his dark eyes.

"I thought nothing could bother me more than letting you come between me and my work until I was faced with the possibility of never seeing you again." His hands settled on her shoulders. "While

I was trying to deal with that unthinkable possibility, Pointe was cozying up to you. I was so busy plotting his demise that I didn't realize until minutes ago that, despite my poor behavior, you were trying to pacify him to help me." He took the necessary steps until the heat of their bodies mingled. "You're an incredible woman. Tell me what I have to do to see you again."

Ayanna stared up into his face. No one had to tell her Tanner didn't ask for second chances or admit to being wrong very often. They were both dealing with emotions that were new and frightening to them. She could walk or do something she hadn't dared in a very long time. She took a deep breath and said, "I never did get a tour."

He hugged her. "Thank you," he said, as the chef reappeared, carrying a plate.

"Now that you've stopped sulking, perhaps you will taste the food I worked since dawn to prepare," Stephen said.

Tanner took the peace offering, but his arm remained around Ayanna. "Ayanna has to get back to work and I haven't shown her around."

The chef retrieved the eighteen-karat gold-trimmed plate. "Then show her. By the time you finish I will have prepared Ms. Hardcastle a few take-aways. Food should not be wasted."

"Tyrell, my cousin and the chef at Leo's, will have a fit. Please don't forget the steamed rice, the clams with black bean sauce, and the dim sum."

Both men laughed.

Ayanna had been right in her prediction of Tyrell's behavior when she came into Leo's with a shopping bag half full of food. She had sailed on past him, ignoring his protests. Tanner was coming over around seven that night to help her finish off the food. All she could think about was nibbling on him.

Grinning, she slipped the food into one of Leo's oversized refrigerators, then went to her office to work. Somehow she made herself not glance at the clock every few minutes, but it was hard. By five she was heading out the front door. After a quick stop at a corner flower shop, she was on her way home, formulating in her mind a romantic evening. She didn't know where the relationship was going, but she wasn't frightened anymore.

Arriving home, she put the food away, lit candles, then went to take her bath and get dressed. Instead of setting the dining room table, she prepared a place for them in front of the red brick fireplace, then lit fat white vanilla-scented candles on the hearth and brick mantel.

Her doorbell rang exactly at seven, and she opened the door before the musical chime had ended. Her heart skittered. "Hi," she greeted, her voice slightly husky.

"Hi," he said, closing the door behind him and taking her in his arms. His mouth unerringly found hers. It was a long, leisurely kiss that made her body hum. Lifting his head, he stared down at her. "You taste better every time I kiss you."

"So do you," she said. Watching his eyes darken, she knew if they didn't eat now they might not in a long time. "Come on, I have everything ready." Taking him by the hand, she led him into the den and gestured for him to sit on the blanket in front of a sky-blue linen tablecloth. "I thought it would be cozier this way."

"Works for me." Unbuttoning his cream-colored, lightweight sports coat, he sat on the floor and drew his long legs under him. When Ayanna started to the place across from him, he caught her hand and tugged. "You're not moving out of arm's reach."

She moistened her lips. His gaze followed and heat spiked though her. "It might be wiser."

"I'd still want to make love to you," he said bluntly, feeling her pulse leap beneath his fingertips. "But I can wait, now that I know you're willing to give us a chance. I want you close to me."

She sank down beside him. "I told you a woman couldn't say no to you."

Palming her face with hands that weren't quite steady, he turned her toward him. "When I'm with you, when I look at you, I can't remember another woman."

The words were said with such aching sincerity that tears came to her eyes. It would be so easy and so very foolish to forget this wasn't forever. "Oh, Tanner."

"If you keep looking at me like that I'm going to kiss you again, and I'm not sure if I'll be able to turn you loose until I've made you mine."

Ayanna warred within herself. She wanted to make love with Tanner, but it was too soon. She picked up his plate. "Everything is good. You're fortunate to have Stephen."

"So he keeps telling me," Tanner said without rancor as he took his plate. "I was afraid Tyrell might toss all this out."

"He wanted to." She leaned forward to pick up her plate and gave a yelp when Tanner drew her into his lap. "We only need one plate. Now, say grace, then you can tell me about your day while we eat."

She stared at Tanner. He stared back.

She could attempt to get off his lap or argue about it, but in the end she'd lose because she would be fighting against herself. There was no place else she'd rather be. She enjoyed looking at him, touching him, being with him. She even admired his relentless determination to have his way.

He'd never be an easy man. He was a renegade, but he touched a responsive cord within her no other man ever had. Bowing her head, she blessed their food.

# SEVEN

Tanner and Ayanna went to a political fund-raising event on Tuesday, a gallery reception on Wednesday, and a charity function on Thursday. By Friday he was getting polite inquiries about Ayanna from business associates and acquaintances. Oddly, he wasn't pleased. He wanted to keep their relationship quiet. He was used to being in the spotlight, but he wasn't sure how Ayanna felt about it.

From the conversation he'd overheard her having with Sheri, he knew Ayanna hadn't been dating lately. He only had to look at her or recall the number of men trying to get her attention when they were out to know that it was by choice. On the other hand, the newspapers had made much of his romantic liaisons, and his past escapades were making it difficult to gain her trust. He didn't want her to think of herself as just another woman in a long line of them. She definitely wasn't. Her vulnerability and intelligence, as much as her beauty, drew him to her.

He'd never cared about what others thought of him in the past, but with Ayanna it was different. It wasn't just so they could be intimate, although if he didn't make love to her soon he might go out of his mind, it was because her opinion of him mattered. He wanted her to be proud of him when she introduced him to her family and friends.

*the blind date*

He was doing his best to go slow and give her time to learn to have faith in him and herself, but it was interfering with his concentration and thus the opening of the hotel. He kept catching himself thinking of her instead of working, like now.

Fingers steepled beneath his chin, he leaned back in the desk chair in an office cluttered with a jumble of sample china patterns, swatches of bright fabric, and objets d'art that he'd promised the interior designer he'd have narrowed down by six that afternoon, and he knew if he didn't get his act together he wouldn't make the deadline.

He glanced at the Seth Thomas clock on his desk. Five-fifteen. It was going to be a very long two hours and forty-five minutes before he picked up Ayanna to take her to a movie. Shaking his head, he picked up the fabric swatches for the bedspreads and curtains in the suites and began flipping through them. He hadn't been to a movie in years. Maybe they could sit in the back and he could get in some serious necking.

He frowned. It was becoming harder and harder for him to pull away. In a dark theater he might lose it.

The phone rang, interrupting his troubled thoughts. Since he had asked his secretary to hold his calls, unless important, he picked it up. "Rafferty here."

"Tanner, this is George Marcel. How are you?"

Rafferty immediately placed the ring of swatches on his desk and came to attention. Marcel didn't make idle calls. He had ocean-front property on Hilton Head that Tanner had been trying to buy for three years. "Fine. I'm about to open another hotel. I hope you'll be able to attend."

"Sounds as if you're busy, but I'm hoping you can come down for a few days," he said. "I think it's time we talked again."

Slaughter had already reported that Marcel had lost heavily in the stock market, and he'd compounded the problem by borrowing money from his company, which he promptly lost to more bad investments. He was in financial quicksand.

Excitement rushed though Tanner, but his voice was cool. "What date were you looking at?"

"Tomorrow," came the quick reply. "I'll have my housekeeper prepare a room and we can play golf and discuss ways to keep both of us happy."

Tanner closed his eyes, cursed fate, and said the only thing he could: "I'll see you tomorrow."

Ayanna had just finished her bubble bath and was smoothing on lotion when she heard the phone ring in the adjoining bedroom. She ignored it as Tanner would be there soon to pick her up for their date. Humming softly, she pulled on her terry-cloth robe and went to her closet.

It was difficult to believe they'd only known each other for a short period of time. Whenever she talked with her mother and Sheri, both were quick to point out what a fabulous catch Tanner was. Ayanna always reminded them that catching him wasn't the problem, it was holding on. Many women had tried and failed.

They always laughed and disregarded her trepidations. Neither appeared to see the pitfalls of caring for a man like Tanner, a man with a love 'em and leave 'em reputation. It didn't help that he had to travel a great deal. And whenever he went, woman would be waiting. The only way Ayanna could handle the situation was to guard her heart and not think about his past or about moving on. She was taking their relationship one day at a time.

The answering machine clicked on as she drew out a long floral-print dress. Noah's voice asked the caller to leave a message.

"Please be at home, Ayanna. This is my second call. Your cousins don't know where you are. I want to see you before I leave."

*Tanner.* She whirled, jerking up the receiver. "I'm here. Please tell me you're joking."

"I wish I were. I'm at the front door; please let me in."

Hanging up the phone, she rushed to the front door and jerked it open. In an instant he was closing the door behind him. He gathered her in his arms, his mouth greedily devouring hers. She kissed him back with the same hunger.

"You smell good and taste better." He nibbled on her ear.

"I just got out of the tub," she said, arching her neck to give him greater access.

He groaned and tightened his hold. "Guess that's why you didn't hear the doorbell. If I didn't have to go, that robe would already be off."

She shivered. "When will you be back?"

He lifted his head. "I'm not sure. The owner of a prime piece of property is finally ready to discuss terms. I have to go. But before my plane leaves in the morning I have several loose ends to tie up."

She understood the trip was necessary. She just didn't like it very much. "You'll probably be up most of the night."

"I've already had my secretary call several of my key people to meet me in my office by seven," he told her. "I don't suppose you'd consider going with me to Hilton Head for the weekend?"

Much as she wanted to, she pushed herself out of his arms, then picked up a tapestry throw pillow from the sofa and hugged it to her chest. "I can't. I guess you have to take a lot of unexpected business trips."

"Occasionally," he said, frowning at her.

She nodded. "You'd better get going. You'll be cutting it close as it is to make it back by seven. Thanks for coming by when you could have called."

He didn't move. "Did I miss something here?"

Ayanna hugged the pillow tighter to her churning stomach. "I respect what you do, but my father was gone a great deal. His work came first. I've always promised myself that I'd never be in a relationship like that."

"I can't change who I am," he said, his expression unfathomable.

"I didn't ask you to," she said.

"Didn't you?" he said, his voice taking on a bit of an edge. "My time isn't my own, just like yours isn't with Leo's. We both do what we have to do. There's nothing I can do about that."

"Would you if you could?" she said before she could stop herself.

"Would you?" he countered, his gaze intense.

Leo's had been her salvation. Tanner's hotels were his passion. It was impossible to weigh one more heavily than the other. "No. Have a good trip."

"How can I when you're letting it come between us?" he said, his voice tight.

"I don't want it to," she whispered.

"Then don't." He took the pillow from her, tossing it back on the sofa, and took her in his arms. "If it wasn't important I wouldn't go."

How many times had she heard her father say those same words? Without another thought she repeated what her mother always said, "Be safe and hurry back."

His eyes were dark and narrowed. "I will. I'm calling you the minute I know I'm on the way back. Pointe will cook us another dinner."

She tried to smile. "I'll be waiting."

"If I kiss you again I may not let go," he said, his voice tight with suppressed longing.

"Have a safe trip," she said.

"Good-bye." Turning on his heels, he opened the door and walked to the waiting limo.

the blind date

Ayanna watched the car pull away from the curb, then went to her room and sat on the side of the bed. This was not how she had planned to spend her evening. But if she continued to see Tanner she might as well get used to spending the evening alone. The phone rang, interrupting her thoughts. She planned to ignore the call until she heard her mother's cheery voice.

"Hi, sweetheart. I know you're getting dressed for your date with Tanner, but I wanted to see if you wanted to go shopping with me in the morning. It will probably be late when you get in so call—"

"Hi, Mother."

"Ayanna, I didn't expect you to pick up," her mother said, surprise in her voice.

She pulled her legs under her. "Tanner had to cancel. He's leaving in the morning on a business trip so he has to work tonight."

"I know you're disappointed, but at least he called," her mother consoled.

"He came by," Ayanna told her, no happier about the situation.

"That was very considerate of him. Your father was the same way," her mother said. "He didn't always get a chance to come home, of course, but he always called. I wasn't always happy, but I knew he was a policeman when I fell in love with him."

"Dad loved what he did."

"Yes, he did, and he was good at it. He had a very high percentage of solved cases," she said proudly. "He was dedicated, honest, and hard working. It always amazed me when some of the other wives became upset when their husbands had to break engagements. A lot of the officers' marriages broke up needlessly because of their work. The women were upset by the same qualities in their men that had attracted them in the first place. Isn't that silly?"

Ayanna's brows knitted as she remembered her conversation with Tanner. At the time, she had thought she was being reasonable about his out-of-town trips, but now she wasn't so sure. Even if she could, she didn't want to change him. Her head fell forward. In her own selfish need to come first, she had forgotten the type of man Tanner was.

"Ayanna, are you there?"

"I was about to become one of those silly women, but you probably already guessed that," Ayanna said in a wry tone.

"The thought had crossed my mind. You hid your disappointment from your father when he couldn't make some of your school functions, but not from me."

"But he always made a point to ask me the next day how it went and take time, just for the two of us," Ayanna said softly. How had she forgotten that?

"He loved you," her mother said.

Despite his missing school events or extracurricular activities, Ayanna had never doubted her father's devotion. He wanted to make the city a safer, better place for his family and the community. His job hadn't been easy, but he had never complained or shirked his duty. He was a man of principle. Just like Tanner. "Mama, you're the best mother in the world," Ayanna said, making her way to her lingerie drawer.

Her mother chuckled. "That's nice to hear."

"I'll call you in the morning." Juggling the phone, she shimmied into her panties and snapped her bra. "Right now I have to go apologize."

"Tell Tanner to have a nice trip."

"I will." Ayanna stepped into her dress. "Bye and thanks." Hanging up the phone, she zipped up her dress, picked up her purse, and hurried out the door.

"Mr. Rafferty, the security guard says Ms. Hardcastle is downstairs requesting entrance," his secretary said, holding her slender hand over the receiver. "Would you like for me to go down and escort her up?"

Tanner couldn't keep the surprise from his face, or the unease that followed. "Thank you, Mrs. Cater. I'll take care of it." Tanner rose from the head of the conference table where seven of his top executives were seated. "Please continue. I'll be back shortly."

"Very good, sir," his secretary said, but Tanner was already heading for the door. He hit the stairs at a fast clip. If Ayanna came to break up with him, she could save her breath. He stepped off the bottom rung of the curved stairwell and started for the lobby. The instant he rounded the corner he saw her through the glass entry door. Her back was to him, and she was speaking to the security guard. The young man was grinning like a loon and standing much too close, Tanner thought with a savage twist of jealously.

He came to an abrupt halt. He had never been jealous of anyone or anything in his life. He searched his mind for another word to describe how he felt and couldn't find one. Disturbed, he stared at Ayanna's slim back, her sleek body in a soft dress that molded itself to her shapely curves with each breath of wind. Need clamored though him. He wanted her as he'd never wanted before. Ayanna was *his.*

The statement somehow smoothed the wrinkles from his forehead. He was just being his usual possessive self. He wasn't jealous. Satisfied, he started toward them again.

As if sensing him, she turned while he was still several feet away. He didn't expect the breathtaking smile on her face or her excited waving. Relief and pleasure rushed through him.

He couldn't get to her fast enough. He pushed open the heavy glass door and was hit again by how beautiful and desirable she was. "Hi, Ayanna."

"I know you're busy but I wanted to talk to you if you have the time," she said, smiling up at him.

Francis Ray

344

"Come with me," he said, leading her to a little alcove off the lobby. The area was empty, the lighting low and intimate.

"I came to apologize for my poor behavior. It was selfish of me not to want you to go. After you've acquired that property, maybe you'll invite me down."

"You can count on it," he said, settling his large hands on her waist, bringing her closer. "I thought you were coming to tell me to take a hike. You surprised me."

She rested her hands on his chest and enjoyed the unsteady beat of his heart. "I don't think people do that very often."

"They don't," he muttered as if she had insulted him.

"Let's see if I can do it again." She put her mouth on his, letting her body sink against him, soften against him as she took his mouth in a kiss that drugged his senses and make him forget everything but the woman in his arms. Their tongues touched, tasted, savored, and greedily sought more.

Feeling the edges of sanity blur, Tanner fought for control and barely won. Lifting his head, he stared down at her flushed face, her slighted parted lips, wet and swollen from his mouth, and cursed Marcel once again for making the trip to Hilton Head necessary. His breathing labored, his body and loins clamoring for something he could not give, he leaned his forehead against hers. "Right now I'd like to take you to bed and forget I have eight people in my office waiting for me."

"Me too."

In her face he saw desire equal to his own. "You're certainly making it hard for me to go."

Her trembling hand cupped his jaw. "I wanted to make it easier."

"I realize that." He turned his head, kissing her palm, then drew her tightly into his arms again. "The problem is, I don't want to let you go."

the blind date

She pressed closer, feeling the heat, the hardness of his arousal, and the unwavering strength of his arms around her. "They're waiting."

"In a minute." His hand made lazy circles on her back while he breathed in her unique scent, then he let his hand continue down to cup her hips against that part of him that ached to be inside of her. He moaned in sweet torture. If he didn't stop now he wouldn't until after he'd made her his.

"Is there anything I can help you with?" she asked, rubbing her cheek over the spot where his heart beat rapidly. "Do you need me to make a run for food or coffee?"

He kissed her on the side of the neck, inhaled her scent, and wished he could wallow in it, in her. His teeth closed delicately on her ear. She shivered.

"D-Does that mean you're hungry?"

His ragged laughter sent more shivers rippling through her.

"T-Tanner?"

He heard the hunger of that one word. Now wasn't the time to unleash it. He stepped back. "Go home while I have the strength to let you."

"I wish I could help so you could finish up earlier," she said.

"Thanks. We're trying to decide on vendors...." His voice trailed off and he stared down at her. "Maybe you can help." Taking her by the hand he started for his office. "That place where you ordered Judge Wyman's basket, could they do customized candy?"

"Sweet Temptation can do anything with chocolate. Julia Ferrington-Braxton is the owner. She has three stores. She came up with the idea of doing the basket for lovers that we sell at Leo's." Ayanna hurried to keep up with Tanner as he climbed the curved staircase. "She met her husband Chase, a Texas Ranger, on sort of a blind date at Leo's."

About to open the door to his office, Tanner paused and stared down at Ayanna. "It's a smart man who sees what he wants and goes after it."

"What about what the woman wants?" Ayanna asked, her brow delicately arched.

He answered without hesitation. "Since a smart man would only be attracted to a smart, intelligent woman, she, of course, would see the advantage of dating him."

She shook her head. "How many years were you on the debate team?"

He chuckled. "All though high school and college."

"Figures," she said, a smile reluctantly tugging the corners of her mouth.

Still smiling, he opened the door and escorted her inside. The men in their tailored shirts stood as his secretary's eyes narrowed behind her tortoise-shell eyeglasses. Tanner had left cranky and had come back smiling. All eyes went to the stunning and happy woman by his side, then to their joined hands. Tanner didn't bring his lady friends to business meetings. Speculation ran rampant in their minds, but graciousness was their bread and butter. The executive manager immediately gave up his seat next to Tanner and moved to the end of the table.

The introductions were quickly made and the reason for Ayanna's presence explained. For the next thirty minutes she gave them the names of several reputable vendors she dealt with who met her demands for high quality and dependability. Although price wasn't an issue to Tanner, she gave the business manager facts and figures, which would be multiplied many times over for the one-hundred-forty-six-room hotel.

Tanner listened approvingly. Ayanna knew her stuff. "Any chance you might leave Leo's and come to work for me?"

She smiled at the teasing glint in his eyes. "Thank, but no thanks."

He stood and reached for her hand. She immediately placed hers in his and came to her feet. "I'll see Ms. Hardcastle to her car."

Saying good-bye, she left, her steps slowing as they made their way to the lobby. She stopped and faced him a few feet from the door where the security guard waited. "I'll miss you."

"Not as much as I'll miss you."

He pulled her into his arms and kissed her. After a long moment he stepped away, his eyes fierce. "I'm coming over as soon as I get back."

Ayanna understood. The next time they were together they would make love. Her body burned. "I'll be waiting." Kissing him on the chin, she walked away on shaky legs.

# EIGHT

Tanner had a bumpy flight and a miserable night. By the time his plane landed, he was in a foul mood. None of his irritation showed when Marcel greeted him, however. Nor did it later that afternoon when Tanner kept missing putts on the golf course. The higher his score, the more amicable his host became. By the time they reached the eighteenth hole, they were deep into discussion. Winning apparently put Marcel in a good frame of mind, but he was no pushover.

Tanner, his disposition unimproved, retired to his room that night, judging it would take at least a couple of days longer to cinch the deal. Deciding that calling Ayanna would make him miss her more and thus worsen his irritability, he woke his secretary from a sound sleep and gave her three specific requests. Finished, he went to take a shower. A very cold shower.

Ayanna couldn't believe it. After three very long days and tortuous nights, Tanner had gotten the property and returned. Rushing into her bedroom after taking a quick bath, she threw a glance at the clock on the bedside table. 4:48 A.M. He'd be there in less than twenty-five minutes.

Quickly she slipped on the new peach-colored silk charmeuse

pajama bottoms, then the dyed-to-match lace bed jacket over a mesh sleeveless baby tee with lattice edging. She'd debated a long time over the lingerie, wanting to appear alluring without being too eager, then groaned. She had passed eager days ago. She'd probably rip his clothes off.

Shaking her head, she picked up her comb. She had just completed her first sweep through her curly hair when the doorbell rang. *Tanner.* The comb fell from her hand. Her heart thudded. She didn't think about how her hair was tangled and in disarray, that she wore no makeup, that he was earlier than she expected, that the intimate setting with candles and soft music was not ready. She just ran to the front door and jerked it open.

In his white shirt and jeans he looked good enough to gulp down whole.

They reached for each other at the same time. Their greeting was a long, hot kiss that left both shaking and eager for more.

"I missed you," she said, her arms still around his neck.

"I didn't think it possible, but you're more beautiful than ever," he said softly.

*Beautiful.* Her eyes rounded as she suddenly recalled her condition. Her nose probably outshone Rudolph's. She pushed away his arms and took another backward step. "Please have a seat. I'll be right back." Without waiting for a reply, she tore off.

In her bedroom, she saw the rumpled sheets from another restless night of thinking about Tanner and decided to straighten them up first. Smoothing out the wrinkles in the pale blue Egyptian cotton sheets, she lamented that she hadn't had time to put on the new ones or spray the sheets with perfume.

"Why bother?"

Ayanna jerked around. Tanner stood in the bedroom door. Slow and purposeful, he started toward her.

"You got my flowers, I see."

"Thank you," she whispered. Saturday she'd received a white basket overflowing with exotic flowers. She'd put them on the marble top of her chest of drawers across from her bed. Sunday she'd been surprised to receive white roses in a heavy crystal vase. She couldn't imagine how he'd had them delivered. She went to sleep breathing in their lush scent and wishing Tanner was there. "They're beautiful."

"This is for today."

Ayanna's eyes widened and her mouth formed a silent O as Tanner lifted a large basket wrapped in iridescent cellophane from behind his back. She recognized it immediately as the one Leo's sold in partnership with Sweet Temptation. Inside were lush strawberries dipped in white and dark chocolate, vintage champagne, a corkscrew, and two flutes and monogrammed napkins with the initial *L*. She had been so intent on him that she hadn't noticed anything else.

"Should I open the champagne here, or do you want to go into the kitchen or den?" he asked.

Once again he was giving her a choice, but she had already made it. She sat on the side of the bed. "Here is fine."

"Thank goodness." Sitting beside her, he reached for the bottle of chilled champagne.

Ayanna smiled and plucked the glasses from the bed of shredded lavender paper. "Prepared, I see."

"I was afraid my hands wouldn't be steady enough," he admitted as the cork gave a loud pop.

The stems wobbled in her hands. Tanner was a strong, self-assured man. Hearing him admit she affected him in such a way touched her deeply.

He filled both glasses, set the bottle back in the basket, then stared down at her. "To no more lonely nights."

She shivered. "To no more lonely nights." Their glasses clinked, their eyes locked on each other as they drank.

Tanner took her glass and set it with his on the nightstand. Standing, he dimmed the overhead lights, casting the room in intimate shadows, then came back to sit beside her. He slipped free the first satin-covered button on her bed jacket. "What time do you have to be at work?"

Her breathing quickened as he slipped the jacket off and kissed her bare shoulder. "After you called, I phoned Noah and told them not to expect me today."

"You just saved my sanity." His hot, greedy mouth fastened on hers as they tumbled back on the queen-sized brass bed, then he rolled, taking her with him, until he was stretched out on top of her.

With a hand that refused to steady, Tanner pulled the tee over her head. Her breasts were full and high, the nipples pouting. "You're exquisite."

Ayanna pushed up his shirt to find a chest ridged with muscles. "You're gorgeous." She put her mouth to his nipple and felt him shudder, then she was on her back and he was staring down at her.

"My turn."

Ayanna felt the incredible heat and hardness of his body aligned with hers, watched in excitement and fascination as his dark head lowered. She heard him murmur her name just before his lips fastened on her aching nipple. She arched on the bed with a sharp moan of pleasure, her nails sinking into his shoulders.

He tugged on the hard peak, then the other, until she withered on the bed. When the pleasure built to a point she wanted to scream, his hand moved down her flushed body, finding the most secretive and intimate part of her. She cried out again and then again as he brought them together in a single thrust.

Nothing had ever prepared her for this moment. It was wild and glorious and frightening. She felt herself losing control, but even as her mind shied away, her hips lifted to take him in deeper and deeper.

"Come with me."

The raspy voice, strained with passion and need, lured her as much as his body. She couldn't deny either. She let go and felt herself spinning out of control, but even as she did she knew he would be there with her.

Tanner stared down at Ayanna, her face damp with perspiration, her nostrils delicately flared, her lips curved slightly upward, and realized she had surprised him once again. He hadn't thought making love to her would negate the jagged claws of need, but he did think it would lessen. He had been wrong.

His hand swept away the sheet he'd pulled over her after they had made love. She was slim, elegant, lovely. His body stirred and hardened. He wanted her with a fierceness that shook him to the core. Possessing her body wasn't enough. What would be? Her eyelashes fluttered, then lifted. The smile that had been forming on her mouth blossomed. Something tugged at him, a curious warmth. Possession might not be enough, but it would do until he figured out what was. Pulling her into his arms, he joined their bodies again.

Ayanna awoke sprawled across Tanner's muscled chest, her leg sandwiched between his. Sunlight shone though the sheer curtains in her bedroom. Closing her eyes, she sighed in contentment as she felt Tanner's hand stroke her back.

"It's almost ten. You want me to fix you breakfast?"

Her mouth curved into a winsome smile at the thought of having a renegade prepare breakfast. "Would it be edible?"

"Let's find out." In one smooth motion he had her in his arms and was striding toward the bathroom.

*the blind date*

Tightening her arms around his neck, she kissed his chin. "If you're cooking breakfast, why am I getting up?"

He set her down in the shower stall and began adjusting the water temperature. "Because I want you near me."

Her heart melted all over again. Looking at the hard muscles of his conditioned body made her shiver. She loved him deeply, irrevocably. There was no going back.

He turned, letting the spray of water pummel his broad back. "Then, too, I have this fantasy of us in the shower." Taking scented soap from a dish, he worked up lather and began to spread it over her breasts, her stomach.

Her eyes drifted shut as his hands went to the inside of her thighs. "T-Tanner. I don't think I can take this."

"Let's see," he said, proceeding to cover every inch of her body with lather. When she was weak with longing, he put her arms around his neck, wrapped her legs around his waist, and drove into her moist heat.

Ayanna closed around him, then melted, quivered. Tanner stroked her until she was clinging to him again, taking and giving pleasure. The next time they finished together.

Breakfast was champagne, chocolate-covered strawberries and whipped cream, French toast, bacon, and grits. Tanner had never tasted anything better. "Thanks for helping."

In jeans and a knit top, Ayanna smiled at Tanner sitting next to her at the kitchen table. "You don't know the first thing about cooking."

"But I would have tried," he said, holding out a strawberry dipped in whipped cream.

Too touched to speak, Ayanna bit into the lush fruit. She was thoroughly enjoying getting acquainted with the tender, caring side of Tanner, which was even more captivating than the renegade. It would be impossible not to love him. But could he love her back?

He frowned. "What's the matter?"

She shook her head. She wasn't going to let doubts ruin their time together. "I'm just glad you're home."

Scooting his armless side chair around, he picked her up by the waist, settled her in his lap, then tucked her head beneath his chin. "I started to call the first night, but I knew if I heard your voice it would make the loneliness worse."

She nodded. "I guessed that was why you didn't call. I'm glad you got what you went after."

"My lawyers are down there now working on the papers. I have to go back to sign, but it will be a day trip," he said.

Sitting up, she gazed at him. "I'm selfish to want you here all the time."

"No you're not, because I feel the same way." His hand tangled in her hair. "When the hotel opens in four weeks there will be a month-long celebration with various events that I'll have to attend. I want you with me."

She couldn't hide her amazement. "Are you sure?"

His eyes fierce, he brought her face closer to his. "The more I'm with you, the more I want to be. Buried deep inside you or being near you is a pleasure I've never experienced before. Does that answer your question?"

Her breath fluttered out over her lips. "Eloquently, and I'd love to go."

He kissed her, then lifted his head, his eyes dark and narrowed. "Grab the bottle of champagne, the strawberries, and the whipped cream. There were a couple of other fantasies I haven't gotten around to yet."

Her body vibrating with excitement, Ayanna grabbed the things from the table. Clutching them to her chest, she smiled and wondered how many more fantasies Tanner had. She was looking forward to fulfilling each one.

"The cab is waiting."

Tanner stared down at Ayanna and wished he could send the cab away. It was almost midnight. They had been together almost nineteen hours, never farther than a few feet apart, and yet, he didn't want to leave. Another first. He'd been with numerous women, but always made it a point to go home. A woman tended to become possessive and start thinking long term when she woke up with a man in her bed or in his.

"Come with me?" The request just slipped out, but he had no wish to withdraw the offer.

She blushed. They'd made love countless ways and she could still blush. "My mother sometimes calls in the mornings."

"Have the calls transferred," he suggested.

Her gaze drifted away from his. "I don't think I could talk to her with you there."

His body stirred. The cabbie honked, and Tanner gritted his teeth. He wasn't winning this time and was disappointed, but another part of him was glad Ayanna woke up in her own bed in the mornings... not that he didn't plan to change that. "Pointe is preparing us dinner at my place tomorrow night. I'll pick you up at six."

Since she'd turned down his earlier invitation and had held firm, she let him get away with telling her about dinner instead of asking her. "Isn't that early?"

"That's about as long as I can stand being away from you." He kissed her, then was out the door.

A bemused expression on her face, Ayanna watched from the window as Tanner got into the taxi. She was already counting the hours until she saw him again. By then she might have enough nerve to enact one of her own fantasies. With a grin on her face, she went to bed.

Dinner at Tanner's condo exceeded her expectations. The sea bass baked with pistachio was scrumptious, the vintage wine delicious, the setting with soft lighting romantic, and the air scented with the fragrance of jasmine intoxicating, but it was Tanner who made her burn with desire and her heart sing with joy.

"This is wonderful," she said, sipping her wine on the balcony, feeling content and happy. Music drifted out to them from inside. "Thank you for inviting me."

"My pleasure," he said, taking the glass from her hand and pulling her into his arms.

She sank against him, enjoying the hardness of his muscled body, the way they fit. He danced as he did everything, with supreme confidence and ability.

He chuckled, kissing her on top of the head. "You wouldn't go to sleep on a guy, would you?"

She smiled without lifting her head. "If I did, what would you do?"

"I'd have to wake you up." Still moving to the slow beat of the music, he tilted her face and proceeded to nibble at her mouth, the curve of her jaw, her ear.

By the time he reached her mouth again, sleep was the furthest thing from her mind. "I like your method much better than an alarm clock."

"Let's see what else about me you like." Picking her up, he headed for the bedroom.

"I already know," she said, unbuttoning his shirt.

"Such as?" he said, amusement in his voice.

"Why don't I show you?" She laughed softly when he quickened his pace.

# NINE

Tanner was rushing out of his bedroom when the phone rang. He had a full day planned at the hotel, and in the evening he and Ayanna were finally getting around to that movie. They had gone out almost every night since his return from the business trip two weeks ago. His interest in her showed no signs of abating. If anything, he was becoming more fascinated.

He grinned on recalling a particular evening at her place when she'd given him a full body massage. By the time she'd finished he barely knew his name. Maybe he could talk her into staying the night and letting him give *her* a massage.

Planning to ignore the caller, he grabbed his car keys on the credenza table by the front door just as he heard Raine's excited voice on the answering machine. He picked up the receiver, as they had been playing phone tag for the past week.

"Hello, big brother. I wanted you to be the first in the family to know I'm ready to make my move against Leo's."

Tanner couldn't get to the phone fast enough. "What? What did you say?"

She laughed, a bright happy sound. "You didn't think I'd be able to pull it off this fast, did you?"

Stunned, Tanner plopped down on the arm of the chair. "Raine, please start over."

She laughed again. "Leo's is going to be the next supper club I add to my growing list. Don't act so surprised. You've known from the first that's what I planned to do. You said so."

He felt like a man who'd been sucker punched. They all had complete autonomy and the considerable resources of Rafferty Enterprises to get what they wanted. He shut his eyes. This could not be happening. "I thought you wanted to know about Leo's to check out the competition."

"Well, now you know."

"You can't do this." His hand tightened on the receiver.

"Things are already in motion and your information about the one-way street helped cinch the deal." Her voice took on a hard edge. "They can either sell to me at a profit or watch their business dwindle to nothing when I tie up traffic every evening and night on very slow renovation of a building two blocks up from Leo's."

He had given Raine the means to hurt Ayanna. His stomach churned. "I didn't tell you that for you to use against Ayanna. We've been dating for over three weeks. We're going out tonight."

"Ayanna? Tanner, usually by now you've already become bored and moved on. I've run out of fingers and toes to count the number of women you've dated in the past year."

"This is different," he said, getting up to pace. "I care about Ayanna."

"Sure you do," his sister said lightly. "That what makes you such a fabulous guy. You're genuinely fond of the women you date. Just answer me one thing, if our situations were reversed, given both our track records, would you back out of a potentially lucrative deal because I was dating one of the owners?"

Since neither their brother in St. Thomas nor his sister were known for long-term relationships, he felt trapped by the damning truth. "Not usually, but it's different this time. You have to back off, Ra."

"No can do, Tanner. I'm flying into D.C. in a few days to push the deal through personally."

Raine was as stubborn as he was. "They won't sell. It's more than a restaurant to them, especially Ayanna."

"I don't plan to give them a choice," she said, the edge back in her voice.

"Ra, we don't do business this way," he told her, anger creeping into his voice. "We come at people from the front, not behind."

"I've sent three men down to make inquiries and Noah Hardcastle refuses to even discuss the matter."

"Then give up, find another restaurant. Have Slaughter scout another location out for you."

"I don't need Slaughter to do anything for me," she said tightly. "He was the last man I sent. He doesn't think I can pull this off, but I'll show him."

Tanner shoved his hand through his hair. Things were going from bad to worse. Raine and Slaughter had been at odds since the day they met. Having him as her bodyguard while she was dating in high school and college didn't help. Having Slaughter telling her what could and couldn't be done was like waving a red flag in front of a bull. "You've never cared for being in the same city with me or near the water. Why now?"

"Demographics counted in my decision as well. There wasn't the large percentage of African Americans I wanted in your other locations. We're both in Charleston."

Raine always did her homework. Too well it seemed. "Don't do this, Ra, please."

There was a slight pause. "If I thought you were serious about her,

I'd drop my plans in a heartbeat, but none of us have been lucky like our parents. The deal is going through. Good-bye, Tanner."

Tanner closed his eyes. What was he going to do?

"Stop whatever you're doing and get Raine on the phone. Now," Tanner instructed his secretary the instant he came through the door. He'd already called her place and talked to her answering machine. "Buzz me as soon as you locate her."

"Yes, sir." Ms. Cater took one look at his grim face and immediately hit "save" on the computer and reached for the phone.

Tanner continued into his office. He plopped his brief case on the desk and prowled. Somehow he'd make her understand. He had to.

The phone rang and he pounced on it. "Raine."

"I'm sorry, Mr. Rafferty. Her secretary doesn't know where she is."

Tanner cursed softly under his breath. Didn't know or wasn't telling. "Find Slaughter."

"I missed him by a few minutes. His plane just took off from San Francisco, heading back to Charleston. He plane is due to arrive at 12:15 our time," she said, already anticipating the next question.

"As soon as he lands I want him on the phone," Tanner told her.

"Yes sir," she said. "Your first appointment with the head of banquet services is in ten minutes."

Her words were a statement and a question. He rubbed the back of his neck. The food for the opening had to be perfect in every detail. "We'll keep on schedule, but interrupt me when you have Slaughter on the phone." Hanging up, Tanner sat behind his desk, his brow creased. "Ra, where the devil are you?"

"Ayanna, please come to my office," Noah requested over the telephone intercom.

Sitting in her office at her desk, she frowned on hearing the tightness in her cousin's voice. "Is everything all right?"

"You'll find out when you get here."

Her frown deepened as she listened to the dial tone. She quickly went down the hall to Noah's office and opened the door. Her gaze narrowed on seeing an elegantly beautiful woman in a tailored black pantsuit with a white blouse sitting in front of his desk.

"Since this concerns you on a personal level, I thought you'd like to be here," Noah said, his arms propped on his desk.

Ayanna's gaze went to Tyrone and Tyrell. Their jaws were tight and they were staring daggers at the woman who sat relaxed in the leather wing chair. "Noah, I don't understand."

"It's very simple, Ayanna," the woman said. "I want Leo's and I intend to have it. Mr. Hardcastle has turned me down three times, but this time, if you refuse my very generous offer, you'll see your business dry up to a trickle when I tie up traffic with renovations."

"Who the hell are you?" Ayanna said, her anger growing toward the poised woman who calmly threatened their dream.

"She's Tanner's sister," Noah said, biting out each word.

Ayanna pulled up short, her eyes wide. All too clearly she recalled telling Tanner about the one-way street. Pain lanced through her. She clenched her fists. "He used me."

Anger flashed in Raine's black eyes "My brother doesn't use anyone."

The door behind her abruptly opened, revealing Tanner. He took one look at the angry faces of the men, the hurt, confused face of Ayanna, and knew he was too late. He went to her and took her arms. "I didn't know about her plans until this morning."

"But you told her what happens when traffic is tied up, didn't you?"

He looked into her eyes and knew regret. "Yes."

She swallowed convulsively and looked away. "Please turn me loose."

"No."

Tyrell and Tyrone moved from behind the desk toward him. So did Noah.

"Think about my very generous offer," Raine said, drawing the men's attention back to her. She drew her sunglasses from the top of her head to her eyes. "Tanner, walk me outside."

His hands flexed, then he released Ayanna. He wasn't afraid of her cousins, but having every bone in his body broken would bring the considerable wrath of the Rafferty clan down on the Hardcastles through no fault of their own. Taking Raine by the arm, he led her out the door.

"You shouldn't have come. I know you can handle yourself, but not three against one. To spare you this, I called Jim and asked him to get the Gulf Stream ready after we got off the phone." She wrinkled her nose in annoyance. "Since I know my secretary can keep a secret, Slaughter must have blabbed. The jet doesn't move unless he knows the itinerary." She glanced longingly at the fifty-foot Rosewood bar with brass railing. "I can't wait to own this place."

Tanner stopped and faced her. "Call it off."

"We already had this discussion." She ran her slim fingers over a small Tiffany-style lamp. "I think I'll get rid of the colored oil candles."

"Ra, listen to me," he said through gritted teeth. "Do this and Ayanna will never forgive me."

Raine finally gave him her full attention. "Tanner, why do you care?"

"Because I love her."

Slowly Raine lifted the oversize designer sunshades, astonishment and disbelief in her large eyes.

"I love her," Tanner repeated, his conviction growing each second. "I'll do whatever it takes for Leo's to stay in the Hardcastle family."

"Does that include going against me and the family?"

"No!"

Tanner whirled to see Ayanna standing behind him, her face pale, her body trembling. He reached for her.

Holding up her hands, she stepped back. Tanner muttered and let his hands drop to his side.

"I won't come between you and your family." Ayanna lifted her chin and faced his sister. "I came to tell you to do your worst. Leo's is not for sale at any price. We have loyal customers. We'll survive."

"I love her, Raine," Tanner said, looking tenderly at Ayanna, willing her to believe. "I'll fight through hell to keep her safe and happy."

"You don't love me!" Ayanna cried, fighting tears and so much misery and pain.

Tanner grabbed her arms and held her when she tried to pull away. "Ayanna, please listen. I didn't know what she planned."

"I believe you, but it doesn't make any difference."

Now he was the one surprised. "How can you say that? I love you."

Tears sparkled in her brown eyes. Once she would have given anything to hear those words. "And I love my cousins. Betraying them was bad enough. I can't compound it by continuing to see you."

"You didn't betray them," Tanner said, desperate for her to believe and forgive him. "I keep telling you that I had no idea Raine was going to use that information against you."

"The point is, she did, and she wouldn't have known if I hadn't told you. That makes me responsible." When she pulled away this time, he let her go. "Good-bye, Tanner. If you care for me at all, you won't try to contact me again." She turned and walked away.

Fury pulsing though him, he went to find the person who had

caused all this trouble. He caught up with Raine as she was about to get into the limo at the curb. "Wait."

She turned. "I would have called later. I wanted to give you some privacy." This time it was she who took his arm. "This is not a rash decision, Tanner. There was another reason I didn't want to go where you and Adrian were. I didn't want people to think I was trading off your names." She let her hand fall. "I've proven to myself that I can make my restaurants a success. I don't care what others think."

"Does that include me, Ra?"

Shock and regret shown on her face. "You shouldn't have to ask that."

"Back off," he ordered, his voice sharp.

"If I really thought what you felt for her was lasting, I'd call off the whole operation. You like challenges. You are easily bored with the same routine, the same city, the same woman." She tentatively touched his rigid shoulder. "I'm taking the jet back to Charleston. I'll call this weekend."

Tanner watched the car pull off, then looked back at Leo's. There could be only one winner in this—his sister or the woman he loved. All things considered, there was only one choice. He got into his car and drove off.

# TEN

"You all right?"

Noah had spoken, but all of her cousins were looking at her with a mixture of concern, pity, and rage.

"I'm so sorry," Ayanna said.

Noah came around his desk and took her into his arms. "There's nothing to be sorry for. You didn't know the kind of man Tanner was, and if I hear you say you're sorry again, I'll personally turn you over my knee."

She wiped the moisture away from her eyes, refusing to give into self-pity or try to defend Tanner. "I don't think she's bluffing."

"Neither do I," Noah agreed, his expression thunderous. "Business might fall off a bit but, thanks to you, we're in good shape financially."

Ayanna refused to think that might change if Raine's renovations went on for a long period of time. "I plan for us to stay that way." She picked up a pen and sheet of paper from Noah's desk. "I suggest we adjust immediately by extending happy hour by at least thirty minutes. Perhaps have Max create a special drink."

She tapped her pen on the paper, then began to write. "It wouldn't hurt to create a few new dinners with food that is plentiful and therefore reasonable at a special price. Perhaps have a drawing for a weekly dinner for two. Bill it as a way of thanking our loyal customers and welcoming new ones by making it well worth their effort to fight snarls to get here. We could also add another night to amateur/open mike night to draw in customers. What do you think?"

"The new meals shouldn't be a problem." Tyrell nodded his head. "I'll let you know what I come up with and you can add it to the menu."

"I think it should be a special pull-out section with maybe a hard hat," Ayanna said. "I'll work up a couple of ideas and we can decided on it later."

Tyrone leaned against the desk. "I don't see a difficulty with adding Thursday to amateur/open mike night. We always have disappointed people who wanted to go on."

"I think we should plan to have everything in place by next week." She tore the sheet of paper from the notepad and replaced the pad on Noah's desk. "It might not be a bad idea to make the customers aware of what's going to happen and let them know the plans we have to keep them."

"This should work," Noah said, looking at Ayanna with admiration. "Once again, you've proven we made a good business decision by making you a full partner."

"You're the only one we thought to ask," Tyrone said.

"Yeah," Tyrell agreed. "You helped make Leo's a success. Your father is probably looking down on you, smiling."

Ayanna knew they were trying to bolster her and she felt tears sting her eyes. They didn't blame her, but she blamed herself. If it took her last penny, Leo's would survive. "I better start working on the design for the new menu." She went to the door, opened it, then turned to face them. "Until we see how things shake out I'll plan on staying at least until nine or ten each night to help with seating and PR."

Tyrell and Tyrone started to protest, but Noah, always in command, held up his hand and they quieted. He understood her need to help and to stay busy. "I'd appreciate your lending a hand."

Closing the door behind her, she swallowed the huge knot in her throat and went to her office. There would be time enough for heartache later; saving Leo's had to come first.

Three days later Raine's threat became a reality. Ayanna sat in her car behind several other vehicles as they waited for a heavy piece of machinery to move so they could pass. Fear knotted her stomach. She'd boasted to Raine they'd survive, but she knew of a number of establishments that had closed when construction made it difficult for people to reach their place of business.

Finally, after waiting over five minutes, her car and the others were waved though. Driving by, she saw at least twenty-odd men in hard hats. She cut a glance at the new hard-hat menu inserts she had just picked up from the printer. There were enough men at the work site to do the renovation of the two-story brick building if that had been Raine's intent, but it wasn't. She was intent on destroying, not building.

Ayanna's hand flexed on the steering wheel. She couldn't think of Raine without thinking of Tanner. Her heart ached for him. But they could never be together. He'd respected her wishes to not contact her, and for that, she was thankful. Seeing him or hearing his voice would have only made the ache worse.

Arriving at the restaurant a little after six, she was glad to see the cars pulling into the parking lot ahead of her and behind her. Leo's would survive, just as she would without Tanner.

A week and a half later, Ayanna gazed out at the diners scattered around the restaurant and accepted that they were in trouble. On a Friday night every table should have been occupied. The restaurant was half empty. She glanced at her watch, then at the reservations. At 8:30 it was still early. People might still be coming after the theater or other events.

"It will be all right," Noah said, coming up to drape his arms around her shoulder.

"I know," she said, praying he was right.

He stared at the dark circles beneath her eyes. "I blame Tanner more for hurting you than for anything else."

"I'm fine," she told him, adding another lie to her growing list. She'd long since stopped worrying about what would happen to her. Once her mother and Sheri had found out what had happened, they constantly asked how she was doing. Her cousins and their wives were just as bad. None of them had said one word of blame or acted any differently toward her, which made her betrayal all the more painful.

"Go home and get some sleep," Noah said with a frown. "There is no need for you to come back here every night. You've gone over the books, instigating cost-cutting maneuvers. There's nothing more you can do."

She was about to tell him she wanted to do more when the double doors opened and an attractive woman in her late fifties came in. The pale pink suit was Dior, the hair fashionably cut. Twin furrows raced across Ayanna's brow. There was something vaguely familiar about the woman.

"Welcome to Leo's," Ayanna said, stepping forward.

"Thank you," the woman said, her voice soft, the words slow and drawn out like a lazy river. "Reservations for Dawson."

Ayanna already knew it was for five people. She'd booked them. "Would you like to be seated or wait for the rest of your party?"

"We're all here," she said, beaming at Ayanna. "He's parking the car. I didn't want to wait another minute so I had him let me out at the front door."

Ayanna smiled at the woman's enthusiasm. "You must have heard about our wonderful menu. Tyrell is a master chef."

"Actually I was in a hurry to meet you," she said. "Tanner said you were beautiful and he was right as usual."

Ayanna tensed as the double mahogany doors in front of her opened again. Tanner stood poised in the doorway. Unable to conceal her longing, her gaze clung to him. Raine and two men stepped around him. Together the family resemblance was unmistakable. No one had to tell Ayanna the younger man was his brother Adrian and the other man an older version of Tanner, his father.

Noah moved past her to block Tanner. "You're not welcome here."

"I have reservations." Tanner pulled a sheet of paper from his pocket. "My faxed confirmation."

Noah cut a sharp glace at the paper. "The name says Dawson."

"My mother's maiden name," Tanner answered, folding the paper and returning it to the inside of his dove gray tailored jacket. "We're ready to be seated."

"I don't give a—"

"Noah," Ayanna interrupted and grabbed five menus. "I'll seat them. This way." Every step shredded her heart a little bit more. The Rafferty Grand's grand opening was tomorrow night. His family must have come to town to celebrate Tanner's and Raine's success . . . and rub it in Ayanna's face. She hadn't thought he would be that cruel.

"Your table," she said, seating them, then handing them each a menu. "Enjoy your meal."

She started to leave, but Tanner caught her hand. A flash of awareness caused her body to tremble. He closed her fingers around a large brown envelope.

"I love you," he whispered.

Tears threatening to spill, she hurried away, the envelope clutched in her hand. She didn't stop until she was alone in the hallway by the ladies' room. Or so she thought.

"What did he give you?" Noah demanded, taking the envelope and opening it. "If he's trying to harass you I'm going to ram this—" He held the papers out to her. "Read them, Ayanna."

She started to shake her head, but Noah stuck them in front of her face. Her eyes widened as she began to read. The papers were deeds to Raine's property and the one directly behind them. He hadn't lied. "He does love me," she whispered, finally taking the legal papers.

"Looks like it," Noah said with a wide grin. "Leo's has struck again. This time the champagne is on me."

Ayanna ran back into the restaurant and straight into Tanner's arms. "Tanner!" she cried. "Thank you! Leo's will never be vulnerable again. Somehow I'll pay you back."

He stared down into her face. "Since you're going to marry me, it's all in the family."

Her heart threatened to beat out of her chest. "You want to marry me?"

"I *am* going to marry you. However, anytime you're ready to put me out of my misery and tell me you love me too, I'd be grateful."

She grinned up at him. "Who wouldn't love a renegade?" Then she sobered and looked at Raine. "On the other hand, I'm not so sure about you. But I'd like for us to at least try to be friends."

Raine extended her slender hand. "I hope so. Tanner made me an offer I couldn't refuse... management of The Ming Room and first dibs on the restaurants in his future hotels."

"Did you take it?" Ayanna asked, not moving to take Raine's hand. The deal would mean a small fortune, but it was nothing less than bribery.

the blind date

Raine held Ayanna's gaze. "No. Family will always mean more than money. Besides, I make my own way or not at all. I miscalculated with Leo's and I always admit my mistakes."

Ayanna ignored the hand and hugged Raine. "I think I'm going to like you." Straightening, she looked up at Tanner. "I've been miserable without you. I love you more than words can say." Her arms went around his neck. "How soon can we get married?"

"How about tonight?" he asked, kissing her deeply.

"Tanner, you have to have a large wedding," his mother protested. "The family would be outraged."

Tanner's father affectionally patted his wife of forty years on her hand. "I have a feeling they aren't listening."

Raine looked amused; Adrian, a die-hard bachelor, stunned.

Patrons began applauding. Tyrell popped the cork on the first bottle of champagne and Tyrone opened the second while Noah called Ayanna's mother.

Sheri and Ayanna's mother arrived minutes apart. Both were crying. Both voiced their objections to a quick wedding. Tanner just smiled. He had no intention of sleeping another night without Ayanna.

Two hours later the Gulf Stream raced down the runway, then banked left, heading for Las Vegas. Another jet raced after it.

Ayanna smiled at Tanner in the bedroom of the aircraft. "I could have told both our mothers that they wouldn't win against a renegade."

"Not when it's this important." He brushed his hand across her cheek. "After Raine realized I was serious about fighting her over Leo's, she knew I loved you and sold her property to me. Then I had to obtain the lot behind Leo's, find a minister, who, by the way, is waiting at the suite at the Mandalay to marry us. The reception was the easiest part. Pointe was delighted to prepare your favorite foods.

"We'll fly back after the ceremony and go straight to The Rafferty Grand. I've given up the condo and moved us into my suite at the hotel. You have a complete wardrobe with appropriate jewelry waiting for you for the month-long grand opening celebrations."

She stared at the flawless five-caret diamond on the third finger of her left hand. She'd cried buckets when he'd given it to her in the limo ride to the airport. He said he wanted them to be alone when he gave it to her so they'd remember the moment always. Who would have thought a renegade could be sentimental?

"What if I had said no?"

He pulled her fiercely into his arms. "I would have found a way to change your mind. You're going to be Mrs. Tanner Rafferty and, in less than eighteen hours, we'll greet the guests at our hotel."

She didn't think she'd ever get used to hearing that he was hers, and she his. "Since you have the wedding party in the plane following ours, perhaps we should make the most of this time," she told him.

He grinned, following her down onto the bed. "My thoughts exactly."